RAMAGE

Lord Nicholas Ramage, eldest son of the Tenth
Earl of Blazey, Admiral of the White, was born
in 1775 at Blazey Hall, St Kew, Cornwall. He
entered the Royal Navy as a midshipman in 1788,
at the age of thirteen. He has served with
distinction in the Mediterranean, the Caribbean,
and home waters during the war against France,
participating in several major sea battles and
numerous minor engagements. Despite political
difficulties, his rise through the ranks has been
rapid.

In *Ramage*, his first recorded
adventure, Third Lieutenant
Ramage takes his first command
while serving in the Mediterranean
under Nelson.

Dudley Pope, who comes from an old Cornish family and whose great-great-grandfather was a Plymouth shipowner in Nelson's time, is well known both as the creator of Lord Ramage and as a distinguished and entertaining naval historian, the author of ten scholarly works.

Actively encouraged by the late C. S. Forester, he has now written sixteen 'Ramage' novels about life at sea in Nelson's day. They are based on his own wartime experiences in the navy and peacetime exploits as a yachtsman as well as immense research into the naval history of the eighteenth century.

Available in Fontana by the same author

DUDLEY POPE

Ramage

FONTANA/Collins

First published by George Weidenfeld & Nicolson Ltd 1965
First issued in Fontana Paperbacks 1979
Ninth impression July 1988

© 1965 by The Ramage Company Limited

Printed and bound in Great Britain by
William Collins Sons & Co. Ltd, Glasgow

For three friends –
Jane and Antonio
and Imek

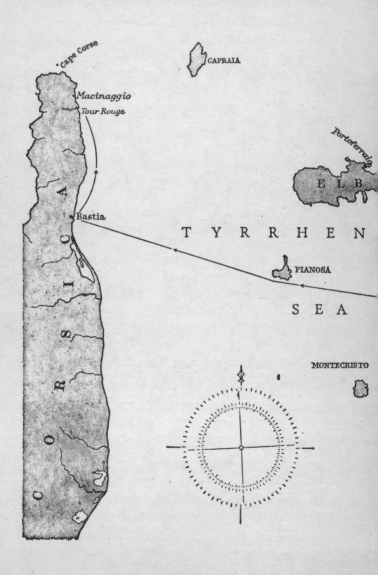

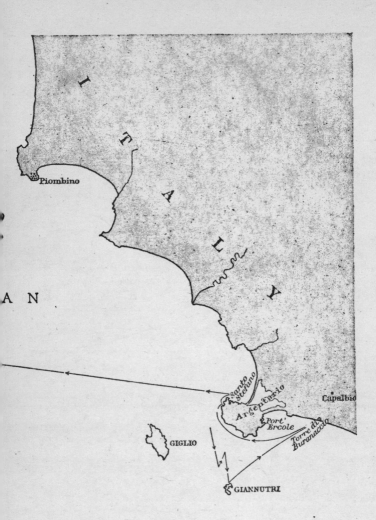

The VOYAGES of LT. RAMAGE RN
while carrying out the orders of
Vice-Admiral Sir John Jervis &
Commodore Horatio Nelson
September–October 1796

Chapter 1

RAMAGE FELT dazed and grabbed at the thoughts rushing through his head: he guessed it was a nightmare, so he would soon wake up safely in his cabin; but for the moment his mind was apparently separated from his body, floating along free like a puff of smoke in the wind. All that noise sounded like continuous thunder and now he was beginning to wake up, hesitating and unwilling to open his eyes and slide from blissful and contented drowsiness into the sharp bright light of consciousness.

Yet he felt a vague uneasiness, wondering if he had overslept and would be late on watch. Uneasiness gave way to apprehension as slowly he realized the thunder was of gunfire: from an enemy's broadsides, punctuated by the occasional deep-chested, bronchitic cough of his own ship's 12-pounder cannons firing, followed by the familiar cartwheels-across-a-wooden-bridge rumble of the trucks as the carriages jerked back in recoil until they reached the limits of the thick rope breechings, which groaned under the strain of halting them.

Then, as his sense of smell returned and the acrid fumes of gun smoke burnt the back of his nostrils, he realized—

'Mr Ramage, sir! . . . Mr Ramage, sir!'

It was his name, but they were shouting from a long way off, reminding him of his childhood when he had gone over the fields and into the woods and one of the servants called him back for a meal. 'Master Nicholas,' they'd shout, 'you come this minute; 'is Lordship's terrible angry when you're late.' But Father was never angry; in fact—

'Mr Ramage! Mr Ramage – wake up, sir!'

But that isn't a servant's voice – there's no Cornish burr: it's a boy calling – a frightened and almost hysterical boy with a sharp cockney accent.

'Mr Ramage – ohmygawd *do* wake up, sir!'

Now a man's voice joined in, and they began shaking him

9

as well. Heavens, his head hurt: he felt as if he had been bludgeoned. The enormous grunt and rumbling interrupting them must be another 12-pounder going off close by and slamming back in recoil.

Ramage opened his eyes. His body still seemed remote and he was startled to find himself lying with his face pressed against the deck. The pattern on the planking was really most extraordinary. He noticed – as if seeing it for the first time – that constant scrubbing and holystoning with sand and water had worn away little alleys of soft wood between the harder ridges of the grain. And someone must swab up the blood.

Blood staining the scrubbed planks: the words forming in his mind shocked him into realizing he was now conscious, but still curiously detached, as if looking down from the masthead at his own body sprawled flat on its face between two guns, nose pressed against the deck, arms and legs flung out, like a rag doll on a rubbish heap.

They shook him violently and then rolled him over.

'Come on, sor . . . come, Mr Ramage, wake up!'

He opened his eyes reluctantly but his head spun for several moments before he could see their faces, and even then they were distant, as though viewed through the wrong end of a telescope. Finally, by concentrating hard he managed to focus the boy's face more clearly.

'Yes?'

God, was that his voice – a rasping croak like a holystone being dragged across a dry deck?

'Yes – what's the matter?'

The effort of speaking brought Ramage's memory back with a rush: it was a stupid question: everything was the matter when late one sunny September afternoon in the year of Our Lord 1796 a French 74-gun line-of-battle ship, the *Barras*, trapped His Majesty's frigate *Sibella*, of 28 guns. . . .

'Ohmygawdsir, it's awful,' gabbled the boy. 'All dead they are, sir, an' a shot caught the Captain right—'

'Steady boy: who sent you?'

'Bosun, sir – said to tell you you was in command now, sir: everyone else's killed and the Carpenter's Mate says there's four feet o'water in the well and the pumps smashed, sir – *can't* you come on deck, sir? 'Ere, I'll 'elp you,' he added pleadingly.

The urgent, terrified note in the boy's voice and the phrase 'You was in command now, sir' helped clear Ramage's head (which was beginning to throb in time with the pumping of his heart) but the significance was chilling. Every junior lieutenant dreamed of commanding a frigate in action; but that terrible rumbling a few hundred yards away – as though some giant god of mythology was hurling bolts of lightning through the frigate's hull, butchering men and timber alike – was the French line-of-battle ship firing her broadside, some 35 heavy guns. The spasmodic coughs and grunts close by were obviously all that remained of the frigate's puny broadside of 14 light guns.

No, that was not included in a junior lieutenant's dream of glory; nor was having the command thrust upon him when most of his wits had been scattered by a blow on the head and so far refused to return. Still, this deck was deuced comfortable . . .

'Come on, sor: I'll 'elp you up.'

Ramage opened his eyes again and, as he recognized one of the seamen – a fellow Cornishman named Higgins, or Briggins, or some such name – realized he had been slithering back into sleep or unconsciousness, or whatever it was that drained the strength from his body and befogged his brain.

Higgins – or was it Briggins? Oh, it didn't matter – stank of sweat: cloying yet sharp, but it did not burn the nostrils like smoke from the guns. As they hoisted him to his feet Ramage closed his eyes to stop his head spinning, and he heard Higgins or Briggins roundly cursing another seaman: 'Wrop his bloddy arm round yor bloddy neck, else 'e'll fall down. Now hold his wrist. That's it. Now walk 'im, you heathen Patlander!'

Ramage's legs flopped one in front of the other while the Cornishman on one side and the Irishman on the other dragged him along: they probably had plenty of experience of getting a drunken shipmate out of a tavern.

In front, through the smoke swirling across the decks and curling into strange wreathing patterns as it was caught by eddies of wind coming in at the gun ports, danced the boy, whom he now recognized as the First Lieutenant's servant. The *late* First Lieutenant's servant, he corrected himself.

'What the 'ell now? 'Ow are we ter get 'im up the ladder?'

The ladder from the main deck up to the gangway and quarter-deck has eight rungs – Ramage was pleased with himself for remembering that – and is only wide enough for one man. Eight rungs mean nine steps to the top, and every one of those eight rungs is mine to command.

The stupidity of the thought shocked Ramage into realizing he was making no real effort to pull himself together: the two seamen could carry him no farther: he was on his own: up those eight rungs was the quarter-deck where, as the new commanding officer, he now belonged: where several score men were looking to him as their leader.

'Where's a tub?' he asked, freeing himself from the men's grasp.

'Just here, sor.'

He lurched a couple of paces and knelt beside it. When the ship beat to quarters before the action began, small tubs of water had been placed near the guns for the men to soak the sponges used to swab the barrels of the guns. As he plunged his head into the water he gave a gasp of pain, and groping fingers found a big swelling and a long gash across the back of his scalp. The gash was not deep, but enough to explain why he had been unconscious: probably a flying splinter of wood.

Ducking his head again, he swilled water round in his mouth, and spat it out, then pulled the wet hair back from his forehead, took several deep breaths, and stood up. The sudden movement set his head spinning again but already he felt stronger; the muscles were coming back to his legs.

At the foot of the ladder he paused, a spasm of fear twisting his stomach: at the top carnage and chaos awaited him. Decisions, vital decisions, had to be made and orders given – by someone who had been below, commanding one division of the guns for most of the action, his field of view restricted to what could be seen through a gun port, and unconscious for the rest of the time.

As he struggled up the ladder Ramage found he was talking to himself, like a child learning something by rote: the Captain, First and Second Lieutenants must have been killed, which leaves me the next senior. The boy said the Bosun had sent word that I'm in command, so presumably the Master was also dead, otherwise the message would have come from him. Well, thank God the Bosun survived, and let's hope the Surgeon's been spared and stayed sober.

How many of the *Sibella*'s guns have fired in the last few minutes? Four or five, and they are all on the main-deck, which means the upper-deck guns and carronades must be out of action. With only four or five guns firing on the engaged side, how many of the ship's company are still alive? There'd been 164 answering last Sunday's muster.

Two more rungs and I'll be at the top. Another broadside from the *Barras* on its way: strange how gunfire across water sounds like thunder – and now the tearing canvas sound of passing round shot, and the horrible punching which shook the ship to the keel as more shot crashed into the hull.

More screams and more men killed. His fault, too: if only he'd hurried he might have done something that'd saved them.

Now his head was level with the narrow gangway running the length of the ship, joining fo'c'sle to quarter-deck, and he realized it would soon be twilight. Then he was on the gangway itself, staggering over to the bulwark. But he hardly recognized the ship: on the fo'c'sle the carronade on each bow had been wrenched from its slide and piles of bodies showed the crews had been killed at the same time. The ornamented belfry and galley chimney had vanished; great sections of the bulwark along the starboard side were smashed in and dozens of rolled-up hammocks lay scattered across the deck, torn from their usual stowed positions in nettings on top of the bulwarks.

Looking right aft across the quarter-deck he saw that all the rest of the carronades had been torn from their slides, and round each of those on the starboard side were more bodies.

One section of the main capstan was smashed in, leaving the gilded crown on top hanging askew; and instead of the double wheel just forward of the mizenmast, manned by a couple of quartermasters, there was just a gaping hole in the deck. Shot had bitten chunks out of the mizenmast – and the mainmast. And the foremast, too. And bodies – it seemed to Ramage there were more bodies sprawled about the deck than men in the whole ship's company; yet seamen were still running about – and others were working the remaining guns on the deck below. He saw four or five Marines crouching down behind the bulwark abreast the mizenmast re-loading their muskets.

And the *Barras*? Just as Ramage looked out through a gun port the Bosun ran up, but he told him to wait a moment. God, what a terrifying sight she was! Silhouetted against the western horizon, below which the sun had set some ten minutes ago, the great ship seemed like a huge island fortress in the sea, black and menacing, apparently impregnable. And so far as the *Sibella* is concerned, Ramage thought bitterly, she is impregnable. She was under a maintopsail only and steering parallel with the *Sibella* about 800 yards away.

Ramage glanced across the ship, over the larboard side. Almost abeam and perhaps a couple of miles away was the solid bulk of the Argentario peninsula, a sprawling mass of rock joined to the mainland of Italy by a couple of narrow causeways. Monte Argentario itself, the highest of the peaks, was just abaft the beam. The *Barras*, ranging up to seaward, had the *Sibella* neatly trapped, like an assassin with his victim against a wall.

'Well, Bosun . . .'

'Thank Christ you're 'ere, sir: I thought you'd gone too. You all right sir? You're covered in blood.'

'A bang on the head. What's the position?'

The Bosun's face, blackened by smoke from the guns, was striped where runs of perspiration following the wrinkles showed the tanned skin beneath and gave him an almost comical appearance, like a sorrowful bloodhound.

Obviously making a great effort to keep his voice calm and

14

not forget anything in his report to the new commanding officer, he waved a hand aft. 'You can see this lot, sir: wheel's smashed and so's the tiller and rudder head – can't rig tackles 'cos the rudder pendents is shot away. Ship's just about steering herself, with us helping with the sheets and braces. Chain pump's smashed, so's the head pumps. The Carpenter's Mate says there's four feet o' water in the well and rising fast. The foremast will go by the board any minute – just look at it, I dunno what's holding it up. Mainmast is sprung in two places with shot still embedded, and the mizen in three.'

'And the butcher's bill?'

'About fifty dead and sixty or so wounded, sir. One round of grapeshot did for the Captain and the First Lieutenant. The Surgeon and Purser were—'

'Belay all that: where's the Carpenter's Mate? Pass the word for him.'

While the Bosun turned away, Ramage glanced back at the *Barras*. Hadn't she just come round to larboard a little, just a few degrees, so her course was now converging slightly with the *Sibella*'s? He thought he could see a movement indicating seamen trimming the maintopsail yard round a fraction. Did they want to get even closer?

The *Sibella* was sailing at about four knots and yawing through four points. She would steer herself better if the sail aft was reduced, so that the foretopsail pulled her along.

'Bosun! Clew up the main and mizen topsails and set the spritsail.'

With no sails drawing on main and mizen masts, the wind would not tend to push the ship's stern round, and the spritsail, set under the bowsprit, would help the foretopsail, though it was almost too small to help much in such a light wind.

As the Bosun's shouts set the men to work, Ramage saw the Carpenter's Mate approaching: he seemed to have smeared more tallow on his body than on the cone-shaped wooden shot plugs which he had been hammering into the holes in the hull.

'Well, make your report.'

'More'n four feet o' water in the well, no pumps, six or

15

more shot betwixt wind and water, an' three or more below the waterline – must have hit as she rolled, sir.'

'Very well: sound the well again and report to me at once.'

Four feet of water. Mathematics was Ramage's weak point and he tried to concentrate, knowing the *Barras*'s next broadside was due any moment. Four feet of water: well, the *Sibella*'s draught is just over fifteen feet, and every seven tons of stores taken on board put her an inch lower in the water. How many tons did that four feet of water swilling about down below represent? What did it matter, anyway, he thought impatiently: what matters is the Carpenter's Mate's next report.

'Bosun – have some men cut away the anchors. Tell them to keep their heads down: we don't want any more casualties.'

Might as well try to get rid of some weight to compensate for the water flooding in. That would save about five tons in weight – decrease the *Sibella*'s draught by just over half an inch. It's almost ludicrous, but it'll give the men something to do: with so many guns out of action seamen were now wandering around aimlessly, waiting for orders. He could save plenty of weight by heaving damaged guns over the side, but with the few men available it would take too long.

The Carpenter's Mate was back. 'Five feet, sir, and the more she goes down the more shot holes there are being submerged.'

And, thought Ramage, the deeper the holes the more the pressure of water . . .

'Can't you plug them?'

'Most of 'em are too big, sir – all jagged. We could fother a sail over 'em if we got the way off the ship . . .'

'When did you last sound?'

'Not above quarter of an hour all told, sir.'

One foot of water in fifteen minutes. If it took about seven tons to put her down an inch, how many for a foot? Twelve inches times seven tons – eighty-four: that meant in fifteen minutes at most eighty-four tons had flooded in. How much more could she take before she sank or capsized? God knows – nothing about that in seamanship manuals. Nor would the Carpenter's Mate know. Nor the constructors, even if they were within hail. Right, let's have some action Lieutenant Ramage.

'Carpenter's Mate – sound the well every five minutes and report to me each time. Get some more men to help plug shot holes – any within a couple of feet of the present water level: stuff in hammocks – anything to slow up the leaks.'

Ramage walked to the rail at the forward end of the quarter-deck from force of habit, since it was there he had spent much of his seagoing life while on watch.

Now, he thought: what do we know? The *Barras* can do what she likes: she's the cat, we are the mouse. We can't manoeuvre, but she's just come round to a slightly converging course. How many degrees? Perhaps twenty. When would the two ships meet?

More bloody sums, Ramage thought crossly. The *Barras* was 800 yards away when she altered course. So – take the 800 yards as the base of the triangle, the *Barras*'s course as the hypotenuse, and the *Sibella*'s course the opposite side. Question: the length of the opposite side . . . He could not think of a formula and ended up guessing that the *Barras* – providing she did not alter her present course again – would finally converge and collide with the *Sibella* at a point a mile ahead. The frigate was making a little over three knots. Three into sixty minutes . . . they'd meet in twenty minutes: by then it would be almost dark.

Again red flashes rippling along the *Barras*'s side; again the thunder. The French are firing raggedly – or, more likely, each gun is being carefully aimed by an officer, since they have no opposition to fear. But none of the shots hit the hull: crashes and the noise of tearing canvas warned him the French were aiming at the masts and spars.

If he was the *Barras*'s captain, what would he do? Well, make sure the *Sibella* is crippled – which is why he's now firing at the rigging – then run alongside in the last few minutes before darkness, board – and tow the *Sibella* back to Toulon in triumph. And that, he thought, is just what he *is* going to do: her captain is timing it beautifully, and he knows that for the last few hundred yards before he gets alongside, we'll be so close he can call on us to surrender. He'll know we can't repel boarders . . .

Ramage realized his own position was almost ludicrous: he was in command of a ship which, ghost-like, was sailing herself without a man at the wheel – without a wheel for that matter; but it didn't matter a damn anyway, because within half an hour he'd have to surrender. Unable to fight, and with the ship full of wounded, he had no alternative.

And you, Lieutenant Nicholas Ramage, he told himself bitterly, since you're the son of the discredited tenth Earl of Blazey, Admiral of the White, can expect little mercy from the Admiralty if you surrender one of the King's ships, no matter the reason. The sins – alleged sins, rather – of the father shall be visited on the sons, yea even unto the something or other generation, according to the Bible.

But looking around the *Sibella*'s deck, it's hard to believe in God: that severed trunk with the legs encased in bloody silk stockings and the feet still shod in shoes fitted with elegant silver buckles, is the frigate's former Captain, and next to it presumably the First Lieutenant, whose days of toadying are finished. Ironic that a man with an ingratiating smile permanently on his face should lose his head. What a shambles: a seaman, naked except for trousers, sprawled over the wreckage of a carronade slide as if in a loving embrace, his hair still bound up in a long queue, a strip of cloth round his forehead to stop perspiration running into his eyes – and his stomach ripped open. Beside him another man who seems unmarked until you realize his arm is cut off at the shoulder—

'Orders, sir?'

It was the Bosun. Orders – he'd been daydreaming while all these men left alive in the *Sibella* waited, confident he would perform some miracle and save their lives: save them from ending their days rotting in a French prison. The devil take it: he felt shaky. Ramage made a great effort to think, and at that moment saw the foremast swaying. Presumably it had been swaying for some time, since the Bosun had already wondered why it had not gone by the board. Gone by the board . . .

18

Yes! Why the devil hadn't he thought of that before: he wanted to cheer: Lieutenant Ramage has woken up: stand by, men: stand by *Barras* ... He felt a sudden elation, as though he was half drunk, and rubbed a scar on his forehead.

The Bosun looked startled and Ramage realized he must be grinning.

'Right, Bosun,' he said briskly, 'let's get to work. I want every wounded man brought up on deck. It doesn't matter how bad he is: get him up here on the quarter-deck.'

'But sir—'

'You have five minutes . . .'

The Bosun was every day of sixty years old: his hair – what was left of it – was white. And the man knew that bringing the wounded on deck risked them being slaughtered by a broad-side from the *Barras*. Only he hasn't realized yet, Ramage thought to himself, that now the *Barras* is firing only at the rigging; she's stopped sweeping the decks with full broadsides of grapeshot because she knows she's killed enough men. If she fires into the hull again the wounded below are just as likely to be hit by the ghastly great jagged wood splinters which the shot rip up – he'd seen several pieces more than five feet long.

Wounded on deck. Now for the boats. Ramage ran aft to the taffrail and peered over: some boats were still towing astern in the *Sibella*'s wake, having been put over the side out of harm's way as the ship cleared for action. Two were missing, but the remaining four would serve his purpose. The wounded, the boats – next, food and water.

By now the Bosun was back.

'We'll soon be abandoning ship,' Ramage told him. 'We must leave the wounded on board. We have four boats. Pick four reliable hands, one to be responsible for each boat. Tell them to take a couple of men – more if they wish – and get sacks of bread and water breakers ready at the aftermost gun ports on the starboard side. A compass for each boat, and a lantern. Make sure each lantern is lit and the boats have oars. Join me here in three minutes. I am going down to the cabin.'

The Bosun gave him a questioning look before turning

away. The 'cabin' in a frigate could mean only the Captain's cabin, and Ramage knew that to mention going below to a man accustomed to seeing armed Marine sentries at every gangway and ladder when in action, to stop people bolting to safety – oh, the devil take him; there isn't time to explain. How much will the fellow remember when he gives evidence at the court martial that always followed the loss of one of the King's ships? If they live to face one . . .

In the cabin it was dark, and Ramage ducked his head to avoid hitting the beams overhead. He found the Captain's desk, and was thankful there had been no time to stow the furniture below when the ship cleared for action. Now, he said, deliberately talking aloud to himself to make sure he forgot nothing: first, the Admiral's orders: second, the Captain's letter book and order book; third, the Fighting Instructions; lastly – damn, the signal book would be in the hands of one of the midshipmen, and all the midshipmen were dead. Yet above all else the signal book with its secret codes mustn't fall into French hands.

He fumbled for the top right-hand drawer – he'd often seen the Captain put his secret papers in there. It was locked – blast, of course it was locked, and he had neither sword nor pistol to force it open. At that moment he saw a light appear behind him, filling the cabin with strange shadows, and as he swung round a nasal voice said:

'Can I help you, sir?'

It was the Captain's cox'n, a cadaverous-faced American named Thomas Jackson, and he was holding a battle lantern in one hand and a pistol in the other.

'Yes, open this drawer.'

Jackson thrust the pistol in his belt and walked over to one of the cannon on the larboard side of the cabin. The carriage had been smashed by a shot and the barrel lay across the wreckage. In the light of the lantern Ramage was startled to see the bodies of three men – they must have been killed by the shot that dismounted the gun.

The American came back carrying a bloodstained handspike, the long wooden bar made of ash and tipped with a metal shoe, used to lever round the carriages of the guns when training them.

'If you'd hold the lantern and stand back, sir ...' he said politely.

He swung the handspike so that the shoe smashed the corner of the desk. Ramage wrenched the drawer open with one hand and gave the lantern to Jackson.

'Hold it up a bit.'

He pulled the drawer right out. On top of several books and papers was a linen envelope with a broken seal. Ramage opened it and took out a two-page letter, which was headed 'Secret' and signed 'J. Jervis'. They were the orders, and he put them back in the envelope and tucked it into his pocket. He glanced at the books, the first of which, labelled 'Letter Book', contained copies of all recent official letters received in the *Sibella* and all those written. The second, labelled 'Order Book', contained copies of all orders the Captain had given and received, except, probably, the last one from Admiral Jervis. Next came the Captain's Log – usually little more than a copy of the one kept by the Master.

Then there was a sheaf of forms and signed documents – the Admiralty believed the King's ships could not float without having a vast number of papers on board to give them buoyancy. 'Cooper's Affidavit to Leakage of Beer' – hmm, that concerned the five casks found to be damaged at Gibraltar; 'Bounty List', 'Conduct List', 'Account of Paper Expended' ... Ramage tore them up. Here was the copy of the Fighting Instructions – it was sufficient to destroy that – and the slim volume containing the Articles of War, the set of laws by which the Navy was governed. They were far from secret; indeed by law had to be read aloud to the ship's company at least once a month, and the French were welcome to them.

Apart from the signal book, and some charts, that was all he needed.

Ramage turned to Jackson. 'Go to the Master's cabin and collect all the western Mediterranean charts and sailing instructions you can lay your hands on, and the Master's log. Bring them to me on the quarter-deck. Put them all in a seabag with a shot in the bottom, in case we have to dump them over the side in a hurry.'

He noticed a strange quietness beginning to settle over the ship and as he made his way out of the dark cabin, fumbling for the companionway leading to the quarter-deck, he realized wounded men had stopped moaning – or maybe they'd all been taken on deck out of earshot – and he could hear once again the familiar creak of the masts and yards, and the squeak of ropes rendering through blocks. And there was a less familiar noise – the slop of water down in the hold, and strange bumpings: presumably casks of meat, powder and various provisions floating around.

The ship herself felt sluggish beneath his feet: all the life, the normal quick reaction of the hull to the slightest movement of the rudder, the exhilarating surge forward as an extra strong gust of wind caught the sails, the lively pitch and roll as she rode the crests of the swell waves and plunged across the troughs – all that has gone. Instead, as if she has suffered some ghastly internal haemorrhage, the ton upon ton of water swilling and surging about down below as she rolls is exerting its weight first on one side and then on the other, constantly changing her centres of gravity and buoyancy, and playing fantastic juggling tricks with her stability.

The Sibella, he thought, shivering involuntarily, is dying, like some great animal lurching through the jungle, mortally wounded and capable of only a few more steps. If a sudden surge of water to one side or the other doesn't capsize her first, then once the weight of the water pouring in through the ragged shot holes in her hull equals the weight of the ship herself, she will sink. That's a scientific fact and only pumps, not prayers, can prevent it.

As Ramage climbed up to the quarter-deck he had a momentary impression of stepping into a cow shed: the stifled moans and gasps of the wounded men sounded like the lowing and snuffling of cattle. The Bosun was carrying out his orders quickly, and the last of the wounded were being brought up: Ramage stepped back a moment to let two limping men drag a third, who appeared to have a broken leg, to join the rest of them lying in rough rows at the forward end of the quarter-deck.

None of the *Sibella*'s guns had fired for several minutes and the wind blowing through the ports had dispersed the smoke; but the smell of burnt gunpowder lingered on, clinging to his clothes, like the curious odour that hangs about a house long after flames have gutted it.

Yes, the *Barras* was where he had expected to see her – just forward of the beam and perhaps five hundred yards away. He suddenly realized she had not fired for three or four minutes. She had no need to: the damage was done. It was hard to believe that less than ten minutes had passed since the *Barras* made that slight change of course; even harder to realize that she first came in sight over the horizon only an hour ago.

Ramage heard the mewing of some gulls which had returned after the gunfire and were now wheeling in the *Sibella*'s wake, waiting hopefully for the cook's mate to throw some succulent rubbish over the side.

Over the larboard beam, the north-western end of the Argentario peninsula was beginning to fade in the darkness rapidly spreading across the dome of the sky from the eastward. Just here the land curved away and flattened out into the marshland and swamp forming the Maremma, which stretch southward for almost a hundred miles, to the gates of Rome. The next big port was Civita Vecchia, thirty-five miles to the south. That was shut, on the Pope's orders, to both French and British ships.

To seaward, beyond and above the *Barras* – which was now, in the gathering night, little more than a silhouette – the Dog Star sparkled, a pale blue pinpoint of light like a diamond on dark velvet. The Dog Star, the chilly downdraught of wind from the maintopsail, the rattle of blocks, occasional hails from lookouts, and the creak of the masts and of the timbers in the ship's hull – for many months they had been as much a part of his life as hunger and chill, heat and tiredness. And all of it reduced to a shattered ship manned by shattered seamen within a few minutes of the sails on the horizon being recognized as belonging to a French line-of-battle ship. There had been no time to escape, and as the *Barras* ran down towards them she had seemed a thing of great beauty, gently dipping and rising in elegant curtsies as the swell waves passed under her, every stitch of canvas set, including studding sails. Even as she ranged herself abeam to windward, her ports open, and the stubby black barrels of her guns poking out like threatening fingers, she had still been a thing of beauty.

Suddenly she had vomited spurts of greyish yellow smoke which, quickly merging into one great bank, had hidden her hull from view. Then she had sailed out of it, trailing thin wisps of smoke from her gun ports, while the *Sibella* appeared to lurch as she was hit by an invisible hail of shot: iron shot ranging in size from small melons to large oranges and which at that range cut through three feet of solid timber, sloughing up splinters as thick as a man's thigh and as sharp as a sword blade.

The first broadside had seemed more than the *Sibella* could stand; but she had sailed on, while the French used grapeshot in several guns for their next broadside. Ramage had seen these egg-sized shot fling a man from one side of the ship to another, as if punched by an invisible fist; others had collapsed suddenly with a grunt or a scream, death heavy inside them. He had seen several of the *Sibella*'s 12-pounder cannon, each weighing more than a quarter of a ton, thrown aside by the *Barras*'s round shot as though they were wooden dummies. Then he had been knocked unconscious.

After the little *Sibella* had been battered until she was a leaking wooden box full of smoke and flame, agonizing wounds, screams, defiant yells and death; after the majority of the eight score men who had made her a living thing and sailed her halfway round the world were at this moment lying dead or wounded, staining with their blood the decks they twice-daily scrubbed, it now seemed incongruous – blasphemous almost – that the stars could begin to twinkle and the sea still chatter merrily round the *Sibella*'s cut-water and gurgle as it creamed away in the wake astern, showing for a few brief moments the path the frigate had sailed before smoothing away the memory that she had ever passed.

Ramage forced himself to turn away from the bulwark: day-dreaming again when all he intended to do was assure himself the *Barras* was still holding her course. He now had only ten minutes or so left in which to finish his plan, which would either save his men's lives or kill them. These were, he supposed, the minutes for which eight years of life at sea should have trained him to meet.

The Bosun came up and said, 'We've got most of 'em up now, sir: about another dozen left. An' I reckon there's less than fifty of us still on our pins.'

He saw the Carpenter's Mate waiting.

'Just under six feet, sir. It's them new holes going under as she settles deeper.'

Ramage realized several dozen men near by, including many of the wounded, were listening.

'Fine – the old bitch will swim a lot longer yet. There'll be no need for anyone to get their feet wet.'

Brave talk; but these poor devils need some reassurance. He glanced across at the *Barras*. Does her captain realize the *Sibella* isn't under control? With his telescope he can see the shattered wheel, and guess that if she could be manoeuvred her officers would have already tried to wear round in an attempt to escape.

'Bosun, as soon as the last wounded man is on deck, muster the unwounded here. I want a couple of dozen axes as well. By the way, who was the signal midshipman?'

'Mr Scott.'

'Have some hands look for his body and find the signal book. None of us leaves the ship until it's found, and you can tell the men that.'

The American cox'n, Jackson, came up to him, holding a canvas sea bag.

'All the Master's charts and sailing directions, the log book, and muster book, which I found in the Purser's cabin, sir.'

Ramage gave him the documents from the cabin, with the

25

exception of the Admiral's orders. 'Put these in the bag. Men are looking for the signal book. Take charge of it when it's found. Now find me a cutlass.'

'The signal book, sir,' said a seaman, holding out a slim and blood-sodden volume.

'I'll take it,' said Jackson, and put it in the bag.

Ramage glanced across once again at the *Barras*. There was not much time left.

'Bosun! Those axes?'

'Ready, sir.'

Jackson came back, a couple of cutlasses under one arm. 'You'll be needing this, sir,' he said, handing him a speaking trumpet. The bloody man thought of everything. Ramage walked aft and scrambled up on to the hammocks along the top of the bulwark. Let's hope the French don't open fire now, he thought grimly. He put the speaking trumpet on his lips.

'Listen carefully, you men, and don't be afraid to ask about anything you don't understand. If you carry out my orders to the letter we can get away in the boats. We can't help the wounded: for their sakes we must leave them for the French surgeon to look after.

'We've got four boats that can still swim. From the moment I give the word you'll have only two or three minutes to get into those boats and pull like the devil.'

'Excuse me, sir, but how can we stop the ship to get into the boats?' asked the Bosun.

'You'll see in a moment. Now, the Frenchman out there.' He gestured with his hand. 'He's converging on us. In eight or ten minutes he'll be almost alongside, ready to board. And we can't stop him.'

At that moment the ship gave a lurch, reminding him of the water still flooding in below.

'If we haul down our flag, obviously we won't get away in the boats. So we've got to fool him to gain time. If we wait until he's almost alongside, then suddenly stop the ship, he'll probably be taken by surprise and sail on past us. But we've got to do it so quickly he doesn't get a chance to open fire.'

Before he has time to wear round again we've got away in the boats – after putting the ensign halyard in the hands of one of the wounded, so he can surrender the ship!'

'Beggin' your pardon, sir, but 'ow can we stop the ship?' a Marine asked.

'There's only one way: drop something over the side so that it acts as an anchor. And to make absolutely certain the French don't have time to fire we want to turn hard a' port at the same time. In soldiers' language,' he said to the Marine, 'We "left wheel" while Johnny Frenchman marches on ahead.'

'What do we drop over the side, sir?' the same Marine asked gloomily, as though he'd heard it all before and knew it would not work. He sucked his teeth, as if they were all he had left to relish.

'We stop the ship like this,' said Ramage, restraining a sudden urge to shake the man and wishing he hadn't given permission for them to ask questions. He spoke slowly and clearly: he wanted no mistakes. 'The foremast is almost gone: nearly all the shrouds and backstays on the starboard side are cut. A dozen men with axes can cut the rest in a few moments and the mast will go by the board – over the larboard side. That's our anchor. More than five tons of mast, yards and sails dumped in the water but still held by the larboard shrouds will suddenly drag the ship's head to larboard – which is the way we want it to go.

'And we help her by setting the mizentopsail and spanker the moment the foremast goes by the board. That'll give the stern a shove just as the wreckage of the foremast is pulling the bow round.'

'Aye, sir, but what about the Frenchman?'

It was another seaman and he genuinely wanted to know: he was not a professional Doubting Thomas like the tooth-sucker.

'If she's running almost alongside us and we suddenly turn away in not much more than our own length, she'll have only a few seconds to fire. If she does fire,' he remembered to add as a warning to the men there must be no delay, 'then she'll rake us. None of you'll see Portsmouth Point again if we get even half a broadside coming in through the transom, so say your prayers and don't make any mistakes.'

Only a few minutes to go. What else? Oh yes—

'Now the boats: Bosun, you'll command the red cutter; Carpenter's Mate, the black cutter. You, the captain of the maintop – Wilson, isn't it – you'll have the gig. I'll take the launch.

'Now – final orders. You there' – he gestured to a dozen men nearest the taffrail – 'you are axemen. Get axes from the Bosun, then go forward and stand by the all remaining fore shrouds and back stays on the starboard side. Sort yourselves out and wait for the Bosun to give the order to start cutting: that'll be the minute he hears me shouting in French.'

Ramage remembered to look across at the *Barras*. Still closing the gap. The sands of time . . .

'Right, carry on, then.'

He gestured to Wilson: 'Collect some topmen and stand by to set the mizentopsail and spanker. Do nothing until I give the word: then haul as if you were heaving for Heaven. Then get the boats round to the ports at the half-deck, starboard side.'

The *Barras* was less than three hundred yards away now: hard to judge in this light. Perhaps five minutes to go. Providing, he thought with a sick feeling of apprehension, the Frenchman does what he's supposed to . . .

'Bosun, Carpenter's Mate, Wilson—'

He jumped down from the bulwark as the three men gathered round. 'As soon as we've turned and the way's off the ship, go below and get the men into the boats. Cast off as soon as you've enough on board. Try to keep in touch – we'll pass a line from boat to boat as soon as we can. Otherwise we'll rendezvous five hundred strokes due north: that's roughly five minutes' rowing towards the Pole Star. Any questions?'

There was none. The Bosun was calm enough: now someone was giving him orders he was reacting smartly and efficiently. The Carpenter's Mate was a phlegmatic soul and Wilson was a devil-may-care sort of man.

'Carry on, then.'

The Bosun hesitated a moment as the other two turned away and from his stance seemed embarrassed.

'I wish your Pa was 'ere, sir.'

'Don't you trust me, then?'

'No, no!' the Bosun said hastily. 'I mean – well, I was with 'im that last time, sir. It was all wrong what they did. But 'e'd be proud, sir!'

With that he disappeared forward. Strange, thought Ramage, that he's never previously mentioned sailing with Father. Hardly encouraging to remind the son of 'what they did' at this particular moment – although it is, in a way; as if the Bosun intended to reaffirm his loyalty.

Two more things remained and yet another glance at the *Barras* warned him he had very little time. He looked round to make sure Jackson was near by, and the American said wryly, 'You'd just about reach her with that knife of yours, sir!'

Ramage laughed: his prowess at knife throwing – he had learnt the art as a child in Italy from his father's Sicilian coachman – was well known.

He walked across to where the wounded were lying, careful not to trip over the dead men sprawled in grotesque attitudes.

'You men – I'll be seeing you soon at Greenwich!'

One or two of them raised a wry cheer as he mentioned the home for disabled seamen.

'We have to leave you, but we're not abandoning you!' (Would they understand the difference? He doubted it.)

'With half a dozen guns left we can't fight and they' – he pointed towards the *Barras* – 'can board us whenever they like. They've a surgeon and medical supplies while we haven't. Your best chance is to be taken prisoner. One of you will be given the ensign halyard: let it go as soon as we leave the ship, so that the French just walk on board: that will make sure none of you gets more wounds. We who haven't been wounded – well, I suppose we're running away – but to fight another day. People will always talk of the *Sibella*'s last fight. So – well . . . thank you . . . and good luck.'

It sounded lame enough and he was embarrassed because emotion tightened his throat so he had to force out the last platitudes. Yet it brought a cheer from the men.

'Bosun – all ready forward?'

'Aye aye, sir.'

'By the way,' he told Jackson, 'if the French open fire and anything happens to me, tell the Bosun at once, and destroy the letter you saw me put in my pocket: that's absolutely vital. Now give the ensign halyard to one of the wounded and make sure he understands what he is to do.'

'Aye aye, sir.'

Curious how reassuring that American was, Ramage thought.

Chapter 2

RAMAGE CLIMBED up to the hammocks on the bulwark. God, the *Barras* was close now – a hundred yards perhaps, and just about abeam. He could see her bow wave, a little smother of white at the stem. He put the mouthpiece of the speaking trumpet to his ear and pointed the open end towards the *Barras*, but could hear nothing.

For the moment it seemed the French captain intended to bring his ship alongside without undue haste. Anyway, that was the seamanlike thing to do – no point in crashing alongside and risk the yards of the two ships locking together.

Unless – Ramage shivered momentarily, shocked by an awful fear: unless I'm completely wrong. I must be wrong, because the Frenchman must know just how badly damaged the *Sibella* is: she's low in the water and rolling sluggishly: he knows she'll never be towed back to Toulon. And he's slowly closing to administer the *coup de grâce*: it'll come any moment now: a sheet of flame rippling along the *Barras*'s rows of gun ports like summer lightning on the horizon, and I and the rest of the Sibellas will be dead.

I've been so clever, convincing myself the Frenchman's

vanity will make him want to tow the *Sibella* home as a prize; but I persuaded myself because I want to live: I didn't consider any other possibilities. Now – well, I've as good as murdered the wounded on the quarter-deck: men who gave me a cheer a few moments ago.

While these thoughts milled round his head he was listening intently; but he took the speaking trumpet from his ear. What's the use, he thought bitterly: I'll never hear the French captain's order to open fire at this distance; and what difference does it make, anyway?

Suddenly anger with himself drove away his fears: there was still a way out. It involved a gamble, certainly: he had to gamble that *Barras* would come within hailing distance before firing her final broadside. At the moment she was too far away from him to be certain they would hear if he shouted.

Ramage found himself thinking about the XVth Article of War, which laid down with harsh brevity that 'Every person in or belonging to the Fleet—' (God what a time to be reciting this) who yielded his ship 'cowardly or treacherously to the enemy . . . being convicted . . . shall suffer death.'

Well, if he was a coward or traitor, at least he would have to be alive for them to sentence him to death, and the way he'd been muddling along so far that possibility was fast becoming remote.

How far was she now? It was damned difficult to judge in the near darkness. Seventy yards? He put the speaking trumpet to his ear. Yes, he could hear French voices calling to each other now: just the normal order and acknowledgement. They must be pretty sure of themselves (and why not?) otherwise there'd be a lot of chattering. Would they open fire too soon? If only something would happen in the *Barras* to create a little confusion and uncertainty: that would gain him the time. Ramage put the speaking trumpet to his lips: he'd confuse them, he thought grimly.

He stopped himself from shouting just in time, and called forward: 'Bosun! Belay what I said about cutting when you hear me speaking French: don't start until I give the order.'

'Aye aye, sir.'

He put the speaking trumpet to his lips again and bellowed across the water at the French ship:

'*Bon soir, messieurs!*'

With the mouthpiece to his ear he heard, after what seemed an age, a puzzled '*Comment?*' being shouted back from the *Barras*'s quarter-deck. He could imagine their astonishment at being wished good evening. Well, keep the initiative.

'*Ho detto "Buona sera".*'

He almost laughed at the thought of the expressions on the Frenchmen's faces as they heard themselves being told in Italian that they had just been wished 'Good evening'. There was an appreciable pause before the voice repeated:

'*Comment?*'

By now the *Barras* was not more than fifty yards away: the bow wave was sharply defined and he could pick out the delicate tracery of her rigging against the night sky, whereas a few moments ago it had been an indistinct blur.

This is the moment: once again he lifted the speaking trumpet to his lips. Now, he thought, let us commend ourselves unto the XVth Article of War and still take as long as we can about it, and he yelled in English:

'Mister Frenchman – the ship is sinking.'

The same voice answered: 'Vot say you?'

'I said, "The ship is sinking." '

He sensed Jackson anxiously shifting from one foot to another. There was a strange hush in the *Sibella* and he realized the wounded were not making a sound. The *Sibella* was a phantom ship, sailing along with no one at the helm, and manned by tense and silent men.

Then through the speaking trumpet he heard someone say in French, 'It's a trick.' It was the voice of a man who held authority and who'd reached a difficult decision. He guessed the next thing he'd hear would be that voice giving the order to open fire.

'You surrender?' came back the question, in English this time.

Hurriedly Ramage turned his head towards the Bosun and called softly:

'Bosun – start chopping.'

He had to avoid a direct reply: if he surrendered the ship and then escaped the Admiralty would be just as angry as the French at a breach of the accepted code.

Putting the speaking trumpet back to his lips he shouted: 'Surrender? Who? Our wheel is destroyed – we cannot steer – we have many wounded . . .'

He heard the thud of the axes and hoped the noise would not travel across to the *Barras*: he must drown it with his own voice, or at least distract the Frenchmen's attention.

'—We cannot steer and we have most of our men killed or wounded – we are sinking fast – we've lost our captain—'

Damn, he couldn't think of anything else to say. Jackson suddenly whispered, 'Livestock's killed, guns dismounted, burgoo's spoiled . . .'

'Yes, Mister, ' Ramage yelled, 'all our pigs and the cow have been killed – all the guns are dismounted—'

'*Comment?*'

'Pigs – you've killed our pigs!'

'*Je ne comprend pas!* You surrender?'

'You've killed our pigs—'

The devil take it, would that foremast never go by the board?

'—The cow has been dismounted – the guns don't give any more milk – the pig's making water at the rate of a foot every fifteen minutes!'

He heard Jackson chuckling and at that moment there was a crackling from forward and a whiplash noise as several ropes parted under strain. Then there was a fearful groan, like a giant in pain, and against the night sky he could see the foremast beginning to topple. It went slowly at first; then crashed over the side, taking the yards with it.

'Wilson! the topsail and spanker!'

He saw the spanker being sheeted home to the boom end as the topsail was let fall from the yard. A few moments later, when he looked back at the *Barras,* she had vanished: He realized the *Sibella* was swinging round to larboard faster than he expected, and he glanced aft. The *Barras* had been caught unawares – she was still sailing on her original course and had gone too far for her guns to be able to rake the *Sibella*'s completely unprotected stern.

He felt shaky with relief and his clothes were soaked with perspiration. He scrambled down from the bulwark, and as he jumped to the deck his knees gave way slightly and Jackson caught him. 'Pity about that cow, sir,' he said dryly, 'I just fancy a mug o' milk.'

Chapter 3

FOR MORE THAN half an hour Lieutenant Nicholas Ramage's little world had been limited to the boat, the sea and the great blue-back dome of the night sky, which was cloudless and glittering with so many stars and planets it seemed to hold every spark that had ever fallen from a blacksmith's anvil.

The launch was heavy, but the men sitting on the thwarts facing him were rowing with a will: as they leaned back in unison, pulling with all their strength, the oars creaked against the wooden sides of the rowlocks. Who was it who said in ancient times, 'Give me a fulcrum and I'll move the Earth'?

At the end of each stroke the men involuntarily gasped for breath, at the same time pushing downward on the looms of the oars to bring the blades clear of the water. Then, leaning forward like rows of seated tenants bowing to the landlord, they thrust the looms in front of them, and at the end of the movement dipped the blades into the water to haul back and begin the new stroke.

Lean back, creak, gasp, lean forward; lean back, creak, gasp, lean forward . . . Ramage, his arm resting along the top of the tiller as he steered, could feel the boat spurting forward under the thrust of each stroke. Occasionally he glanced astern, where the Bosun's cutter and the other two boats followed, each linked by a line to the next ahead.

'Sir!' exclaimed Jackson, gesturing astern: there was a

small red glow in the distance but, even while Ramage watched, tongues of flame spurted up, as if a blacksmith's bellows suddenly fanned new life into a forge fire.

Half an hour: the French would have taken off the wounded. God knows they must have suffered as they were carried across to the *Barras*. Still, the sea was calm enough for the two ships to lie alongside each other, which would save them being ferried in boats. Ramage could picture the French officers leading the boarding party having the well sounded and reporting back the depth of water in the ship and the damage.

Now, with the magazine flooded, they've set fire to the ship. . . . He turned away and saw some of the men wiping their eyes. It was ridiculous how a ship's company became fond of a few hundred tons of wood, rope and canvas which had for months been their home, and for the last hour and all eternity a tomb for many of them.

The men were rowing unevenly as they watched the *Sibella* burn. A sudden tug on the line to the cutter, followed by a string of curses from the Bosun, told him that he might as well let the men watch the *Sibella*'s funeral pyre and have a rest at the same time, and he shouted the order into the darkness.

At last he could read the orders to the *Sibella*'s late captain: he had been burning with curiosity from the time the oarsmen had settled into a steady rhythm and given him time to think.

'The lantern, Jackson, and keep it shielded with the canvas, I want to read something.'

Pulling the linen envelope from his pocket, Ramage took out the sheet of paper and smoothed it. The letter had been written on board the *Victory* on September 1, a week earlier, and was an order from Admiral Sir John Jervis, K.B., telling the *Sibella*'s late captain, in neat and flowing script, 'Whereas I have received information that following the French occupation of Leghorn and other towns inland, several leading members of influential families in Tuscany sympathetic to our cause have succeeded in escaping and made their way southward to the coast off Capalbio, from whence they have requested assistance, you are, therefore, hereby required and directed to proceed with all possible despatch in His Majesty's ship *Sibella* under your command, off Capalbio, taking care that your intentions should not become known to anyone on shore.'

So that was what brought them down here ... Ramage turned over the page and continued reading.

'You will then under the cover of night send a party on shore to the fortified tower situated between Lake Burano and the shore and commonly known as "Torre Buranaccio", and take off the party of refugees, believed to be six in number, and who are named in the margin.

'From the information I have received, the Tower is not in use by the Neapolitan troops, nor occupied by the French (who are known to have passed through the area); and the refugees have arranged that a charcoal burner, whose name they have omitted to communicate to me but whose hut is one half a mile southward along the beach from the tower and five hundred yards inland, shall be kept informed of their whereabouts.

'Since negotiations will have to be carried on in the native language, the landing party should be under the command of Lieutenant Nicholas Ramage in virtue of his knowledge of the Italian language.

'Great importance is attached to the safety and well-being of these refugees in view of the influence they can command on the Italian mainland; and as soon as they and any others with them are safely embarked in His Majesty's frigate under your command, you are to make the best of your way to Rendezvous Number Seven, where you will find one of His Majesty's ships whose commanding officer will give you further orders for your subsequent proceedings.'

Hmm, thought Ramage, considering the length of the letter and details, 'Old Jarvie' really means what he says about the importance of these people: he was notorious for the brevity of his orders.

Ramage folded the letter and put it back in his pocket. As orders for the *Sibella's* late captain, they were simple enough; but for his successor they presented difficulties undreamed of when dictated by Sir John, who was the strictest disciplinarian on the flag list. Ramage realized he did not even know where Rendezvous Number Seven was . . .

A sudden kick on the shin stopped his reverie.

'Sorry, sir,' said Jackson, 'I'm getting cramp in my leg.'

Ramage knew the men were waiting expectantly. Well, let them wait.

What must he do? What would the Admiral expect him to do? What would the *Sibella*'s late captain, cremated a few moments ago, have done if he were sitting here in the launch's stern sheets?

He could ask the opinions of the senior men, showing them the order: hold a council of war, in fact. But his pride prevented that and anyway his father had once said – 'Nicholas, my boy: if you ever want to achieve anything in the Service, never call a council of war.' Yet when the old boy had acted on his own advice, Ramage thought bitterly, look what had happened . . .

Then in his imagination he saw, for a fleeting second, a group of thoroughly frightened civilians staring seaward through the narrow window of a peasant's hut, plagued by mosquitoes, too frightened to light a lamp at night, and waiting for a ship of the Royal Navy to rescue them from – from France's guillotines or possibly the unspeakable horrors of the Grand Duke of Tuscany's dungeons, since the Grand Duke's attempts to remain neutral had been feeble, and he had even entertained Napoleon to dinner, from all accounts.

Who were they, anyway? He'd forgotten to look at the names in the margin.

'Lantern, Jackson.'

He unfolded the letter once more and read the names of five men and a woman listed one below the other in the margin: the Duke of Venturino, the Marquis of Sassofortino, Count Chiusi, Count Pisano, Count Pitti and the Marchioness of Volterra.

It took him a moment or two to register the shock of reading the anglicized version of the Marchesa di Volterra's name: he had a sudden picture in his mind of a tall, white-haired

37

woman with a patrician face whom he had known, for much of his childhood, as 'Aunt Lucia'. She was no relation, but as one of his mother's closest friends she was a frequent visitor when his parents lived in Siena; and they in turn had often stayed at the Marchesa's palace at Volterra. So now the little boy she used to bully because he could not (would not, too) quote yards of Dante, was back – almost back, anyway – in Italy, to haul her off the beach. . . .

Sir John Jervis's determination that they should be rescued made sense now: the Marchesa, and the Duke of Venturino, were two of the most influential and powerful figures in Tuscany: it had been said for years that if they could agree with each other for long enough, they could probably overthrow the Grand Duke and rid Tuscany for ever of the dreary Hapsburgs.

Ramage was glad he'd decided to attempt the rescue before reading the names. If he'd previously decided against it, he would have changed his mind later. There was some satisfaction in attempting what he hoped was the right thing for the right reason.

Yet when it came to rescuing refugees, it shouldn't matter who they are: when a head rolls into the wicker basket from the guillotine blade, a peasant's head is a human head as much as the duke's; which was what Shakespeare meant when he made Shylock say 'Hath not a Jew eyes? Hath not a Jew hands?'

Ramage could imagine the president of the court trying him for the loss of the *Sibella* asking, 'Why did you decide to attempt to execute with an open boat the Admiral's orders, which were intended to be carried out by a frigate?'

'Well, sir, I was thinking about Shylock . . .'

He could imagine the sneers; could hear, almost, the whispered 'Yes, he's his father's son all right.' And that's the crux of it: he was his father's son and so much more vulnerable than other lieutenants because he had many more potential enemies waiting to strike at him to wound his father. A Service vendetta was a long-drawn-out affair and when admirals were involved everyone was forced to take sides because promotion and patronage were involved. To become the protégé of a particular admiral was a good thing, as long as the admiral was in favour, because he would push opportunities your way. But if the admiral supported a political party, as several of them did, then the moment his party lost power, the fact you were one of his protégés was a millstone round your neck.

Poor Father: a braver man never lived, and many still considered him the most brilliant strategist and tactician the Navy ever had. Which was, of course, the reason for his downfall. When you give the command of a fleet to a born leader with a keen brain, and provide him with a textbook containing a limited set of regulations telling him how to fight a battle, you're asking for trouble.

Ramage was seven when his father was brought to trial; but later, when he was old enough to understand, he had read the minutes of the trial of John Uglow Ramage, tenth Earl of Blazey and Admiral of the White many times. It was easy to see how the court had found Father guilty; indeed, since he had refused to be tied down by the Fighting Instructions and had used his own tactics instead, they had no alternative. But the King's refusal to quash the verdict – which only he had the power to do – was naked politics: Father had an independent mind and had refused to pay court to either Whigs or Tories, so he expected help from no one.

Ramage realized that since he had only four open boats to carry out orders intended for a frigate his own position was, in a microcosm, similar to the one facing his father fifteen years earlier. Then, the Government, ignoring all warnings about the size of the French forces, sent a small fleet to the West Indies under the Earl of Blazey. And when the Earl arrived to find himself attacked by a French Fleet which was twice as powerful and in circumstances not covered in the Fighting Instructions – which dealt only with a few eventualities – he had used brilliant and original tactics to extricate himself, losing only one line-of-battle ship.

But, of course, he had lost the battle: against those odds no one could have won it. Any British admiral feeling himself bound by the Fighting Instructions – but unable to get any guidance from them – would have fought an orthodox battle and lost many more ships. In fact, considering he only lost one ship, Father had won a tactical victory. However, there was a fatal combination: first, as usual, the Government had sent too few ships, but when the mobs began to yell in protest over the defeat, it was determined to shift the blame on to someone else's shoulders; secondly, the Admiral who fought and lost the battle had ignored the Fighting Instructions. That was enough for the politicians: they had a ready-made scapegoat.

The mobs were never told the Fighting Instructions were not flexible enough to cover that kind of battle; instead a flow of pamphlets and newspaper articles led them to think that had he followed the Instructions he would have won. The fact that his own tactics were brilliant and avoided the heavy losses an attempt to follow the Fighting Instructions would have entailed was never brought out – except when Father made his defence at the trial. Even then the newspapers, which were in the Government's pay anyway, distorted or omitted what he said.

The old chap's speech had been almost too clever; he presented such a well-reasoned argument that the layman's suspicion of an expert – and the professional's jealousy – were soon aroused.

How had Father described the Fighting Instructions? Oh yes, he'd likened them to instructions for a coachman when a highwayman standing in his path orders him to halt. Ramage could almost see the actual print in the leather-bound copy of the minutes of the trial, which was kept in the library at home.

'The Fighting Instructions in effect order the coachman,' Father had said, 'to aim his blunderbuss directly over his horses' heads, and fire at the highwayman. But they do not tell him what to do if there are two or a dozen highwaymen standing to one side of the path or another. They assume it will never happen. But at the same time their orders contain a clause which ensures that, if it happens, whatever the coachman does is wrong: if he fires to the left, to the right, surrenders or runs away.'

The court could have sentenced him to death; but since the affair of Admiral Byng the Articles of War had been amended to allow a lesser penalty. The court had ordered him to be dismissed the Service. Ramage had often wondered whether this was, for his father, a lesser penalty than death.

The man who had emerged from the trial as his father's enemy had been a member of the Court, a captain low down on the post list but high up in the King's esteem: Captain Goddard, now a rear-admiral, who was a man with little intelligence or ability but full of corrosive jealousy. Marriage into the outer fringe of the royal family had, so far as promotion was concerned, made up for his other deficiencies.

Since Goddard had so much influence with the crazy King – indeed, it was said he was one of the few men who could get any sense at all out of His Majesty during his not infrequent bouts of insanity – he had attracted a large following in the Navy when he became a rear-admiral: many captains – and flag officers – were prepared to sink their pride in order to provide Goddard with the sycophantic circle of admirers his pride required, receiving preferment and promotion in return.

Unfortunately, Goddard was serving in the Mediterranean at the moment, although apparently neither the Commander-in-Chief, Admiral Sir John Jervis, nor the third in command, Captain Horatio Nelson, had much time for him. Ramage was not sure, but suspected it was due only to Sir John Jervis's influence that he was himself employed. But the fourth in seniority, Captain Croucher, was a close friend of Goddard's. If he was president at the court martial trying him for the loss of the *Sibella*, Ramage thought, the verdict could be given even before the first witness was sworn in.

Anyway, Ramage told himself, it's time we were under way: the seamen have had enough rest. Those in authority can always put a subordinate in the wrong: that's an indisputable fact and it's no good brooding over it.

Chapter 4

'LET ME HAVE the charts, Jackson.' The American handed over the canvas bag, and Ramage selected one from the roll which covered the area from the Vada Rocks, off Livorno – or Leghorn as the British insisted on calling it – to Civita Vecchia. Before looking at it he glanced at the Master's log and found it had been filled in up to six o'clock that evening, when the last entry gave a bearing and distance of the peak of Monte Argentario and the north end of the island of Giglio and added: 'Enemy sail in sight to north-west.'

Ramage unrolled the chart, folded it on his knee, and pulled the throwing knife from its sheath inside the top of his boot, using the blade to measure the distance from Monte Argentario at 6 pm, taking it off the latitude scale at the side of the chart. He then twisted the knife round so he could use the blade to transfer the bearing from the compass rose.

He then pricked a point on the chart. That was the 6 pm position of the *Sibella*. After estimating the course she'd steered and the distance covered until the French boarded, he pricked the chart once again. That was where she had sunk. Then he made a third mark – their present position, as accurately as guesswork based on experience could permit.

Where did it put them? Roughly midway between the Argentario promontory and the island of Giglio. The channel between the two – he used the knife to measure it approximately – is twelve miles wide. So they were about six miles from Capo d'Uomo, the high cliff where one of Argentario's mountainous ridges meets the sea.

Ironic, he thought, that we've been rowing north-westward, away from Capalbio and the refugees, for the past half hour.

The chart showed that to reach the Tower at Capalbio they must first round the southern end of Argentario, which is almost an island joined to the mainland by two causeways. Odd how on the chart Argentario looked like a fat bat hanging

42

upside down from a beam, with its two legs forming the causeways and the beam the mainland. The Tower is on the coast about five miles south of where the southern causeway meets the mainland, with the village of Capalbio on a hill five or six miles inland.

Well, it's more than fifteen miles, and without knowing the coast it will be impossible to find the Tower before daylight. That means we must hide somewhere before daylight. But where? The south-eastern side of Argentario is too risky: Port' Ercole, just round the corner, would have plenty of fishing boats coming and going. No, we'll have to keep clear of Argentario and spend daylight on Friday hiding at Giannutri, another small island athwart the channel to the south-east. From there, on Friday night, we can reach the Formiche di Burano, a tiny reef only a few feet high and offshore of Capalbio. From our present position to Giannutri is ... about seven miles: we can hide near Punta Secca.

He saw they would have to cover twelve miles on Friday night to reach the Formiche, and another three to the Tower. But in the meantime he would have a chance to study the mainland through his glass.

That meant he had Friday night to find the refugees; they would have to stay in hiding Saturday and sail from Capalbio on Saturday night ...

'Bosun, Carpenter's Mate, Wilson – come on board!'

A sandy beach at Capalbio – that would mean hauling the boat up. Only the gig would be light enough to be hauled on shore by its crew. Six men to row, plus Jackson and himself, for the trip to Capalbio. Then half a dozen refugees. Fourteen in the gig for the return journey ... it would be overloaded only if they ran into bad weather, since it could carry sixteen when used for cutting out expeditions. But he had no choice: the boat would have to be hauled up and hidden: finding the Italians might take time – he dare not gamble on landing, finding them and getting to sea again the same night.

The Bosun hauled the cutter up to the launch's transom and scrambled on board, followed by the Carpenter's Mate and

43

Wilson. As the three men sat waiting in the darkness, Ramage would have given a lot to know their thoughts. . . .

'I've opened the Captain's orders and propose carrying them out . . .'

He tended to have difficulty in pronouncing the letter 'r' when he became excited: the faint hint of 'pwopose' warned him to keep calm.

'I shall take Jackson and six men in the gig. Bosun, you'll transfer to the launch, and Wilson can take over your cutter.

'Bosun, you'll be in command of the three boats.'

Damned difficult giving orders to men in the dark when you couldn't see their faces.

'You will take them to Bastia, in Corsica.'

'But it's—'

'A long way: over seventy miles, but it's the nearest place where you'll find any British ships, and as you know the Corsican coast, you won't get lost. Take the muster book and master's log. When you arrive, report to the senior British naval officer, giving him a full account of what has happened and – now listen carefully, this is most important – ask him to communicate to Sir John Jervis at once that Lieutenant Ramage is proceeding in execution of Sir John's orders concerning the *Sibella*. Also request him to send a ship to rendezvous with me five miles off the north end of Giglio at dawn on Sunday and, if I'm not there, again at dawn on Monday.

'If you are unlucky enough to get caught by the French on the way, throw the log over the side, and at all costs convince them you are the only survivors from the *Sibella*. Don't mention me or the gig. Now—'

Swiftly he settled the details of the courses the Bosun was to steer. He remembered to ask if any of the boats had wine on board and found the Carpenter's Mate's boat had a barrel, which he was ordered to empty over the side. His protests were met with a curt, 'Can you guarantee to control a couple of dozen drunken men?'

After telling the Bosun to send the six best men over to the gig, Ramage shook hands with the three men in the darkness, and prepared to scramble over the boats to join his latest command. This, he thought to himself, must be a record – to have held the command of a frigate, a launch, and finally a gig, all in the space of an hour.

Just before ordering the other three boats away, Ramage remembered to gather them round and, to back up the Bosun's authority, warned all the seamen that they were still governed by the Articles of War. They listened in silence broken only by the slapping of the water against the sides of the boats and the occasional scraping as one or other of the boats fended off.

Then, to Ramage's surprise, just as he was about to tell the Bosun to carry on, one of the seamen called out in a low voice, 'Three cheers for 'is Lordship – 'ip, 'ip . . . ooray!' The men had kept their voices low; yet he sensed the emotion in their voices. He was so startled – both by the unexpected cheers and the significant use of his title – that he was groping for a suitable reply when several of the men called across, 'Good luck, sir!' which allowed him to respond with a gruff, 'Thank you, lads: now bend your backs; you've a long way to go.'

With that he sat down in the stern sheets, took the tiller and waited for the other boats to get clear before setting the gig's crew to work at the oars.

Glancing over towards Argentario he saw a faint, silvery glow below the horizon which was just beginning to dim some of the stars: the moon was rising behind the mountains, and a few minutes later he could distinguish the faces of the men sitting on the nearest thwarts, and noticed they were shiny with perspiration.

Well, he told himself, there are fewer worries in commanding a gig twenty-four feet long and weighing about thirteen hundredweight than a frigate of 150 feet displacing nearly seven hundred tons: less comfortable though, he thought, easing himself round so that the transom knee did not dig into his hip.

As the moon, a great oyster-pink orb, rose from behind Argentario it sharpened the silhouetted peaks of the mountains. They were, he mused, comfortable mountains with the peaks and ridges well rounded, compared with the jagged, tooth-edged Alps: more like gargantuan ant-hills. But as the moon climbed higher, shortening the shadows, the silhouette faded, and the whole of Argentario was tinted in a warm, silvery-pink light. A silver light on Monte Argentario ... Why was it named the Silver Mountain? Was silver ever mined there? Surely not. Perhaps the wind ruffling the leaves of the olive trees made it look silvery in daylight – he remembered noticing their foliage sometimes gave that effect to a hillside.

Now he could see all the men in the gig and recognized them as topmen: the Bosun had given him the survivors of the finest seamen in the *Sibella*: the men who reefed or furled aloft high up and out on the yards.

In the moonlight, unshaven and raggedly dressed, they looked more like the crew of a privateer's boat than King's men, and privateersmen were as bad as pirates – worse, in fact, since they usually served on a shares-in-the-prize basis, which made them much more cruel and daring than pirates, whose rewards depended on the whim of their captain.

One of the men on the nearest thwart, naked from the waist up, a rag round his brow to stop the perspiration running into his eyes, and his hair tied in a pigtail, still had his face begrimed with smoke from the guns. Why the devil didn't I tell them to put some hammocks in the boats? thought Ramage: even though they are tanned, a day half stripped under a hot sun will scorch their skin and exhaust them more than a spell at the oars, apart from an increasing thirst.

That man rowing stroke – wasn't his face streaked with blood?

'You – stroke! Have you been hurt?'

'It's nothing, sir: just a cut on the forehead. Why, is me face bloody?'

'Looks it from here.'

They were an extraordinary bunch: give them the slightest opportunity to shirk a job and they'll seize it, he thought. Give the majority of them a chance to desert and they will, even though they risk death, or the certainty of a flogging round the fleet. But in battle they are new men: the shirker, the drunkard, the fool – all become fighting demons. In an emergency each has the strength of two men. Even now, after half a day's bitter battle, they'll haul on their oars, if necessary, until they drop from exhaustion. Yet if there was a cask of wine in the boat and he went to sleep, he'd find them all blind drunk when he woke.

They were like children in many ways, and even though several of the Sibellas were old enough to be his father, he was always conscious of their basic simplicity: their sudden childlike enthusiasms, waywardness, lack of responsibility and unpredictability.

Dreaming again, Ramage . . . He decided to let them rest while he gave them a word or two about their task.

'Well, men, you may be curious to know where we are going – if you haven't already heard at the scuttle butt . . .'

This raised a laugh: many an officer first heard details of his captain's secret orders by way of the scuttle butt, which was the tub of water placed on deck, guarded by a Marine sentry, and from which the men could drink at set times during the day. There the day's gossip was exchanged, and although the route the news travelled from the cabin to the scuttle butt was often devious, the news itself was nearly always accurate. A captain's steward's eyes and ears rarely missed anything, and a lowly captain's writer – virtually a clerk – became someone of importance among his shipmates only if he had some information to pass on.

'In case you haven't, I'll tell you as much as I can. There are half a dozen Italian refugees – important people: important enough for the Admiral to risk a frigate – to be rescued from the mainland. That was the job the *Sibella* started. Well, we've got to finish it.

'We'll get as close as we can to this place tonight, but we daren't risk being seen in daylight, so we'll have to hide and finish the trip tomorrow night. Now you know about as much as I do.'

'A question, sir?'

'Yes.'

' 'Ow far's this Bonaparte chap got down this way? Who owns this bit o' the coast, sir?'

'Bonaparte occupied Leghorn a couple of months ago. Leghorn's a free port, but that bit of the coast and almost as far down as here belongs to the Grand Duke of Tuscany, and he's signed a pact with Napoleon.

'But all along the coast there are enclaves – little countries, as it were – belonging to other people: Piombino, for instance, opposite Elba, belongs to the Buoncampagno family. Half of Elba and a narrow strip of the coast running south as far as here, and including Argentario, which you can see over there, belong to the King of Naples and Sicily.'

'Whose side is he on, sir?'

'He was on ours, but he's ceased hostilities.'

'Surrendered, sir? Why the French ain't reached Naples or Sicily, yet!'

'No, but the King's afraid they'll march on Naples, I suppose. Anyway, just beyond Argentario is the town of Orbetello and that's the capital of the King's enclave here. I'm not sure how far south it stretches. Southward of that the land belongs to the Pope.'

' 'Ow about 'im, sir?' asked the seaman with the bloodstained face. 'Is 'e on our side?'

'Well, he's signed an armistice with Bonaparte and shut his ports to British ships.'

'Looks as though we ain't got many friends round these parts, do it,' one of the seamen commented to no one in particular.

'No,' laughed Ramage. 'None we can count on. And where we are going to land we might find Bonaparte's troops, or Neapolitans – we shan't know whose side they'll be on – or even the Pope's troops.'

'Are these people we're taking off Eyetalians, sir?'

'Yes.'

'Then why ain't they put their names down in Boney's muster book like the rest on 'em, sir, begging your pardon?'

'These particular ones don't like him any more than we do:

nor does he like them: in fact if he gets his hands on them, they'll end up being married to the Widow.'

The men murmured among themselves: they knew well enough the French slang for the guillotine. Ramage heard one of them say, 'They seem a rum lot, these Eyetalians. Some sign on with Boney, while the others bolt. 'Ow the hell do they know which to do?'

That, thought Ramage, sums it up fairly neatly. And now after eight years he was about to return to this beautiful, lazy, flamboyant country, which was so full of contradictions that only an insensitive fool could say with any certainty that he loved or hated it, or any stage in between.

'Beggin' your pardon, sir: you speak the lingo, don't you?'

'Yes.'

Heavens, the men either trusted him so much they felt they could ask questions without getting a savage snub, or they were taking advantage of him, 'being familiar', as some officers called it. But their interest was genuine enough.

'How's that, sir?' asked the same nasal voice.

Why not tell them? They'd all stopped talking to hear his reply, and for the next couple of days he needed every ounce of trust they'd give him.

'Well, when my father sailed in '77 to command the American Station – when your people showed signs of wanting to be independent,' he said jokingly to Jackson, 'my mother came out to Italy to stay with various friends: she loved travelling – she still does, for that matter. I was two years old. I had an Italian nurse and began to speak Italian almost as soon as I did English.

'We went back to England in '82 when I was seven. Most of you know the reason ... In '83, after my father's trial, he decided to leave England for a few years, and we came back to Italy. So I was out here again from the time I was eight until just before I was thirteen, when we returned to England and I first went to sea.'

'That was when the press caught you, was it, sir?'

The rest of them roared with laughter at the blood-stained

man's joke. A good half of the men had been hauled in by press gangs and brought on board one or other of the King's ships, where they were given the chance to 'volunteer', which meant they received a bounty of a few shillings, and had 'vol' instead of 'prest' written against their names in the muster book.

'Yes,' said Ramage, joining in the laughter, 'but I took the bounty.'

The men had rested enough and he gave the orders for them to start rowing again. Ahead, lying low in the water like a sea monster, was the flat-topped islet of Giannutri. Although the chart did not give much detail, the nearest point to the mainland, Punta Secca, had a scattering of inlets just south of it. But the name, Dry Point, did not hold out much hope of finding drinking water.

Ramage ran his fingers through his hair and winced as they caught in clotted blood at the back of his scalp. He had forgotten about the cut. At least it had dried up quickly. At Giannutri, he thought to himself, he would have to do something towards tidying himself: at the moment he must look more like a highwayman than a naval officer.

Chapter 5

JACKSON WATCHED as the upper rim of the sun finally dropped below the low hills of Giannutri and spread a welcome cool shadow across the eastern side of the island. He glanced at the watch: another half an hour before his spell as lookout ended and he had to wake Mr Ramage.

They had been luck in finding this little inlet, which was cut out of the rock as neatly as if someone had sliced it with a knife. The boat was almost invisible to a man standing on the shore five yards away, whereas the sides of the inlet, only a few inches higher than the gunwale of the boat, meant they could keep a lookout all round them.

For much of the morning Mr Ramage had been sitting on the side of the hill, glass to his eye, studying the mainland. As soon as he had located the Tower of Buranaccio, just at the back of the beach, its base hidden by the sand dunes and the curvature of the earth, he had ordered all the seamen to be brought up, two at a time, to look at it through the glass and study the coast on either side.

In the meantime, Jackson had set one of the sailors to work scrubbing the Lieutenant's jacket to remove some of the blood-stains, carefully smoothing the cloth with his hand as he laid it out to dry. The silk stock looked far from ironed; but flatten-ing it out on a smooth rock while still wet had given it a new lease of life. At least, thought Jackson, Mr Ramage will look smart enough in the dark when he meets these dukes and people. Pity he had lost his hat.

Looking down at the sleeping lieutenant, Jackson saw that occasionally the muscles of his face twitched. Curious, the habit he had of blinking, particularly when thinking hard, or if he was tired or excited. It seemed deliberate, as though squeezing the eyelids together helped him concentrate.

The Bosun had said Mr Ramage looked just like his father, the Earl of Blazey – old 'Blaze-Away', as the Navy called him. Jackson felt a twinge of embarrassment as he remembered when, a few months ago, he said he hoped old 'Blaze-Away's' son had more guts than his father, and the Bosun had brought him up all standing by getting into a fury. Seemed the trial was all political ... Well, the Bosun served in the old boy's flagship at the battle, so he ought to know. Anyway, whether or not the father had been a coward, the son seemed man enough.

The lad had a good face, Jackson thought to himself; there had never been an opportunity to study it before. On the thin side, though, with the nose straight and cheekbones high. But with Mr Ramage it was always his eyes that attracted you. Deep set and brown, they were slung under a pair of bushy eyebrows, and when he was really angry they seemed to bore right through you. What was it one of the men in Mr Ramage's division had said when hauled before the captain for some crime or other, and asked if he was guilty? Something to the effect it was no use pleading not guilty as Mr Ramage knew different; and when the Captain had said Mr Ramage had not been on deck at that particular moment, the sailor replied, 'That don't signify because Mr Ramage can see through oak planks.'

Yet, mused Jackson, he had never come across an officer quite like him: none of the sarcasm and hoity-toity of so many junior lieutenants. But everyone respected him – perhaps because the hands knew he could beat any of them up to the maintop. He could knot and splice like a rigger, and handle a boat as though he'd been born under a thwart. And, more important, he was approachable. Somehow he seemed to know instinctively how the men felt: when it was necessary to encourage them with a quiet joke, and when to threaten them with a 'starting' – not that Jackson ever remembered actually seeing him allow a bosun's mate to hit the men with a rope's end. Nor had he ever had to take a man before the captain.

It was curious how, when he was angry or excited, he had trouble pronouncing the letter 'r'. You could see him tensing himself to say it correctly. But Jackson remembered a topman – that fellow there with a cut forehead – making a pun once, 'When you see his bloody young Lordship blinking his eyes and wobbling his "r's", it's time to go about on the other tack!' Why was it he never used his title on board? After all, he was a real Lord. Something to do with his father, maybe.

Christ, he thought, that lad's lying there like a worn-out hawser. Ramage was curled up on the stern sheets, arms above his head and using his hands as a pillow. Although he was obviously in a deep sleep, Jackson guessed he was not relaxed: the corners of the rather full lips were turned down slightly; his forehead was wrinkled, as if he was concentrating, and his eyebrows were lowered. If he had his eyes open, Jackson thought, you'd imagine he was trying to sight something on the horizon. And where did he collect that scar above the right eyebrow? He always rubbed it when he was tired or under a strain. Looked like a sword cut.

By now the east side of the island, which had been mauve as the sun set, was darkening in the twilight, and Jackson looked towards the mainland. Over to his left was the great hump of Argentario, and he could see one of the two semi-circular causeways which joined it to the mainland. In front, he could just see a small, flat reef of rocks, the Formiche de Burano, a black spot in the sea in line with Mount Capalbio. Just to the right of Mount Capalbio was Mount Maggiore, and on the coast in line with its peak was the little square tower, which Mr Ramage said they had to visit. It was too dark against the eastern sky to see it now, and anyway half of it was below the horizon.

The chart showed there was a big oblong-shaped lake behind the tower, running parallel with the beach and less than half a mile inland. From the middle of the nearest side a little river left the lake, running towards the sea past the north side of the tower, making a dog-leg turn to flow along the west wall – so the tower had a moat on two sides – and then straight for another couple of hundred yards, parallel with the shore, before curving round to flow into the sea.

Oh well, Jackson thought to himself, it will be nice to be on shore again, even if only for an hour or two. He looked at the watch. Another five minutes before he was due to rouse Mr Ramage.

Some of the seamen had already woken. One had persuaded another to retie his pigtail, while a third leaned over the side of the boat and began to hone his knife against the rock until Jackson told him to be quiet.

The American glanced round the gig and began checking off various items. The tiller was ready to be shipped; the oars were safely stowed; the two precious breakers of water were lashed under the thwarts, as were the bags of bread; the lantern was trimmed and ready for lighting; the bag of charts and papers was at his feet.

The seaman with the cut on his forehead rolled up a trouser leg and swore viciously, pointing at the mosquito bites on his ankle. He fished a rough canvas shirt from under a thwart and pulled it over his head.

'Can't we have a drink, Jacko?' asked another sailor.

'You heard what Mr Ramage said.'

'You're just a damned mean Jonathan.'

'Ask Mr Ramage when he wakes.'

'You like pushing us Limeys around.'

'All right, you're a Limey and I'm a Jonathan,' retorted Jackson, 'but that don't make me any less thirsty than you.'

'Anyway that thirsty bastard ain't a Limey, he's a Patlander,' a man lying on the bottom boards said to Jackson. 'He's so Irish he salutes when we ship a green sea.'

'Listen, the lot of you,' growled Jackson. 'Mr Ramage has two minutes' more sleep and he deserves 'em; so put a couple of reefs in your tongues.'

'Is he doing the right thing, Jacko?' one of the men whispered. 'After all, this gig ain't a bleedin' frigate.'

'Scared? Anyway, we'd have had to do this last bit in a boat even if the *Sibella* was still swimming.'

'Yus, but we wouldn't have to row all the way there and back like a lot of bumboatmen.'

'Well,' Jackson said crisply, 'make up your mind whether you're scared or lazy. If you're scared then you've no need to be, with him on board' – he jerked a thumb in Ramage's direction – 'and if you're lazy you'd better watch out with this one on board—' he jabbed a thumb to his own chest.

'All right, all right, Jacko; I'd sooner 'ave 'im than you any day, so put me down as just being scared.'

Jackson glanced once again at the watch, and then climbed over a thwart to rouse Ramage.

The skin of Ramage's face felt taut and stiff, scorched by the sun despite the tan; and a band across the top of his forehead, normally protected by his hat, was hot and sore. He opened his eyes and they felt full of sand. Realizing someone was gently shaking him and calling his name, he sat up, conscious of a momentary feeling of fear as he remembered the last time he had woken.

Almost nightfall; yet he would have sworn he'd been asleep only five minutes.

'Everything all right, Jackson?'

'Yes, sir.'

With that Ramage stripped off his clothes and climbed over the transom into the water. It was warm, but chilly enough to be refreshing. As he climbed back on board again Jackson handed him a piece of cloth.

'Do as a towel, sir.'

'What is it?'

'His shirt, sir,' he said, pointing to one of the man and adding, 'he offered it!'

Ramage nodded his thanks, rubbed himself down and pulled on his stockings, breeches and shirt. He glanced up in surprise as Jackson said, 'We've tidied up your stock, weskit and coat, sir. If you don't want 'em yet I'll stow 'em so they don't get creased.'

'Oh – yes, do that please.'

Trust Jackson, thought Ramage: he realizes I look like a pirate. If only I had a razor, he thought, feeling his chin, which crackled as he ran his hand over it.

Jackson handed him his boots and, as soon as he had pulled them on, gave him the throwing knife, which he slid into the top and did up the button which held the sheath in place.

It would be safer to wait a few more minutes, until it was completely dark: anyone on Giannutri who saw them leaving could swiftly light the pile of firewood he had seen on the platform of the signal tower at the north side of the island.

He was surprised by the number of signal towers on Argentario: from its nearest point to Giannutri there was one on every headland along the coast northwards, presumably round as far as Santo Stefano, the little port on the north-east side, and also round the south coast, probably to link with Port' Ercole. Some of the towers looked Spanish; others Arab: tall warnings of the threats of Barbary pirates, who were still busy in the Mediterranean.

Finally it was dark enough to get under way, but as he gave the order Ramage felt nervousness sweeping over him, like a chill from a sudden cold breeze.

In the darkness the sea, the boat and even Ramage's own body, seemed remote. To seaward it was impossible to see where horizon ended and night sky began, despite the glittering stars and the light from the sharply etched moon, which had just risen over the mainland. The boat seemed to be gliding along like a gull, suspended between sea and sky.

Ramage found it hard to believe the crazy attempt he was making with seven men in a small boat was reality. Was this gig supposed to be a suitable substitute for a frigate to rescue men of great political influence so that they could rally their people to carry on – start, in some cases – a war against Bonaparte?

Was Ramage himself a suitable substitute for a post captain, welcoming them on board amid grandiose assurances for their future? Was he the man to inspire and overawe them with Britain's sea power in the Mediterranean? The whole situation was either tragic or ludicrous.

Jackson's lean face, dancing with strange shadows as he lifted the canvas shade of the lantern to glance at the compass, brought Ramage's thoughts back to the immediate present. He noticed Jackson was going bald: the sandy-coloured hair was receding . . . in the darkness the American's head reminded him of the rounded low-lying rocks of the Formiche de Burano, which they had passed an hour ago.

If his estimate of the current was correct, they were less than a mile from the beach and it was time to get rid of the Admiral's orders and the secret signal book – in fact everything but the charts – since the chances of capture were increasing rapidly.

He gave instructions to Jackson, then spoke to the seamen. Should he and Jackson be caught or killed it would be criminal to leave the seamen in ignorance of their position.

'You all saw the Tower through the glass this morning,' he told them. 'There's a small stream just south of it, and we may be able to hide the boat there. Jackson and I will try to find these people, and it may take the rest of the night. If we haven't returned by sunset tomorrow – that's Saturday – you'll leave in the boat at nightfall and make your way to a point five miles north of Giglio, where a frigate should be there to meet you at dawn on Sunday and again on Monday. If it doesn't turn up, you'll have to make for Bastia.'

A splash near by showed Jackson had flung the weighted canvas bag overboard, and Ramage told him to go forward with the lead line – the American had fashioned one from a length of marline and a smooth, heavy pebble – ready to give a cast.

Ramage took the tiller. 'Right men: steady strokes and no noise: give way together.'

The boat's erratic rolling and pitching stopped as the blades of the oars bit and thrust it ahead once again; the tiller came to life as the water surged past the rudder and bubbled away astern, talking to itself.

They were lucky it was calm: a wind with any west or south in it – a *maestrale libeccio* or *scirocco*, for instance – whipped up such a sea along this coast that beaching the boat or getting into the river would be impossible. And the same went for launching again afterwards: any of these winds, which often came up suddenly with little or no warning, could maroon them on shore for several days, so that they would miss the frigate off Giglio.

'A cast, Jackson.'

'Two fathoms, sir.'

The beach was now very close. The noise on board a ship or boat was usually sharp and clear, not muffled by echoes and deadened by trees or buildings; but now the creak of the gig and the slop of the sea were becoming overladen with the faint – for the moment – mechanical buzzing of thousands of cicadas and the squawks, barks and grunts of wild animals and birds. The heavy yet astringent, austere resin smell of the juniper and pines, floating seaward like an invisible fog, permeated everything, its sharpness emphasized for Ramage because for years he had been accustomed to the ever-present, sickly odours of sweat, reeking bilges, tarred rope, damp wood and damp clothing.

The dark green pines – their smell was as sharp in the nostrils as burnt gunpowder and as unforgettable. It was odd how smell, much more than sight or sound, brought back memories. What could he remember best of the years in Tuscany? The pines, larches and cicadas, of course; and the white dust clouds trailing behind carriages; the dark and heavy green of the cypress trees growing narrow and pointed, jutting up along the side of a hill like boarding pikes stowed in racks. He particularly remembered the sharp contrast between the deep green of pine and cypress, with their sturdy solidity which no wind could ruffle, and the silver-green scattering of leaves which seemed too young, too fluttering, to grow from the tortured, twisted olive trunks. And the creamy-skinned oxen with their huge horns, so massive and so gentle; he could picture their steady plodding, a pair always working together, so accustomed to leaning in towards each other that they could never be changed round. And the poverty of the peasants, the *contadini*, who lived like the slaves he had seen labouring in the plantations in the West Indies, but who were in many ways worse off, because a plantation owner who had paid several pounds a head for slaves was careful to keep them alive, while the Tuscan peasants, breeding and dying like flies, were free labour for the landowners. . . .

'Another cast, Jackson.'

'Fathom and a half, sir.'

In a few minutes, Ramage thought, he would be on Tuscan soil. Was it Tuscan, though? Or did the King of Naples' enclave stretch as far south as this? What a patchwork quilt Italy was: a dozen or so small, self-centred states, kingdoms, princedoms, dukedoms or republics, each jealous of the other, each a centre of intrigue and villainy, where politicians made more use of an assassin's dagger than a vote in council. They'd long since learned that sharpened steel always beat logic.

'Jackson!'

'A fathom, sir.'

Yes, he could see the beach now: the little wavelets were reflecting in the moonlight as they danced towards the shore and sprawled on the sand. He heard a buzzing round his head: they'd all provide a feast for the mosquitoes which made life a misery in this area. And he only hoped none of the men would pick up the ague which was part of the normal life on the marshy Maremma, the flat plain stretching from here down to Rome and beyond.

'Five feet, sir.'

The water was shoaling fast and the beach was perhaps fifty yards away. The cicadas were making the night ring, sounding like the ticking of a million clocks; and occasionally a frog gave a hoarse croak, as if complaining about the cicadas. From farther inland he heard a series of deep grunts: a wild boar grouting around under the pines and cork oaks.

Where the devil was the Tower? The narrow strip of sandy beach was clear enough, and he could make out the dunes behind, topped by a dark band formed of masses of juniper bushes and rock roses, and the thick carpet-like plant sprouting thousands of podgy green fingers – what did they call it? some odd name: *fico degli Ottentoti*, fig of the Hottentots.

'My boy,' his mother had said when he was much younger, 'you must go back to Italy one day when you are older; old enough to understand and judge her.' And now he was doing just that; though his mother's judgement was that of a woman born into a family which for centuries had wielded power and influence, and a friend of several similar families in Italy who had seen their rights and power usurped and, in their view, anyway, wrongly used by upstarts and degenerate, half-witted Hapsburg or Bourbon second sons, with a following of Aus- trians and Spanish grandees who had been given estates in Italy to get them out of the way. Or they had seen their land given away as a king's payment to a temporary mistress's family. Worse still, they had seen their own and Church lands fall into the clutches of papal princelings, the bastard offspring of ostensibly celibate popes who had been born of broken sacred vows, made noble by the twitch of the same popes' be- jewelled little fingers, and given vast estates: a nobility created from deceitful lust and made rich by corruption.

But this was nothing to do with the job on hand: his thoughts were only the reflection, or the echo, rather, of his mother's often, and usually strongly, expressed opinions. He did not know if she was always right in her judgements; but she and her friend Lady Roddam were women famous for their outspoken and advanced views – they had even been labelled as republicans by their enemies.

To the devil with advanced views, he told himself: how far are we from the Tower? Suddenly he saw it quite close, squat and square, the stonework pale in the moonlight, and half hidden by the sand dunes at the back of the beach. How had he missed seeing it before? He realized he'd been looking for something dark and shadowy, not thinking of the effect the moonlight would have. Hell! If the French had only a couple of guns and even a sleepy lookout on top of that Tower . . .

He pulled the tiller towards him to turn the boat southward, parallel to the beach: they were so vulnerable, even to pistol fire, that he wanted to spot the entrance to the river first, so they could run straight in without delay. At that moment he saw a wide but short band of silver spread inland across the beach like a carpet over the sand: the river, with the moonlight on it. He promptly altered course straight for it.

'Jackson, a cast!' he called as loud as he dare.

'A fathom, sir . . . five feet . . . four . . . four . . .'

Blast, it was shoaling fast.

'Keep it going.'

'Four feet . . . four . . . three . . .'

Damn, damn – they'd touch in a moment, but they were a good thirty yards from the beach: a long way for the men to haul the boat. He saw that Jackson was dropping the lead line like a boy fishing from the quay: there was not room, need nor time to heave it.

'Four feet : . . four . . . five . . . four . . . five . . . a fathom.'

Ramage breathed a sigh of relief: they must have been crossing a sandbank running parallel with the beach. Twenty yards to go and they'd be in the river, which seemed to get narrower the nearer they approached. With this flat sandy coastline there was certain to be a bar across the mouth.

'Four feet, sir . . . three . . .'

And this was it.

'Three . . . three . . .'

They might just as well wade the last few yards, hauling

60

the boat along by hand. He was just going to order the men over the side when he remembered the wretched *riccio*, the prickly sea urchin which looked like a rich brown chestnut husk, and whose spines broke off when they stuck into bare flesh, causing suppuration if not pulled out at once. It was rare to find them on sand; but there'd be small rocks around and they would be covered with them.

'Avast there with that lead, Jackson,' he called, keeping his voice low. 'Lay in on your oars, men. Who are wearing shoes?'

Four or five men answered and he ordered: 'Right, over the side with you and haul the boat up. Watch out for small rocks. The rest of you come aft.'

Their weight in the stern would cock the bow up a little, enabling the men in the water to run the boat farther over the bar before her keel dug into the sand.

'Unship the rudder,' he told Jackson, and jumped over the side.

Leaving the men to haul the boat, he splashed through the last few feet of water and reached the beach on the left bank of the river. As he stepped on to the hard sand at the water's edge his boots squelched; but after three or four paces, beyond where the waves lapped, the sand was so soft that at every step he sank in almost up to his ankles. The beach was steep, and as he looked over to the left he noticed the Tower was out of sight behind the dunes: no prying eyes could see the boat now.

By the time Ramage had walked and scrambled thirty paces he was five or six feet above sea level, with the rounded tops of the dunes still some twenty feet above him, but it suddenly became steeper and as he climbed upwards his feet kicked aside tufts of sharp-spined sea holly. Halfway up the side of the dune he met the first of the waist-high clumps of juniper bushes and rock roses and had to thread his way round them to avoid tearing his clothes.

He reached the top of the dune only to find it was the first of several which extended inland for fifty yards, looking like vast waves, until they dropped down to form one bank of the river curving round behind them.

Ah – now he could just see the top of the Tower: the stone-work gleamed in the moonlight and he could see the hard, angular shadows formed by the embrasures. The top of the Tower was so sharply etched against the blue-black night sky he was sure that had there been any sentries he could see them, but there was no sign of movement; nor did there seem to be any cannon poking their muzzles through the embrasures.

Well, he had to know just where the river went. Between him and the next juniper-capped dune was a deep depression, like the trough between two big waves. He began running down the side, but after half a dozen paces his feet sank deep into the sand and the momentum of his body sent him sprawling. Not the place to be chased by cavalry, he thought as he picked himself up, spitting sand from his mouth and slapping his clothes to shake off the worst of it.

As he stood up again it seemed he had suddenly gone deaf: the dune behind deadened all sound of the waves on the beach, and for the first time for many months he could hear nothing connected with the sea: he might be a hundred miles inland.

From the top of the next dune Ramage could see a little more of the Tower, and he walked down the side and up to the top of the third and last dune. Several feet below, to his right as he stood with his back to the sea, the river came straight inland for about fifty yards and then turned left to pass in front of him, rushes growing in thick clumps along the banks. It went on for two hundred yards, parallel with the sea, passing within a few yards of the seaward side of the Tower before turning sharply inland again, close against the north wall.

The Tower had been built in a good place, Ramage realized: with the river guarding it on the north and west sides, and the lake beyond covering it to the east, any attackers could approach only along the beaches.

And it was a solid construction, designed like a chessman castle, only square instead of round. From the ground the walls sloped gently inward until just below the embrasures, then sloped outward again for the last few feet, like the nipped-in waist of a woman's dress.

Ramage had seen enough for the moment. How deep was the river? He climbed down the steep bank to the rushes. The fact they grew there at all indicated the water was at worst brackish and ran from the fresh-water lake to the sea. For a second he froze with fear, then realized the sudden movement was a coot or moorhen which streaked out from almost underfoot, flying so low its wings beat the water. Gingerly he walked through the rushes, the water pouring over the tops of his boots, and turned right to follow the river round to its mouth and meet the men with the gig.

Rounding the corner, he found the men had pulled the boat over the bar. Jackson splashed over towards him.

'Where do you want it, sir?'

'Here,' Ramage said, indicating the northern bank. 'Snug it in close among the reeds.'

There was no point trying to hide it under branches of bushes: a pile of juniper among the reeds would be more conspicuous than the boat itself.

Well, there was no time to waste: the charcoal burner's hut mentioned in the Admiral's orders was half a mile southward down the coast and five hundred yards inland, and the sooner they found it the better, although a nagging question kept popping up in his mind.

Ramage splashed over to the men and glanced at the boat. 'That's fine. I want one of you to act as a sentry up there. The rest can sleep in the boat or very near it.' He indicated the sloping side of the dune. 'Hand me out a couple of cutlasses ... Thank you. Now, come on Jackson.'

'Good luck, sir,' one of the seamen said, and the rest echoed his words.

Ramage walked along the river's edge to the sea, followed by Jackson, wading out thigh-deep until he felt the sand bar under his feet. He then walked across it to the far bank.

'We'll walk along here just in the water to avoid making footprints,' he said. 'Anyway, it'll take too long if we climb up and down the dunes.'

Chapter 6

RAMAGE STROLLED along a path of silver foam: the wavelets lazed their way up to the beach and gently rolled over in orderly rows, shattering into myriads of droplets, each sparkling in the moonlight. The droplets then joined together and gurgled back in little cascades.

The sand along the water's edge was littered with branches of trees which must have been washed out to sea when a sudden storm flooded a river, and months later thrown up on the beach again, stripped of their bark, bleached by the sun, and polished by the sand, so they looked like the bones of a sea-monster. Twigs which had suffered the same fate were like twisted slivers of ivory, and occasionally he passed scatterings of sea shells which crunched beneath his feet.

The seamen should be all right: they had food and water, but no money or liquor, so with wine and women eliminated the only risk was discovery by French patrols or peasants. That was unlikely: this *macchia* would not attract many peasants, and as for French patrols – well, the town of Orbetello, between the two causeways leading to Argentario, was near by. But the main road to the south, the Via Aurelia, along which Caesar had marched back to Rome, was four or five miles inland, and he doubted if the French would bother to patrol the swamps and sand dunes between the Via Aurelia and the sea.

Ramage was thankful he had brought Jackson along, because the dangerous part was just about to begin, and there was no point in pushing the nagging question out of his mind any longer.

The question itself was simple enough: how to ask peasants where the refugees were without revealing that he was looking for them? If the French were in the neighbourhood they would certainly reward anyone bringing in important information or prisoners.

'Jackson – there might be more than one charcoal burner's hut—'

'I was just thinking that, sir.'

'—and we daren't risk giving ourselves away. Or why we're here.'

'No, sir.'

'So we're going to pretend we're French.'

'French, sir?'

Jackson could not disguise the note of surprise – or doubt – in his voice.

'French, French troops hunting the same refugees.'

'But – well, sir,' Jackson said hurriedly rephrasing his question more politely, 'the local folk will hardly help us if they think we are Frogs.'

'No, but it'll be fairly easy to see if they're lying. But more important, if they think we're French, obviously they won't take it into their heads to report us.'

'There's something in that, sir.'

'But we don't look much like a search party, so when I knock on a door, you keep out of sight and make a noise like a whole patrol!'

'Aye aye, sir. But your uniform, sir?'

'They won't know the difference.'

As they trudged along the beach, Ramage began to feel weary. He'd been at sea so long that he felt unbalanced when walking on land, as though he was drunk; and the hours in the open boat had exaggerated the effect so that, although the beach was flat, he felt he was walking uphill. It would wear off in a few hours; but combined with the weariness, it left him dazed and drained of strength. Nor did the thought of having to wake up and threaten simple peasants arouse any enthusiasm for the task ahead.

He ran his hand through his hair and cursed as his fingers caught in a tangle at the back of his scalp: the wound must have opened again and bled a little.

How far had they walked? He glanced back and just glimpsed the top of the Tower. Less than half a mile. This was a damned unlikely area to find a charcoal burner's hut: only a few larch, pine, cork oak and ilex stuck up out of the undergrowth ... Still, the poor beggars living here had little choice: this side of the lake there were no fields to cultivate, no land fit for olives or vines. That left only fishing – and the beach was too exposed for that – or collecting wood and making charcoal.

Thirty yards ahead the dunes came closer to the water's edge and the juniper bushes grew almost down to the sea: a good place to strike inland without leaving conspicuous foot-prints in the sand.

Inland, beyond the dunes, the ground in many places was marshy underfoot, and they had to make several detours to avoid stagnant ponds sprawling across their path. Soon they were threading their way among bushes eight or ten feet high, with a scattering of cork oak. Even in the moonlight Ramage could distinguish the bare and smooth, reddish-brown boles where the cork bark had been stripped off.

Suddenly Ramage felt Jackson tugging his coat. 'Smoke, sir: can you smell it? Wood smoke.'

Ramage sniffed: yes, it was faint, but unmistakable. They must be very close to the igloo-shaped oven of turf used by a charcoal burner, because there was not a breath of wind to spread the smoke: not even the usual inshore breeze.

Reaching down to his boot, Ramage eased the heavy-bladed throwing knife in its sheath, and drew his cutlass. Then the two men cautiously continued walking.

Three or four minutes later they found themselves on the edge of a small, flat clearing. In the centre Ramage saw a dull red glow where the oven had been left damped down for the night, completely covered in thick turf except for a tiny hole in one side.

Jackson nudged him and pointed. Beyond the furnace, on the far side of the clearing, Ramage could just make out the outline of a small stone hut.

'Can you see any others?'

'No, sir. That's likely to be the only one: downwind of the furnace.'

It certainly was to leeward of the night's offshore winds, but the certainty in Jackson's voice made Ramage curious, since there was no prevailing wind in this area.

'Why so sure?'

'Downwind of the furnace means the smoke is nearly always drifting round the hut at night. Drives the mosquitoes away.'

'Where did you learn that?'

'Ah,' whispered Jackson, 'I spent my boyhood in the woods.'

'This way,' said Ramage, pointing to the right. 'The moon won't give us away. As soon as I get to the door you go round the back of the hut and sound like a platoon of Marines.'

'Oh sir!' whispered Jackson, giving a mock groan. Ramage smiled to himself; seamen had a friendly contempt for Marines and soldiers.

After smoothing his hair, adjusting his stock and brushing sand from his breeches, Ramage walked up to the door, gripping the cutlass in his right hand. Jackson had disappeared round the back.

Well, he thought, we might as well get on with it, and banged on the door several times with the cutlass blade. He waited a couple of moments and then yelled in French: 'Open the door: open the door this minute.'

A sleepily spoken stream of blasphemy came from inside. 'Who is it?' demanded a hoarse voice in Italian.

'Open the door!' he repeated in a bullying voice.

A few moments later the door rattled and then squeaked open.

'Who is it?' growled the Italian from the darkness inside the hut.

Now was the time to start speaking Italian.

'Come out into the moonlight, you pig: exhibit the respect for a French officer. Let's see what you look like.'

The man shuffled out while a woman's voice from inside the hut hissed, 'Be careful, Nino!' At that moment Ramage heard a din from behind the hut. Jackson was doing his job well: from the shouted orders and crackling of undergrowth he sounded like a platoon of men.

Nino stood in the moonlight, rubbing his eyes with the back of his hand.

'Well?' demanded Ramage.

'Yes, yes, your Grace,' he said hastily, using the most formal

67

method of address he could think of. 'What does your Grace wish?'

Ramage prodded him in the stomach with the point of his cutlass. 'Where,' he demanded sternly, 'are these pigs of aristocrats hidden?'

He watched Nino closely.

Yes, there was a reaction: a movement of the shoulders, as if bracing himself slightly against an unexpected gust of wind.

'Aristocrats, your Grace? We have no aristocrats here.'

'That I know, fool; but you know where they are hiding.'

'No, no, your Grace: I swear by the Madonna we have no aristocrats here.'

Inside the hut a woman alternately prayed and wept with long, dry sobs; but Ramage realized the man was denying only that anyone was hidden in the hut, apparently avoiding a direct denial that he knew where they were.

'How many have you in your family?' he demanded.

'Seven, your Grace: my widowed mother, my wife, my four children and my brother.'

'Do you want them all to starve, ungrateful pig?'

'No – no, your Grace. Why should they?' he asked in surprise.

'Because in ten seconds, if you don't tell me where the aristocrats are, you'll join your dead father and the Madonna and all those saints your stupid priests tell you about!'

It would do no harm to give these peasants perhaps their first warning that Bonaparte's men, despite their Red Cap of Liberty and bold talk of freedom, were atheists.

But the effect on the peasant was extraordinary: he straightened himself up and faced Ramage squarely. As the woman continued sobbing inside the hut, he said with calm simplicity: 'Kill me, then: I tell you nothing.' He stood waiting for Ramage's cutlass to drive into his belly.

This fellow, thought Ramage, had a sense of honour: if some of those damned effete Italian *aristocrati*, mincing and dancing and gossiping their lives away in Siena and Florence – at least until Bonaparte arrived – could see the courage shown on their behalf by one of the *contadini* they might not despise them so much.

The man was simple, brave and honourable; but the last two virtues also revealed he knew where the refugees were. The Admiral's orders had mentioned the charcoal burner's hut', which implied there was only one; so surely this must be the charcoal burner in question ... Ramage decided to take the chance.

The peasant was still waiting for the cutlass to plunge into his stomach, so Ramage stepped back a pace, as if to gain more room to strike the fatal blow, then suddenly thrust the blade down vertically into the ground. Before the startled peasant realized what was happening Ramage seized him by the arm, leaving the cutlass in the ground, pushed him back into the hut – remembering to duck under the low doorway – and said gaily:

'*Allora, Nino, siamo amici!*'

'*Dio! Perche? Chi siete voi?*'

'Why? We are friends because I am an English naval officer and I have come to help these people. Now, Nino, before we join them, what about some wine and bread; we have come a long way and we are hungry.'

' "We", *signor*?'

It was working: the suddenly friendly voice, the request for wine ...

'Jackson, come in here,' he called in English, 'and say something to me in English; anything man!'

Damn, it was dark in the hut: they could easily stick a knife in his ribs ...

Jackson came in, stopping just inside the door, uncertain where Ramage was standing. 'Do you think this chap knows where they are, sir?'

'Yes, he does,' said Ramage, also speaking slowly. 'But I've got to convince him we are English.' He turned to the Italian. 'Nino, let us have some light with the wine, then you can look at me well.'

He heard the rustling of straw: it sounded as though a man – not Nino, whose arm he was still holding – was moving.

'Who is that?'

'My brother.'

The woman stopped sobbing: that was a good sign: some reassurance was spreading through the hut, which stank of sweat, urine, cheese and sour, spilled wine.

The wine, only a few days old, would still be soaking into the casks and seeping out between the staves, so that it had to be topped up each day to expel the air which would otherwise turn it into vinegar.

The brother began striking a flint to light a candle, but Nino told him impatiently to use embers from the charcoal furnace outside. In a few moments he returned, one hand cupping the flame of a rush candle. The light was dim, but enough to illuminate the tiny hut. The wife, a black-eyed dumpling, was sitting up on a straw mattress in a corner, hands clasped across her breasts, as if she was naked, instead of being dressed in a flannel nightdress reaching up to her chin. An old woman, presumably the mother, with a face brown and wrinkled like a walnut, was crouching beside her, clearly terrified and plucking at the well-worn beads of a rosary with claw-like fingers. In another corner a goat munched contentedly and began to urinate with odorous unconcern.

Ramage saw that Nino was a stocky, black-haired man. Several days' growth of beard sprouted out from a smoke-grimed but open face, and his eyes were bloodshot. He wore black corduroy trousers and, despite the heat, a thick woollen vest – he 'turned in all standing', as a seaman would say, except for his corduroy jacket, which was slung across the only chair in the room. Black corduroy – the uniform of the *carbonaio*, the charcoal burner.

'Where are the children, Nino?'

'I sent them to stay with my sister in Orbetello.'

'Yes, they would be safer there at a time like this.'

Nino fell into the trap. 'Yes, we thought so.'

'Some wine, Nino, eh?'

'I am sorry, *Commandante*, of course,' said Nino, 'we are not used to having visitors in the night.'

'But in the daytime?'

The Italian did not answer as he took his coat from the chair and flung it towards his wife.

'Will you be seated, *Commandante*? We are poor people. There is no chair for your attendant.'

Ramage sat down, and while Nino collected some bottles from the far corner of the room, his brother reached up into the rafters and brought down a round cheese and the remains of a long sausage. 'We have no bread,' he apologized.

The brother took a clasp knife from his pocket, opened out the curved blade, and wiped it on his trouser leg before cutting two segments of cheese and several slices of sausage. In the meantime Nino retrieved his jacket and used it to wipe the neck of two bottles.

'My uncle's wine, from near Port' Ercole,' said Nino, proffering a bottle to each of them.

Suddenly there was a raucous bellow outside and Jackson sprang to the door, cutlass in hand, shouting, 'What the hell's that?'

Nino roared with laughter and, guessing Jackson's question, said: 'At least I know you are not French soldiers: that's my donkey.'

Ramage laughed too: although for a moment alarmed, he recognized the noise almost at once. Presumably Jackson's seafaring life had prevented him recognizing the hoarse and agonized, starved-of-air bellowing of a peasant's most valued possession, his *somaro*.

'It's all right, Jackson, it's only a donkey.'

'My God, I thought someone was being strangled!'

'It's done the trick, though; he's realized a French soldier would recognize it immediately.'

Then Ramage remembered a remark Jackson had made earlier.

'If you were a woodsman, why didn't you recognize it?'

Jackson snorted indignantly, 'Sir! We used horses, not bloody mules!'

Ramage sipped the wine and Nino watched him carefully, for the moment more concerned about the stranger's verdict on the wine than the reason for the midnight visit.

'It's good, Nino: very good. It's a long time since I tasted such as this. A very long time,' he repeated, hoping Nino would start questioning him.

'You speak Italian very well, *Commandante*.'

'Before I entered the Navy I lived for many years in Italy.'

'In Tuscany, no doubt.'

'Yes – Siena, most of the time. And Volterra.'

'With friends, perhaps?'

'No, with my parents. But we had many friends there.'

'Yes?' said Nino politely. Then as if satisfied with the information: 'The *Commandante* was asking about some nobles, I believe?'

Could one be sure of these peasants, even now? Yet Ramage had to take a risk, otherwise this polite talk would go on all night.

'Nino, I think you are a man of honour. *Allora*, I will be honest with you because I trust you. If you cannot help, I ask only that you do not betray me. My Admiral has sent me not to kill people, not to destroy lives, but to save them.'

The two brothers were watching him, listening carefully and patiently. He found himself using his hands to emphasize words: strange how difficult it was to speak Italian without gesticulating.

The candle flickered because the sacking normally covering the tiny window had been drawn back to let some air in. Not sufficient, God knows, to get rid of the stench of goat, wine, urine, sweat and cheese, but enough to make the flame dance. The shadows it threw across the brothers' faces, and their natural peasant impassiveness, made it hard to guess their thoughts.

'My Admiral told me' (the exaggeration was permissible, Ramage thought) 'that at least five nobles escaped to here when the French entered Leghorn. My Admiral also told me there was a lady among them; a famous lady, a lady who would know about such things as alabaster . . .'

He paused, wondering if the two men knew of the alabaster mines at Volterra and would therefore guess he was referring to the Marchesa. If they did, then he'd soon gain their confidence.

Nino gave a nod which implied that although he agreed there might be a lady who knew about alabaster, it did not mean he knew her.

'Nino, I will be frank: there is no reason why you should trust me, so I won't ask you to take me to these people. . . .'

'Where is the *Commandante*'s ship?'

'Out there,' said Ramage, pointing seaward, 'beyond the reach of prying French eyes.'

'You landed by boat?'

'Yes.'

'The *Commandante*'s hair is matted with dried blood, or something similar.'

'It is dried blood: we had a battle and I was wounded by the French.'

'Would you like my wife to make a poultice for it, *Commandante*?'

'No,' said Ramage rather too hastily for politeness. 'No, thank you: there is no need: it heals itself well. Now,' he said, indicating he assumed they were satisfied, 'as I said, I do not ask you to take me to these people; only that you take a message.'

'If it was possible that we could help the *Commandante* by taking a message to someone he wished to receive a message,' Nino said guardedly, speaking formally and still not admitting he knew anything, 'it would have need to be in Italian.'

'Of course,' Ramage replied, adopting Nino's roundabout manner. 'The message I have in mind would be to a lady who knew about alabaster, telling her the English have arrived to take her and her friends on a voyage. And to reassure this lady – so that she can identify the English officer – tell her that when he was a boy she made him recite Dante in Italian, and she was angry with him because of his bad accent. And she said to this boy, that of all Dante wrote, to remember specially one line: "*L'amor che muove il sole e l'altre stelle*" – "The love that moves the sun and the other stars".'

Nino repeated the phrase. 'Did this man Dante write that?'

Ramage nodded.

'It is beautiful,' said the brother, speaking for the first time. 'But why was the lady angry because of your accent, *Commandante*? You pronounce it as if you were a real Tuscan.'

'Now I do, but then I was a small boy; still learning the language in fact.'

'This message, *Commandante*. Supposing it could be delivered: where would you like to wait?'

'Where you wish. My sword – that is outside, and you may take it, and that of my attendant, and hide them where you wish.'

Nino stood up as if he had decided what he must do.

'*Commandante*, you and your attendant are tired. Perhaps you would care to sleep here—' he waved towards the mattresses. 'In the meantime, I have some work to do. My brother has no work, so he will stay here.'

Ramage and Jackson stretched out on one mattress. The old woman whimpered – her eyes were watery, and she had long since ceased to do anything with her life but eat and sleep. The wife whispered something reassuring.

The brother put the candle in a corner behind a box, and draped a jacket round it to hide most of the light. Ramage suddenly realized how tired he was, and the cut in his head was throbbing. Just before he slid into a deep sleep he felt a spasm of fear: he had trusted the peasants, but would the next bang on the door herald the arrival of real French troops?

Chapter 7

'*Commandante! Commandante!*' Someone was shaking him. In an instant – thanks to many years' training and several scares in the past couple of days – he was wide awake and felt Jackson spring up beside him. It took a moment to realize where he was, but the inside of the tiny hut quickly came into focus. Strange shadows chased each other across the walls as the candle Nino held in his hand wobbled slightly.

'Oh – Nino, all goes well?'

'No, *Commandante* – at least, not entirely so.'

'Why is that?'

'We have to move from here.'

'Why – are the French coming?'

'No, *Commandante*; but it will be more convenient for us to talk elsewhere.'

'Where do we go?'

'To a place near here.'

Was it a trap? Ramage decided not, since the Italian could have brought back French soldiers who would have seized them as they slept. There was no choice; he would have to go with Nino. Perhaps Nino was going to take them to the refugees . . .

He and Jackson followed the two brothers along a track which, from the stars, Ramage could see ran almost parallel with the coast. After about fifteen minutes, through a break in the bushes, he could see they had been skirting Lake Burano only a few yards away on the right, and the Tower was just ahead. He quickly slipped his knife, hilt first, up his sleeve.

The moon had moved round far enough to leave the nearest side of the Tower in deep shadow, and it looked so menacing that Ramage could not repress a shiver.

Soon they were beside the Tower and Ramage looked up at it. Curious how the walls sloped in to the bottom of the embrasures and then out again. He leaned against the wall, looked up and saw the reason: slots cut under the embrasures, out of sight until you were right below the wall, allowed the defenders to shoot down vertically while still protected by the parapet.

The entrance was a door almost halfway up the north wall, but the stone steps did not reach the Tower: between the wall and the structure of the steps was a gap eight feet wide, spanned by a temporary wooden platform, like a drawbridge. In case of attack the defenders merely had to remove the platform and no one could reach the door.

As he started climbing the steps he saw the two brothers waiting for him at the top. They must have gone ahead. The wooden platform creaked as he stepped on it – he noted that the noise would give him a useful warning of intruders.

'After you,' he said to Nino, disguising his wariness with politeness.

'Certainly, *Commandante*,' the Italian said, as if he understood Ramage's caution. 'Wait while I light a candle.'

As soon as the light began to flicker, Ramage walked inside. The room was huge, like a cavern, occupying the whole length and width of the Tower. Overhead the domed ceiling was at least twenty feet high. He looked round for the staircase leading to the roof, but there was none: only a small door in the wall on his left – the wall facing the lake. Presumably it led to the staircase, so the wall must be double.

Nino put the candle on a small table, which, with a chair, was the only furniture in the room. Ramage saw a large fireplace just to the left of the entrance door and went over to it. There were some pieces of charcoal in the hearth, but, judging from the cobwebs hanging down like miniature fishing nets, it had not been used for a long time.

'Well, Nino?'

'As I told you, *Commandante*, there are difficulties. The message you mentioned, *Commandante*. By chance I met a person who knew something of alabaster but nothing about a little boy and Dante. This person was expecting friends, *Commandante*, but is worried.'

Ramage guessed the Italian was deliberately not referring to the person's sex. Well, it was many years ago, and there was no particular reason, he supposed, why the Marchesa di Volterra should remember his Dante. But she must remember his mother. Perhaps she was so old her memory had gone. She must be – well, more than seventy now ... A sudden thought struck him.

'This lady of the alabaster, Nino: is she very old?'

Nino's eyes narrowed. 'No, she is not old. On the contrary!' he exclaimed, as if the idea outraged him.

So the person *is* a woman, Ramage thought, and she is very young. Therefore the old Marchesa must be dead, and this is her daughter. Yes! Gina ... Gianna: that's it: she was younger than himself; pretty too, from what he could remember, but impulsive and unpredictable, and very self-possessed for a child. Wasn't there some bitterness in the family because the old Marchesa had no son? The girl must have inherited the title by some dispensation or other, and those vast estates: hmm, she'll be a handful for a man to handle unless she's changed a lot.

'Nino, perhaps the old lady I refer to is dead and this is her daughter. I cannot be certain.'

'*Commandante*, name this lady, and tell us yours, or we cannot help you.'

Ramage hesitated: there was sudden tension in the cavernous room: it seemed to reach out from the two brothers, from each dark corner and from the shadowy vaulted ceiling. The Italians, standing by the table, were facing him squarely while Jackson, who had been examining the small door which apparently led to the stairs, quietly turned and watched, recognizing the threatening tone of their voices although not understanding the words.

'Are we having trouble, sir?'

'No, I don't think so.'

Ramage looked at Nino straight in the eyes.

'I give you my name willingly, because it is of no consequence; but' – he searched for a strong phrase – 'but may the Madonna strike you dead if you ever repeat the lady's name. It is – the Marchesa di Volterra.'

'Ah,' the relief was obvious in Nino's voice.

The little door creaked for a moment and was flung wide open. Jackson leapt to one side and as the draught made the candle flicker, putting the room almost in darkness for a few moments, there was a swirl of movement. As the flame recovered, Ramage saw someone almost completely hidden in a long black-hooded cape standing just inside the room.

How it happened, Ramage was not quite sure; but equally suddenly Jackson made a quick cat-like movement which put him behind the hooded figure, the point of his cutlass pressing between the stranger's shoulder blades. He kicked back and

77

shut the door. Ramage was surprised to see how small the stranger was, compared with Jackson.

A hand – a small hand, Ramage noticed – came from among the folds of the cape, and it was holding a pistol: a pistol whose blue steel barrel, shining dully in the candlelight, was pointing straight at his stomach, and which was cocked, ready for firing. He glanced from the muzzle – which in a moment seemed to have grown to the calibre of a cannon – to the stranger's face, but it was hidden in the shadows thrown by the hood. Just as he glanced sideways at the candle, measuring the distance to it, the hooded figure spoke.

'If the gentleman behind me does not remove his sword, I shall be forced to use my pistol.'

The voice spoke in English, but had a heavy accent; it was calm but quite determined; and it was a girl's voice. From sheer relief Ramage started laughing and just stopped himself in time from gesturing to Jackson: a sudden movement might lead the girl to squeeze the trigger. . . .

'Stow the cutlass, Jackson.'

The American sheepishly put the cutlass behind his back. The two brothers did not understand what had been said, but smiled when they saw Jackson's embarrassed movement and heard Ramage's spontaneous laugh: not, Ramage felt, because they saw anything funny in the situation, but their peasant instinct – stronger and wiser than that of more cultured people – told them only maniacs killed while laughing.

However, the girl in the black cape merely took a few steps sideways to avoid having Jackson behind her, and told the two brothers to stand to one side, which they hastily did. Getting them out of the line of fire, Ramage noted, because the pistol still pointed unwaveringly at his stomach.

She said: 'Teli your friend to stand beside you.'

'Come over here, Jackson.'

Ramage had an uneasy feeling the girl not only knew how to handle the pistol but would use it without hesitation. But what had gone wrong? For a moment he had thought she must be the Marchesa; yet now . . . He wriggled his right forearm slightly to make sure the throwing knife in his sleeve would fly clear, and was thankful he had transferred it there from the sheath in his boot.

Obviously she had been listening at the door – she came in as soon as he mentioned the Marchesa's name. Why the pistol, then? Perhaps Jackson's sudden movement had startled her into producing it. Where were the rest of them? Were the men even now waiting behind that door? Supposing they came in and startled the girl, so that she accidentally squeezed the trigger?

'What,' the girl said icily, 'is this about alabaster and "*L'amor che muove il sole*"?'

'May I introduce myself: I am Lieutenant Nicholas Ramage of the Royal Navy.' He decided to risk being wrong and continued: 'I am sorry your mother is dead, madam: she was one of my mother's closest friends. My message was intended for her: the quotation from Dante was one of her favourites – she often made me recite it when I was a boy and I knew she'd recognize me when she remembered it. I thought it safer not to name names . . .'

'And who, sir, was your mother?'

The voice was still icy: she was not a girl who had an attack of vapours when a servant dropped a wine glass: she was used to giving commands and having them obeyed. Hardly surprising, since she was the head of such a powerful family. But why did she not know his name or remember him? Then he realized she would never have heard his family surname, since Father had inherited the earldom long before they lived in Italy.

'My mother is Lady Blazey. My father is Admiral Lord Blazey. Perhaps you remember me as their son "Nico"?'

The pistol was withdrawn into the folds of the cloak, and with the other hand the girl swept back the hood, shaking her head to tidy her hair. It shone blue-black, like sun on a raven's wing feathers. Then she looked up at him.

His head swam, and it seemed he had to gasp for breath. God, she was beautiful: not paintings-on-the-wall beautiful, but the beauty of a face moulded by strength of character and determination, assurance and courage, and an expression

79

deriving from the confidence of a woman knowing her own beauty and accustomed to being obeyed.

Even by candlelight he could see the finely chiselled features: high cheekbones, large, widely spaced eyes, a small, slightly hooked nose. The mouth – it was a little too wide, with lips a fraction too full, for classic perfection. It was as though a sculptor had deliberately carved a sensuous goddess. Yes! Except for the nose, she might have been the model for – he searched his memory, Siena – no, Florence: Ghiberti's beautiful carving of 'The Creation of Eve' on the east doors of the Baptistry. Had she the naked Eve's same bold, slim, body, the same small, jutting breasts, the same glorious shoulders, flat belly and rounded thighs? The girl's face was certainly a little fuller and more sensuous. Ramage glanced down at her breasts; but the cape ... she might as well be wrapped in a parcel.

'It was fortunate I did not shoot you, Lieutenant Ramage,' she said calmly.

Goddess! he thought, jerked suddenly back to reality. Diana the Huntress, maybe; not one of the peaceful kind. But she was self-possessed and her mind worked like lightning: Ramage realized there had been a moment's hesitation before calling him 'Lieutenant': she knew an earl's son might have a courtesy title even if not one in his own right; and although he had introduced himself without using it, she was obviously trying to avoid a mistake in the way she addressed him.

'It was doubly fortunate,' he replied, 'since my man had his cutlass at your back.'

'Very well, Lieutenant,' she said, indicating formalities were over. 'This man' – she indicated Nino – 'will fetch the others, and then we will sail in your ship for England.'

The impulsive but self-possessed child had not changed in the transition to womanhood, and Ramage knew that he must grab the initiative from her to avoid the next few days being extremely difficult.

'Madam, there are details to explain before we start.'

'Very well, but please be brief, because we have waited a long time: you are very late.'

Her tone was so patronizing that as anger flooded through Ramage, he realized he now had both the chance and the wish to reduce this girl to more manageable proportions. He indicated the chair beside the able: 'Will you please be seated: I repeat – there are some things to explain.'

He waited until she gathered the cape round herself, nonchalantly placed the pistol in her lap as though it was a peacock-feather fan, and then looked up at him coldly, as if he was a tiresome servant. Then he spoke in a voice that surprised him for its bitterness.

'Madam, to enable me to be here tonight – late as I am – more than fifty of my men have been killed; another fifty have been wounded and taken prisoner by the French; and fifty or more are now rowing for their lives towards Corsica. . . .'

'Yes?' her voice was cold, polite and utterly impersonal: it was as if the cook was proposing the menu for the day.

'Of less importance,' he said bitterly, 'is the fact that I have been forced to surrender one of His Majesty's ships.'

'That can hardly be your fault: you are too young: your Admiral should not trust the command of a ship to a youth.'

He struggled with his temper, aware of the warning signs for one of his blind rages: he was blinking quickly, rubbing the scar on his brow, and in a moment he'd be fighting to avoid mispronouncing 'r'.

'In fact my Admiral did place three officers over me, but they've all been killed. No doubt he will consider the loss of life so far a small price to pay for your safety. I mention all this pettifogging detail only to explain my lateness – and why you and your friends are not going direct to England.'

The girl lowered her head, turning slightly away from the candle, so that her face was in shadow. She was smaller, more frail even, than he'd first thought, and his anger passed quickly, spent like a shout echoing down a valley. For all her outward calm, she was young and probably very frightened and now he was embarrassed at his bitter outburst.

'May I ask why some of the men in your party are not here?'

'There was no need. The peasant was satisfied you were not French, but the message was garbled. We thought it just possible you were trying to identify yourself to one of the party by referring to a past meeting. Obviously "alabaster" could only mean the mines at Volterra, or the Volterra family; but I remembered nothing of a small boy and "*L'amor che muove ile sole*".'

'Why did you come then, not one of the men?'

'Because the Volterra family were concerned,' she said impatiently. 'As soon as I heard you explaining to Nino I realized you thought my mother was still alive. After that, this man' – she nodded towards Jackson – 'startled me.'

'You did not fear a trap?'

'No, I trusted the judgement of the peasant – his family have worked for us for generations and this' – she waved her hand – 'is my land. Anyway, it would have been difficult for you to trap me because on the way to us he searched all this area.'

'But he didn't find my men!'

'Oh yes he did! You have a boat hidden among the rushes and your sentry is just above, on top of the dunes. He was asleep, incidentally, and so were the five men in the boat.'

Ramage glanced at Jackson, who was clearly making a mental note to deal with the man – and, from the look on his face, obviously wished he could deal with the girl as well.

'If you didn't think it a trap, I hope you trust me now.'

She smiled as if offering an olive branch, and said lightly, 'I do: I hope the rest of the party do, too. Such men are used to the intrigue of Court life: they find it hard to trust anyone, even among themselves.'

'Well, they've no choice: they'll have to trust me; and what's more, they'll be under my orders,' he said grimly, to avoid any misunderstanding over the extent of his authority; and to tide him over the uncomfortable silence that followed he added, 'Madam: I am very tired, so forgive me for being short-tempered and a little *aspro*. I meant that I have my orders concerning their safety and will carry them out as best I can.'

The girl, her olive branch brushed aside, was cold again.

'You have surrendered your ship. What can you do with this little boat?'

'If your party will forgo comfortable cabins and servants to wait on you, it will take us to meet a ship off Giglio, or failing that, to Bastia. There is water and plenty of bread. By bread, I mean ship's bread, which is a type of hard biscuit. The boat will be crowded: will you explain this to your party?'

'Supposing we are seen by a French warship and captured?'

'There's a risk, but not very great.'

'But there is a risk.' It was a statement, not a question.

'Of course there is a risk, madam: of gales, too. Perhaps as much of a risk as being caught by Bonaparte's men if you stay here.'

He found it hard to avoid sounding contemptuous when he added: 'If your companions wish to continue their journey in the boat, I am at your service.'

'And if they do not wish? If they do not like the idea of such a long voyage in such a small boat?'

There was nothing in his orders concerning that – except the Admiral regarded these people as very important, which in a way covered the point.

'The only alternative is for me to leave you here and try to arrange for a warship to pick you up later, but I can't give any guarantee.'

'I will explain this to them,' said the Marchesa. The patronizing tone had gone from her voice; but the self-assurance remained. 'When do you wish to leave?'

'Tomorrow night, as soon as it is dark – I mean tonight, of course: dawn's not far off. By the way, do you know anything about French troops round here?'

'Very little: a few cavalry patrols pass along the Via Aurelia – some have been searching the villages for us.'

'And the political situation?'

'The Grand Duke of Tuscany – well, he's a weak man, and you probably know he allowed this Bonaparte to occupy Leghorn on June 27. There's talk of certain Corsicans starting a revolution against the British in Corsica: Bonaparte is calling for volunteers. Since Corsica placed herself under British protection, I suppose this Bonaparte is embarrassed to find he could be called a British subject,' she added dryly. 'He risks being hanged as a traitor – if you can catch him.'

He was amused at the contemptuous way she referred to 'this Bonaparte'. Still, 'this Bonaparte' had achieved the impossible by crossing the Alps with his armies and capturing, one after another, the Italian states, like a farmer striding through his orchards plucking ripe fruit.

'For the rest,' she said, ' – well, there is talk of the Austrians defeating the French in two battles: at Lonato, and somewhere else – I cannot remember the name. And the Pope has suspended the armistice he signed with this Bonaparte.'

'What about Elba?'

'I do not know: there were French plans to capture it after Leghorn: it is very near the coast. Oh yes, I forgot: the Spanish have signed an alliance with France.'

'Declared war on the British, you mean?' exclaimed Ramage.

She shrugged her shoulders. 'I do not know: I imagine so.'

Ramage envied her unconcern – if Spain joined the French, then the Royal Navy would be overwhelmed in the Mediterranean: the Admiral was fighting against heavy odds even now ... And a full-scale revolution in Corsica could mean the British would have to clear out because they had very few troops there. The capture of Elba would deprive them of yet another base. And the Spanish Fleet joining the French ... Well, there'll be enough battles and casualties to make every junior lieutenant a post captain before the war ends, he thought viciously.

He found himself tapping the palm of his left hand with his throwing knife: quite unconsciously he must have taken it out while listening to the Marchesa.

'Do you usually have such a knife up your sleeve?' she asked.

'Yes,' he answered sourly. 'Invariably. Like all good card players.'

'You mean you like to cheat.'

He imagined her outlined against the little door: and before he realized what he was doing, his right hand swung up over his head, then suddenly chopped down. The knife blade flashed for a moment before thudding into the door, the hilt vibrating for a few moments.

'No,' he replied, walking over to pull it out of the wood. 'Not to cheat: just to win. Too many kings, courtiers, courtesans and politicians think war's just a game of cards and realize their mistake only when they find an uncouth Corsican artilleryman has strolled across the Alps and trumped all their aces.'

'So we in Tuscany have been playing cards?'

'Madam, could we continue this discussion another time?'

'Certainly: I was really only interested to know if you cheated. Now,' she said, picking up her pistol and standing, 'shall we meet here this evening?'

'No – it will save time if you all come to the boat. Nino can guide you. Bring water, if you can, and food. But no possessions and no servants.'

'Why?'

'Because servants take no risk by staying – they and possessions take up space in the boat. We have no spare space.'

'But jewellery, money?'

'Yes, within reason. So, Madam, will you be at the boat at nine o'clock: that should give you half an hour of darkness to get here. Are you hiding far away?'

'At—'

'No, don't tell me exactly where: the less we know, the less we could be forced to tell if we were captured. Just the direction and the time to get here.'

'Towards Monte Capalbio. Half an hour at the most.'

'Excellent: nine o'clock at the boat, then.'

'Yes. I will send Nino during the day to tell you what the others have decided. One of the party, Count Pitti, has yet to arrive: we expect him hourly.'

Ramage suddenly realized she already intended to come, whatever her companions decided.

'You anticipate difficulties?'

'Perhaps.' The flat tone indicated she did not propose to discuss it.

'Until this evening, then.'

She held out her hand and he lifted it to his lips. She was trembling very slightly, but so little that she must have thought allowing him to kiss her hand would not reveal it.

Chapter 8

LYING IN THE SAND later that day, shaded from the fierce heat of the sun by a juniper bush, Ramage alternately dozed and woke, relieved that for the moment there were no decisions to make and no particular risks to run. All that bothered him for the time being were the flies and mosquitoes which attacked him with a determination quite alien to the country.

He ran over in his mind the plan he had already outlined to Jackson and the men. Just before nine o'clock – providing the wind did not come up and bring a bit of a sea with it – the gig would be hauled out to the sand bar, where it could be held by a couple of seamen so that the party could wade out to it. That was the easiest way of making a hurried departure in case of an emergency. But if there was no urgency, the boat could be hauled up the river again so the refugees could embark without getting wet.

Now all that remained was for Nino to arrive with a message from the Marchesa telling him how many of the men were coming.

How he hated these men he had never seen: these names, these (probably) scented fops, whose very existence had sunk the *Sibella* and decimated her crew. The violence of the spasm of hatred made him sit up, as if to shake it off, and when he lay back again he despised himself for being so irrational: they might well be brave men anxious to carry on the fight against the French.

'A drink of water, sir?'

The ever-wakeful Jackson: he'd miss that Yankee twang and cadaverous face when they reached Bastia and Jackson was sent off to some other ship.

He took the dipper and drank. It was warm and brackish; like all water stored in a ship it stank, but years of practice taught a seaman to drink with the back of his nose blocked, so the smell was delayed until after the water was down his throat, past regret or recall.

Maybe it was unfair to blame these refugees; but with their money and influence, surely they could have chartered – stolen, even – a fishing boat and made their way to Corsica, instead of requesting a British warship? Did they want a warship for comfort or security? If comfort, because they found the idea of a fishing boat too disgusting, then the devil take them. If security: well, they had lost their lands, their homes, and probably their wealth – temporarily anyway – so perhaps one could not blame them. But he had a suspicion it was for luxury; for pride; so that they should not make a *brutta figura*, cut a figure, the cheap vanity that was – and presumably always would be – the curse of Italy.

He thought, many Italians – but by no means all – are like Van der Dekken, the Flying Dutchman; only the curse on them is that they're doomed to roam the world, their vanity raw and exposed to every chill wind, open to every slight, until they find something to give them confidence and the natural dignity that goes with it.

Yet, apart from the *brutta figura*, if he was honest he was blaming them for his own forebodings: that much he admitted. He stared up at the deep blue of the sky. Foreboding . . . apprehension . . . fear: the same commodity, but with different names stencilled on the casks. The fear was of – well, not so much when he thought about it: only the consequences of surrendering the *Sibella*. There were plenty of his father's enemies still carrying on the vendetta. He only hoped Captain Nelson would be at Bastia when he arrived; but if it was Admiral Goddard or one of his followers, which was quite possible – well . . . ·

He heard a man puffing and grunting, and as Jackson leapt to his feet, cutlass in hand, Nino came into the clearing.

'Ah, *Commandante*,' he said, 'this heat!' He rubbed his face vigorously with a piece of cloth, smearing the soot which always begrimed a *carbonaio*'s face across the areas of skin which had been washed clean by streams of perspiration. 'Your sentry was not asleep this time!'

'What news, Nino? Sit down – we have no wine, only water.'

Nino grinned. 'In the name of my uncle at Port' Ercole, *Commandante*, I took the liberty of bringing you something.'

He untied the neck of a small sack and took out three bottles of the deep golden white wine for which the district was famous, followed by several cheeses and half a dozen long, thin loaves of bread.

'Those biscuits,' he said. 'The Marchesa told me of your ship's biscuits, and so I found you some bread.'

'It was kind of you, Nino.'

'*Prego, Commandante*; it was nothing, you are welcome. The bread is made from my uncle's grain.'

Drinking wine in the heat of the sun always gave Ramage a headache; but he knew Nino would be hurt if he did not. 'We'll have a little now and keep the rest for the voyage.'

'Drink it all now, *Commandante*; the two gentlemen will be bringing supplies for the voyage.'

Ramage glanced up at the peasant. 'The two gentlemen, Nino?'

'I have a message from the Marchesa, *Commandante*. She said to tell you that three of the gentlemen have decided their duty keeps them here.'

Nino's voice was polite, but there was no mistaking his views on the reluctant trio.

'The two gentlemen: who are they?'

'I do not know their names: they are young and I think they are cousins. Now, *Commandante*, I must leave you: I have work to do before I meet you again at nine o'clock. *Permesso, Commandante?*'

'Yes, and thank you, Nino: my greetings to your brother and your mother and your wife, and my apologies for disturbing them last night.'

'It was nothing, *Commandante*.'

With that he was gone. Ramage told Jackson to take some wine and food to the seamen and then lay back on the sand again, watching the insects zig-zagging among the spines of the junipers. The air was alive with the buzzing of the cicadas; the noise seemed to come from everywhere and yet nowhere; almost as though it was being produced inside one's head.

The sleep had done Ramage good: now he felt restless and full of energy. With the immediate problems solved, he found himself thinking of the girl: he re-created a dozen times the episode in the Tower, dwelling again and again on the quality of her voice. It was hard to define – soft, yet it had the ring of authority; precise in the way she spoke, but musical to the ear. Clear – and yet always on the verge of huskiness. He started to wonder how husky it would become when she made love, and hurriedly forced the idea out of his mind: the sun was hot enough without thinking of that: he'd already disturbed himself enough with memories of Ghiberti's naked Eve and speculations about the body beneath the black cape.

He felt a deep and powerful longing to roam free over the Tuscan hills once again: to ride the tracks and stir up the white dust; to see the lines of dark green cypress growing up the side of hills, stark against the hard blue sky. To watch a pair of creamy oxen plodding along, tails lazily flicking the flies from their flanks, and the owner asleep in the cart. To see a walled hill town, ride up the twisting path to the gate, his horse's hooves clattering on the cobbles of the narrow streets, and glance up at a window to see a pair of beautiful eyes watching him curiously. To go back in time, to his boyhood, when Gianna was a little girl the Marchesa brought to the house. . . .

The cicadas still buzzed in the darkness – did they never sleep? – as Ramage watched the moon rising over Mount Capalbio. Earlier in the day, looking at a flat stone set high in the south wall of the Tower, Ramage had just been able to distinguish some Latin words, a name and a date carved into it, recording that a certain Alfiero Nicolo Verdeco was 'the architect of this edifice' in AD 1606. Had Signor Verdeco stood on this spot nearly two centuries earlier and seen his 'edifice' bathed in the warm, oyster-pink glow of a full moon – a harvest moon?

Ramage heard some splashing near by and from the top of the dune looked down at the mouth of the river: the boat was being held by three seamen, up to their knees in water, so that the after end of the keel rested on the sand bar. The rest of the men were already in the boat, waiting to help the refugees on board.

He called down to Smith, asking the time.

He saw a faint glow as Smith lifted up the canvas shield over the lantern and held the watch close to the light. Thank God someone had brought a good supply of candles.

'Five minutes short o' nine o'clock, sir.'

Time to walk along the top of the dunes towards the Tower, to keep an eye open for the refugees. Let's hope they'll be punctual. Nine o'clock in Italy could mean anything between ten o'clock and midnight.

He guessed they had been hiding somewhere near the little hill town of Capalbio, inland on the far side of the lake. Their shortest route to the boat would be round the northern edge of the lake, where they would pick up the track running parallel with the beach, forty yards or so inland, and linking the Tower with the little village of Ansedonia, farther up the coast towards the causeways. Nino had said it was called the *Strada di Cavalleggeri*, the Road of the Horsemen, but no one used it now. The track was hard sand, built up with an underlay of rocks where it crossed patches of marshy ground, and it ended at the bridge of narrow planks over the river by the Tower. The refugees need only walk along it until they met the bridge, turn right and climb up on top of the dunes, then carry on beside the river until they reached its mouth, where the boat waited.

The moon was coming up fast, losing its pinkness the higher it rose, and seeming to shrink in size. Damn, thought Ramage, it must be nearly half past nine.

Jackson seemed to sense his mounting annoyance and anxiety.

'Reckon they're all right, sir?'

'I imagine so: I've never yet met a punctual Italian.'

'Still, she said half an hour. If they left at dusk they've been nearly an hour, sir.'

'I know, man,' Ramage said impatiently. 'But we don't know whether they left on time, or where they started from or how they're coming, so we can only wait.'

'Sorry, sir. Reckon those men with her ladyship have had a rough time today.'

'Why? How do you mean?'

'I wouldn't like admitting to her I was scared of doing something. . . .'

'No.'

Jackson was in a talkative mood, and obviously nothing short of a direct order would stop him.

'. . . I guess she could make a man feel pretty small, sir.'

'Yes.'

'But there's another side to it, sir . . .'

Ramage guessed Jackson knew he was anxious and was deliberately making conversation to help him over the waiting.

'Is there?'

'Yes – if a man had a woman like that to encourage him, he could push the world over.'

'She'd push it for him, more likely.'

'No, sir. Although she's small and dainty, I reckon she's – well, tough like a man; not all "fetch my smelling salts, Willy" as you might say. But I reckon it's only because she's boss of the family and has to be like that. I guess that inside her she's all woman.'

He wanted Jackson to talk. The American was not being familiar: dammit, he was old enough to be his father, and his salty wisdom obviously came from experience. But more important, Ramage realized, that low-pitched nasal voice was helping beat off the waves of loneliness and despair that were threatening to drown him. He looked once again over the flat marshes of the Maremma to the distant mountains silhouetted by the moonlight; then he stared up at the moon itself, now looking with all its pockmarks like a polished silver coin; and the stars, so clear and so close together it'd be hard to jab the sky with the point of a sword without touching one of them. They all seemed to be saying 'You are very insignificant, very inexperienced, very frightened . . . What little you know; and what a short time you have in which to learn . . .'

A musket shot whiplashed over to his left, a thousand yards or more along the *Strada di Cavalleggeri*. And another – and a third.

'There!' exclaimed Jackson, pointing. 'Did you see the flash?'

'No.'

Damn, damn, damn! He was helpless: he'd left his cutlass in the boat.

Another flash and a moment later the sound of the shot.

'I saw that one: just near the track. Must be a French patrol chasing them.'

'Yes,' said Jackson, 'the flashes are scattered.'

Realizing he could not help from where he was, Ramage snapped: 'Come on, we'll make for the end of the track and pilot 'em in!'

They dashed along the top of the dunes but every dozen or so paces one or other of them toppled over as his feet sank into a patch of particularly soft sand. The juniper and sea holly tore at their legs and thighs, and they had to dodge round the bigger bushes.

Then, almost sobbing for breath, they were level with the Tower and running down the side of the dunes to follow the river's sudden curve inland towards the lake.

As the land flattened out they burst through a wall of bushes and found themselves at the edge of the hard track: to the right it ended abruptly at the little bridge; to the left it ran straight, disappearing into the darkness towards Ansedonia.

Three more shots rang out and Ramage saw the flashes – all inland of the track. Jackson suddenly dropped on all fours and for a moment Ramage thought he had been hit by a stray ball, then realized the American had an ear to the ground.

'Cavalry — a dozen horses, at a guess, but scattered,' he said.

'Can you hear people running?'

'No, sir: sound don't travel well through this sandy stuff.'

Should they both run along the track and try to fight off the pursuers? No, they'd only add to the refugees' confusion: better wait here. No — make a diversion and draw the fire: that was the only hope.

'Jackson!' In his enthusiasm he seized the American by the shoulder. 'Listen — they can get to the boat either along this track or by crossing the dunes farther up there and then along the beach. I'll stay on the track and you go up on the dunes. As the Italians pass we make sure they're going in the right direction, then make a diversion as the cavalry reach us. When I shout "boat" bolt back and get on board: horses won't be able to gallop on the dunes. Understand?'

'Aye aye, sir!'

With that Jackson was scrambling up the side of the dune. An American who, a few years ago, was fighting the British, was now serving in the British Navy risking his neck on Tuscan soil to save some Italians from the French, who were once his allies against the British. It didn't make sense.

Ramage stared along the track, trying to glimpse a hint of movement in the distance. Realizing he was too close to the boat to make an effective diversion which would give the Italians time to get over the dunes, he ran fifty yards along the track.

He pulled the throwing knife from his boot and waited in the shadows of a big bush. God, except for the thumping of his heart it was now as silent as the grave. Even the cicadas had stopped their buzzing. Just shadows, and the moonlight, which bleached colours and courage alike.

A crackle of branches up the track: a faint rhythmic thumping of running feet. Another flash — someone shooting towards the track, from the seaward side this time. Then another shot, from landward. Now shouts — in French, calling on people to halt. Another flash and bang: a pistol shot, fired back up the track — the refugees were defending themselves. People

93

running, calling desperately to each other in Italian, cursing breathlessly.

Now he could just distinguish a small group running towards him, jinking from one side of the track to the other to make themselves more elusive targets.

There was a jangle of horses' harness on the seaward side of the track – more cavalry coming along the beach?

'Jackson.'

'Here, sir!'

The American was up on the dune, thirty yards ahead.

'You divert the Frogs – I'll help the Italians: they must be all in!'

'Aye aye, sir.'

Ramage ran along the track calling. *'Qui, siamo qui!'*

'Where?' It was Nino's voice.

'Here – ahead of you: keep running!'

'Madonna, we are nearly finished! The Marchesa is wounded!'

In a few moments he was among them: two men, presumably the refugees, were carrying the girl by the arms, her legs dragging in the sand. She was conscious. Nino and his brother were behind, guarding the rear.

Ramage thrust the two strangers aside, grabbed the girl's right hand in his left and pulled it towards him as he bent down, doubling her body over his right shoulder. Straightening himself up he gripped her right ankle as well with his left hand, leaving his right hand free, and still holding the knife. He began running along the track, towards the Tower.

'How near are the French?'

'Not fifty paces behind – a dozen cavalry or more,' one of the men gasped: 'We had pistols – that's why they aren't getting too close – but they're empty.'

She was light, thank God, but how badly hurt? Her head was hanging down over his back.

'In pain?'

'A little: I can bear it.'

'Madonna!' shouted Nino, 'look out!'

A sudden thudding of hooves close behind sent him bolting

sideways into a gap between the bushes. He flung the girl clear and spun round to find two horsemen plunging after him through the gap, one behind the other, sabre blades glinting in the moonlight. They'd fired their muskets and had no time to reload.

Six yards, five . . . Ramage stood blocking the horsemen's path, deliberately showing himself. Four yards – up went the Frenchman's sabre . . . Ramage gripped the knife and swung his arm over his shoulder . . . The horse turned slightly as the rider reined it to one side, giving himself room to slash with the sabre. Ramage's arm swung down and the knife blade flashed for a second in the moonlight.

The sabre dropped and the man gurgled as he fell backwards, still holding the reins in one hand. The horse reared up, whinnying in fear, and the following horse ran into it; but the second rider pulled it round and galloped back out of the gap. The first horse turned and followed as its rider fell to the ground.

Ramage ran to the body, pulled the knife from the man's shoulder, slung the girl over his shoulder once again, and went back to the track. The second horseman had disappeared into the darkness and he called to the Italians, who emerged from the bushes near by.

'Come on!' Ramage yelled and ran along the track.

He heard a whistle to his right: Jackson was imitating the reedy note of a boatswain's call.

'We're carrying on to the boat, Jackson: hold on and cover us!'

'Aye aye, sir. Sorry about those two: they cut in ahead of me.'

The girl's getting heavy: it'll be almost impossible running along soft sand on the top of the dunes. Should he risk the water's edge, where the sand is hard?

'Nino!'

'Yes, *Commandante*?'

'We must split up: take your people along the track. I'm going over the dunes and along the beach – I can't manage the soft sand!'

'Yes, *Commandante*, I understand!'

This is as good a place to cross as anywhere. 'Hold tight,' he told the girl, and ran up the side of the dune, managing to use the momentum of their bodies to reach the top without stopping. He plunged on down the other side, but suddenly his feet sank too deep in the sand and he pitched over, sending the girl flying.

Hurriedly he untangled himself. 'Are you all right?'

'Yes – I can walk: it is easier in this sand. I've been trying to tell you that ever since you picked me up.'

'You're sure?'

'Yes,' she said impatiently, and he took her hand. She shook it free and a moment later he realized she had to hold up her skirts.

'My left elbow!'

He grasped it and together they reached the top of the next dune: now there was only one more valley and one more crest. Down they plunged and up again, then down the shallower slope to the water's edge. A moment later they were running along the tide-line, splashing through occasional shallow pools of water.

He glanced back along the beach: oh Christ! Four dark shapes, men on horseback, galloping straight towards them, fifty yards away. Obviously they'd both been seen. Could they get back up the dune in time?

'Quick, back up there and hide in the bushes.'

He pushed her when she paused for a second.

'You, too!'

'No – go on, hurry, for God's sake!'

'If you stay, I stay!'

He pushed her again: 'Go on or we'll both be killed.'

Two people arguing while four horsemen galloped up to kill them. Ludicrous, but anyway it was too late – she'd never make the bushes: the horsemen need swerve only slightly to cut her down. The sea? Not a chance – the horses could plunge out farther and faster.

Forty yards away, perhaps less. Ramage gripped his knife: one of them would die with him, he vowed viciously.

'When I say "Go", duck and run round the horsemen, then up to the dunes.'

He'd go for the leading horse and hope she could dart past in the confusion, escaping before they could rein round and give chase. If he leapt low, knife at the horse's throat, perhaps he could escape the sabre; but anyway the hooves would get him. Jesus, what a way to die.

Suddenly from the top of the dunes above and just ahead of the horsemen a dark shape appeared: a strange figure uttering weird cries which made Ramage's blood run cold.

The leading horse promptly reared up on its hind legs, sending the rider crashing backwards to the ground: the second horse, unable to stop in time, cannoned into it, and the rider slid over its head. The third horse shied and then bolted back the way it had come, hitting the fourth horse a glancing blow and apparently unseating the rider, who fell off but, with one foot tangled in the stirrup, was dragged along the ground as all four horses galloped back along the beach, leaving three men lying on the sand.

It had taken perhaps ten seconds and it was Jackson again – waving branches he'd wrenched off the bushes. The American ran down to the three men, cutlass in hand. Ramage shuddered, but it had to be done.

'Quick!' Ramage grabbed the girl's arm, and ran towards the boat. A few moments later he could see the break in the line of the beach where the river met the sea: there was the gig.

'Not far now!'

But she was staggering from side to side, swaying as if about to faint. He hurriedly stuck the knife in his boot, picked her up, and ran to the boat where eager hands waited to lift her on board.

'We've got one Italian here already, sir,' called Smith. 'Another couple of chaps came and went away again.'

'Right – I'll be back in a moment.'

Jackson and one refugee to come. But what about Nino and his brother? He could not leave them here – they'd never escape.

He ran up the side of the dune. A few hours earlier he'd been lying there in the shade of a juniper, day-dreaming . . .

'Nino! Nino!'

'Here, *Commandante*!'

The Italian was by the river bank, thirty yards away, towards the Tower.

Ramage ran towards him.

'*Commandante* – Count Pitti is lost!'

'What happened?'

Shots rang out farther back along the dunes as Nino explained.

'He was with us as we ran to the boat. But when we got there he was missing. Count Pisano is on board.'

'So is the Marchesa. Nino – do you and your brother want to come with us?'

'No, thank you, *Commandante*: we can escape.'

'How?'

'Over there.' He gestured across the river.

'Go now, then, and hurry!'

He held out his hand and each man shook it.

'But Count Pitti, *Commandante*!'

'I'll find him – now go, quickly!'

More shots, closer now. 'You can do no more: now go, and God be with you.'

'And you, *Commandante*. Farewell then, and *buon viaggio*.'

With that they ran down the bank and plunged across the river.

Ramage could hear harness rattling to his left, the seaward side of the dunes. He ran along the ridge but a flash only twenty yards away made him fling himself sideways into the shelter of some bushes. The Frenchman must be a poor shot to miss at that range.

As Ramage broke through the other side of the bushes he heard more shots and suddenly five yards ahead of him saw a body sprawled face downwards in the sand. He ran over and found it was a man wearing a long cape. He knelt down, pulling the man over on to his back.

The shock made his head spin: in the moonlight he could

see there was no face, just pulp: a shot through the back of the head . . .

So that was the remains of Count Pitti. Now there was only Jackson to account for.

He ran to the top of the ridge and yelled:

'Jackson – boat! Jackson – boat!'

'Aye aye, sir.'

The American was still back there among the dunes.

Ramage knew his responsibility was now with the boat and its precious passengers, and ran down the river bank. A few moments later Smith was hauling him on board.

'Just Jackson to come. Haul her off the bar – ship the tiller. Now, inboard you men,' he said to the seamen in the water as soon as he felt the boat floating free of the bottom.

When they had scrambled over the gunwale and reached their places on the thwarts he snapped, 'Oars ready! Oars out! When I say "Give way", give way smartly: our lives depend on it.'

Where the hell was Jackson? He spotted a group of men fifty yards away along the beach: they were kneeling – French soldiers taking aim! Choose, man: Jackson's life or the lives of six seamen and two Italian aristocrats highly valued by Admiral Jervis? What a bloody choice.

Wait, though: the soldiers had been galloping hard: they won't be able to take a steady aim.

He saw a man silhouetted for a moment against the top of the nearest dune, but the glimpse was enough for him to recognize Jackson's thin, loose-limbed figure.

'Hurry, blast you!'

He unshipped the tiller again, put it on the thwart, and swivelled round, leaning over the transom ready to grab him. The American reached the water's edge and ran with the high step of a trotting horse as the water deepened.

Ramage was conscious of a stream of oaths babbled almost hysterically in Italian behind him just as he realized the French troops farther along the beach were firing. Someone was tugging his coat and pummelling him. Jackson had four yards to go.

99

The tugging and pummelling was more insistent: then he noticed a relationship between the Italian curses and the tugs. Now the man was pleading in high-pitched Italian. 'For God's sake let us get away: hurry for the love of God.'

Three yards, two yards, one – he grabbed Jackson's wrists and yelled, 'Right men, give way together – handsomely now!'

He gave an enormous heave which brought Jackson sprawling inboard over the transom, and from the grunt the American gave it was obvious the rudder head had caught him in the groin.

'Come on, out of the way!'

Ramage helped him with a shove and hurriedly shipped the tiller: the men had been rowing straight out to sea, which would keep them in range of the French that much longer. He put the tiller over, steering directly away from the soldiers, so the boat presented a smaller target. Just as he glanced back there were three flashes at the water's edge and one of the seamen groaned and fell forward, letting go of his oar.

Jackson leapt across just in time to grab the oar before it went over the side.

'Fix him up, Jackson, then take his place.'

By the time the French had reloaded, the boat would be almost out of sight, down-moon and against the darker western horizon.

The Italian was now squatting down on the floor boards, almost at his feet: Ramage realized he was there only after hearing a low, monotonous, gabbling of prayers in Latin and noticing some of the seamen muttering uneasily, not understanding what was going on. Prayers are all right in their place, he thought, but if gabbling them like a panic-stricken priest upsets the seamen, then the boat isn't the right place – fear spreads like fire.

He prodded the man with his foot and snapped in Italian, '*Basta!* Enough of that: pray later, or in silence.'

The moaning stopped. The soldiers would have reloaded by now. Ramage looked back and could still distinguish the beach.

He sensed the men were jumpy and it was hardly surprising, since they'd been sitting in the boat, or standing beside it up to their waists in water, while a good deal of shooting was going on near by.

'Jackson,' he said conversationally, to reassure the men, 'that was a frightful noise you made on the beach. Where did you pick up the trick of charging cavalry single-handed?'

'Well, sir,' Jackson replied, an apologetic note in his voice, 'I was with Colonel Pickens at Cowpens in the last war, sir, and it was mighty effective in the woods against your dragoons: they hadn't met that sort of thing before.'

'I imagine not,' Ramage said politely, turning the boat half a point to starboard.

'No, sir,' Jackson said emphatically. 'Only the last time I did it, 'twas against a whole troop of 'em in a narrow lane. They were chasing me, you see.'

'Is that so? Did it work?' he asked, conscious the men were listening to the conversation as they rowed.

'Most effective, sir: I had 'em all off, except one or two at the rear.'

'How did you learn this sort of – er, business?'

'Woodsman, sir; I was brought up in South Carolina.'

'Madonna!' exclaimed a voice in heavy-accented English from under the thwarts. 'Madonna! They talk of horses and cow pens at a time like this.'

Ramage looked round at the girl, conscious he had not given her a thought since he climbed on board the boat.

'Would you please tell your friend to hold his tongue.'

She leant down to the man, who was almost at her feet; but he already understood.

'Hold my tongue?' he exclaimed in Italian. 'How can I *hold* my tongue? And why should I?'

Ramage said coldly in Italian: 'I did not mean "hold your tongue" literally. I was telling you to stop talking.'

'Stop talking! When you run away and leave my cousin lying wounded on the beach! When you desert him! When you bolt like a rabbit and your friend screams with fright like a woman! Madonna, so I *am* to stop talking, eh?'

The girl bent down and hissed something at him, keeping her voice low. Ramage, tensed with cold rage, was thankful the seamen did not understand: then suddenly the Italian scrambled out from under the thwarts and stood up in the boat, making one of the oarsmen lose his balance and miss a stroke.

'Sit down!' Ramage said sharply in Italian.

The man ignored him and began swearing.

Ramage said curtly: 'I order you to sit down. If you do not obey, one of the men will force you.'

Ramage looked at the girl and asked in Italian: 'Who is he? Why is he behaving like this?'

'He is Count Pisano. He blames you for leaving his cousin behind.'

'His cousin is dead.'

'But he called out: he shouted for help.'

'He couldn't have done.'

'Count Pisano said he did.'

Did she believe Pisano? She turned away from him, so that once again the hood of her cape hid her face. Clearly she did. He remembered the Tower: did she think he cheated at cards, too?

'Well, *he* didn't go back to help his cousin,' Ramage said defensively.

She turned and faced him. 'Why should he? *You* are supposed to be rescuing *us*.'

How could one argue against that sort of attitude? He felt too sick at heart even to try, shrugged his shoulders, and then remembered to say: 'Any further conversation about that episode will also be in Italian: tell Pisano that. I don't want the discipline in this boat upset.'

'How can it upset discipline?'

'You must take my word for it. Apart from anything else, if these men understood what he was saying, they'd throw him over the side.'

'How barbarous!'

'Possibly,' he said bitterly. 'You forget what they've been through to rescue you.'

He lapsed into gloomy silence, then said: 'Jackson – the compass: how are we heading? Don't use the lantern.'

The American leaned over the bowl of the boat compass for

several seconds, twisting his head one way and then the other, trying to see the compass needle in the moonlight.

'About south-west by west, sir.'

'Tell me when I'm on west.'

Ramage slowly put the tiller over.

'Now!'

'Right.' He noted a few stars to steer by. They had ten miles to go before passing a couple of miles off the south-western tip of Argentario. The wounded oarsman argued with Jackson, who finally let him row again and climbed aft to sit on the sternsheets opposite the Marchesa.

The girl suddenly said quietly, as if to herself, 'Count Pitti was my cousin, too,' and wrapped the cape round her more closely.

'The lady's all wet,' Jackson said.

'I've no doubt she is,' Ramage replied acidly. 'We all are.'

To hell with it: why should he concern himself about the damp petticoats of a woman who considered him a coward. Then she sighed, slowly pitched forward against Jackson, and slid into the bottom of the boat.

Ramage was too shocked for a moment to do anything: even as she sighed, he suddenly remembered she was wounded: he was the only one in the boat who knew – except Pisano.

Chapter 9

B Y PUTTING floor boards fore and aft across thwarts, Jackson managed to rig up a rough cot for the Marchesa; but before they could lift her on to it, the seamen stopped rowing of their own accord and stripped off their shirts, handing them to the American to make a pillow.

The men began rowing again – a slight onshore breeze was raising a short lop which made the boat roll violently when stopped – and Ramage and Jackson lifted the girl on to the rudimentary cot. Ramage dare not let himself think how much blood she had lost; he did not even know exactly where she was wounded.

The two men wrapped the lower part of the girl's body in her cape and Ramage's jacket. While lifting her they saw the right shoulder of her dress was soaked with blood and Ramage decided it was worth risking using the lantern to examine the wound. If only he had a surgeon's mate on board. . . .

He told Jackson to pass the compass to Smith who was rowing stroke and sitting nearest to them in the boat, only a foot or two away from the girl's head.

'Put the compass where you can set it, Smith: line up some stars and try to keep the boat heading west.'

He reached out and unshipped the tiller. Smith would have to keep the boat on course with the oars.

Now – to cut away the clothing and look at the wound. He pulled his throwing knife from his boot: ironic that it was still stained with the French cavalryman's blood. He held it over the side, washing the steel clean with sea water.

A ripping of cloth made him glance across at Jackson: the American was busy tearing a shirt into strips to use as bandages.

'Ready, sir?'

'Yes.'

He leaned over the girl – God, her face was pale, a paleness emphasized by the cold moonlight. Lying on her back, eyes closed, she might have been a corpse on an altar ready for a ritual burial. Didn't the Saxons put a warrior's body in a boat with a dead dog at the feet and then set fire to the boat?

Gripping the knife in his right hand, he took the neck of her dress with his left. Difficult – oh, to the devil with modesty: he was so shaky with worry for the girl's very life that the chance of seamen seeing a bared breast in the moonlight didn't matter.

As he began carefully to cut the material he saw her eyes flicker open.

'*Dove sono Io?*' she whispered.

'*Sta tranquilla: Lei e con amici.*'

Jackson was looking at him anxiously.

'She asked where she is.'

He knelt on the bottom boards so that by bending slightly his head was level with hers, and said: 'Don't worry: we are going to attend to your wound.'

'Thank you.'

'The light, Jackson.'

The American held up the lantern while Ramage slit the shoulder and sleeve seams of her dress, then the lace and silk of her petticoat and shift. They were stiff, and the bloodstains appeared black in the lantern light. With the last stitch cut he slipped the knife back in his boot and gently pulled away the layers of material. Each piece had an identical hole torn in it. The top of her shoulder showed white, almost like part of an alabaster statue, but just below, beneath the outer end of the collarbone, the skin was dark and swollen from an enormous bruise. Jackson moved the lantern slightly, so the light showed at a better angle, and Ramage saw the wound itself, in the centre of the bruise.

'Other side, sir . . .' whispered Jackson.

In other words, Ramage thought, did the shot go right through?

He stood up and bent over, tucking his left hand behind her and gently raising her left side until he could slide his right hand down the back of her dress, running his fingers softly over the shoulder blade and left side of her back. There was no corresponding wound: the skin was smooth – and cold, a cold which seemed to run up his arm into his body. He wanted to clasp her; to give her some of his own warmth; to comfort her. The shot, an alien, powder-scorched lump of lead, was still in her body, and the thought made him feel sick.

'Ask her if she knows how far away the Frog was, sir,' suggested Jackson.

Ramage leaned over and said gently: 'When the man fired, were you facing him?'

'Yes . . . we didn't know the horsemen were there until the peasant called out. One of them fired just as I turned round.'

'How far away were they?'

'A long way: it was a lucky shot.'

Lucky! thought Ramage.

When Ramage translated, Jackson said: 'That's good, sir: at that range the shot must have been almost spent. We might be able to get it out.'

Might! thought Ramage: to save her life they had to, before gangrene set in.

'You'll have to help me.'

Jackson put the lantern on the thwart, tore more pieces of shirt, and leaned over the side to soak them in sea water. Then, holding the lantern in one hand, he passed the wet cloths to Ramage.

'Tell me if it hurts too much,' Ramage whispered, and she nodded. He began bathing away the encrusted blood.

For what seemed like hours, but must have been at the most fifteen minutes, he tried to find where the shot was lodged in her flesh, using the point of his knife as a probe. She never flinched, never groaned, never once whispered that he was hurting her. Occasionally she just shivered, as though she had ague; but Ramage did not know whether it was from cold, fear, fever or reaction – he'd often seen men shaking violently after receiving a bad wound.

As he stood up, back aching and hands trembling, she seemed smaller, as if the intense pain made her shrink.

'It's no good,' he said quietly to Jackson. 'I daren't probe any deeper.'

The American gave him some dry cloth, which he folded into a pad and put on the wound. Finally, with the last strip of bandage tied in place, he re-arranged her clothing as well as possible, and wrapped the coat round her.

'That's as comfortable as I can manage,' he said apologetically.

'I am all right,' she said, 'I think you have suffered much more than I.'

She reached up with her left hand and touched his brow, and he realized he was soaking wet with perspiration. She turned to Jackson, and said, 'Thank you, too.'

Now he needed time to think.

'Give me the charts and lantern, Jackson; then get the compass and take the tiller. Continue steering due west for the time being.'

Ramage leaned back against the gunwale, lantern in one hand and charts in the other. His body felt shaky; his mind was full of a great black bruise; in fact the sea, the land, his whole life, was one black bruise. . . .

The essentials, he told himself; concentrate on the essentials. If he could not get the Marchesa to a doctor within a few hours, the wound would go gangrenous; and gangrene in the shoulder meant death.

He had brought death to her cousin, Pitti. Had he brought – or rather, was he bringing – death to this girl? It seemed a long time ago – although it was only a couple of nights – that he'd read Sir John's orders. If only he'd returned to Bastia and raised the alarm, so that another frigate could have gone to pick them up . . .

Anyway, what for the moment could be salvaged? The Marchesa's safety was now his immediate concern. That solved the problem of his next move, and he unrolled the chart.

He needed a place where he could find – temporarily kidnap, if necessary – a doctor; and it had to be somewhere with a small bay or cove close by, so that he could hide the boat and get the girl on shore.

The neatly drawn chart stared up at him: the carefully inked outline of the islands stood out almost in relief, and the handwriting of the *Sibella*'s late master – for it was his chart – showed the ports available. Port' Ercole was the nearest – he could see roughly where it was, almost in line with the peak of Monte Argentario. But the chart showed it was too rock-bound to be sure of finding a suitable place for hiding.

But following the coast of Argentario as it trended round in an almost complete circle from Port' Ercole, he saw a large bay only two or three miles short of the port of Santo Stefano: a bay called Cala Grande, with several little inlets and, more important, the cliffs almost sheer on all three sides.

Cala Grande – the Large Bay. Behind it, he noticed, were two small mountain peaks, Spadino and Spaccabellezze. How did they get their names? 'Little Sword' and 'Beautiful Cleft'. Like the cleft between her breasts, perhaps.

My God, he thought to himself, why can't I ever concentrate? He measured the distance. The men would have to put their backs into rowing. He rolled up the chart and put down the lantern. The sudden movements made the seamen glance up from their oars.

'Men,' he said. 'We are putting in to a bay about a dozen miles ahead, so that I can get a doctor for the lady. We've got to get there by dawn so that we can hide the boat.'

'How is the lady, sir?'

The man with the shot wound in the wrist was asking. Ramage was annoyed with himself for not telling them: after all, they had given the shirts off their backs for her – apart from risking their lives in the rescue.

'The Marchesa is about as well as we can hope. She has a shot in her shoulder, but I can't get the ball out. That's why we need a doctor. . . .'

There were murmurs of sympathy: they knew much better than she how an untreated shot wound could end.

A man suddenly stood up in the bow. He had no oar and Ramage almost groaned: Pisano again.

'I demand . . .'

'*Parla Italiano*,' snapped Ramage, not wanting the seamen to know whatever it was that Pisano intended demanding.

The man lapsed into Italian. 'I demand we continue to the rendezvous.'

'Why?'

'Because it is too dangerous to go to Santo Stefano: the French are in occupation.'

'We are not going to Santo Stefano.'

'But you just said—'

'I said we were going to a bay, and that I was going to get a doctor from Santo Stefano.'

'It is madness!' shouted Pisano. 'We will all be captured.'

Ramage said icily: 'I must make your position clear. In this boat you are under my orders, so control yourself. If you have anything to say, say it in a conversational tone: you are alarming the sailors—'

'I—'

'—and making a fool of yourself by squealing like a sow in farrow.'

'You! You—' Pisano was lost for words for a moment. '—You coward, you poltroon – how dare you talk to me like that! Assassin! It's your fault Gianna lies there wounded! And you deserted my cousin Pitti over there' – he gave a histrionic sweep with his arm and almost overbalanced – 'you, you who are supposed to rescue us!'

Ramage sat back. Perhaps if he let the man get it off his chest it would put an end to the tirade – for the time being at least.

'What's he on about, sir?' asked Jackson.

'Oh, he's upset about the Marchesa, and the other chap.'

'It's upsetting the men, sir,' Jackson said as Pisano continued shouting.

And it was: the man rowing just abaft where Pisano stood in the bow suddenly lost his stroke, so the blade of his oar struck that of the man in front of him.

'Pisano!' snapped Ramage, 'be quiet! That's an order. Otherwise I'll have you bound and gagged.'

'You wouldn't dare!'

'If you don't sit down at once I shall order the two men nearest you to tie you to the seat.'

The hard note in Ramage's voice warned Pisano it was no idle threat. He sat down abruptly just as the Marchesa, in a weak voice, called out:

'Luigi – please!'

She was trying to sit up, but Ramage reached out in time to stop her, his hand in the darkness accidentally pressing down on one of her breasts. He said in Italian:

'Madam – don't distress yourself. I let him talk in the hope his tongue would tire. But we can't waste any more time.'

She did not answer; and Ramage leaned back against the gunwale. If he'd been in Florence when he told Pisano he was squealing like a sow having piglets, the man would plan swift revenge. For a shallow fop like Pisano, the only thing that mattered in life was that he shouldn't make a *brutta figura*. Pisano's type could never understand honour in the normal sense: he would break an oath without compunction; cheat, lie and deceive without giving it a thought. In fact these things were part of his code; the code by which he and his kind lived their lives, so that anyone doing the same to him would not upset him unduly, since he would have been expecting it. But let anyone laugh because he tripped over a loose carpet, let someone even hint that he was not a real man, not the finest horseman, the most courteous fellow that ever entered a drawing-room, the most accomplished lover in Tuscany: let anyone cast a slur on his vulgar virility: then that person had a mortal, albeit cowardly, enemy. Someone like Pisano would never make an open challenge unless he had an overwhelming advantage: no, it would be a case of a few whispered words to a man with a dagger. Pisano's honour would be satisfied the moment he paid cash to the hired assassin reporting that he had completed the task.

Ramage noticed the outline of the boat and men was getting clearer. The oarsmen in the darkness looked like tombstones constantly bowing to him; but now their silhouettes were turning from black to dark grey, and the stars were growing dimmer. The false dawn, Nature's daily deceit. They had been rowing without rest for nearly three hours.

Once they reached Cala Grande, the port of Santo Stefano would be separated from them overland by the short and thick peninsula of Punta Lividonia. With luck, he'd be able to find a track from the cliffs above Cala Grande leading across the high ridge of rock forming the neck of the peninsula direct to the town — probably between the twin peaks of Spaccabellezze and Spadino.

Grey, grey, grey . . . the men were grey; the girl on her altar of bottom boards was grey; the waves surging past the boat in small toppling pyramids were grey and steely, cold and menacing to the eye. The wind was increasing slightly from the south and the boat was pitching gently like a see-saw as each wave coming up behind lifted for a few moments first the stern and then the bow as it swept forward.

Chapter 10

THE SEAMEN hauled the gig up the narrow beach at Cala Grande. Without waiting for orders from Ramage, two of them found a way to the top of the cliff and were soon hurling down bundles of light brushwood and dry grass which the others hurriedly made into a rough bed, using the grass as a mattress.

At a signal from Ramage, they lifted the Marchesa from the boat, using the bottom boards as a stretcher. They handled her with a gentleness which a stranger would not have credited: Ramage saw that each man showed a curious mixture of a proud but timid father holding his baby for the first time, and a well-trained seaman picking up a smoking grenade that might explode any moment.

Ramage had purposely not interfered, realizing their genuine concern for her. He also sensed there was no hint of lewd curiosity – although that would have been natural enough since most of them had not seen a woman for many months. Nor did it enter his head that they might be doing it for his sake as much as hers.

The seamen completely ignored Pisano as they went about their work; in fact they avoided him as though he was a leper. The Italian, unused to such treatment, reacted curiously, since in his estimation seamen were on the same level as peasants. He tried to start a conversation with Smith, no doubt realizing he was in effect third in command of the party. Although Pisano's English had a heavy accent, he spoke clearly; but Smith merely shook his head politely and said, 'Non savvy, Mr Jaw-me-down,' and Pisano had nodded, not realizing he was being answered in a mixture of sailor's pidgin English and slang, as though he was a Negro who was also loud-mouthed. When he asked another sailor for a drink of water, the man just looked him up and down and continued his work.

'Why do they not answer me?' Pisano asked Ramage.

'They are not obliged to do so.'

Looking at his watch, Ramage saw it was 8.30 am: high time he and Jackson were on their way to the town. He glanced along the beach, where two of the seamen were sweeping the sand, using the branch of a bush to smooth out footprints and the deep furrow left by the keel of the boat.

Already the air was hot, warning of a scorching day. Seaward he could see the island of Giglio a dozen miles away, a low, triple hump. The sun sparkled off the sea, and haze hung low on the horizon, faintly purple, blurring the line where sea and sky joined.

The rest of the men were sitting on the sand near the boat munching the bread and sipping the water that Jackson had just issued to them. Ramage called to Jackson and Smith. As soon as they stood before him he said:

'Listen carefully, you two: Jackson, you'll come with me to the village, and Smith, you'll be in charge here. If the Italian gentleman wishes to stay with the boat he'll be under your care' – he chose his words carefully – 'just as if he's one of the crew. You understand me, Smith?'

'Aye aye, sir.'

'The lady, Smith, is to be protected at all costs. I expect we'll be away two or three hours; but if we aren't back by sunset we shan't be back at all. In that case you'll launch the boat as soon as it is dark and take the lady to the rendezvous off Giglio. Report what's happened as soon as you get on board the frigate. You know the urgency . . . Can you read a chart?'

'Sort of, sir.'

'Well, here it is: study it while I'm gone. If you don't meet the frigate, go on to Bastia. You understand? Carry on, then.'

As soon as Smith had gone back to the boat, out of earshot, Jackson said, 'Sir, would you like me to make absolutely sure that he . . .'

'Yes, but be discreet: I don't want them to fetch him a clout with the flat edge of a cutlass just because he sneezes.'

As soon as Ramage saw no one was within earshot of the

girl, he went over and knelt down beside her. She was awake: her face was pale and her eyes bright, and he saw she had been trying to tidy her hair with her left hand.

'Madam,' he said quietly, and she at once put out a hand towards him. He was too surprised to do anything for a moment, then he took it in his, and she whispered:

'Where is my cousin?'

'Some distance away.'

'Lieutenant, I want to ask you a question. My other cousin, Pitti: you went back to him on the beach, did you not?'

The question was so unexpected that he stiffened, and the hand squeezed his, as if trying to tell him something she could not, or would not, put into words.

'Madam, I don't want to go over all that again; not now, anyway.'

'But you did?' she insisted. When he made no reply she said impulsively, 'I know you did.'

Oh, to hell with it. 'You didn't see me: how *can* you know?'

'I just know: I am a woman. He was dead?'

Again he did not answer, but was puzzled by his own silence. What was stopping him? Suddenly he knew it was just pride – he was angry that anyone should doubt him. As soon as he realized that, he decided to tell her the whole story, but just as he was trying to think how to begin, she whispered, 'You need not answer. But Lieutenant . . .'

'Yes . . .?'

Her voice was very soft; he had to lean over to hear.

'Lieutenant . . . my cousin Pisano is also a proud man . . .'

Also! he thought. Too proud to risk his skin for his cousin Pitti; but no matter.

'. . . I think he spoke in haste last night.'

'Quite. I gathered that.'

'With us,' she said gently, 'our men care only for *una bella figura,* while the English care only for their honour. Yet you men are all equally as touchy about it, whatever name you call it by.'

Again she squeezed his hand softly, as if aware an invisible wall was building up between them.

'For my sake,' she said, 'if for no other reason, be patient with him and with me. And' – her lower lip was trembling – 'and I am sorry for the trouble and danger I have caused you and your men.'

'We have our duty to do,' he said coldly.

She let go of his hand. Although it had been his voice, a vicious stranger inside him had spilled those six words without warning and without reason, while he wanted desperately to hold her in his arms and comfort her: to say he understood about Pisano; that he'd push over mountains, swim the Atlantic, lift the world on his shoulder for her sake.

He said, almost shyly: 'I am sorry: let us forget it. May I tidy your hair?'

She looked at him, wide-eyed with surprise, then said in sudden alarm, 'Is it *too* untidy?'

'No; but you left your maid behind . . .'

She snatched at the olive branch.

'Yes, wretched girl: she was pregnant. I left her in Volterra. It was as well I did; the ruthless Lieutenant Ramage would not allow me to bring such a luxury.'

'There was no need: I can do your hair.'

'Half a dozen times a day?' she asked mockingly. 'Anyway, there are other things a maid does for her mistress.'

Ramage felt himself blushing.

'You'll find a comb in the pocket of my cape,' she said.

He tapped the grains of sand from the teeth of the comb, took out the pins holding her hair in place, and began combing. Yes, it was wasting time – valuable time; but in an hour he would be walking in the same streets as enemy soldiers who would shoot him as a spy if they caught him, since he would not be in uniform. Should he tell her how he was going to disguise himself? No, not now: not to spoil these few moments.

'This is the first time a man has ever combed my hair . . .'

'And the first time I've ever combed a lady's hair.'

They both laughed, and he glanced towards the men, suddenly feeling sheepish at the thought of the ribald remarks they were probably making, but they were taking no notice.

'I'm not the only barber in business on this beach.'

'Oh?'

'No – some of the seamen are tying each other's queues.'

' "Queues"? What are they?'

'Pigtails. Sailors call them queues. Very proud of them, too.'

Finally her hair was combed enough: it was black as a raven's wing feathers and curly, and he wanted to run his fingers through it; ruffle it and make her laugh and then tidy it again. Instead he began putting the pins back in, fumbling as he tried to arrange it as it was before.

'Tie it in a "queue" instead, Lieutenant.'

'All right, but keep still; I'll tie it to one side. We'll start a new fashion.'

'Your hair needs combing too, Lieutenant. It's all prickly at the back!'

'Prickly?' He put a hand to the back of his scalp and found the hair still tangled with dried blood and several matted ends stood up like a cockerel's comb.

'Why does it stick up like that?'

'I cut my head: the blood has dried.'

'How did you cut it?'

'It happened when the French attacked my ship.'

'The French did it? You were wounded?'

'Only slightly,' he said, putting the comb back in the cape and conscious of the watch ticking away in his pocket. 'Well, Madam – once again you're the most beautiful young woman at the ball. Now you must excuse me – I have a disagreeable task before I go off to the village.'

'Disagreeable?'

'Yes, but it won't take long. I'll soon be back with a doctor.'

He wanted to kiss her mouth; but instead he kissed her hand with an exaggerated flourish. '*A presto* . . .'

He walked over to Pisano, was was sitting against a rock a few yards from the men.

'Come with me,' he said curtly.

Pisano followed Ramage beyond a group of large boulders. When they were out of sight of the seamen, Ramage said:

'I am now going to the village. In view of your remarks

earlier today, you may prefer to stay on the mainland, instead of continuing the voyage.'

'Why do you think that?' Pisano asked warily.

'Do you or don't you?'

'I want to know—'

'Answer my question,' Ramage insisted.

'I wish to come in the boat, of course; it would be suicide to stay!'

'Very well. We are the same build, and your clothes are more suitable than mine for strolling through the village. I should be grateful for the loan of them.'

Pisano spluttered and began to argue, but Ramage cut him short.

'We are dealing with human lives, not vanity: the lives of seven of my men and the Marchesa, apart from you. So I don't intend taking unnecessary risks. Walking around in the uniform of a British naval officer is an unnecessary risk.'

'This ... this ... this is an outrage!' gasped Pisano. 'I shall protest to your Admiral!'

'You can add it to your list of protests,' Ramage said sourly.

With that, Pisano lost control of himself: jumping up and down, hands gesticulating violently, as if he was trying to catch flies, his face working with excitement, he began a long harangue.

Ramage began blinking rapidly and rubbing the scar on his forehead; cold perspiration was spreading over his body like dew falling in the darkness. He knew he was very near the limit of his self-control and in a moment or two he would pass it; then he could fight without mercy, or kill without compunction.

Pisano paused for breath and, as if for the first time, saw the Englishman's face: the thick eyebrows were drawn into a straight line, and looking into the brown eyes reminded Pisano of staring into a pair of pistol barrels. The long diagonal scar over the right eye and across the forehead made a sudden sharp white line across the tanned skin, the blood squeezed from the flesh by the intensity of the man's frown. The lower lip curved outwards slightly and the skin over the cheek bones and nose

116

was drawn, as if too tight. For a moment, Pisano was very frightened.

Ramage made a great effort to keep his voice low and under control, and tried to phrase what he had to say so that he used as few words as possible containing the letter 'r'.

'Of all the things you say, only one concerns you: Count Pitti. I assure you he was killed on the beach. For the rest, how I ca – how I obey my orders concerns only me: I am wespons – I am answerable to my superior officers.'

The apparent calmness of Ramage's voice was such a relief to Pisano that, suddenly finding his tongue, he yelled, 'Poltroon, liar! No doubt you surrendered your ship like the coward you are!'

'I suggest you remove your top clothing and stockings,' Ramage said coldly, disgust giving way to anger. 'The loan of your clothing to help save the Marchesa's life is not an unreasonable request. Shall I call a couple of my men to assist you?'

Pisano stripped off his jacket, waistcoat and lace stock, and flung them on the sand. He stood on one leg to take off a shoe before removing a stocking, fell down, and when he sat up again asked:

'You want my breeches as well?'

'No,' said Ramage, 'that would be too much.'

From the overhanging top of the cliff above Cala Grande Ramage looked down at the bay. There was no sign of the boat, nor where it had been beached: the men had made a good job of smoothing the sand. Below him seagulls were gliding almost motionless on the wind currents, watching for fish.

Until he and Jackson reached the cliff top, Ramage had not realized just how steep were the mountains of Argentario: he'd expected to find Spaccabellezze and Spadino not far above them, with only a gentle climb up to the cleft between the two peaks. Instead there was a steep slope of several hundred yards even to reach where the cleft began curving up to cross the ridge.

He guessed the long ridge continued to his left until it ended at the sea, forming the promontory of Punta Lividonia, and they had to cross it through the cleft to reach Santo Stefano. Jackson pointed to a mule track. It was halfway up the slope, running parallel with the ridge for half a mile before turning upwards to cross it at right angles.

'Yes,' said Ramage, 'that's the one for us.'

Once the two men reached the track they could look back down the slope and see the edge of Cala Grande. The sea, now the sun had risen higher, was the living blue of a kingfisher's wing feathers.

They came to the end of the level section of track and followed it round to the left, beginning the last part of the climb that would take them over the top of the ridge. Now they passed through cultivated land – if that was not too grandiose a name for tiny terraces jutting out of the hillside, like balconies. The walls of each terrace were made of interlocking stones and built to form three sides of a shallow box, the hill making the fourth side, and filled with red earth. Stumpy grapevines threw out shoots which the peasants trained along low frames of twigs and twine. Already the leaves were a mottled red and golden yellow and Ramage realized the vines were still laden with grapes. They were tiny, their topaz flesh tinged with red, and he had not noticed them at first because they blended with the leaves.

'Look,' he said, pointing.

In a moment Jackson had scrambled up on to the terrace and picked several bunches, which they ate.

'Not too bad – they are wine grapes,' Ramage explained. 'The peasants will pick them after the next rain.'

'What if it doesn't rain, sir?'

'Well, they'll pick them just the same and get less wine: it's the day of rain at the right time that makes all the difference to the harvest.'

Twenty minutes later they reached the middle of the cleft so they were astride the great ridge: on their right was Spadino, on their left the higher and nearer peak of Spaccabellezze. The track in front of them now began to drop down and curve to the left, following round the foot of Spaccabellezze, and for several hundred yards they walked between the high walls of terraces as if in an ornamental maze, and from among the complicated pattern of differently shaped rocks and stones the inquisitive heads of lizards, now turned brown to match the autumn colours, watched them pass with unwinking beady eyes.

Suddenly the walls ended on both sides and the two men found themselves looking down into a valley running parallel with the ridge on which they stood. The effect was dramatic: on the far side was a lower ridge with several more beyond, each higher than the other, so that the land rose and fell in great crests and troughs, like huge petrified waves beating at the foot of Monte Argentario itself.

Just to their right, astride the nearest ridge, was a very tall, narrow rectangular tower, like a thin box standing on end: another link, Ramage saw, in the chain of signal towers round Argentario which led to the fortress of Filipo Secondo in Santo Stefano itself. This one, well inland, was obviously specially built as a centre for those on the west coast, which formed a half-circle round it, like spokes radiating from the axle of a wheel. Most – the larger ones, anyway – were in sight of it, so presumably it could be used as a short cut to Santo Stefano, to save an urgent signal having to be relayed laboriously from one tower to another right round the coast.

Ramage paused for a few minutes, both for a rest and to study the wild, open beauty of the view. The great ridges and plunging valleys were a curious mixture of grey jagged rock and, where the slopes were less steep, geometrically precise plots of terraced land. The lower slopes were criss-crossed with what, in the distance, seemed to be fluffy balls of silver-green wool: olive trees, with grapevines growing among them, and between them yielding the oil and wine which were the peasant's life-blood.

'Come on,' he said to Jackson. They began walking again and almost immediately found themselves in an olive grove.

How lovely these slim, silver-green leaves: how twisted, gnarled and tortured-looking the stumpy trees and boughs, as if they symbolized the back-breaking toil that was a peasant's life, whether man or woman, from before puberty to rheumatic old age and despairing death.

Up here, high over the valleys, there was still the buzz of the cicadas, but less insistent than on the beach by Lake Buranaccio; and instead of the all-pervading perfume of the juniper, there were many odd smells: the occasional sour stench of donkey dung and the catmint odour which warned them snakes were near. Surely that was sage – Ramage snatched up some leaves as he passed and crushed them in his fingers. And rosemary – the heavy perfume of rosemary: 'There's rosemary, that's for remembrance' – and Ophelia lying on a bed of branches, almost à bier, down in Cala Grande. And that's fennel, and here are daisies. 'I would give you some violets, but they withered all when my father died' – and, Ramage thought to himself, maybe I'm going mad as well, trotting along here quoting *Hamlet* to myself. But he realized that if he survived the next day or so he'd understand better Hamlet's desperate sense of loneliness.

As they rounded a bend the land suddenly dropped away in front of them: the main ridge curved to the left, towards Punta Lividonia, while a smaller ridge, like a wide buttress, ran downwards in a series of steps, ending at the sea to form a narrow peninsula separating the two small bays round which Santa Stefano was built.

Two-thirds of the way down the ridge, on a natural flat platform, stood the great, squat sand-coloured fortress of Filipo Secondo. It had a big courtyard on its landward side, nearest them, with wide stone steps leading up to the drawbridge.

In shape, harsh beauty and position it was typically Spanish, and from his position, a hundred feet above, Ramage could see that its guns completely dominated the bays.

La Fortezza di Filipo Secondo – the Fort of Philip the Second: the old tyrant of the Escorial who had launched his Armada against England. Spain's arm had been long in the days of its greatness, whether it held a threatening sword or a plump bride to a state it wanted to add to its Empire.

Now, a couple of centuries later, Filipo's alien fortress, standing astride an Italian fishing port, was flying the Tricolor of Revolutionary France: symbolic, in a way, of how the heavy seas of history constantly swept Tuscany – and yet never really changed it.

'What do you make of the guns?'

'The half-dozen facing seaward are 32-pounders, I reckon, sir. The half dozen on either side – well, they look like long eighteens.'

Jackson's estimate agreed with Ramage's own. Thirty-two pounders – when fired from sea level they had a range of over a mile; but perched 150 feet up in the fortress it would be much more. He could imagine their effect on a frigate like the *Sibella*, with each shot more than six inches in diameter, the size of a small pumpkin, and weighing thirty-two pounds, plunging down on to her deck at an angle; on the weakest part of the ship.

Certainly those guns, if handled properly, could cover the half-dozen or so ships he could see at anchor in the bay to the left of the fortress, although the ships would have been wiser to have anchored between the two bays, right in front of the fort. Without thinking he noted the types of vessels – a brig, heavily laden, two small schooners, and two tartanes.

Jackson suddenly nudged him and Ramage saw a peasant and his donkey coming up the steep track towards them. The donkey, laden with brushwood, almost hid its owner, who was getting a lift to windward by holding on to the animal's tail. As he passed, he eyed the two men with a mixture of suspicion and curiosity.

Ramage said a polite good morning and received a grunt in reply. He realized he was still holding his jacket and waistcoat over his arm and his black leather boots were covered in thick dust. He waited until the donkey had towed its owner round the bend in the track, then knelt down to brush his boots with the inside of the waistcoat. Thorns had scratched the leather and sea water had dried to leave salt encrusted in the cracks and round the welts. He rubbed harder and then gave up: only a brush and polish would do much good. He tied the stock and put on the waistcoat and jacket.

He was thankful a seaman's dress was almost universal: Jackson, apart from his light brown hair, would pass for a sailor of almost any nationality from one of the ships in the bay.

'Suits you, sir,' Jackson said with a grin: it was the first time he had seen Ramage out of uniform.

'I feel like a Florentine dancing master.'

They began to walk down the steep track to the town, stepping on stones and exposed pieces of bare rock worn smooth by scores of years' use by donkeys and human beings.

'Hmm, you could find this village in the dark just by following your nose,' grumbled Jackson, sniffing the air which was becoming overladen with the stench of refuse and sewage rotting in the hot sun.

And Ramage, alone with his thoughts, thought to himself, we are looking for a doctor, but we might end up needing an undertaker.

Chapter 11

AN UNSHAVEN, shifty-looking manservant ushered Ramage into a long, high-ceilinged drawing-room sparsely furnished in the usual middle-class Italian style – a couple of over-elaborate gilded armchairs, a Murano glass chandelier almost opaque with dust hanging from the ceiling and sprouting stubs of candles, a chest of dark wood with the inevitable coat of arms carved on the front covered with peeling paint and gilt, and a long, sad-looking couch covered with silk, the woodwork crudely lacquered.

The two small, high windows facing south had glass in them, but little light penetrated the layer of grime and fly spots. Just why did the sofa look sad?

'The doctor will be down in a little moment,' said the servant and went out, closing the door.

The man had not seemed suspicious; nor the peasant who had directed them to where 'Il Dottore' lived, at the Casa del Leone, the House of the Lion, which was just below the Fortress and almost completely overshadowed by it.

Ramage, who had left Jackson outside on guard, waited for

more than ten minutes before the small door opened at the far end of the room and a tubby little man in spectacles trotted in. He wore a *velada*, the long coat with tails which, gathered at the waist, spread out behind like a fan and gave him the air of a self-important pigeon. Nevertheless, his manner was deferential.

'It is indeed an honour to receive a visit from *Il Conte*,' he said, rubbing his hands as though washing them.

Ramage, when asked his name by the manservant had merely said 'Conte Brrrra', deliberately slurring the name: it was too risky either to use a real name, or invent one. He went through the ritual of introducing himself, again slurring the name, knowing the little doctor would never dare risk a snub by asking him to repeat it.

'How can I assist your Grace?' asked the doctor.

'A small matter – of no vast importance,' said Ramage, playing on the man's vanity, 'and one for which it grieves me to bother you; but one of my suite has been hurt in an accident: some damage to the shoulder . . . I would wish that . . .'

'Of course, of course, your Grace.'

The little man was perhaps a little suspicious: he was still rubbing his hands, but at the same time studying Ramage warily over the top of his spectacles. Was it the accent?

'. . . Where is the patient, your Grace?'

'Not far from here.'

'On the road to Orbetello?'

'Yes, on the road to Orbetello.'

'Your Grace . . . your Grace will forgive the question – your Grace is a foreigner?'

So it was the accent. 'No, but I have lived abroad since childhood.'

Ramage saw the doctor was covertly eyeing his boots: but they would reveal nothing because, though scratched and torn, they were obviously of good quality. The little man inspected the coat and waistcoat. Again, excellent quality, with the finest embroidery and gold buttons – thanks to Pisano.

'Would your Grace bring the patient here, please?' he asked finally.

'Unfortunately that is not possible: I am afraid to move her.'

'A lady? But a shoulder injury – there would be no risk if she came in your Grace's carriage.'

'That is the difficulty: all three of my carriages are damaged – hence the injury to this lady,' said Ramage, surprised at how easily the lies came but annoyed he'd forgotten to make up a convincing story. 'And as for moving her – I would not like to take the responsibility: she is . . .' He hesitated deliberately, careful to put the emphasis in such a way that the doctor's curiosity would be aroused, '. . . she is someone very dear to me, you understand.'

Clearly the doctor did not: Ramage hoped he would imagine they were an eloping couple, but instead the little man seemed to have made up his mind about something.

'Your carriages, your Grace: where did the accident occur?'

'About two miles outside the town: a wheel came off the first coach and the other two ran into it. A wretched business.'

The doctor looked down at his hands and then brought them together, so the fingertips touched. He glanced up over the top of his spectacles again, and said cautiously, as if unsure of Ramage's reaction to what he was about to say:

'Your Grace will probably understand my reluctance to rush to your assistance when I tell you the road from Orbetello cannot be used by carriages: it is simply a track. Therefore I have difficulty in understanding how the accident occurred . . .'

He obviously had more to say and Ramage waited.

'However, we have just received reports that a British warship is in these waters: indeed, just before dawn today it sent boats into Port' Ercole, stormed the batteries, and captured several ships at anchor there. Your Grace speaks perfect Italian, but he does pronounce one or two words with just a hint – no more, I assure you – of an English accent. . . .'

A cutting-out expedition just before dawn! Hell, he must have missed seeing the damned frigate by only a few hours. Had she been sent to meet him at the rendezvous? Hardly – there would not have been time.

So the doctor was suspicious – but not unfriendly. Well, here goes, he thought.

'Do you mean to say those impudent English have dared attack Port' Ercole?'

'Why yes,' exclaimed the doctor, obviously taken aback. 'From under the guns of the fortresses they towed out two French ships, and burnt others, in spite of the fact that we are neutral in this present unhappy conflict, even if we cannot stop the French coming and going as they please. But the British . . .'

'They are scoundrels! Do you think their ships will come here?'

'Oh no,' exclaimed the doctor, puzzled by Ramage's attitude. 'No, no – you have seen the fortress: how it guards the port. Those guns – my God, the last time the garrison fired them they broke all the glass in my windows! They are big guns: no ship could survive. And French artillerymen have taken them over.'

Ramage stopped himself glancing up, but remembered noticing the glass had not been cleaned for months: yet they faced the muzzles of the guns on the seaward side of the fortress. So much for the amount of firing practice the gunners were allowed.

But from the way the little doctor was watching, Ramage realized he did not believe a word of his story. On the other hand, it seemed he discounted any link with the British frigate. Yet Ramage sensed the little man's curiosity was roused. It was time to go about on the other tack: his only chance – if he was to avoid violence – was to gain the little man's sympathy.

'Doctor, I will be honest with you: you are far, far too intelligent and far-seeing for me to succeed in my gentle attempt at deception. Yes, I am a British naval officer – although nothing to do with the frigate at Port' Ercole. I give you my word of honour that I have in my care a lady who has been shot in the shoulder: the ball is still in the wound. She is not far from here, and if she does not receive skilled treatment very quickly, I fear for her life. Will you give her that treatment?'

'But – but that is impossible! The authorities – why they would guillotine me for doing such a thing.'

'Who are "the authorities" – the French?'

'Yes, and our Governor is also friendly towards them since our King signed the armistice.'

'Are you certain they would kill you?'

'Well, probably: I am not without influence; but it would be hard to explain away.'

Sympathy had failed: time was getting short.

'But you are not certain they would kill you?'

'Well, not entirely; they might shut me in the dungeons for a few years.'

'Then there is one thing you *can* be certain of, Doctor.' Ramage reached down to his right boot and came up with the knife in his hand. 'You can be quite certain that if you don't help this lady, then I'll kill you – now.'

The little man glanced at the knife and whipped off his spectacles.

'But this is monstrous! You would never escape! I have only to call out—'

'Doctor, look carefully at this knife: it is not an ordinary one. You see I am holding it by the point of the blade, and that the blade is thick and the hilt thin. That is because it is a throwing knife. If you open your mouth to shout, I flick my hand and before you utter a sound this blade is sticking in your throat . . .'

The little doctor began perspiring – not profusely, but in a genteel fashion of which no doubt he would be proud if he thought about it.

'If I come with you . . .?'

'If you come with me and attend the lady, you will be unharmed and when you've finished you'll go free: I give you my word I am concerned only with saving a life, not taking one.'

'All right, I agree – not that I have any choice since you'll murder me otherwise. But no one must know.'

'We have a mutual concern for secrecy. But in case you change your mind out in the street and call for help, or even raise a warning eyebrow to a passer-by, then this knife will kill you. I learned knife throwing and anatomy, Doctor, from a

Neapolitan, so you need entertain no hopes of the blade glancing off bone.'

'No, no, quite,' the doctor said hurriedly, 'I must get my bag of instruments.'

'I will come with you: you may need help in carrying them.'

'No, no, I assure you—'

'It will be no trouble, Doctor: none at all.'

One of the seamen acting as sentry at the northern end of the beach had already spotted the track and stationed himself halfway along it. The doctor's alarm when a half-naked seaman suddenly stood up from behind a bush a yard away, pointing a cutlass at the little man's stomach, sent him scuttling back to Ramage for protection.

Walking across the sand the doctor, whose eyesight was keen enough without spectacles – they were worn as part of his social and professional uniform and were probably made of plain glass – spotted the girl's couch of juniper branches and at once his manner changed: the doctor, the practical man of medicine, took over.

Knowing she could not see over the edge of the boughs, Ramage called a warning to her in English that they were bringing a doctor.

'Judging by his manner, he must have trained in Florence,' he added, a bantering note in his voice. 'I hadn't time to look farther afield.'

'Lieutenant, I had not realized your sense of humour was as highly cultivated as your sense of duty!'

'It flourishes in the sun,' he said dryly. 'Now speak only in English: I'll pretend to interpret.'

'May I examine the lady?' asked the doctor.

'Yes,' said Ramage. 'We will dispense with introductions. If we do not know each other's names then we cannot be forced to reveal them, can we Doctor?'

'Assuredly not,' the doctor declared wholeheartedly. He knelt by the girl, unstrapped his bag of instruments, and removed his jacket.

'The lady speaks Italian?'

'No,' said Ramage.

The doctor ceased to be a puffed up – and puffed out – fat little man: in cutting away the crude bandage his podgy fingers handled the scissors with the same assurance and gentle deftness of a woman making fine lace.

Ramage told the doctor to call him if necessary and walked away, sick and faint, and angry at his inability to help the girl or ease her pain. Anyway, the next move had to be planned.

At the northern end of the beach he sat on a low rock, cursing to himself because there was hardly any shade from the cliff towering up almost vertically above him. If the girl can be moved tonight – what then? Well, I know one of our frigates attacked Port' Ercole last night but it's unlikely she's the one I've asked to be at the rendezvous. The merchantmen at anchor in Santo Stefano are a good bait, and if the doctor's complacency about the strength of the fortress is shared by the Governor and the French, they won't expect the British to try to cut out the ships.

So much for the fortress: what's the frigate doing here? Three possible reasons: first, because of the danger of Bonaparte's troops trying to invade Corsica, Sir John has sent frigates to capture or destroy any craft that can be used as transports; second, the frigate is under orders to capture a particular ship because of her cargo – though that's unlikely because she wouldn't have endangered the enterprise by bothering with other craft in the harbour; third, the frigate spotted the ships while passing Port' Ercole and her captain couldn't resist the chance of a few prizes. Yet that's unlikely because it's difficult to see into the harbour from seaward.

That leaves the first explanation: Sir John is dealing with possible enemy transports. In that case Santo Stefano can also expect a visitor . . .

Right – supposing I was the frigate's captain: what would I do after attacking Port' Ercole? There are only a few harbours and anchorages around here worth bothering with – Port' Ercole and Santo Stefano on Argentario; Talamone on the mainland to the north, and Giglio Porto.

So if I was the frigate's captain I'd tack out to sea before dawn with the Port' Ercole prizes; wait today out of sight over the horizon, sorting out prize crews and prisoners; then tack in again after dark with the land breeze and deal with an unsuspecting Santo Stefano tonight.

Taking it a stage further, how would I attack? Well, since I've already tackled Port' Ercole with its three fortresses, obviously I wouldn't be worried by a single fortress at Santo Stefano. And I can see from the chart that a cutting-out expedition needn't risk the fortress's guns until the last moment.

Although the Fortress is well placed to defend ships anchored immediately in front of it, the chart shows its one massive blind spot – Punta Lividonia, jutting seaward and masking its fire at the approach to the port.

Ramage retrieved the chart from Smith to refresh his memory. Yes – if he was going to cut out those ships, he'd heave-to the frigate there – a mile or so north-west of Punta Lividonia. The Point would hide the ship from the Fortress, and he'd also be down-moon, with no danger of being silhouetted from the shore.

He'd order the cutting-out boats to steer south-east until they were close under the Point; then they'd row round it and on to Santo Stefano, keeping just far enough off the beach to avoid anyone on shore hearing the oars, yet safe from the Fortress's guns because the twists and turns of the coast would block their fire until they were about half a mile from the anchored ships.

The sun sets this evening about seven o'clock; it will be almost dark by seven thirty; and the moon rises only a few minutes later. The frigate will take at most three hours to sail in, which will bring her off Punta Lividonia at ten thirty. The boats would be off the point by eleven. And that's about the most perfect timetable I could wish for.

Where's the snag? What have I forgotten? Ramage could think of nothing and glanced down at the chart again. From where he was at the moment in Cala Grande, the northern tip of Punta Lividonia was just over a mile away. If he waited with the gig there – just off the Point – the boats of the cutting-out party should pass him on their way in to attack. Even if he missed them in the darkness, he'd be able to follow them back to the frigate after the attack, when they wouldn't be worrying about being quiet.

Supposing the frigate went to Giglio or Talamone instead? Well, from off Punta Lividonia he could watch both ports, and although he'd never reach the frigate in time if she attacked either, the gunfire would tell him his guess was wrong and he could still reach the rendezvous off Giglio before dawn, having gone only a couple of miles out of his way. He had nothing to lose by chancing it; in fact everything to gain, since the Bosun might not have reached Bastia, or a frigate might not have been available to send to the rendezvous.

At that moment a shadow fell over him and he glanced up to see Jackson standing there.

'Well?'

'Thought you'd like to know, sir: he's got the ball out. A small one. From a pistol.'

'How is she?'

'A bit shaky, sir; she fainted once or twice, but she's got plenty of pluck. Old Sawbones seems to know his stuff.'

'Has he finished?'

' 'nother ten minutes – I'll let you know, sir.'

Jackson strode off and Ramage saw Smith was also helping the doctor, who was kneeling beside the couch. In his imagination he could see forceps and probes digging deep into that great punctured bruise. He shivered and looked back at the chart, but the lines of the coast, the neatly written names, the tiny figures showing the soundings, all became a blur; the black ink spread across the paper until Argentario was a great bruise set in the Tyrrhenian Sea.

'It has gone well,' the doctor said, holding a handkerchief in a bloodstained hand and mopping the perspiration from his face. 'Very well indeed: the bullet was lodged deep in the muscle and fortunately did not carry many fragments of cloth with it into the wound. Most fortunate, most fortunate.'

Ramage felt his head swimming.

'My dear sir, are you all right?'

'Yes – just tiredness.'

The doctor looked at him quizzically. 'Well, you've nothing to worry about – at least as far as the lady is concerned. For you I prescribe a *siesta*.'

Ramage smiled. 'I'll just have a word with her.'

Jackson and Smith walked away as he approached, to leave them alone.

'The doctor tells me all went well.'

'Yes, he was very gentle.'

God, her voice was weak and she was pale: those glorious brown eyes – which looked at him so imperiously when her pistol was aimed at his stomach – were full of pain, and the soft skin below them dark with exhaustion.

Yet she looked even more beautiful: the pain emphasized how exquisitely carved were the brow, the cheekbones, nose, chin, the line of her jaw ... Her mouth – yes, the lips were just a little too sensuously full to make her features classical. He suddenly noticed the lips were shaping themselves into a tired smile.

'May I ask, Lieutenant, what you are looking at with such concentration? Has this rather frail vessel some defect in its design which a sailor finds displeasing?'

He laughed. 'On the contrary: this sailor was admiring the vessel: he hasn't had much opportunity to examine her closely before.'

'Do your orders include flirtation, Lieutenant?'

Irony? A sly dig at his sour 'We have our duty, Madam' remark earlier in the day, or mischievousness?

'The Admiral would expect my behaviour to be that befitting a gentleman!'

'You have considerable latitude, then,' she said. 'But on a more serious note, Lieutenant, how much does one pay this doctor?'

'I'm afraid I have no money.'

'Then would you take my purse' – she offered it with her left hand – 'and pay him what he asks.'

'Yes, certainly. I must go and discuss a few details with him.'

He found the doctor still mopping his brow, but he had washed the blood from his hands.

'Now, Doctor, how strong is the patient, and when will she need further treatment?'

'Considering all things, the patient is strong. Much depends on what your plans are. Further treatment? Well, she should be seen by a surgeon within a day or two to inspect the sutures.'

'Can she be moved, I mean?'

'Where to? And by what means?'

'To – to a port many miles away. In this boat.'

'It is a long way: the boat is small: the sun is hot. . . .'

'Doctor, please be precise. The longer we stay, the more chance of capture, and the longer we must retain you. I have to decide which is the lesser risk.'

'The lesser risk . . .' The doctor was talking to himself. '. . . I have applied the necessary ligatures, which must be removed in seven days . . . There is much contusion but not enough to interfere with the natural healing processes. Yet – yet one must watch in case suppuration begins, because if it does . . .' He gestured with his hand, as if cutting his throat. 'Some time in an open boat, the hot sun, poor food, to be weighed against the dungeon of Filipo Secondo . . . She is young, well nourished and healthy . . .'

He looked up at Ramage. 'My friend: there must, of course, be considerable risk if you take her in the boat. But providing she receives professional medical attention within thirty-six hours, then that is the lesser risk. The lesser of two evils, you understand: not the best course to follow. When do you propose leaving?'

'At nightfall.'

The doctor burrowed into a waistcoat pocket and took out an enormous watch. 'Then you'll have an extra eight hours if I examine her again just before you leave.'

'I was hoping you'd suggest that, Doctor,' Ramage said, and thought, isn't that relief on the little man's face?

'Tell me, Doctor, when I brought you down here did you think you would live to see tomorrow?'

'To be frank, my young friend, no.'

'But I gave you my word.'

'I know; but sometimes, to do the greatest good, a man is forced to accept the lesser of two evils. . . .'

Ramage laughed. 'Yes, perhaps. By the way, I . . . er . . . the question of a fee. . . .'

The doctor looked shocked. 'Sir! I would not think of it!'

'Please, Doctor: I appreciate your gesture, but we are not poor people.'

'No – I thank you, but what little I've been able to do I did willingly. And since you know I cannot betray you even if I wished, I will tell you that I am not unaware of the identity of the person I have had the honour to attend, although she does not know that.'

'Oh?'

'I do not need a second sight; the town is full of posters offering rewards . . .'

'How much?'

'A great deal of money.'

Ramage guessed the Marchesa's purse also contained a great deal of money. By not betraying them, by not asking him for even a percentage of the reward . . .

The doctor said, 'I know what you are thinking and I know the Marchesa gave you her purse. But you will offend me if you even suggest it.'

Ramage held out his hand, and the doctor shook it firmly.

'My friend,' the little man said, 'we are strangers: I can therefore speak with a certain frankness. Inside me here' – he tapped his left breast – 'I have more sympathy for the cause you are helping than I would dare admit to one of my fellow countrymen. But then you English – you must find us strange people: people apparently without morals, without lasting loyalties, without traditions that mean anything. But have you ever wondered *why*? Have you?'

'No,' Ramage admitted.

'You are an island race. For more than seven hundred years no enemy has ever occupied your island, even for a day. No one in your family's history has had to bow to a foreign conqueror to prevent his family being murdered and his estates confiscated.

'But we' – he gave a despairing shrug – 'we of the Italian states are invaded, occupied, liberated and invaded again nearly every decade: it is as inevitable as the passing of the seasons. Yet, my friend, we have to stay alive. Just as a ship has to alter course, to tack, when the wind changes, if she is to arrive at her destination, so do we, if we are to get to our destination. My destination – and I am honest about it – is to reach old age and meet death sitting up comfortably in my bed.

'Years ago, my friend, the wind of history was the *Libeccio*, blowing us invaders from Spain; then from the north-west came the Hapsburgs. Today it is the *Tramontana*, coming across the Alps from France. Although our Grand Duke made us the first state in Europe to recognize the French Republic, little good it has done us: Bonaparte walks through our cities like a conqueror.

'For myself, I am a royalist and I hate them – or, rather, the anarchy and atheism they stand for. But who are we real Tuscans (as opposed to the Hapsburg Tuscans) against so many? So let us hope the wind changes again before long.

'Forgive this long speech: I am nearly at the end of it. I want to say' – and now he spoke in an embarrassed rush – 'that although I have to alter course, I recognize in you a brave man – one who, because of his island tradition, would die rather than alter course. I also recognize a brave woman, and she' – he pointed to the Marchesa – 'is such a one. Although she has inherited a different tradition from yours, it is a family one which is just as strong. So, my friend, until the wind changes again, I shall remember nothing of today's events.'

'Thank you,' Ramage said. It seemed an inadequate reply; but there was little else he could say.

Chapter 12

WITH THE bright moon making a sharp mosaic of light and shadow it was hard to judge the distance to the beach, but as far as Ramage could make out the gig was now half a mile off Punta Lividonia.

'Are you comfortable?' he whispered to the girl in Italian.

'Yes, thank you. Will your people come?'

'I hope so. We deserve some good luck.'

'Yes – touch iron!'

'Touch some wood as well.'

'Why?'

'In England we touch wood for luck, not iron.'

He saw her reach out and feel for the bottom boards on which she was lying. He then took her hand and guided it to the metal tiller. 'That will do for iron!'

The men, whispering among themselves, seemed completely unworried; quite happy to live for the present moment and leave the next one to him. If only he had as much confidence in his own judgement as apparently they had ... Now the gig was out here, Ramage could think of a dozen reasons why the frigate would not arrive.

A few moments later the girl said in a low voice: 'May I ask you something, if I whisper?'

'Yes,' he said, bending so that his head was near hers.

'Your parents – where are they now?'

'Living in England: at the family home in Cornwall.'

'Tell me about your home.'

'It's called Blazey Hall: it was a priory once.' That was a tactless remark to make to a Catholic.

'A priory?'

'Yes – Henry VIII confiscated much land from the Catholic Church and gave or sold it to his favourites.'

'Your family were his favourites?'

'I suppose so: it is a long time ago.'

'What is it like – the *palazzo*?'

How could he describe the mellowed stone against the background of great spreading oaks, the riot of colour in the flower gardens his mother supervised so lovingly, the sense of peace, the polished yet comfortable furniture, to an Italian used to the flamboyant yet strangely arid Tuscan countryside and the *palazzi* which could never be homes because of their sparse furniture and the attitude of their owners? And a measure of the difficulty was that English was one of the few – if not the only – languages which had the word 'home' in it. *Vado a casa mia* – I'm going to my house.

'It's hard to describe. You must go and stay with my parents and see for yourself.'

'Yes. The idea frightens me a little. Your father – he must be too old to be at sea with a fleet?'

'No – he ... well, I'll explain when there is more time: politics are involved: there was a trial and now he is out of favour with the Government.'

'Does this affect you too?'

'In a way, yes – my father has many enemies.'

'And through you, they try to wound him?'

'Yes. It's natural, I suppose.'

'Normal,' she said with unexpected bitterness, 'but scarcely natural!'

'You don't remember me from when you were a little girl?'

'No – at least, sometimes I can picture your parents and a little boy – a very shy boy; then when I try to remember another time my mind is empty. Do you remember me?' she asked shyly, almost cautiously.

'I don't remember you: I remember a little girl who, for the mischief she caused, was more like a little boy!'

'Yes, I can imagine that. My mother wanted a son so desperately: she treated me as if I was a boy – I had to ride a horse as well as my male cousins, use a pistol and fence – oh, everything. I loved it, too.'

'And now?'

'Now it has to be different: when my mother died I became responsible for five big estates and more than a thousand people: overnight I became a Marchesa. Every morning is taken up with estate affairs and I have to be *molto serio* and every evening with social affairs, when I have to be *molto sociale*. No more riding, except in a carriage with postilions, no more—'

'Don't say "No more pistols"!'

'Well, that was the first time for years. Did I frighten you?'

'Yes – mainly because I thought you didn't know how to handle it. How did the estates descend to you and not a cousin?'

'Some ancient decree or dispensation: if there is no son everything passes through the female line until there is a son. If I marry—'

Ramage touched her to stop her talking: one or two of the men were pointing uncertainly over the starboard quarter. He turned and saw several small, indistinct darker patches on the sea. They were too big, and moving too steadily, for dolphins, which loved to leap and jink, playing in the sea like children, and which lookouts often mistook for small craft. But maybe they were fishermen, returning from a day's fishing.

'Five boats, sir,' whispered Jackson. 'Full o' men and oars muffled. I reckon it's them, sir!'

'Ready, men – we'll cut across their bows: quietly, then – oars ready . . . out . . . give way together. . . .'

Now came the most dangerous part: he had to attract the boats' attention and identify himself without raising the alarm on shore. A quick hail, using a typically English expression, would do the job, Ramage decided.

How far now? About fifty yards and the beach was at least another five hundred yards beyond. He stood up and cupped his hands to his mouth to aim his voice:

'Ahoy there: ahoy there: hold your horses a minute!'

The boats neither slowed down nor speeded up. Supposing they were guard boats from the French ships, packed with soldiers and patrolling the approach to the harbour? Another hail or not? But a hundred muskets – not to mention boat guns – fired into the gig at this range . . .

'Ahoy there!' he repeated, 'we're survivors from a British ship. Ahoy there, do you know the flags eight-oh-eight?'

That had been the *Sibella*'s number: if challenged or wanting to identify herself, she would hoist flags representing that number, and anyone referring to the signal book could read her name against it in the list.

'Name the ship!' demanded a voice from the leading boat.

'*Sibella*.'

'Toss and boat your oars, then, and don't try any funny business.'

He saw the five boats were turning and fanning out: the officer in charge had obviously ordered them to approach from different directions, avoiding a trap.

'Do as he says, Jackson,' said Ramage, 'and speak up!'

'Way enough, me boys,' the American yelled. 'Toss your oars ... Beat your oars. Look alive there or the Admiral'll stop yer grog.'

Ramage smiled: Jackson had adopted a Cockney accent and used just the kind of threat a British naval officer would recognize as genuine.

A few minutes later one of the boats came closer alongside: the oarsmen backed water and took the way off the craft just as the officer growled at the Marines to be ready with their muskets.

'Stand up whoever hailed me.'

He stood up. 'Lieutenant Nicholas Ramage, late of the *Sibella*, or rather of the late *Sibella*.'

'Good God, Nick, what on earth are you doing here?' exclaimed the voice.

'Who's that?'

'Jack Dawlish!'

Coincidences were normally too frequent in the Navy for anyone to pay much attention, but he had spent two years with Dawlish as a midshipman in the *Superb*. Indeed, Dawlish and that fellow Hornblower had done their best to teach him spherical trigonometry.

'Hold on, Jack – I'm coming on board.'

He scrambled into Dawlish's launch, leaping from thwart to thwart until he reached the sternsheets, where he shook Dawlish's proffered hand.

'What the devil are you doing here, Nick? But give it a fair wind, we've a job to do!'

'The *Sibella* was sunk: I'm the senior surviving officer. I've important refugees in my boat – one of them's badly wounded and must see a surgeon. Where's your ship?'

'One and a half miles due north of this point,' Dawlish gestured towards Punta Lividonia. 'About a mile from here, in other words. His Majesty's frigate *Lively*, commanded by my gallant Lord Probus, and despatched by Commodore Nelson to capture or destroy any ships that might try to carry Bonaparte's rude soldiery across to Corsica and disturb the peace,' said Dawlish, assuming a mock pompous voice.

'*Commodore* Nelson?'

'Yes, got his broad pendant a week or so ago. He'll soon get his flag, mark my words. Little chap with big ideas.'

'Never met him. Well,' Ramage said airily, 'I won't delay you. Paddle on a bit farther, Jack, and at anchor in the first bay, half a mile this side of the Fortress, you'll find a heavily laden brig, two small schooners and a couple of tartanes. If you keep this distance off the beach they'll mask the guns in the Fortress. The brig's nearest.'

'Oh?' exclaimed Dawlish in surprise. 'Been into the town lately?'

'Yes, I had a stroll through it this morning. By the way – six 32-pounders on the Fort facing seaward: they'll depress enough to fire at you. And on this side there are six long 18-pounders. None of 'em fired for months. Keep close in and the merchantmen will be in their line of fire.'

'Thanks! Did you tell them we were coming?'

'No – you aren't the most punctual of people, Jack: I didn't want them to wait up unnecessarily!'

'Most thoughtful. Well, tell my Lord Probus his First Lieutenant was last seen charging down a cannon's mouth!'

'By the way,' said Ramage, 'is your Surgeon any good?'

'At swilling wine, yes. For butcher's work – well, we've had more clap and costive complaints than gunshot wounds lately, so I don't know.'

'Well, we'll soon find out. See you later.' He scrambled across to the gig just as Dawlish called after him the *Lively*'s challenge and the reply.

He sat down in the sternsheets of the gig. 'Carry on, Jackson: the *Lively*'s a mile due north of here. The challenge is "Hercules" and the reply "Stephen".'

Hercules and Stephen: so Captain Lord Probus, the heir to the earldom of Buckler, had a sense of occasion. Ramage thought he'd test Jackson's reaction.

'Why "Hercules", Jackson?'

'Er – don't know, sir.'

'Port' Ercole. The port of Hercules. And "Stephen" is obvious.'

'Yes, sir,' said Jackson, but his mind was clearly on the tot of rum awaiting him in the *Lively*.

'Just over there, sir: fine on the starboard bow,' said Jackson suddenly.

The ship was so black in silhouette that it made the night sky seem a very deep blue.

Within a few minutes a challenge rang out from the ship, brassy as it issued from a speaking trumpet.

'Hercules!'

'Stephen!' yelled Jackson.

It was the moment he had been praying for since before the *Sibella* had been surrendered, but it had arrived and Ramage was curiously disappointed. Now, as he crouched in a tiny cabin on board the *Lively*, washing himself thoroughly, he had no responsibilities: Gianna had been put in Lord Probus's sleeping cabin, and the Surgeon was busy attending her; the seven former Sibellas, Jackson among them, were now feeding and would soon be listed in the *Lively*'s muster book as 'Supernumeraries'.

So now Ramage had no lives on his hands; no decisions to make where a mistake would lose those lives; no urgent questions requiring equally urgent answers. He should be relieved but instead felt lonely and unsettled, without knowing the reason. The only possible explanation seemed both ridiculous and sentimental. The ten of them in the gig had, with one exception, become in effect a family; a small group of people knitted together by the invisible bond of shared dangers and hardships.

Lord Probus's steward soon arrived to say his Lordship wanted to see him on deck. Probus must be a puzzled man, Ramage thought; apart from a brief explanation when the gig first arrived alongside in the darkness, he can have no idea why the Marchesa and Pisano are on board.

Ramage found Probus standing by the wheel, looking towards Punta Lividonia. The frigate was lying hove-to in a very light breeze, guns run out and the men at quarters.

'Ah, Ramage – your folk are being looked after properly?'

'Yes, thank you, sir.'

'Well, while we're waiting for my men to give the signal – I'm going in to pick 'em up and tow out any worthwhile prizes – you'd better give me a short verbal report.'

With that Probus led the way aft to the taffrail, out of earshot of the men.

Briefly Ramage explained how the *Barras* had caught the *Sibella*, listed the British casualties, and described how, after finding himself in command, he was forced to quit the ship, leaving the wounded to surrender her. Finally, after he had outlined the story from then until the gig arrived alongside the *Lively* – omitting only Pisano's allegations against him – Probus said, 'You've had a busy time. Let me have a written report in the forenoon.'

'Ah!' he exclaimed as several flashes lit up Santo Stefano, 'Dawlish has woken 'em up! My God, he took long enough to get there. Cox'n! My night glass.'

In a few moments, telescope to his eye, he was trying to get a glimpse of boats in the gun flashes. He said to Ramage, 'You'd better turn in and get some sleep. I've told the junior lieutenant to shift into the midshipmen's berth and give you his cabin. By the way, who is this fellow Pisano?'

'The Marchesa's cousin, sir.'

'I know that! What's he like?'

'Hard to say, sir. A bit excitable.'

There was more firing from the direction of the port and Probus said, 'Hmm . . . all right, we'll discusss it further in the morning.'

'Aye aye, sir; good night.'

' 'Night.'

Discuss what further? Ramage wondered; but he was too tired to let it bother him.

Chapter 13

NEXT MORNING Ramage thought sleepily that he was beginning to be nervous about waking. The cot swung gently as the ship rolled, suspended at each end by ropes from eyebolts in the deckhead above, and the creaking of the ship's timbers showed the *Lively* was under way with a fair breeze. Had they any prizes in company?

The ship stank: he'd been too tired to notice it last night, but the past few days spent out in the fresh air emphasized the extent and variety of unpleasant smells in a ship of war. From the bilges came the village pond stench of stagnant water, the last few inches in the bottom of the well that the pumps never sucked out, and which was a reservoir for all sorts of muck, from the mess made by the cows and pigs in the mangers forward to seepage from salt meat and beer casks. The gunroom itself reeked of damp woodwork and mildewed clothing, and was overfull of the thick atmosphere resulting from many men sleeping in a confined space which neither daylight nor fresh air penetrated.

A wash, shave, and something to eat and drink.

'Steward!' he called. 'Sentry! Pass the word for the gunroom steward.'

A moment later the steward knocked on the door. Since the cabin was one of a row of boxes formed by stretching painted canvas over wooden frames, and was five feet four inches high, six feet long and five feet wide, the knock was simply a courtesy.

'Sir?'

'Is the galley fire alight?'

'Yes, sir.'

'Right, hot water, soap and towel for washing; and please borrow a razor from one of the other officers. And some hot tea, if there is any. None of your baked breadcrumbs coffee.'

'Aye aye, sir.'

A few minutes later he was sitting at the gunroom table freshly washed and shaved, with half a pint of weak but almost scalding tea inside him. He was about to dress in his old clothes when the gunroom steward went to a cabin. After rummaging around he came out with a pair of white breeches, a shirt, waistcoat, jacket and various other oddments of clothing over his arm.

'Mr Dawlish told me to give you these, sir, so I can have a chance of cleaning up your clothes. And the Captain passed the word 'e wants to see you when you're ready, sir, but says it's not urgent.'

'Right. Thank Mr Dawlish and put the clothes in my cabin, please. Take my boots and give them a good blacking.'

The steward left and Ramage sat at the table for a minute or two, reading the names of the ship's officers over the cabin doors opening off each side of the gunroom. Apart from that of Jack Dawlish, he did not recognize any of them. The Marchesa was lying in a cot only a few feet away, one deck higher . . . for a moment he felt guilty because he had given her hardly a thought since waking.

Lord Probus was in an amiable mood, standing on the windward side of the quarter-deck and surveying his little wooden kingdom. The bright sun was blinding after the half darkness of the gunroom, and Ramage could see that towing astern of the *Lively* was the small brig he'd last seen at anchor in Santo Stefano.

'Did you sleep well?' asked Probus.

'Very well, sir, and too long, by the look of it.'

'You probably needed it. Now,' he said lowering his voice and glancing round to make sure no one else was within hearing, 'tell me more about this fellow Pisano.'

'Pisano, sir? There's nothing more to tell: you know he's the Marchesa's cousin—'

'Blast it, Ramage, don't back and fill like a bumboatman! Last night he made an official verbal complaint about you to me. He went on for hours, I might say. Now he's presented me with it in writing. And you haven't even mentioned the episode.'

'There's not much to mention, sir. A question of his word against mine.'

'Well?' Probus asked, 'what's that got to do with it?'

'I believe Admiral Goddard is at Bastia . . .'

'Goddard? What's that got – oh, I see: for the court martial.'

'Yes, sir.'

Probus tapped a foot on the deck. 'Yes, he'll almost certainly be there. But you were carrying out Sir John Jervis's orders, so your report will go to him. Anyway,' he said abruptly, as though he had just decided something, 'don't write anything until you've seen Pisano's complaint. I shan't show it to you, and you must word your report as if the complaint didn't exist. Only make sure you cover all the allegations he makes.'

'But how can I—'

'Come on,' interrupted Probus, pointing to the companionway, 'your protégée wants to see you.'

'How is she, sir? I'm afraid I dozed off last night before the Surgeon came down.'

'Judge for yourself,' Probus replied, knocking on the door.

She looked even smaller, even more frail in the cot: a delicately made and raven-haired doll in a shallow box. Fortunately Probus was a man of taste, and the sides of the cot and the quilt were covered in embroidered silk instead of scrubbed canvas. She was wearing a silk shirt as a nightdress and had made a brave attempt with one hand to tidy her hair – he was pleased she had kept to the style he had made for her on the beach, combing it to one side. A comb and ivory-backed brush were at the foot of the cot.

She held up her left hand, and Ramage raised it to his lips.

Keep it formal, he warned himself, conscious that the worldly Probus was obviously curious about their relationship.

'How are you, Madam?'

She looked happy enough.

'Much better, thank you, Lieutenant. The doctor is most encouraging: he tells Lord Probus that I shall have a small scar but no disability *permanente*.'

'Is that so, sir?'

He'd reacted too quickly and Probus would be quick to spot it. . . .

'Yes, Ramage: our Sawbones, old Jessup, is a hard drinker and I expect his flow of blasphemy while treating her must have shocked the Marchesa; but he's a good surgeon for all that, and he says she'll be up and about in a couple of days.'

'I'm very glad, sir.'

'I'm sure you are,' Probus said dryly, adding hurriedly, 'we all are. But although we wish her a speedy recovery, we want an excuse to keep such a charming young lady on board for as long as possible—'

'Lord Probus is *molto gentile*,' Gianna said. 'I have given the Lieutenant much trouble, too.'

'No,' Probus said quickly, 'you have been no bother to anyone.'

Ramage was puzzled for a moment by the faint emphasis on 'you'.

'Well,' said Probus, 'I have a lot to do: Mr Ramage, will you please go to my cabin in fifteen minutes' time and write your report: use my desk – I've left you pen, ink and papers. If you will excuse me, Madam?' he said to the girl, and left the cabin.

For a moment Ramage reflected: Probus said he could stay with Gianna for fifteen minutes: most considerate of him. But why make a point that he should use his desk? And he had left pen, ink and papers. Why papers, not paper?

'My Lord Probus is very *simpatico*,' Gianna said, breaking the silence. '*Allora*, how are you, *Commandante*?' she asked with gentle mockery.

'No longer a *commandante*: just a *tenente*. But I slept for hours. Apart from your shoulder, Madam, how do you really feel?'

'Physically, very well, *Tenente*,' she said very formally and added with more than a hint of a blush:

'Nicholas, "Madam's" name is Gianna: have you forgotten? "Madam" makes me feel very old.'

When he made no reply – he was repeating 'Gianna' to himself and marvelling at its musical sound – she said, rushing the words as if embarrassed at her boldness: 'Lieutenant! Repeat after me: "Gianna".'

' "Gee-ah-na",' he said dutifully, and they both laughed.

He pulled over a chair and sat by the cot. Momentarily he saw Ghiberti's 'Eve', naked and held by cherubs. One of the cherubs had its hand resting on her flat belly and, glancing at Gianna, he realized that she too was naked beneath a thin silk shirt, a quilt and a sheet. He could see the outline of her legs and then the curve of her thighs: they were as slim as those Ghiberti created. And there the cherub rested his hand: and her breasts, too, were as small as Eve's.

'The Captain – he is an old friend?' she said calmly, and he flushed as he realized she had been watching his eyes.

'No – I've not met him before. What made you think that?' Silly question, but he could think only of her breasts. . . .

'Well, he is friendly, and you call him "Sir" and not "My Lord" like everyone else, so I thought you must know each other.'

'No, there's another reason.'

'*Secreti?*' she asked cautiously.

He laughed. 'No, simply that I'm also a "Lord".'

'Yes, of course,' she said, her brow wrinkling. 'But that also puzzles me. The men in the boat – why did they not call you "My Lord"?'

'In the Service I do not use my title.'

'Would it be indiscreet to ask why? Because of your . . .' she left the sentence unfinished, once again embarrassed at her boldness.

'No, not entirely because of my father. No – simply that I am a very junior lieutenant, and when the captain and officers are invited to dine on shore many hostesses are puzzled who has precedence at table – a junior lieutenant with a peerage, or a captain without one. If they choose the lieutenant, his captain can feel very insulted. So . . .'

'So it is more tactful to be just "Mister".'

'Exactly.'

She suddenly changed the subject. 'Have you talked with my cousin?'

'No – where is he?' Ramage realized he had not seen him since they came on board.

'He had a bed in the captain's dining-room,' she said.

'In the "coach".'

'Coach? *Carròzza?* The type with horses?'

'Are you going to be a sailor or a groom?' he asked teasingly. 'In a ship like this, the captain's quarters are called "The Cabin", but there are really three. The biggest one is aft, through that door, and runs the whole width of the ship, with all the windows in the stern. It's called "the great cabin", and the captain uses it during the day.

'This cabin is the "bed place", or sleeping cabin. The one your cousin occupies, next to this, is called "the coach". Some captains use it as a dining-room, others as an office.'

'I understand,' she said, and he realized they both felt strangers now they were in more formal surroundings. The neatness and polish of the captain's quarters, with its odd mixture of elegant and warlike furnishings – only a few feet away a black-barrelled 12-pounder cannon sat squat on its buff-coloured carriage, secured to the ship's side by heavy ropes and tackles – were far removed from the intimacy of an open boat. The orderliness forced on them a shyness which had previously been crowded out by the dangers of the first hectic hours of their meeting.

'Nicholas,' she said shyly, pronouncing it 'Nee-koh-lass', 'this is the first time in my adult life I've been alone in a room – or a cabin, for that matter! – with a young man who was not a servant or a member of my family. . . .'

Before Ramage realized what he was doing, he knelt beside the cot and kissed her full on the lips; and what seemed hours later, while they both stared as if seeing each other for the first time, she smiled and said, 'Now I know why always I had a chaperone . . .'

She raised her left hand and delicately traced the long scar on his forehead. 'How did this happen, Nico?'

Nico, he thought. The affectionate diminutive.

'A sword cut.'

'You were duelling!'

It was an accusation but – it seemed to him – an accusation revealing her alarm that he should have risked his life.

'No, I wasn't. I was boarding a French ship.'

Suddenly she remembered something: 'Your head! The wound on your head! Has it healed?'

'I think so.'

'Turn round.'

Obediently he turned and felt her hand gently moving his hair aside at the back of the scalp.

'Ow!'

'That did not hurt! The blood has dried in the hair. It did not *really* hurt, did it?'

She sounded both doubtful and contrite and he wished he could see the expression on her face.

'No – I was teasing.'

'Well, keep still . . . yes, it is healing well. But you must wash away the blood. I wonder,' she added dreamily, 'if you will have no hair where the scar is, like a mule track through *macchia*?'

There was a knock at the door and he just had time to regain his seat before Lord Probus came in, although his sudden movement made the cot swing rather more than the ship's roll could account for.

'Come along, young man,' Probus said in mock severity, 'your fifteen minutes are up. The Surgeon says the Marchesa must rest.'

'Aye aye, sir.'

'But I have rested *sufficiente*,' the girl protested mischievously. 'I enjoy having visitors.'

'Well, you'll have to make do with my poor company,' said

Probus, 'because Mr Ramage has a report to write.'

In the great cabin Ramage found an elegantly carved desk, with an inlaid top set facing the stern lights. He sat down and looked out at the smooth wake the frigate was leaving across the surface of the almost harsh blue sea. The prize brig, sails furled on the yards, a white ensign over the Tricolor, was towing astern. The cable, led out of one of the frigate's stern chase gun ports, made a long and graceful curve, its weight making it dip down into the sea before it rose up again to the brig's bow. Occasionally, as the brig yawed and took a sheer to larboard or starboard, the extra strain flattened the curve, and Ramage could hear the grumbling of the tiller ropes running down to the deck below as the men at the wheel put the *Lively*'s helm up or down, to counteract the cable's sudden tug.

Several miles beyond the brig was Argentario, distance and heat haze colouring it pearl-grey and smoothing the cliffs and peaks into rounded humps. The sun playing on the olive groves made them look like tiny inlaid squares of silver. The island of Giglio, a dozen miles nearer, was like a whale on the surface basking in the sun. Even closer, and farther to the right, Monte Cristo, with its sheer cliffs, sat like a big, rich brown cake on a vivid blue tablecloth.

Ramage reached for the quill and as he dipped it in the silver ink-well, saw a letter partly hidden under the sheets of blank paper. He was just going to put it to one side when he remembered Probus's curious phrase about not writing his report until he'd read Pisano's complaint.

Yes, it was from Pisano, written in a sprawling hand, each letter tumbling over its neighbour. So that was why Probus insisted he used the desk. . . .

The wording of Pisano's complaint was difficult to understand: a combination of indignation and near-hysteria played havoc with both his English grammar and vocabulary. As he read it, Ramage realized the words were an echo of the tirade he had last heard – spoken in high-pitched Italian – on the beach at Cala Grande. The letter concluded first with a demand that *Tenente* Ramage should be severely (underlined three times) punished for cowardice and negligence; and secondly, with pious expressions of gratitude that God should have been merciful in rescuing them from *Tenente* Ramage's clutches and delivering them into the capable hands of *Il Barone* Probus.

Ramage put the letter down. He felt no anger or resentment, which surprised him. Just how did he feel? Hurt? No – you could be hurt only by someone you respected. Disgust? Yes, just plain straightforward and honest disgust: the same reaction as when you saw some drunken whore caressing a besotted seaman with one hand and stealing his money with the other. She would justify her behaviour by saying a girl had to eat and the sailor could afford the loss, forgetting he'd probably earned the money fighting in half a dozen actions, and for less than a pound a month.

Pisano obviously felt an urgent, overpowering need to save his own reputation, even if it cost a British officer's career; and his justifications would be that a Pisano's reputation and honour (*bella figura*, rather) were of far greater value. Yet, Ramage thought ironically, Pisano's honour was probably like the drunken whore's virginity – she'd lost it without regret at an early age, later sentimentally mourned it, and then for the sake of appearances declared daily she still had it in her possession.

Well, his own report had to be written. How much notice was Probus taking of Pisano's complaint? Or, more to the point, how much notice would Rear-Admiral Goddard, or Sir John Jervis take?

After signing his report, he folded it, tucked the left-hand edge of the paper into the right, and stuck down the flap with a red wafer which he took from an ivory box – he could not be bothered to send for a candle and use wax.

Returning to the smelly depths of the gunroom, he found Dawlish writing his report on the cutting-out expedition. After they exchanged news of their own activities since serving together in the *Superb*, Ramage asked him about the attack on Santo Stefano.

'Simple,' said Dawlish. 'We were a little annoyed you didn't stay up to help us count our chickens! By the way, I hear you've been rescuing beautiful women from the clutches of the Corsican monster. What's she like?'

Remembering Dawlish's reputation as a womanizer, Ramage said warily, 'Depends on what you call beautiful.'

'His Lordship seems impressed, and old Sawbones hasn't stopped talking about her.'

'Any female patient would make a change from a row of venereal seamen.'

'I suppose so,' said Dawlish, disappointment showing in his voice. 'But the chap with her – who's he?'

'A cousin, name of Pisano.'

'Well, you watch him: he had the old man up half the middle watch calling you every name under the sun.'

'I know.'

'Been misbehaving yourself?'

'No.'

'Kept calling you a coward.'

'Yes?'

'You're being very cagey, Nick.'

'So would you be! Don't forget I surrendered one of the King's ships – admittedly to a 74-gun Frenchman. But size doesn't matter: one Englishman equals three Frenchmen, so a frigate should deal with a French line-of-battle ship without inconvenience. And now I've got this damned fellow Pisano yapping at my heels. As if that isn't enough, I hear Goddard's at Bastia.'

'I know,' said Dawlish sympathetically. 'At least, he was when we left.'

When Dawlish went out, Ramage sat down at the gunroom table, thankful that the owners of the cabins on each side were busy about the ship: he was in no mood for questions.

Probus, Dawlish – both were sympathetic; neither tried to make light of the danger of Goddard's enmity and the consequences if he was still at Bastia when the *Lively* arrived in a few hours, since it would be his duty to order the trial.

The fact both Probus and Dawlish thought he was in a dangerous situation showed he was not being childish and

151

worrying unnecessarily. Maybe he'd soon be regretting a shot from the *Barras* hadn't knocked his head off. . . .

Ramage began to realize how lonely one was at a time like this, and began to understand better his father's cynicism: the old man had said that when trouble comes, friends melt into the shadows, unwilling to risk giving a hand, yet ashamed to admit it; making polite conversation, yet staying at arm's length.

And the enemies stayed in the shadows, too, using their circle of sycophants to do their dirty work for them.

Neither Probus nor Dawlish owed anything to Goddard's 'interest'; but that didn't mean either would risk Goddard's enmity: he was acknowledged as one of the Navy's most vindictive and politically powerful young flag officers. His power rested on the fact that his own and his wife's families, with their friends, controlled twenty or more votes in the House of Commons. In the last year or so, according to the gossip from London, Goddard had added another name to his list of enemies, that of Commodore Nelson, who seemed to be a protégé of Admiral Sir John Jervis and now an object of Goddard's jealousy. Did it mean Goddard and Jervis were enemies? Or likely to become so? Ramage thought not.

'Old Jarvie' was one of the few admirals who had taken a fair stand over his father's trial. He was not directly concerned in it, but apparently made no secret of his disapproval of the Ministry's behaviour.

Still, Ramage thought to himself, before Sir John reads my report – he was based at San Fiorenzo Bay, on the other side of Corsica, and would probably be at sea anyway – the trial will be over and sentence passed. . . .

A midshipman was knocking on the gunroom door, as if for the third or fourth time.

'Captain's compliments, sir: the lady wishes you to visit her.'

He found Gianna propped up in the cot, leaning against a bank of cushions. She had been crying: even now a sob shook her, and she winced as the involuntary movement gave her a spasm of pain. She motioned him to shut the door quickly.

'Oh, Nico . . .'

'What's the matter?'

He hurried across the room and knelt beside the cot, reaching for her hand.

'My cousin – he came to see me.'

'And—?'

'He is making the trouble for you.'

'I know, but it's nothing: he's overwrought.'

'No – *è molto serioso*. Lord Probus thinks so, too.'

'How do you know? Did he say so?'

'It was what he did not say that worries me. My cousin insisted Lord Probus came with him to see me, and he asked me many, many questions.'

'Probus or your cousin?'

'My cousin.'

'About what?'

'That night at the beach beside the *Torre di Buranaccio*.'

'Well, that's nothing to get upset about: just tell them what you know.'

'But what *do* I know?' she wailed. 'He says you deliberately left our cousin Pitti behind; he says you are a coward; he says—' she was sobbing now and, finding it difficult to continue talking in English, lapsed into Italian '—he says your father was . . . was accused of cowardice. . . .'

Our cousin: the tie of blood: the divided loyalty. No, Ramage thought bitterly, not even divided, since both men were her cousins, but where he was concerned, she'd probably just been indulging in a mild flirtation.

'Pisano is quite correct: my father was accused of cowardice.'

'*O, Madonna aiutame!*' she sobbed. 'What am I to do?'

She was in both mental and physical agony, and Ramage suddenly thought that perhaps it was not a mere flirtation for her. But nevertheless they'd reached a crisis in their brief relationship. How detached he was: as he knelt watching her sobbing he seemed to hear another person inside him whispering, 'If she has any reservations about you; if she thinks you

153

could leave Pitti like that, then you're better off without her ... How can she think you'd quit him after all the risks you'd already taken to get to Capalbio?'

The cold-blooded other self was still in control when, watching her closely, he said in a low voice, 'I've already told you your cousin was dead. Why do you still think I left him wounded?'

She was looking down at the cot cover, and when he saw her right hand, despite the shoulder wound, plucking distractedly at the material, he realized he was still holding – gripping, in fact – her left hand, and he released it.

'I do not think you left him wounded! I do not think anything! I dare not think anything! What *can* I think?' she continued. 'You say he was dead; my cousin says when we were in the boat he heard him crying for help.'

'Did Pisano say *how* he knows his cousin wasn't dead? Did he go back and look? If so, why didn't he help him?'

'How could he go back? The French would have caught him too! And anyway it was not his duty: he says it was *your* duty to rescue *us*.'

Ramage stood up: she'd said that once before: again he'd run into the barrier of the different code, the muddled logic. He could understand her difficulty in deciding whether to believe him or Pisano; but he couldn't understand why Pisano should be exempted from helping his own cousin.

Even as he stood looking down at her he saw himself facing the court martial. If this girl – who appeared to have some affection for him – had difficulty in believing what he said, what chance did he stand against Goddard and his men? What chance in the face of the surrender of the *Sibella*, followed immediately by Pisano's accusations?

There wasn't one witness he could call to defend himself: he was the only one who saw that faceless corpse. Pisano had all the advantages of the accuser: the court would be bound to take the Italian's word – after all, he was one of the people considered important enough to send a frigate to rescue.

Gianna was looking up at him: those deep brown eyes – twinkling an hour ago, but now sad and bewildered – were a window through which he glimpsed her agony of mind. She was holding out both hands (what pain it must be causing her even to move the right hand), pleading with the eloquence with which only Italian hands can plead.

'Madam,' said a strange strangled voice he did not recognize, though it came from his mouth, 'we arrive in Bastia in a few hours. Within a day or two a court martial will decide whether or not I did my duty, and punish me if it thinks I failed.'

'But Nico – I do not want you to be punished.'

'You anticipate the court's verdict.'

'No! I did not mean that. You twist my words! Oh, *Dio Mio*! Please, Nico, do not stand there a hundred miles away. Have you no heart? Have you suddenly become a dummy stuffed with your awful English porridge?'

Great sobs were shaking her; she was clutching her wounded shoulder with her left hand to lessen the pain. And he could do nothing: a ruthless stranger seemed to control him.

'Nico . . . I want to believe you.'

'Then why don't you?' he demanded brutally. 'I'll tell you. If you believe me, you think you have to admit that Pisano is a coward. Other people won't think that, but it doesn't matter. Neither of you realize no one would expect Pisano to go back; that was our job: that's why we are sailors. But Pisano is doing all this needlessly to save his *bella figura*. We were there to save your lives. The same bullet can kill an American sailor like Jackson or a – well, a peer of the realm like myself. Yet we came together to help you all. Death is very egalitarian, you know,' he sneered. 'Why, the same court martial can hang a seaman or a lieutenant, even if he is a peer of the realm.'

'Hang?' She was horrified: instinctively her hand went to her throat.

'Yes. Sometimes they agree to shoot officers, particularly if they are peers,' he added bitterly. He felt cold: his skin was contracting as if too tight for his body: his eyes were focusing more sharply than they'd ever done before: on the cross-stitch embroidery of the cot cover: the tiny blue veins on the backs of her hands: the softness of her mouth. Yet someone else had spoken: surely he couldn't have said all that? Yet—

'If you'll excuse me, Madam.'

'Nicholas . . .'

But he was at the door: a hand – his hand, though it seemed to act of its own accord – reached out, turned the handle and pulled the flimsy door towards him. Some hidden force drew him from the cabin and closed the door behind him, and a moment before it shut he heard her crying as if her heart would break. His own heart was either broken or turned to stone. *Honi soit qui mal y pense:* evil be to him who evil thinks. But why did one deliberately crush a lovely flower? Because it was lovely?

When he reached the top of the quarter-deck ladder he saw Probus, who indicated with a nod of his head that he should walk with him to the taffrail.

'I suppose I shouldn't be telling you this, but Pisano made me be a witness while he questioned the Marchesa.'

'Yes, sir, she's just told me.'

'She knows nothing about the beach episode.'

'But she believes him.'

'Why?' asked Probus flatly.

'They are blood relations – that counts for a lot.'

'You are not hiding anything are you, Ramage? You did go back, didn't you?'

'Yes, he was dead; but I was alone and it was dark. To defend yourself against a charge of cowardice you need witnesses. No one saw me. It's a question of who takes who's word for what, and Pisano's story sounds a likely one.'

'The Marchesa told me earlier she wants to believe you, but you won't tell her anything she can use to force her cousin to stop making these damned accusations. She thinks you're hiding something.'

'But I'm not. What *can* I tell her, sir, except that I went back? That's all there is to it.'

'Believe me, Ramage, you can't afford to have both of them against you. Otherwise Goddard's got you and you're done for.'

'I realize that, sir.'

'And there's the *Sibella*.'

'There are witnesses enough for that.'

'Of course: I only meant you've enough canvas set already and the glass is falling. Anyway, you realize I've spoken to you as a friend, not as a senior officer?'

'Yes, sir, and I appreciate it,' said Ramage, saluting before he turned away.

As a friend, not as an officer: Probus could mean just that; but he might mean, 'Don't get me involved because I shan't risk anything for you.'

Chapter 14

THE GULLS increased their frantic mewing and closed in on the ship, waiting for the cook's mate to throw scraps over the side. With all her canvas furled or clewed up, the *Lively* slowly lost way, and at a signal from Dawlish an anchor splashed into the water and the cable snaked out through the hawsehole, smoking as friction singed the fibres of the rope.

While the prize brig anchored close by, Lord Probus's barge was hoisted over the side and his bargemen, rigged in red jerseys and black straw hats, rowed him briskly across to report on board the 74-gun *Trumpeter*, whose captain was the senior officer present in Bastia. Ramage noted with relief that Admiral Goddard must be at sea. There were two other line-of-battle ships and four frigates in the anchorage.

One of the *Lively*'s quarter boats was lowered and the bosun climbed down into it, to be rowed round the ship to make sure all the yards were squared: that they were all hanging absolutely horizontally.

Already the first of the bumboats was putting off from the quays laden with women, fruit and wine: the first two no doubt overripe and all three too expensive. Dawlish saw them coming and told some Marines the boats were not to approach within twenty-five yards.

'Can't trust these Corsicans,' he commented to Ramage. 'Half are sympathetic to the French and waiting for them to arrive; the other half are so scared we'll be thrown out that they daren't help us for fear of reprisals later. But they're all united in one thing – cheating us.'

'Corsican bumboatmen aren't unique in that.'

'No, I mean the people generally. I wouldn't like to be the Viceroy: old Sir Gilbert must have a deal of patience to handle them. And the Army – you know, we've only about 1,500 soldiers to defend this place.'

'Probably enough to defend the port itself.'

'Yes, I suppose so. How the devil did we ever get landed with Corsica in the first place?' asked Dawlish.

'Well,' said Ramage, 'about three years ago this fellow Paoli led the Corsicans in revolt against the French, threw them out, and asked for British protection. The Government sent out a Viceroy – Sir Gilbert. But I don't think it's much of a success: Paoli and Sir Gilbert don't agree now, and Paoli's quarrelled with his own people. If you've got two Corsicans, you've got two parties on your hands. And Paoli's an old and sick man.'

'I don't see how Bonaparte can possibly invade,' said Dawlish. 'We've searched for transports in every anchorage from Elba to Argentario, and captured or sunk the few we found. They do say, though, that all manner of privateers are sneaking over at night from the mainland with Corsican revolutionaries – on a cash basis, a couple of dozen or so at a time. Some of the prisoners we took in the brig said the French were so sick and tired of the Corsicans in Leghorn they're giving them arms and cash and encouraging 'em to go and liberate Corsica just to get rid of 'em. The French reckon they've nothing to lose: if we capture 'em at sea it means fewer causing trouble in Leghorn, and if they manage to land – well, it's trouble for us.'

Dawlish suddenly put his telescope to his eye. 'Midshipman! Look alive there! The *Trumpeter*'s hoisting a signal.'

A boy scurried to the bulwarks, steadying his telescope against one of the shrouds.

'Four-oh-six,' he called out. 'That's us, sir!'

'Oh, for God's sake, boy!'

'Two-one-four – that's for a lieutenant from ships of the fleet, or ships pointed out, to come on board. Then – Christ! That's funny!'

'What's funny, boy?'

'Next hoist is number eight-oh-eight, sir: a ship, but I don't know her. I'll look in the list.'

'It's all right,' said Ramage, 'that was the *Sibella*'s number. They want me. Acknowledge it, Jack, and let me have a boat, please. By the way, who commands the *Trumpeter* now?'

'Croucher, I'm afraid; one of Goddard's pets.'

'And I can see more than five post captains.' Ramage waved a hand to indicate the warships at anchor.

Dawlish looked puzzled.

'You've forgotten the Courts Martial Statutes,' said Ramage. 'Remember – "If any five or more of His Majesty's ships or vessels of war shall happen to meet together in foreign parts . . . it shall be lawful for the senior officer . . . to hold courts martial and preside thereat . . ." '

'Oh – of course; so Croucher can . . .'

'Exactly – and will, no doubt. Can you lend me a hat and sword?'

The 74-gun *Trumpeter* was very large compared with the *Lively*, and her shiny paintwork and gilding showed Captain Croucher was rich enough to dip deeply into his own purse to keep her looking smart, since the Navy Board's issue of paint was meagre – so meagre, Ramage recalled, as the boat's bowman hooked on and waited for him to climb on board, that one captain was reputed to have asked the Board which side of his ship he should paint with it.

Ramage scrambled up the thick battens forming narrow steps on the ship's side and, saluting the quarter-deck, asked the neatly-dressed lieutenant at the gangway to be taken to the captain.

'Ramage, isn't it?' the lieutenant asked disdainfully.

Ramage glanced at the spotty face and then slowly looked him up and down. A few months over twenty years old – the minimum age for a lieutenant – with very little brain but a great deal of influence to ensure rapid promotion. The spotty face blushed, and Ramage knew its owner guessed his thoughts.

'This way,' he said hurriedly, 'Captain Croucher and Lord Probus are waiting for you.'

Captain Croucher's quarters were vaster than Lord Probus's: more headroom, so that it was possible to stand upright in the great cabin, and more furniture. Too much, in fact, and too much silverware on display.

Croucher was painfully thin. His uniform was elegantly cut and immaculately pressed, but all his tailor's skill could not disguise the fact that Nature had sold him short; as far as flesh was concerned, Croucher had been given 'Purser's measure', in other words only fourteen ounces to the pound.

'Come in, Ramage,' he said as the lieutenant announced him.

Ramage, who had never met Croucher before, almost laughed when he saw the truth in the man's punning nickname, 'The Rake'. The eyes were sunk deep in the skull while the bone of the forehead protruded above them so that each eye looked like some evil serpent glaring out from under a ledge in a rock. The man's mouth was a label which revealed meanness, weakness and viciousness – three constant bed-fellows, thought Ramage. The hands were like claws, attached to the body by wrists as thin as broom handles.

Probus was standing with his back to the stern lights so that his face was in shadow and he looked uncomfortable, as if dragged into something which he could not avoid but which embarrassed him.

'Now, Ramage, I want an account of your proceedings,' said Croucher. His voice was high-pitched and querulous, exactly suited to the mouth.

'In writing, sir, or verbally?'

'Verbally, man, verbally: I've a copy of your report.'

'There's nothing more to say than that, sir.'

'Are you sure?'

'Yes, sir.'

'Well, then, what about this?' asked Croucher, picking

up several sheets of paper from his desk. 'What about this, eh?'

'He can hardly know what that is,' Probus interposed quickly.

'Well, I can soon enlighten him; this, young man, is a complaint, an accusation – a charge, in fact – by Count Pisano, that you are a coward: that you deliberately abandoned his wounded cousin to the French. What have you to say to that?'

'Nothing, sir.'

'Nothing? Nothing? You admit you are a coward?'

'No, sir: I meant I've nothing to say about Count Pisano's accusations. Does he say he knows for certain his cousin was wounded and not dead?'

'Well – hmm . . .' Croucher glanced over the pages. 'Well, he doesn't say so in as many words.'

'I see, sir.'

'Don't be so deuced offhand, Ramage,' Croucher snapped, and added with a sneer, 'it's not the first time one of your family's been involved over the Fifteenth Article, and now perhaps even the Tenth . . .'

The Fifteenth Article of War laid down the punishment for 'every person in or belonging to the Fleet' who might surrender one of the King's ships 'cowardly or treacherously to the enemy'; while the Tenth dealt with anyone who 'shall treacherously or cowardly yield or cry for quarter'.

Croucher's remark was so insulting that Probus stiffened, but Ramage said quietly:

'You'll forgive me for saying the Twenty-second Article prevents me from replying, sir.'

Croucher flushed: the Twenty-second Article, among other things, forbade anyone from drawing, or offering to draw, a weapon against a superior officer: one that prevented a disgruntled junior officer from challenging a senior officer to a duel.

'You're too glib, young man; much too glib. Now, are you not the senior surviving officer of the *Sibella*?'

'Yes, sir.'

'Then the day after tomorrow, Thursday, you will be

brought to trial in the normal way so we can inquire into the cause and circumstances of her loss.'

'Aye aye, sir.'

As the boat took Ramage back to the *Lively*, he was surprised to find he felt reasonably cheerful. Now the trial was imminent, now he'd seen the enemy himself, the prospect seemed less frightening. Obviously Admiral Goddard had received a report from the *Sibella*'s Bosun when the three boats arrived in Bastia, and had left instructions with Croucher telling him what to do when Ramage arrived. Little did Goddard dream that Croucher would have such an easy task. . . .

Next morning, Wednesday, as a prisoner at large, Ramage had no duties in the ship, which seemed curiously empty now the girl and her cousin had been taken on shore to lodge at the Viceroy's house. No doubt, Ramage thought bitterly, Sir Gilbert and Lady Elliot were hearing for the tenth time Pisano's wretched story. Well, Sir Gilbert was a hard-headed Scot who'd known the Ramage family for years. Would he be shocked?

Late that afternoon a boat from the *Trumpeter* arrived alongside the *Lively* and a lieutenant delivered several sealed documents, and after the receipts had been signed went on to visit each of the other ships in the harbour. A few minutes later Lord Probus's clerk brought Ramage a bulky letter addressed to him.

Written on board the *Trumpeter*, dated a day earlier, and signed by someone calling himself 'Deputy Judge Advocate upon the occasion' (presumably her purser) the letter said:

'Captain Aloysius Croucher, commanding officer of His Majesty's ship *Trumpeter* and senior officer of His Majesty's ships and vessels present at Bastia, having directed the assembly of a court martial to inquire into the cause and circumstances of the loss of His Majesty's late frigate *Sibella*, lately under your command, and try yourself as the sole surviving officer for your conduct so far as it may relate to the loss of the said ship; and it being intended so that I shall act as deputy judge advocate at the said court martial, which is to be held on board the *Trumpeter*, Thursday, the 15th instant, at eight o'clock in the morning; I send you herewith a copy of the order. . . . also copies of the papers referred to in the order, and am to desire you will be pleased to transmit me a list of such persons as you may think proper to call to give evidence in your favour, that they may be summoned to attend accordingly.'

The letter was signed 'Horace Barrow'. Ramage glanced at the enclosed documents. One was a copy of Croucher's order appointing Barrow the Deputy Judge Advocate; the second was the order for the trial; the third a copy of Pisano's letter to Lord Probus; the fourth a copy of Ramage's own report, and the last told him that the *Sibella*'s Boatswain and Carpenter's Mate would be called as witnesses in support of the charge.

Ramage sensed that something strange was going on: why was Pisano's letter, which had nothing to do with the loss of the *Sibella*, enclosed among the 'papers referred to' in Croucher's order? Ramage guessed Croucher wanted to get the letter written into the minutes of the trial so that the Admiralty would read it, and this was the only way of doing it. The legality was doubtful; but Ramage guessed the letter was bound to come out in the open some time, so it might as well be now.

He pulled out his watch: he had just eighteen hours to find witnesses and draw up his defence. . . .

He'd need the Bosun, who was next in seniority and the best man to give evidence about the *Sibella*'s casualties; the Carpenter's Mate for her condition at the time he abandoned her; and Jackson, since he was with Ramage for most of the brief period of his command. And the boy who brought the message telling him that he was in command. And the two seamen who helped him up to the quarter-deck: he couldn't remember their names, but Jackson would.

Ramage walked over to the master's mate, who was acting as officer of the watch now that the *Lively* was at anchor – Probus was not one of the fussy captains who insisted lieutenants stood watches while in harbour – and asked him to pass the word for Jackson, but before the master's mate had time to open his mouth Ramage heard Lord Probus's cox'n yelling down the forehatch for him. What did Probus want with Jackson?

'Belay that,' Ramage said. 'I'll wait till the Captain's seen him.'

He did not have to wait long: within three or four minutes of Jackson going down to the Captain's cabin, he came up again, looking for Ramage. He hurried over, saluted and said in an aggrieved voice, 'I've just received orders from the Captain, sir.'

'Well, he's every right to give you orders.'

'I know, sir; but I'm to take our lads over to the *Topaze*, sir: we're all being transferred to her at once, on Captain Croucher's orders.'

Ramage glanced over at the little black-hulled *Topaze*. As a sloop she was small enough to be commanded by a lieutenant or a commander – an officer too junior to sit at his court martial. He saw that the boat from the *Trumpeter* had just left her, having presumably delivered orders from Croucher to her commanding officer.

Jackson, who had followed his gaze, suddenly exclaimed: 'Look – she's getting ready to sail, sir.'

Certainly there was a scurry of men bending on headsails. Ramage felt his stomach knot into a spasm of fear as he realized what Croucher was doing. . . .

The *Trumpeter*'s lieutenant had brought over the order for the trial and the request for Ramage's list of witnesses – but at the same time had delivered to Probus an order to send all the Sibellas to the *Topaze* at once. And the *Topaze*'s commanding officer had obviously just received orders to sail as soon as the Sibellas were on board. . . .

So by the time Ramage's list of witnesses arrived in the *Trumpeter*, the *Topaze* would have gone and the Deputy Judge Advocate would be able to reply, quite truthfully, that many of the witnesses he requested were not in port.

Jackson must have sensed Ramage's sudden tension.

'Anything wrong, sir?' he asked anxiously.

'Everything,' Ramage said bitterly. 'Tomorrow I stand my trial on a charge of cowardice and, apart from the Bosun and Carpenter's Mate, I won't have a single witness in my defence.'

'Cowardice?' Jackson ejaculated. 'How's that, sir? Isn't it just the normal loss-of-ship inquiry?'

Ramage realized that for discipline's sake he had no business discussing the matter with Jackson; but since Jackson would be at sea tomorrow, it didn't matter much.

'Yes, cowardice: at least, I think they'll bring it in.'

'But it's not in the actual charge, is it, sir?'

'No – it's the usual wording.'

'But . . . but how the devil can they bring in cowardice, sir, if you'll pardon me for asking?'

'Easy enough,' Ramage said sourly. 'I've been accused in writing by Count Pisano.'

'Him! Christ, for—'

'Jackson: I've been very indiscreet in telling you all this. Now, quickly, give me some names – the boy the Bosun sent down when I was knocked out, and the two men who helped me up on deck.'

'Can't remember, sir. But some of the lads will: I'll ask 'em while we're getting ready to go over to the *Topaze*, sir.'

Jackson saluted and went forward. The American had an odd expression on his face: was it a look of triumph? Ramage felt a spasm of fear: in the past few days he'd often made indiscreet comments to Jackson, and – although Croucher wouldn't know it from Ramage's own report – the American was the only possible witness who was in a good position, if he was prepared to tell lies, to back up Pisano's charge of cowardice. . . .

Trapped, trapped, trapped! For a moment he felt pure panic as he realized that unless Croucher had kept back some of the other Sibellas who had reached Bastia in the Bosun's party, the only other witness at the trial, apart from the Bosun and Carpenter's Mate, would also be the most influential – Pisano. Gianna, if she was well enough to attend, would at worst back her cousin or, at best, not contradict him.

Jackson came back. 'The two men were Patrick O'Connor and John Higgins, sir; and the boy was Adam Brenton.'

'Thank you,' Ramage said and ran down to the gunroom shouting to the steward to bring pen, ink and paper.

Hurriedly he scribbled a letter to the Deputy Judge Advocate requesting the men named in the attached list to be called as witnesses, and signed it. On a second sheet of paper he wrote the names of the Bosun, Carpenter's Mate, the men Jackson had just mentioned, and rounded the list off with Jackson and Smith. Then, as an afterthought, he added a postscript to his letter saying he would forward a further list as soon as he could see the *Sibella*'s muster book and refresh his memory.

He folded the letter and list together – there was no time for a seal – and ran up on deck again.

Dawlish was by the gangway where Jackson was mustering the six Sibellas, with their hammocks and new seabags, which were pitifully empty since they had been able to buy only a few articles from the purser that morning.

'Jack – can you send this letter across to the *Trumpeter* at once: it's urgent?'

'Certainly – there's a boat from the *Topaze* alongside: she can deliver it on her way back.'

'No, Jack: can you send one of our own boats with it?'

Dawlish realized there must be a good reason for Ramage's insistence.

'Bosun's Mate! Muster the duty boat's crew. Here,' he called to a midshipman, 'take the duty boat and deliver this to the' – he paused and glanced at the letter – 'to the Deputy Judge Advocate in the *Trumpeter*.'

As Jackson began calling out the names of the Sibellas from a list he was holding, Dawlish shouted forward, 'Look alive, there! I don't see the duty boat's crew! Bosun's Mate, hurry those men aft!'

Ramage realized Probus had come up the companionway and was walking towards them.

'What do you want a boat for?' he asked Dawlish. 'The *Topaze* is sending a boat for these men.'

'I know, sir, it's already alongside. Mr Ramage wants a letter delivered to the *Trumpeter*.'

'Well, that can wait, can't it, Ramage? I've some papers to send over later on.'

'It's my list of witnesses, sir.'

'Your *what*?'

'List of witnesses.'

'Have you been asleep?'

'Well, sir, I had the charge delivered to me only ten minutes ago.'

'Ten minutes! Didn't you get it yesterday?'

'No, sir. It came in the last boat from the *Trumpeter*: the same one that brought the orders for these men.' Ramage gestured towards the Sibellas.

'All right then, carry on then, Dawlish.'

Probus walked away, and a few moments later Ramage saw him looking with his telescope first at the *Trumpeter* and then at the *Topaze*. After a moment's glance at the sloop, Probus called:

'Midshipman! What's that the sloop's flying?'

Ramage saw the *Topaze* had just hoisted a wheft at the ensign staff – a signal a ship made for her boats to return, and usually a warning that she was about to sail.

'Wheft, sir,' called the midshipman. 'Boats to return.'

'Mr Dawlish,' said Probus, 'send those men off smartly. Mr Ramage, come over here!'

As soon as Ramage joined him, Probus asked: 'Did you know she was sailing?'

'We saw them bending on headsails a few minutes ago.'

'Why didn't you come and tell me?'

Ramage did not answer: it hadn't occurred to him.

'So you'll lose a lot of your witnesses?'

Ramage said nothing: Probus could work it out for himself.

Finally Probus shut his telescope with a vicious snap, turned as if to say something to Ramage, but apparently thought better of it.

Just at that moment Ramage saw the Sibellas lowering their gear into the boat. Jackson came over towards Probus, as if to make his report. But instead of stopping at a respectful distance and saluting, the American came straight up to him, gave the startled captain a push in the chest, and said in a conversational tone of voice, 'You're in the bloody way.'

Probus was too dumbfounded to react at once, and Jackson then gave Ramage a push. 'You, too!'

Probus recovered first and, his face flushed with anger, turned to Ramage: 'Is this man drunk, or mad?'

'God knows, sir!'

' "Insolence" and probably "Striking a superior officer", sir,' said Jackson. 'I ought to be arrested.'

'You're damned right!' Probus said heatedly. 'Hey, Master-at-Arms! Pass the word for the Master-at-Arms!'

While the Captain turned to repeat the order to Dawlish, Jackson gave Ramage a deliberate wink.

Realizing the significance of what Jackson had done, Ramage stared down at the deck, ashamed of his earlier doubts.

Probus waited impatiently for the Master-at-Arms, banging the telescope against his leg, and finally strode to the quarter-deck rail, bawling to Dawlish.

Ramage seized the opportunity to hiss at Jackson: 'You fool – they can hang you, for this!'

'Yes, but if I'm under arrest I can't sail in the *Topaze*!'

'But—'

'Didn't know you were in special trouble, sir: thought it was routine, although I did wonder why that Italian gentleman kept making all those speeches. If I'd—'

He stopped as he saw Probus turning back from the rail, and Ramage realized that since all the conversation in the gig between himself, Pisano and Gianna had been in Italian, Jackson had no inkling of Pisano's accusations.

Within a minute the heavily-built Master-at-Arms, breathless after running up the ladders from below, was standing before Probus, who pointed at Jackson and said: 'Take that man below.'

Probus told Dawlish: 'Send a lieutenant to the *Topaze* with these men. He's to explain to her commanding officer that one of them has been detained on board this ship on my orders and a report is being sent to Captain Croucher.'

To Ramage he snapped: 'Come down to my cabin.'

The cabin was cool, thanks to the awnings rigged across the

deck overhead. Probus pulled a chair away from the desk and sat down.

'Did he know you are being tried tomorrow?'

'Yes sir – I told him a few minutes ago.'

'And he saw the *Topaze* getting ready to sail?'

'Yes – he saw them bending on headsails, then you mentioned about the wheft.'

'Does he know the charge?'

'No – but I mentioned that Pisano had accused me of cowardice.'

'Very indiscreet.'

'Yes sir, I apologize. May I ask you a personal question?'

'You can ask, though I don't guarantee to answer.'

'Did you know she was sailing?'

'You know I can't answer – but my reaction to seeing the wheft makes your question unnecessary.'

'Thank you, sir.'

'You've nothing to thank me for: I've told you nothing.'

'Aye aye, sir.'

'What sort of man is this dam' cox'n?'

'American, a fine seaman, plenty of initiative and deserves promotion. I don't know why he's never got a discharge with a Protection.'

'Well, that's his affair,' Probus said impatiently. 'We want to know what he's up to now. Obviously he wanted to be arrested to avoid sailing in the *Topaze*. That means he wants to stay here. The reason's obvious enough – he wants to be available as a witness. Why? What can he say that can help you?'

'That's what puzzles me, sir: he can't know much about the Pisano business because we always spoke in Italian.'

'So the only new fact he's learnt in the last few minutes is that Pisano's accusing you of cowardice, and that it'll probably come up at the trial.'

'Yes, sir.'

'Doesn't make sense, does it? He can't have any vital evidence – nothing that'd be in dispute, anyway. But you've been very indiscreet in confiding to a seaman.'

'I realize that, sir.'

'Still, no harm has been done.'

'Except that now Jackson's under arrest as well as me.'

'Oh? who said so?'

'Well, sir—'

'I only ordered him to be taken below. But if I'm going to keep him on board so you can have him as a witness, I've got to have him under arrest. . . .'

Ramage waited for Probus to continue.

'Before I put him under arrest I wanted to be sure of the charge. Not striking me – although he did – because that means he'd have to be tried by court martial and could hang. Insolence – that's it: then I can deal with him. But listen, Ramage: if this conspiracy ever comes out, we're both ruined. So you'd better get hold of Jackson and warn him to be damn' careful.'

'Aye aye, sir.'

'Very well. But Captain Croucher isn't going to be very pleased. Your father had a lot of enemies, my lad.'

'So I'm beginning to find out, sir. But it's rather hard to meet a man for the first time and find he's an enemy.'

'Well, you can console yourself it's a lot worse on shore here in Corsica with the vendetta: Romeo and Juliet – daggers at dead of night – quarrels between families handed down from father to son like an estate. . . .'

'That's just what I've inherited, it seems to me,' Ramage said bitterly.

'Don't be ridiculous! It's quite a different thing.'

Ramage supposed there must be a difference, but for the moment it was hard to distinguish, except for the darkness. A stiletto between the shoulder blades was a more sophisticated weapon than the one Captain Croucher was using.

'Are you in love with this girl?'

Ramage gave a start: Probus's voice sounded almost disinterested, and the question obviously wasn't meant offensively; rather as though he was turning an idea over in his mind.

Well, did he love her? Or had his protective instincts been

170

aroused because she was in danger when they first met? Was he just fascinated by her beauty and her accent, which made English so musical – and sensual, too, for that matter? He simply hadn't thought of it in cold blood: it just happened: one didn't suddenly say 'I'm in love'. He'd known several girls in the past and never regarded them with more than affection, except for a married woman who'd – he felt himself go hot with embarrassment at the thought. Yet . . . now, at this very moment, he realized for the first time (admitted it, rather) that while she was in the ship – even after he'd stalked out of the cabin, ignoring her pleas – merely knowing she was near had been enough. When she'd gone away he became an empty shell, with no reason for existing, no reason – incentive was a better word – for doing anything. Was this love? It certainly wasn't the brash, almost crude feeling he'd felt for the married woman: that was just a lot of tingling below the sword belt and breathing hard above it. No, he felt utterly lost without her; restless and incomplete. But when she—

'You realize she's in love with you?' Probus said.

'With me?'

'My dear fellow,' Probus exclaimed impatiently, 'are you blind?'

'No – but . . .'

'The devil take the "buts". I don't know why I'm getting myself mixed up in your affairs; but do I have to draw a chart? You're in very deep water. Until a few minutes ago I wasn't too sure how much of Pisano's story was true: no smoke without fire, you know. But for the Marchesa, I'd have believed half of it, and I'll tell you why, although' – he held up his hand to stop Ramage interrupting – 'women are sometimes wrong in their judgement, and she wasn't on board the *Sibella* when you struck.

'For me, the *Sibella* was the biggest question mark, of course. Suddenly finding yourself with the responsibility of a badly damaged ship and a lot of wounded men – it's natural enough to do something hasty: something you regret later. But I've had time to size up that fellow Jackson – I shouldn't be telling you this, I suppose – and if he'll risk the noose round his neck to save your reputation, then I'm prepared to believe you did the right thing in striking to the *Barras*.'

'Thank you, sir,' Ramage said lamely. 'It's not the *Sibella* episode that bothers me: it's the beach.'

'Precisely: it did me, until I found the Marchesa wanting to believe you – but getting precious little help from you, I gather. That cousin really was dead?'

'Yes.'

'Then why the bloody hell didn't you convince the girl? She says you won't explain anything. I suppose she thinks you are either a liar or too proud. You've only yourself to blame if she ends up listening to that bag of wind Pisano, haven't you, eh?'

When Ramage made no reply, Probus appeared to lose his temper. 'Answer me, man!'

'Well, sir, to begin with I was pretty shaken at being accused of not going back; then I got angry at being called a coward by Pisano – dammit, sir, he was so yellow he bolted for the beach without so much as *ciao* to Pitti. So – well, I felt they weren't worth wasting my breath on. Pisano's only accusing me of cowardice to cover himself.'

'But you had one very important person prepared to believe any reasonable explanation you gave – and presumably testify on your behalf.'

'Oh? Who, sir?'

'The Marchesa, you fool!' Probus made no effort to hide his exasperation.

Ramage's head whirled and perspiration soaked his clothes as the humiliating thought struck him like a dagger thrust that he had been so full of indignation, so puffed up with outraged pride and stung with injured innocence, that he hadn't sat down and used his brain.

He realized now that Gianna had only wanted to hear from his own lips exactly what he'd seen when he went back: she only needed a few words of explanation and assurance from the stranger with whom she had – according to Probus anyway – fallen in love. Instead, he had just repeated like a pompous parrot that he had done his duty.

'You look as if you're going to pass out, Ramage. Here — sit down.'

Probus stood up and pushed a chair across the deck. As Ramage sat down, Probus took a bottle and glasses from a rack on the bulkhead.

'This brandy's almost too good for a fool like you,' he said, handing Ramage a half-filled glass. After pouring himself out a drink he sat down in another chair and began tapping a finger nail against the glass, appearing to be absorbed in the bell-like note it made, then took a sip of brandy and gave an appreciative sigh.

Ramage took the opportunity of asking a question.

'Why do you think Jackson's doing this for me, sir?'

'How the devil should I know! Pisano acts like that because he's Pisano. Jackson's a seaman. You know a seaman's an odd customer — he'll lie and cheat and get fighting drunk at the sniff of a cork, but he's got one of the highest developed senses of justice on this earth: you've seen enough floggings to know that.

'I always know when I'm flogging the right man — I just look at the faces of the ship's company. Although I'm flogging one of their messmates, if he's guilty, then they accept it. But if he's innocent, I know by their attitude. No murmurings, no mutterings; but I know.

'I'd say that's how Jackson's mind has worked. He probably knows your father was a scapegoat. He's been around long enough to know the Ramage family have enemies. Once he knew they were bringing cowardice into the trial, he realized pretty quickly why he and the rest of the Sibellas were being shipped off to the *Topaze*. Quicker than me, incidentally,' Probus added.

Ramage said: 'All this makes me feel pretty humble. First you, then Jackson. I don't want to sound ungrateful or offend you, sir, but I'd rather you didn't get mixed up in this any further.'

'My dear fellow, I'm not going to! Already I feel quite ill, and soon after midnight I'll be far too sick to think of attending a court martial in the forenoon — as a certificate duly signed by the surgeon will inform the president of the court. Since there are six post captains among the ships here there'll be one more than the necessary five, so the trial can continue.'

'Thank you, sir.'

'Don't thank me: I'm not helping you – I'm looking after myself. I don't propose running foul of Goddard, but I know far too much about the case to be able to sit as a member of the court. Since it'd be a trifle difficult to explain to the president of the court how I came by that knowledge, it's fortunate I now feel quite feverish and sick, and must take to my cot. So good night to you.'

'Jackson, sir?'

'Leave him to me. Insolence, didn't I say? To me, not to you. You were a witness: the only witness. It happened – as far as I can remember – some time before I received the order to transfer him and the rest of the Sibellas to the *Topaze*. I must write a report for Captain Croucher. Oh yes,' he added absentmindedly, 'that reminds me. I've another letter to write, too.'

Ramage waited, thinking Probus had more to say about the letter, but the Captain glanced up and said, 'It's all right, you can go; I'm not writing it to you. Good night.'

Chapter 15

WHEN THE gunroom steward woke him next morning with a cup of tea, Ramage had the usual brassy taste in his mouth and headache resulting from sleeping in the tiny, almost airless cabin. He knew the tea would be tepid and taste awful; it always was, and presumably – for lieutenants, anyway – always would be. His trial was due to begin in an hour or so: the condemned man drank a hearty breakfast.

The steward returned. 'Mr Dawlish said to give you these, sir,' and he put a sword and hat on top of the small chest of drawers. 'There are some other things I've got to get, and there's this, sir: it came off from the shore just now, sir.'

He handed Ramage a letter which had been closed with a blob of red wax but bore no impression of a seal. In the half-darkness of the cabin it was difficult to read, but he saw the writing was bold but jerky, and the calligraphy indicated the writer was probably Italian: certainly not English.

He climbed out of his cot to read the letter under the gunroom skylight. There was no greeting, and no signature. Just three lines of writing:

> *'Nessun maggior dolore,*
> *Che ricordarsi del tempo felice*
> *Nella miseria.'*

He recognized Dante's words from the *Divine Comedy*: there is no greater sorrow than to recall a time of happiness in misery.

True enough, he thought; but who wants to remind me on a morning like this. He held the page to the skylight and could just distinguish a watermark: a crown on a sort of urn, with 'GR' beneath it. So the writer had access to official notepaper . . .

Suddenly he was back in the Tower, standing before a beautiful girl in a black cape who was pointing a pistol at him and demanding: 'What's all this about *L'amor che muove il sole e l'altre stelle*?' So she'd sent the letter, writing jerkily because of the wound in her shoulder, on notepaper borrowed from the Viceroy. But what 'time of happiness' was she recalling?

The steward entering the gunroom brought Ramage back to the present with a start: finding an officer standing naked under the skylight stopped the man as effectively as if he had walked into a wall, and he simply held out an armful of clothing.

'Mr Dawlish, sir. One pair o' shoes is his, but the uvvers belong to uvver officers. Question of which of 'em fits, sir.'

'Quite – leave them in the cabin.'

'And Mr Dawlish said to say for you to pass the word when you was ready, sir, 'cos the Provost Marshal's arrived, and the boat's due to leave in fifteen minutes, sir.'

In fifteen minutes one of the *Trumpeter*'s cannon would

fire, and the Union Flag would be run up at her mizen peak: the signal that a court martial was to be held, and warning everyone concerned to repair on board.

Under the *Regulations and Instructions*, when the senior of five captains ordered a court martial he could also act as president; so that Croucher would preside today and be in the fortunate position of both accuser and judge.

But, Ramage reflected, why think about it? Realizing he was still naked, he hurriedly washed: the water was almost cold because he had not noticed the steward bring it in.

The surgeon, no doubt, was examining Lord Probus and writing the certificate which, by law, was necessary to excuse him from attending the court martial; the Master would be carrying out the usual morning routine of seeing the yards were squared, inspecting the rigging, and probably arranging for empty water casks to be sent on shore to be refilled; while the purser would be preparing to issue victuals. The lieutenants would have made sure the ship was spotless: the decks had been scrubbed at dawn, the brasswork polished with brickdust until it gleamed, and awnings rigged to keep the hot sun off the decks.

The stockings were silk – a thoughtful gesture on Dawlish's part, since lieutenants could rarely afford them – and Ramage straightened them out, heaved on the breeches, tucked in the shirt and carefully tied the stock. The waistcoat and coat fitted quite well and were obviously Dawlish's best; but the shabbiest pair of shoes were the only ones that fitted. He could imagine Pisano having difficulty in getting himself rigged out for the trial – there'd be nothing sufficiently elegant and gaudy to suit the Count's taste in Sir Gilbert's house. . . .

Well, he was ready for the Provost Marshal, and he called to the sentry to pass the word for him to come down to the gunroom. Interesting to see whom Croucher had appointed, since only a flagship had a regular provost marshal.

Someone came clattering down the after ladder and he heard the sentry salute. Suddenly there was a thump and a body hurtled headlong through the gunroom door. In the split second before the man fell flat on his face, cocked hat flying out ahead of him and sword caught between his legs, Ramage recognized the pimply young lieutenant from the *Trumpeter*, Blenkinsop. Ramage swiftly snatched up the hat and hid it behind him. Blenkinsop, his face red, stood up, extricating from between his legs the offending sword which had catapulted him through the door, pulling his coat straight and tugging at his stock. He glanced round for his hat, barely conscious in his embarrassment that Ramage was standing only a few feet away. He looked like an owl on a branch of a tree: the similarity was striking.

'Are you looking for this?' Ramage asked innocently, offering the hat. 'It arrived a few moments before you.'

'Thank you,' he answered stiffly. 'You are Lieutenant Nicholas Ramage?'

'Indeed I am,' he said politely.

'Then I—' he paused, looking for the paper he had been holding as he fell.

'I think you'll find that the warrant appointing you "Provost Marshal on the occasion" has slipped under the table.'

Blenkinsop went down on his knees to retrieve it, his hat falling off in the process. Finally, hat back on his head and the warrant unfolded, he began reading:

'To Reginald Blenkinsop, a lieutenant of His Majesty's ship *Trumpeter*. Captain Aloysius Croucher, of His Majesty's ship *Trumpeter* and senior officer present at the port of Bastia, having ordered a court martial to be assembled to try Lieutenant Nicholas Ramage, formerly of his late Majesty's ship—'

'His Majesty's *late* ship,' interrupted Ramage.

'—formerly of His – His Majesty's late ship *Sibella*, for the loss of the said ship: the aforementioned Captain Croucher hereby authorizes and appoints you to officiate as Provost Marshal on this occasion; and you are to take the person of the said Lieutenant Nicholas Ramage into your custody, and him safely keep, until he shall be delivered by due course of law; and for so doing this shall be your warrant—'

'Oh stow it,' Ramage interrupted impatiently, 'you must like the sound of your own voice.'

'I'm duty bound to read this to you,' Blenkinsop said primly.

'No, you're not. You are supposed to present it to the Captain of this ship as your authority to remove me. But you've already done that, naturally.'

Blenkinsop looked embarrassed. 'Oh – well, I – I say, do I really have to?'

'Well, it's not for your prisoner to tell you what to do; but his Lordship might take a serious view of you removing one of his officers without showing him your authority.'

'Oh dear. Well, I'd better go and do that.'

'Excellent! Capital!' said Ramage. 'But keep your voice low – his Lordship is on his sick bed. Run along, now: I'll wait for you on the gangway.'

Ramage picked up Dawlish's sword, and collected the few papers he had to take with him. There was a letter from the Deputy Judge Advocate which had arrived the previous evening informing him – with an unbecoming briskness, he thought – that of the witnesses he had requested for his defence, only the Bosun and Carpenter's Mate would be available. Ramage had noted down some facts about the wind and weather, times and casualties, and the courses steered before the *Sibella*'s surrender, but had not prepared the usual written defence, since he had no idea what accusations he would eventually be facing.

A few moments later he was standing talking to Dawlish when a flustered Blenkinsop came up from the Captain's cabin and said, 'It seems there's also someone else for me to take over to the *Trumpeter*.'

Dawlish looked blank; then Ramage remembered Jackson. 'Yes, one of my witnesses.'

'Oh, very well,' Blenkinsop said condescendingly.

'By the way,' said Ramage, 'you forgot to ask me to surrender this,' handing Blenkinsop the sword and scabbard.

'And be careful with it,' said Dawlish, 'because it's mine. Tell me' – his voice suddenly became almost deferential – 'aren't you one of the Wiltshire Blenkinsops?'

'Yes,' he answered with affected modesty.

'Am I right in thinking you are the only one in the Service?'

'Yes, that is so.'

'Thank Christ for that!' said Dawlish viciously. 'Now, don't let me delay your departure with all this idle social chatter. Be careful you don't get boarded by one of these bumboats – the women are absolutely riddled with terrible diseases, and the prices they charge are outrageous.'

'Really!' exclaimed Blenkinsop, and bolted for the entry port, blushing furiously.

As he disappeared down the ship's side to the waiting boat, Ramage went to follow him, but Dawlish, with a grin on his face, motioned him to wait a moment and went to the port.

'Mr Blenkinsop – shall I send your prisoner down?'

Chapter 16

THE *Trumpeter*'s great cabin, now in use as the courtroom, looked very different from when Ramage had first seen it two days earlier: the long, polished table was placed athwartships, and six naval captains sat along the far side, facing forward, with Ramage's borrowed sword in front of them.

The captains had Ramage facing them on their left, sitting on a straight-backed wooden chair, and to the right an empty chair was ready for the first witness. To one side of Ramage sat Blenkinsop, a sword across his knees, while behind, at the forward end of the cabin, a dozen chairs for spectators were arranged in two rows, facing the table.

The deck was covered in canvas which had been painted in a pattern of large black and white squares. Ramage noticed the four legs of a chair just fitted inside a square, as though everyone in the court was a chessman. As far as the trial was concerned, he knew what moves the court was allowed by law to make and, providing he kept his head, he might be able to prevent them checkmating him ... He waited for the opening gambit to be made by the Deputy Judge Advocate, who was sitting to his left at the far end of the table.

The man's temporary title could never disguise that he was a purser. Small, steel-rimmed spectacles perched precariously halfway down a long and bulbous red nose, while the nose itself appeared to have been stuck on to a fat face, rather as if some cruel humorist had thrust the thin end of a carrot into an over-ripe pumpkin. It was the face of a prosperous trades-man – as indeed a purser was: a man who knew all there was to know about prices and percentages; who had grown rich serving out provisions to the men in pounds weighing fourteen ounces and, quite legally, pocketing the two ounces' difference.

Mr Horace Barrow, the *Trumpeter*'s purser, could prob-ably buy out a captain any day of the week; but now – equipped with a sheaf of papers, several quill pens, and a knife to sharpen them, a bottle of ink, sandbox, a leather-bound Bible, an ivory and silver Crucifix – in case any witnesses were Catholic – and books of reference, including the slim volume containing the Articles of War and a thicker one, the *Regula-tions and Instructions*, by which the Navy was governed, he was ready to start the trial.

Five of the six captains sitting at the table had watched Ramage as he came in. All were smartly dressed, as befitted the occasion: the order summoning each officer to the court martial always specified that 'it is expected you will attend in your uniform frock'.

Certainly the uniform frock was drabber now, Ramage re-flected; only last year the Admiralty had decreed the white facings of the turned-back lapels should be replaced with blue, although not everyone had yet complied, but the lapels, held back by nine buttons on each side, and the stand-up collar, were still edged with gold. All but one of the captains wore epaulets on each shoulder – another new idea ordered by the Admiralty at the same time that the lapel facings were changed – and not at all popular with some officers, who regarded as Frenchified the gold lace sewn on the shoulder pads, and the tight spirals of gold bullion hanging down in a fringe.

The exception among the captains was the one sitting at

the end next to the Deputy Judge Advocate: he wore only one epaulet, on his right shoulder, indicating he had less than three years' seniority.

The one captain who did not look up when Ramage marched in was Croucher, the president of the court: he was staring down at some papers on the table, and Ramage noticed he also had the *Sibella*'s two logs and muster book in front of him. The other captains were sitting on Croucher's right and left according to seniority. The man on his right – Ramage remembered him from an earlier commission – was Captain Blackman and must be next senior to Croucher, while Captain Herbert, whom he knew by sight, came next and sat on his left. There were two captains Ramage did not recognize, but the most junior, wearing the single epaulet, was Ferris, who commanded a frigate. Was he one of Goddard's clique? Surely not: Ramage remembered him as one of Sir John Jervis's protégés.

Since Ramage was facing aft, the captains were silhouetted against the bright glare of the sunlight reflecting up from the sea through the stern lights. On his right, so close he could almost reach out and pat the breech, was an 18-pounder cannon – the last one in the larboard row that began at the forward end of the quarter-deck and continued through the captain's accommodation which, since the *Trumpeter* was a two-decker and almost twice the size of a frigate, was one deck higher than in the *Lively*. On the other side of the cabin was another cannon, also polished black and resting solidly on its buff-colour carriage, secured by the rope breeching and side tackles, the last of those on the starboard side. They were solid reminders that the *Trumpeter* was first and foremost a fighting ship: when she was in action the furniture would be stowed below and the wooden bulkheads forming the captain's quarters would be hinged up out of the way, so that no enemy shot should shatter them into splinters.

Ramage watched the Deputy Judge Advocate shuffle through his papers and then polish his spectacles. Presumably he had already read to the court Probus's letter asking to be excused on the grounds of illness, and the *Lively*'s surgeon would have been called in to attest on oath his Captain's incapacity. Either Probus had given a realistic impression of a sick man or the surgeon was willing to perjure himself.

After Ramage had been marched in the court was declared open and everyone else concerned or interested entered, among them Pisano. The names of the captains had been read out by Barrow, who then administered the oath. After each of the six men, with his hand on the Bible, had sworn he would 'duly administer justice according to my conscience, the best of my understanding, and the custom of the Navy in like cases ...' Croucher, as president of the court, then administered the oath to Barrow.

The preliminaries are over, Ramage thought to himself; now for the opening gambit. . . .

Barrow stood up and read out the charge, like a priest mechanically reciting a mass, his spectacles sliding down his nose from time to time and interrupting the proceedings while he readjusted them.

The witnesses were ordered out of the court and Ramage turned to watch them go: they scarcely make a crowd, he noted sourly – just the Bosun, the Carpenter's Mate and Jackson. Suddenly he saw someone at the doorway beckoning to Pisano, indicating that he too should leave the court. So Pisano is to be a witness! But he's not on Barrow's list of witnesses. . . .

Well, that'll be a difficult move to counter. Ramage was surprised to find himself using chess similes, since he was an appalling player. He'd always found the game too slow, and had a bad memory. In fact his complete inability to remember the cards already played at those interminable games of whist in the *Superb* used to drive that fellow Hornblower mad. Yet, Ramage remembered with amusement, he sometimes won simply because he was such a bad player: even if Hornblower guessed the cards he held it was no help since his play was completely unpredictable. Nor, when Ramage won, did Hornblower like being reminded that surprise was the vital element in tactics. . . .

After Pisano disappeared through the door Croucher rapped the table. 'The prisoner's report on the surrender of

His Majesty's frigate *Sibella* will now be read to the court.'

Ramage was shocked to find himself being referred to as 'the prisoner'; but of course it was correct.

Barrow wrote down the president's words – it was his job to keep the minutes – and then shuffled among his pile of papers to extract Ramage's report to Probus. It was hardly an impressive-sounding document when read by Barrow, who had an irritating habit of letting his voice drop as he reached the end of a line, and put the page down on the table each time his spectacles slipped, so that he could use both hands to readjust them.

To Ramage's surprise, Barrow continued reading after completing the passage describing the surrender. He was leaning forward, undecided whether or not to protest that the rest of the report had nothing to do with the ship's loss when Captain Ferris, the junior captain, interrupted.

'Surely this has no relevance for the court?'

'Pray allow me to be judge of that,' said Captain Croucher.

'But we are only inquiring into the loss of the ship,' insisted Ferris.

'We are trying the accused for his conduct upon the occasion,' said Croucher, sounding like a parson chiding a wayward parishioner. 'In fairness to the accused, we must satisfy ourselves as to the whole of his conduct during this lamentable episode,' he added, barely able to keep the hypocrisy from his voice.

'But—'

'Captain Ferris,' Croucher said sharply, 'If you wish to argue the point we must clear the court.'

Ferris looked round at the other captains, who stared woodenly in front of them, and then glanced at Ramage as if to indicate it was hopeless for either of them to protest any further.

'Very well,' Croucher told Barrow, 'you may proceed.'

Finally Barrow finished reading, and sat down.

'Since this is an inquiry into the loss of the ship and an examination of the prisoner's conduct,' said Croucher, 'has the prisoner any further facts not contained in his report which he wishes to lay before the court?'

You clever swine, thought Ramage: now you've really trapped me. You want me to introduce the Pisano business so it's set down in the minutes and you can take it further; but if I don't say anything it'll look as though I'm hiding it.

He replied, 'Any facts I may have overlooked in my report will no doubt emerge during the examination of the witnesses, sir,' and was startled by his own smoothness

'*Have* you overlooked any facts?' demanded Croucher.

'No relevant facts that I can remember, sir.'

To hell with you, Ramage thought: it's vital to remember that intonation and emphasis are not important; what matters is how the words will be read by Sir John Jervis and the Admiralty in the minutes of the trial.

Poor Barrow – his pen was trying to keep pace with the rapid dialogue; any minute now, just as soon as he dared, the perspiring little purser would ask for a pause to give him time to catch up.

'Very well,' said Croucher. 'The Deputy Judge Advocate will now read out a second report to Captain Lord Probus.'

A second report? Ramage glanced at Barrow. Was this another gambit?

'This report is dated September 12th, addressed to Lord Probus, and signed by Count Pisano,' said Barrow. 'It begins—'

Just as Ramage was going to protest, Captain Ferris interrupted.

'Is this relevant to the case? The court has no official knowledge of Count Pisano's existence, nor his connexion with the loss of the *Sibella*.'

Captain Croucher put his hands palms downwards on the table and, looking at a point in space about two feet in front of his nose, said silkily, 'It *is* perhaps relevant that I am President of this court and you are its junior member . . .'

Ramage sensed Croucher was not really bothered by Ferris's protests; he had another trick ready.

'. . . However, before introducing the document the court will wait until later in the proceedings, when its relevance will be made clear.'

He looked across at Barrow and said: 'Call the first witness.'

While the word was being passed for the Bosun, Barrow hurriedly scribbled away, darting his pen into the ink pot from time to time with the rapidity of a snake striking.

Ramage could guess what he was writing: the page would be headed 'Minutes of Proceedings at a Court Martial held on board His Majesty's ship *Trumpeter* in Bastia on Thursday the 15th day of September, 1796.' Then would come, under the heading 'Present', the names of the six captains, beginning with Croucher as president, 'being all the captains of post ships according to seniority except Captain Lord Probus who certified the President his inability to attend through ill health.'

He would then scribble 'Insert order for trial' – the wording would be written into the fair copy of the minutes, as well as a record of his own appointment and the administration of oaths. Then there would be a discreet outline of the earlier exchanges with Captain Croucher, and now he would be scribbling a new heading 'Evidence in support of the charge'.

The *Sibella*'s Bosun came into the cabin, pausing just inside the door, obviously bewildered by the array of senior officers looking up at him, and dazzled by the sunlight.

Barrow looked up, motioned him to the table and gave him the Bible. The Bosun straightened his shoulders – he usually walked with a slight stoop – and repeated the Oath.

Captain Croucher told him: 'Don't answer a question until the Deputy Judge Advocate has had time to write it down, and don't speak too quickly.'

'Aye aye, sir.'

For several seconds Ramage had been listening to several men having a violent argument outside the cabin door and, just as Captain Croucher glanced up, thought he could distinguish a woman's voice speaking rapid Italian. Surely – no, he must be day-dreaming. Barrow, busy with his papers, had not noticed anything and began the questioning.

'You are Edward Brown, and were Boatswain of—'

The door was flung open with a violent crash that made

everyone jump, and Gianna, her face white and drawn, emphasizing the fine chiselling of her high cheekbones, swept into the cabin. Her eyes blazed with anger and her whole bearing was that of a proud, impulsive young woman accustomed to being obeyed. Her dress, pale blue embroidered in gold, was partly hidden by a black silk cape which had been flung back carelessly over her shoulders.

A Marine sentry stumbled into the cabin after her, musket in his hands, crying out, 'Come back, ye crazy bitch!' and then one of the *Trumpeter*'s lieutenants, pushing the sentry out of the way, grasped her arm.

'Madam, please! I've told you the court is in session!'

But her beauty, her magnificent anger, was too much for him: he dare not hold her tightly and she waved off his restraining hand as if a fly had settled on her fan. Ramage saw Pisano follow them into the cabin flushed and angry.

Gianna walked straight up to the big table and looked coolly at the six captains, who were so startled and overawed that to Ramage it seemed they shrank in size, ceasing to exist as flesh and blood and becoming six figures painted on canvas, transfixed at a certain moment in time by an artist's brush.

'Who,' demanded Gianna, 'is in charge here?'

Oh, how he loved that voice when it became imperious! He didn't know whether to watch Pisano, the six captains, Gianna, the lieutenant who stood uncertainly a yard or so behind her, Barrow, whose spectacles had slid so far down his nose that it was difficult to know why they did not fall off altogether, or the Marine sentry, who clearly thought the cabin had been invaded by some bumboat woman.

Croucher reacted first but, completely under her magnetic spell, stood and bowed. 'I – er . . . I am the President of the court, Madam.'

'I am the Marchesa di Volterra.'

Her voice and compelling, patrician beauty combined to silence everyone except the Marine sentry, who gasped, 'Gawdorlmighty!'

Ramage doubted if Croucher had ever waited for an admiral to speak with more apprehension than he waited for the girl.

'I have no legal right to appear in a court martial trying Lieutenant Ramage for the loss of his ship,' she said in a tone indicating quite clearly she regarded this as a trifling matter, 'but I have a moral right to appear in a court trying him for cowardice if it is based upon the accusations of my cousin.'

Several people gasped, and Ramage glanced at the white-faced Pisano who made no reaction: he'd obviously already heard all this a minute or two earlier, outside the cabin door.

'I believe my cousin has in writing accused Lieutenant Ramage of cowardice; I believe my cousin accuses Lieutenant Ramage of abandoning my cousin Count Pitti; I believe—'

'How can you possibly know of this, Madam?' exclaimed Croucher.

'But it is true, is it not?'

The sharp and authoritative note in her voice flashed the question at Croucher like the swift, clean *riposte* of an expert fencer, and he was slow to parry.

'Well – er, yes, in a way: Count Pisano has made certain charges—'

'Accusations, not charges,' she corrected him. 'These accusations are without basis. I cannot let loyalty to my family prevent me from making certain that justice is done, so this court must know firstly that Count Pisano does not know Count Pitti was wounded: it was dark and although he says he heard him call out, he has admitted to me he does not know what it was he said.

'Secondly, Lieutenant Ramage carried me to the boat because I was wounded, and put me in it. Count Pisano – who came to the boat by a different route – was already sitting in it. So if he had heard Count Pitti call out, he should have gone back himself.

'Thirdly, after Count Pisano and I were safely in the boat, Lieutenant Ramage went up to the dunes again – I saw him – and called for Mr Jackson. Several minutes passed before he returned, and during that time Count Pisano was impatient because he wanted the boat to leave.

'Fourthly, when Lieutenant Ramage finally returned to the boat and we waited a few seconds for Mr Jackson to arrive

– we could see him coming towards us – Count Pisano was urging the Lieutenant to leave: in other words, he was urging the Lieutenant to abandon Mr Jackson, who had a few minutes earlier attacked four French cavalrymen and saved my life and that of Lieutenant—'

At that moment Pisano ran forward screaming, '*Tu sei una squaldrina!*' and hit her across the face; then there was a heavy, dull thud and a rattle, and Pisano collapsed to the deck at the girl's feet. The stolid Marine sentry, who had lunged forward and hit Pisano on the side of the head with the butt of his musket, took a pace backwards and stood stiffly to attention, a look of doubt beginning to grow on his face.

Ramage leapt forward, realizing the Marine's musket blow had been the unthinking reaction of a person horrified that anyone should strike a woman. . . .

'Good man!' Ramage exclaimed and in a moment Gianna was in his arms. 'Are you all right?' he whispered.

'Yes – yes.' She lapsed into Italian. 'Have I done the correct thing? Have I made a terrible mistake?'

'No! You were magnificent. I—'

'Is the Marchesa all right?'

Ramage realized that Croucher, trapped behind the table and unable to understand what they were saying, was now so agitated that he was shouting the question, probably for the third or fourth time.

'Yes sir, she says she is.'

'Right. You—' Croucher said to the Marine, 'and you, you blithering idiot' – (this to Lieutenant Blenkinsop, who was still standing beside his chair, open-mouthed and sword in hand) – 'take that man down to the Surgeon.'

The Marine put his musket down on the deck, eagerly seized Pisano by the hair and dragged him a couple of yards across the deck before Blenkinsop hurriedly told him to hoist Pisano by the arms while he took the legs.

Ramage sat the girl in the witness's chair. Barrow, whose spectacles had finally fallen on to the table, subsided into his seat. This was the signal for all the captains, except the President, to settle down again. Croucher obviously felt he had to do something to regain control of the situation.

'Clear the court!' he ordered. 'But you stay,' he said to Ramage, 'and you too, Madam, if you please.'

The Bosun, and the few officers who had been sitting in the row of seats behind Ramage, filed out, while Croucher ordered the lieutenant who had followed Gianna into the cabin to put another sentry on the door.

Within two minutes the cabin was quiet again. Gianna quickly composed herself and, womanlike, turned slightly so that the captains saw her left profile, and not the right, which was red from Pisano's blow.

Ramage sat down again in his own chair. Except for the sentry's musket still lying diagonally across the white and black squares of the deck – from butt to muzzle it had made the knight's move, he noticed – there was nothing to indicate what had happened. The chessboard had been swept clean of the pawns . . . who was going to make the next move?

'Well,' said Croucher lamely, 'well . . .'

Ramage promptly put himself in Croucher's position, ran through the courses open to him, and was ready when Croucher said:

'. . . Frankly I don't know how we should proceed now.'

'I am still on trial, sir. . . .'

The perplexity showed in Croucher's thin, foxy face: Ramage sensed the man knew he was standing on a powder barrel and was afraid Ramage was lighting the fuse.

Five minutes ago, the trial was just going as Croucher had planned; but now the Marchesa di Volterra had been assaulted in his own court by his most important witness.

Ramage watched Croucher's face closely and thought he could detect one unpleasant realization after another galloping through the man's mind: the Marchesa must have a great deal of influence in high places . . . What would Rear-Admiral Goddard say and, more important, Sir John Jervis, the Commander-in-Chief . . . Did her influence spread to St James's Palace . . .? Goddard would wash his hands of the whole affair – there might have to be a scapegoat. . . .

And, thought Ramage wryly, his name might well turn out to be Captain Aloysius Croucher. The more he thought about it – and his brain seemed to be working at enormous speed – the angrier Ramage became: although all six captains and Barrow were soaking with perspiration, he began to feel cold – the icy coldness of rage.

He knew he was blinking rapidly and he guessed his face was white; but he felt a violent revulsion against the Pisanos, the Goddards, the Crouchers: he was sick of these men who would go to any lengths – or depths – to satisfy their pride or jealousy. None of them was any better than a Neapolitan hired assassin, who, for a few *centesimi*, would knife anyone in the back. In fact each was worse, because the assassin made no pretence at being any better than he was.

Suddenly Ramage understood something which had puzzled him for years: why, at the trial, his father had eventually refused to make any further defence. His enemies claimed he'd finally admitted his guilt; his friends, for the lack of any other explanation, assumed he was just worn out.

But now Ramage knew his father had decided his accusers were too despicable to warrant him continuing to defend himself against their charges; charges which were so gross that if he was to clear himself he would have to use the same crude and dishonourable weapons.

But why not use them? Why, Ramage thought, should the despicable always win against the honourable? Why should men like Goddard and Croucher, lurking in the shadows, using assassins – whether assassins destroying a man's life with lies in a court of law or with a stiletto in a dark alley – why should such men always escape? They always did: the Duke of Newcastle, Fox, Anson, the Earl of Hardwicke for instance – they'd engineered Admiral Byng's execution and escaped; and less than thirty years later their successors had ruined his own father, although mercifully they hadn't stooped to judicial murder.

The tactics, Ramage realized, were not to waste time with the assassins, but instead go straight for the men who employed them: the men in the shadows.

Ramage suddenly knew he didn't give a damn if his own career was wrecked: that was little enough to gamble if it meant squaring Goddard's yards . . .

Croucher was saying something.

'I beg your pardon, sir?'

'I was announcing, for the second time,' Croucher said acidly, 'that the court feels since the prosecution has not offered any evidence in support of the charge, the court should record the fact and dismiss the charge.'

How blatant can you be, thought Ramage.

'The prosecution has only been interrupted, sir.'

'Yes, I know,' Croucher said testily, 'but—'

'I assume the prosecution actually possesses evidence, sir, so with respect I feel the trial ought to continue.'

Croucher looked wary: he could see many traps ahead. But he had several advisers, apart from the legal books on the table in front of the Deputy Judge Advocate.

'Very well, then, you and the Marchesa will leave the court while the members discuss the situation. You will not, of course, have any conversation together. Tell the sentry to pass the word for the Provost Marshal.'

Chapter 17

FIFTEEN MINUTES later a sentry came into the Captain's clerk's cabin, where Ramage was waiting with Blenkinsop, to tell them the court had re-opened. When Ramage walked back into the great cabin he saw the seats behind his chair were now full: every officer not on duty in the ship had come in to watch, hoping for more excitement.

Captain Croucher looked up at Ramage.

'The court has decided that no reference to the recent interruption shall be recorded in the minutes, and the trial will continue. Do you agree?'

'It is not for me to agree or disagree, sir,' Ramage said coldly. 'With the greatest respect, you are the President of the court. If the court is in error, no doubt the Commander-in-Chief or the Admiralty will take the appropriate steps.'

He wasn't going to fall into that trap; if he agreed, Croucher was cleared of any possible charge of misconduct over the trial. Croucher had set a trap and – thanks to Gianna – was now in danger of himself being caught in it; but that was the risk people took when they set traps. Croucher was a fool anyway, because Gianna wasn't on oath; none of the court seemed to have realized the minutes should record only evidence given on oath: if a ship blew up alongside, there would be no need to record it – unless to explain the court's adjournment. Ramage decided to bluff.

'I think,' Croucher said uncertainly, 'the court has the power to order anything to be omitted from the record.'

His voice did not carry much conviction; clearly he wanted to lure Ramage into a discussion, so that he could suggest in a friendly way that he was causing a lot of unnecessary bother.

Ramage stood up.

'With respect, sir, and admittedly with no knowledge of legal procedure, surely a court can't ignore and thus virtually destroy evidence already given? Otherwise minutes could always be edited or censored, like some penny broadsheet, to prove a guilty man innocent – or an innocent man guilty.'

'Good God, young man, no one's suggesting the minutes should be censored: the court just feels it would be the wisest way of disposing of a very disagreeable situation.'

'By disagreeable, sir,' said Ramage politely, 'I assume you are concerned that it is disagreeable for me; but the court must ignore my feelings and get at the truth, however disagreeable it may be. . . .'

'Very well, then,' Croucher said, obviously admitting defeat, 'call the first witness.'

Ramage interrupted: 'Can we follow the normal procedure, sir, and have the Deputy Judge Advocate read over the minutes from the time the first witness was originally called?'

'My dear boy,' Croucher replied, 'we can't spend all the week on this trial: let's get on with hearing the evidence.'

Ramage rubbed the scar over his right eyebrow and blinked

rapidly: excitement and anger were mounting: he must keep calm: once these men found their victim showed signs of fighting back, they became nervous, and he had to watch for every opportunity to attack: he must continue the bluff.

'With respect, sir, it is only fair to me to have it read.'

'Oh, very well, then.'

Everyone looked at Barrow, who gripped his spectacles in both hands and almost giggled with nervousness.

'I made no note, sir . . .'

'You what?'

'No, sir.'

Ramage interrupted smoothly: 'Then perhaps we can agree on a paraphrased version, sir?'

It only needed someone to point out that Gianna had not been on oath and he'd lost the gamble; but it was worth it. To his relief Croucher finally agreed, and for the next five minutes he and Ramage argued over the wording. Ramage insisted that the Marchesa's remarks should be put in word for word, and when Croucher declared that it was impossible to remember what she said, Ramage suggested she should be called in to repeat her remarks. Croucher, alarmed at the idea, eventually agreed on a short version and asked sarcastically: 'Are you satisfied now?'

'Indeed, sir.'

'Thank God for that. Barrow, make a note of that and recall the first witness!'

The Bosun walked straight to the witness chair, and since there was no need for him to take the oath again, Barrow began the questioning.

'You were formerly Boatswain of His Majesty's late ship *Sibella* on Thursday the eighth of September, when you fell in with the French warship?'

'Aye, I was that!' replied Brown.

'Kindly answer, "yes" or "no",' Barrow said acidly. 'Relate to the court every particular you know concerning the action from the time Captain Letts was killed.'

Ramage was just going to protest that Brown should begin his story earlier, since the court was investigating the loss of the ship as well as trying him, when Captain Ferris interrupted.

'From the wording of the order for the trial, I think the witness should tell what he knows from the time the French ship came in sight. Captain Letts' activities are of equal interest to the court.'

'Since Captain Letts is dead he can hardly be a witness,' said Captain Croucher, trying to avoid openly rejecting Ferris's demand.

'Had the prisoner been killed he would not be on trial either,' retorted Ferris. 'But it would be unfair to blame the prisoner for anything which was Captain Letts' responsibility.'

'Very well,' said Croucher. 'Strike the last part of the question from the record and substitute "from the time the French ship was sighted".'

Brown was a simple man but although nervous at facing so many senior officers he obviously knew that this was no ordinary trial. And since Brown was a simple man, he told his story simply. He had just said he had heard some of the men say they'd been told several of the officers were killed, when Captain Blackman, sitting next to Captain Croucher, interrupted: 'What you heard other people say is not evidence: speak to facts.'

'Them's the facts!' said Brown, taking little trouble to hide his contempt for anyone so stupid as not to understand. 'The orficers were killed. Couldn't see it with me own glims 'cos I couldn't be everywhere at once. But they was dead all right.'

'Carry on,' said Croucher, 'but try and remember that what someone said to you *is* evidence, but what you were told someone said to someone else isn't – that's just hearsay.'

Clearly Brown neither understood nor cared, but launched off again on his narrative, bringing it up to the time that all the officers appeared to have been killed and the Master had taken command. The Master had just given orders for knotting some torn rigging when he was himself cut in two by a shot.

'I thought to meself, "Allo, won't be long afore I'm dragging me anchors fer the next world too", and I didn't fancy taking command of that lot.'

'What "lot"?' asked Croucher icily.

'Well, sir, the ship as she was. A complete wreck by then. Anyway, sir, since I was apparently the senior man alive I sends men to make a tally of 'ow many was dead and 'ow many was winged. They came back and reports there aren't no more'n a third of us left on our pins.'

'Exactly how many were killed and how many wounded?' asked Captain Ferris, indicating to Captain Croucher that he wished to see the ship's muster book.

'Forty-eight dead, sir, and sixty-three wounded – a dozen or so o' them mortually.'

'Mortally,' corrected the Deputy Judge Advocate.

'That's what I said. Mortually. Means they died later.'

'Out of a ship's company of one hundred and sixty-four,' commented Ferris, closing the muster book.

'Wouldn't be knowing, sir.'

'That was the total at the last muster,' Ferris said. 'Note it in the minutes, Barrow. Carry on with your evidence, Brown.'

'Well,' said Brown, 'I was just wishing I could lash up me 'ammick, stow mc bag and go 'ome when the bleeding Master-at-Arms mentions, ever so casual, that he thought one of the orficers on the main deck wasn't dead, sir, only wounded. I sent a lad down to make sure and I heard he found Mr Ramage unconcherous—'

'Unconscious,' said Barrow.

'Hearsay evidence,' Captain Blackman interrupted triumphantly.

'Nor it wasn't!' retorted Brown. 'In a minute the boy came back and told me with 'is own lips as 'e'd found Mr Ramage breathin' but wounded and unconcherous—'

'Unconscious,' said Barrow.

'Unconchirous, then,' said Brown, determined to ram home the point. 'I sent 'im down again to tell Mr Ramage he was in command, and the lad came back and said—'

'Wait a moment,' said Barrow, 'you're talking much too fast.'

Brown could not resist a chance of a dig at a purser – for he had recognized Barrow's trade – and sniffed, 'First time I met a pusser slow with 'is pen!'

'Steady there!' warned Captain Croucher. 'Confine your remarks to the case on hand.'

'Well, as soon as Mr Ramage came on deck I reported the state of the ship and the butcher's bill and told 'im that 'e was in command.'

Captain Ferris asked, 'What condition was Mr Ramage in?'

'He looked as though 'e'd tripped over the standing part o' the fore sheet and bin hauled back on board just in time!' said Brown, and Ramage almost laughed at the simile, since 'Going over the standing part of the fore sheet' was slang for dying, or being killed.

'Be more specific,' said Ferris.

'Well, 'e was groggy on 'is pins: he'd 'ad a terrible bash on the 'ead.'

Why, thought Ramage, can the man tackle one aitch and miss the next? He was just making a mental note to ask Brown a question when it was his turn to cross-examine as Ferris asked:

'Did he appear dazed?'

'Looked like a grampus that'd been luffed into a brick wall, sir.'

Several people in the court laughed, including Ramage: it was an apt description, since, like a grampus, he'd been soaking wet after ducking his head in the water tub; and the picture of a grampus swimming head first into a brick wall seemed to describe how he'd felt at that moment. Ferris seemed satisfied, but Croucher said to Barrow:

'With the witness's consent, you'd better put that down as "Yes, he appeared dazed." Is that correct, Brown?'

'Better make it "very dazed", sir.'

'Carry on, then.'

'Well, there aren't much more to it. Mr Ramage got a round turn on 'iself in a moment or two and took command.'

Brown obviously thought that was all the evidence he needed to give, but Croucher said, 'Well, go on to describe the surrender of the ship.'

Briefly Brown told how by cleverly wearing round the

Sibella at the last moment so that her foremast collapsed over the side and acted as an anchor, Mr Ramage had given the unwounded men a chance to get into the boats and escape in the darkness, and left the wounded to surrender the ship.

'Thus the wounded were abandoned to the French?' asked Captain Blackman.

'You *could* put it like that, sir,' said Brown, making it clear that anyone who did would be a fool or a rogue. 'But we was mustered in three divisions: the dead – and they didn't care; the wounded, who couldn't get a mite o' medical attention 'cos our surgeon and his mate was already dead; and them of us who weren't wounded and didn't want to be prisoners of the Frenchies.

'Apart from that,' he added, 'there's the Harticles of War. Number Ten, last bit, about "if any Person in the Fleet shall treacherously or cowardly yield or cry for quarter", so it wouldn't 'ave been right for us who wasn't wounded to let ourselves be taken prisoner. And it stands to reason our chaps'd get properly treated by the Frenchies, who mightn't be much in a scrap but at least they don't murder the wounded. But even if we'd been able to get the wounded away in the boats – and we couldn't, mind you – we'd 'ave as good as murdered 'em. Christ!' he exclaimed at the thought of it, 'it nearly did for us that trip to Bastia in the boiling 'ot sun, and we wasn't even scratched.'

'Quite,' said Captain Blackman, who had been trying to stop the Bosun's excited speech, partly because he realized the reason behind his question was now blatantly obvious, and partly because the Deputy Judge Advocate was waving desperately with one hand and scribbling away with the other.

'Quite!' he repeated. 'Please pause after each sentence – the Judge Advocate simply cannot write at that speed.'

Clearly Brown thought that at last he had completed his part in the trial, but Captain Croucher said:

'Continue your narrative until the time you arrived in Bastia.'

The look of surprise on Brown's face could hardly be lost on the members of the court, Ramage thought, but if it was, Brown's next remark drew attention to it.

'I hope as 'ow I'm not incrimuanating meself – or anyone else – by going on like this, 'cos that's got nothin' to do with surrendering the ship.'

'You are not charged with anything so you cannot incriminate yourself,' said the Deputy Judge Advocate.

'No, I'm not charged with anything yet,' he retorted, 'but that's not to say the trip to Bastia's got anything to do with sinking the *Sibella* or why Mr Ramage is on trial. Nor's it to say I won't be charged later on.'

'Get on with your evidence, man,' said Captain Croucher impatiently, 'you've nothing to fear if you tell the truth.'

After Brown had described the voyage to Bastia, he declared: 'Well, that's all I've got to say.'

Captain Croucher glanced up. 'That is for us to decide. As it happens I have no questions. Have any of the members of the court anything to ask this witness?'

'Where was Mr Ramage standing when he gave the order to wear ship?' asked Ferris.

'On the nettings by the starboard mizen shrouds,' said Brown. 'He shouted at the Frenchies from there. I thought he was mad to stand up exposed like that, if you'll forgive me saying so, sir, 'cos apart from anything else if 'e got shot it meant I was in command again!'

Ramage realized that Ferris would not be one of Captain Croucher's favourites by the time the trial ended: clearly Ferris wanted to underline the fact that Ramage had not been skulking somewhere out of the way of shot.

'No more questions?' asked Croucher, in a voice that defied anyone to speak. 'Well, the prisoner may cross-examine the witness.'

Anything Ramage said now could only be an anti-climax after Brown's bluff, honest and forthright narrative.

'I have no questions, sir.'

'Oh – oh well, read back the evidence, Mr Barrow.'

Only once did Brown interrupt, to make a correction, and

that was because Barrow had written that Ramage 'appeared dazed'.

'I said "very dazed",' said Brown belligerently. 'Don't you go taking words out of my mouth!'

'Wait a moment, then,' said Barrow, picking up his pen.

When he continued reading, Brown said, 'You read over that last bit again and make sure you've set it to rights!'

The implication startled Barrow, but he slid his spectacles back up his nose and read it.

'That's right: proceed, Mr Purser,' said Brown, making it clear that pursers should know they could not be trusted.

When Barrow finished reading Brown was allowed to leave the court, and the next witness was called.

Matthew Lloyd, the Carpenter's Mate, marched in and stood precisely where the Deputy Judge Advocate's pointing finger indicated. He was as thin as the planks he so often sawed, adzed and chiselled; his face was long and tanned, as if carefully carved from a narrow piece of close-grained mahogany.

When Lloyd answered Barrow's routine questions about his name, rating and where he had been on the evening of the action, his voice was staccato, each word rapped out as if he was hammering in a row of flat-headed scupper nails. When he related what he knew about damage received during the action, he did it as precisely as if he had been marking out a piece of wood before starting to make some delicate cabinet work for the Captain. His answers were equally precise. No, he did not know exactly how many shot hit the hull because as soon as they plugged one hole another would appear. No, he wasn't sure which broadside it was that killed the captain but he thought it was the fifth; yes, he had been sounding the well up to then and at the time Captain Letts was killed there were three feet of water. Soon after that the ship seemed to be making nearly an inch of water a minute. No, he had not timed it with a watch, he told Captain Croucher, but it was a foot in less than fifteen minutes.

There was no chance of keeping the ship afloat, he told Captain Blackman, because several shot had opened up the hull planking in way of the futtocks, and it was impossible to fit shot plugs from inside the ship. No, he had not reported to Captain Letts that the pumps could not keep up with the leaks because by that time Captain Letts had been killed, but he had reported to the Master.

Yes, he told Captain Ferris, there had been a great deal of damage in addition to shot hitting the ship on the waterline; but he'd only mentioned those 'twixt wind and water because there were so many and they were his special concern.

The first he knew of Mr Ramage being in command, he told Captain Blackman, was when Mr Ramage sent for him and asked the extent of the damage. What were Mr Ramage's exact questions? It was difficult to recall precisely but he remembered being very surprised that the Junior Lieutenant – if Mr Ramage would excuse him saying so – should be so thorough; and as soon as he was told the depth of water in the well Mr Ramage had worked out how many tons had flooded into the ship, roughly how much buoyancy remained, and how long – allowing for the fact that the lower the ship sank the faster the water would come in through the shotholes because the pressure increased with depth – the ship could stay afloat.

'Yes, I know you know all about that, sir,' he said to Captain Blackman, 'but I'm giving *my* evidence and I'm describing what Mr Ramage said and did, and he was speaking out loud because – as far as I could see – he'd only just recovered from being knocked unconscious. Marvel to me,' he added, 'that he could work it out in his own head, anyway.'

'Mr Ramage had worked out roughly how long it would be before the ship sank?' asked Ferris.

'Yes – between sixty and seventy-five minutes.'

Ramage noticed Croucher was becoming increasingly restless: Ferris's questions were clearly annoying him, although Ramage knew that Ferris was only concerned with getting at the truth; while Blackman was, from Croucher's point of view, asking the wrong sort of questions: the Carpenter's mate was a steady man with a good memory, not at all intimidated by Blackman's hectoring manner. Blackman's blatant attempts to discredit Ramage were in fact only drawing attention to his thoroughness.

Finally Captain Croucher's restlessness became obvious even to the willing Blackman, who stopped questioning Lloyd.

'Has the court anything else to ask this witness?' asked Croucher. 'Very well, the prisoner may cross-examine.'

There were only two points to make – purely for the record.

'You definitely remember my estimate of the length of time before the ship sank, with the damage there then was and the pumps out of action?'

'Yes, sir, quite clearly: particularly as you said it in minutes, and not "between an hour and an hour and a quarter".'

'How long, in your estimation, passed between my making that estimate and the French setting the ship on fire after we had left?'

'More than half an hour, sir.'

'Why do you think they set her on fire?'

Captain Croucher interrupted: 'Opinion is not evidence, Mr Ramage.'

'If you'll forgive me, sir, I am questioning the beliefs of a professional man about his own subject, not asking his opinion.'

'Don't argue with the court.'

Ramage bowed and turned back to the Carpenter's Mate: the question was perfectly in order, but it was unnecessary to argue with Croucher since it could be asked in another way.

'If I had ordered you to lay a fuse to blow up the ship at that time after I made the estimate, could you have obeyed?'

'No, sir.'

'Why not?'

'The magazine and powder room would have been under water, sir.'

'But if instead I had given you orders to destroy the ship, what would you have done?'

'I could only have set her on fire, sir, like the French did.'

'Now, given that you had an unlimited number of men to help with repairs and that the pumps were working, could you, from the time I took over command, have saved the ship from sinking?'

'No, sir, most definitely not.'

'I have no more questions to put to this witness, sir,' he said to Croucher.

'Very well. The court has nothing else to ask, so call the next witness.'

'Call Count Pisano,' said the Deputy Judge Advocate.

Ramage had been waiting for this moment: so far the trial seemed to be going his way: he'd bluffed Croucher into leaving Gianna's speech in the trial minutes; thwarted his attempt to drop the whole case once the interruption was made; and the Bosun and Carpenter's Mate had given favourable evidence. Now all he had to do was prevent Croucher bringing in Pisano as a witness.

Ramage said to Captain Croucher: 'Would you wait a moment, sir: this gentleman's name does not appear on the list of witnesses in support of the charge which the Deputy Judge Advocate sent to me.'

Croucher gave such a disarming smile that Ramage knew he'd made a mistake: he was not sure what it was, but Croucher was about to checkmate him.

'The Deputy Judge Advocate,' Croucher said politely, 'will explain the position to you.'

Ramage needed time, so he quickly stood up. 'Perhaps the court should be cleared while the point is argued.'

'There is nothing to argue about,' Croucher said sharply. 'Carry on,' he told Barrow.

The man stood up and adjusted his spectacles.

'A similar circumstance arose in a court martial in January of last year,' he said pompously. 'A court martial held, incidentally, here in Bastia. The court referred the question to the authorities in London. The Judge Advocate General gave his opinion on it, in a letter dated May 22, 1795, of which I have an attested copy here, saying: "If any person at hand, and who can without delay be called upon, is supposed to be capable of giving material testimony, I have not a doubt that the court may require his attendance and examine him." '

Ramage leapt to his feet just as Ferris was about to speak.

'Judge Advocate General, did you say?'

'Yes,' Barrow said smugly.

'What has he got to do with it?'

'I do not understand you,' interrupted Croucher.

'The Judge Advocate General, sir,' said Ramage, 'is concerned only with Army affairs. I hardly need remind you that legal matters concerning the Navy would be the responsibility of the Judge Advocate to the Fleet. Am I to conclude the opinion was given on an Army court martial?'

Croucher glanced at the Deputy Judge Advocate, and Barrow said sheepishly, 'Well yes, sir; but we have no reason to suppose the Judge Advocate to the Fleet would differ in opinion.'

'*That* is a matter of opinion, and opinion is not evidence,' said Ramage. 'However, my point is that it's the custom of our Service to notify an accused person of the witnesses being called against him.'

But he knew they'd over-rule him, so he decided to forestall Croucher's little victory.

'However, I'm not objecting to any particular witness, because I am sure the court' – Ramage could not keep the irony out of his voice – 'is anxious to arrive at the truth.'

'Very well,' Croucher said impatiently, and told Barrow to call Pisano, who strode in through the door with an expression on his face as if he regarded himself as the most important guest arriving at a gala ball. He ducked under each beam, although his head would have cleared it by a couple of inches – clearly he had banged himself so much in the smaller *Lively* that he was taking no chances – but, thought Ramage, instead of making an entrance *da grande signore*, he looked more like a puffed-up pigeon strutting jerkily across a *piazza*.

'Would you stand here, please,' Barrow said deferentially. 'You are Luigi Vittorio Umberto Giacomo, Count Pisano?'

'I have several other names, but they will be sufficient to identify me.'

Croucher interrupted: 'You feel sufficiently recovered to give evidence?'

'Yes, thank you,' Pisano replied stiffly, clearly wishing to forget the episode.

'You will forgive me for certain questions I have to ask you,' said Barrow. 'You are of the Roman Catholic faith?'

'I am.'

'And you are – eh – not under excommunication?'

'Indeed not!'

Barrow put the Crucifix on the Bible and placed them nearer Pisano.

'Would you please place your right hand on the Crucifix and repeat the following oath after me.'

Pisano repeated each phrase, eyes uplifted in what he must have thought was a reverent attitude, and sat down.

'Your English is so good I have no need to offer you the services of an interpreter!' Croucher remarked with an ingratiating smile.

Ramage knew exactly how Pisano would react.

'Interpreter? Interpreter? Am I entitled to one?'

'Of course,' said Croucher proudly, 'anyone whose native language is not English is entitled to an interpreter in a British court of law.'

'Then I wish to have an interpreter,' announced Pisano, crossing his legs and folding his arms, as if to indicate he would not speak another word until an interpreter was produced.

'Oh – ah – well, certainly,' said Croucher lamely. 'Send for an interpreter, Barrow.'

The Deputy Judge Advocate gave Captain Croucher what Ramage took to be a warning look, but said: 'Of course, sir.'

'Send for my clerk,' said Croucher. 'He can find one.'

The clerk was brought into the court, instructed to find a translator, told to shut up and look when he began to make some protest, and hurried out again, pursued by Croucher's 'And get a move on!'

Croucher sat back, a self-satisfied smile on his face. Barrow looked wretched – obviously he sensed a squall just over the horizon. Croucher's smile began to dissolve when Captain Blackman whispered something, and he turned and spoke to Captain Herbert, sitting on his left. Herbert shook his head and in turn questioned the captain next to him. He, too, shook his head, while Blackman had in the meantime been whispering to the captain on his right, who shrugged his shoulders and spoke to Ferris, who also shook his head.

Croucher reached out for one of the *Sibella*'s logs and began reading, trying hard to appear unconcerned. Pisano, probably piqued at not holding the centre of the stage, indicated his boredom by picking pieces of fluff from his sky-blue breeches (where on earth did he find them? Ramage wondered) and then inspected his finger nails with more concentration, it seemed to Ramage, than he could ever muster for more serious matters.

And, he thought grimly, matters could not be more serious. Croucher was obviously pinning everything on Pisano's testimony, and he must be the last witness they could produce: then he'd make his defence. Should he call the Bosun and Carpenter's Mate? No – there was nothing they could add to their earlier evidence. So there was only Jackson. He would only corroborate what had been said about the *Sibella*, but he might be useful for the Tower affair and the visit to Argentario.

Yet what *could* Jackson say? All the deference that Croucher was showing Pisano indicated that, despite Gianna's intervention, he was going to make sure the court believed every word he said.

In that case the verdict was a foregone conclusion. Ramage felt his previous elation evaporate: all those fine resolutions about fighting back, he thought bitterly ... You can't fight without weapons. And that's what his father had found.

But – if Pisano's word counted for so much, then so would Gianna's! Perhaps not with the court, but if she gave evidence it would be recorded and appear in the minutes which Sir John Jervis and the Admiralty would read. And – he could kick himself for only just thinking of it – the court had just ruled someone could be called as a witness without previous warning.

At that moment the clerk returned to the cabin and handed a note to Captain Croucher, who read it, looked at Pisano, and said apologetically, 'I am afraid that owing to some oversight there is at the moment in the squadron only one person versed in the Italian language and he's not available to act as an interpreter.'

'Why not?' demanded Pisano insolently.

'I – ah – well . . .' Croucher looked round, as if expecting to see a suitable explanation written on a bulkhead. 'Perhaps you would be kind enough to accept my word for it that he is not available.'

'But if I am entitled to an interpreter I want an interpreter,' insisted Pisano. 'I have a right – you said so yourself: I demand my rights!'

'I regret,' Croucher answered heavily, 'that the only interpreter available is Lieutenant Ramage.'

Pisano's manner had clearly nettled him; Ramage thought he might even be having some regrets at having to use such an unpleasant man as a weapon: even Croucher must have scruples, and probably shared the average British naval officer's distrust of all foreigners.

'Very well,' said Pisano. 'But I make a formal complaint that I have been deprived of my rights.'

'Sir—' Barrow said apologetically to Croucher. 'Would you allow me to express an opinion? If the Count simply wishes the court to note that he had not had the services of an interpreter, all would be well. But if he is making a formal complaint, then it might well cause Their Lordships to declare the trial irregular, and quash the proceedings. . . .'

Croucher looked at Pisano. 'Would you agree to it simply being noted in the minutes that an interpreter was not available?'

'What minutes? What are these minutes? Seconds, minutes, hours?'

'No, no!' Croucher said hastily. 'Minutes in this sense is – are, rather – the written record of the trial.'

'Oh. All right then: anything to finish this. I am a busy man,' Pisano added. 'I have a lot to do.'

Croucher said hurriedly, anxious to take advantage of Pisano's agreement, 'Yes, quite, we will proceed at once. The Deputy Judge Advocate will hand you a document' – he waited while Barrow found it and passed it – 'which I would like you to look at. Do you recognize it?'

'Yes, of course: a letter I wrote.'

'To whom did you address it?'

'That fellow, what is his name? Prodding, Probing . . . Probus . . . anyway the man who commands the little ship.'

'Would you be good enough to read to the court the contents of the document?'

Very neatly done, thought Ramage. But we might as well make it difficult for Pisano. Just give him a minute or two to get into his stride . . .

'I wrote this report on the disgraceful behaviour of Lieutenant Ramage—'

'The witness is requested only to read the document, I believe,' remarked Captain Ferris.

'Er – yes, pray read the document without any prefatory remarks,' said Croucher.

'All right. I read: "Dear Lord Probus, I demand that Lieutenant Ramage be accused of abandoning my cousin Count Pitti to the enemy after he was wounded on the beach at *Torre di Burranaccio* and I demand that he further be accused of causing my cousin the Marchesa di Volterra to be wounded by his rashness, negligence and cowardice . . ."'

Ramage stood up and asked politely, 'Has it been stated if the witness is reading from the original document, or from a copy? If a copy, it should be sworn to.'

'*Mio Dio!*' exclaimed Pisano.

'The point is a valid one, sir,' interposed Barrow.

'It is the letter I wrote: my own calligraphy – I recognize that well enough,' said Pisano heatedly. 'It is not a copy – what an outrageous suggestion!'

'The fault is mine,' Barrow admitted wearily. 'I should have questioned the witness about its validity before he began reading.'

'Please continue,' Croucher said hurriedly.

Pisano raised his voice, as if determined to shut out any further interruptions. Ramage noticed that the letter seemed even more hysterical and unbalanced when read aloud by

Pisano than when he'd seen it in Probus's cabin.

Pisano was now behaving like an actor playing to the gallery – heavy emphasis here, a significant pause there, and the whole narration accompanied by meaningful gestures with his left hand. He thumped his chest when referring to Pitti being wounded (not his head, Ramage noted); he thumped his right shoulder as he mentioned the Marchesa's wound.

The effect on the six captains was interesting and Ramage, tired of watching Pisano's play-acting, began watching them closely. Ferris was embarrassed and drawing idly on a pad. The captain sitting next to him also seemed to be an uncomfortable spectator. Blackman – rather hard to guess what was passing through his mind: he was a deep fellow and was no doubt trying to visualize the effect of Pisano's letter when read by Their Lordships in the quietude of the Admiralty. However, Croucher seemed to be satisfied and oblivious of Pisano's antics. Herbert and the sixth man both clearly wished they were at sea.

Finally Pisano finished reading and threw the letter on to the table with a flourish.

'The court will question you,' said Croucher.

'I am at your service,' he replied with a bow.

'You saw Count Pitti fall?'

'Yes: I heard a shot and I saw him fall.'

'Did you go to his assistance?' Ferris asked.

'No, there was no time.'

'Why?'

'Because I knew the Marchesa was wounded and I wanted to help her.'

'But surely there was time to see how badly wounded he was?' persisted Ferris.

'Chivalry and honour dictates that a lady has preference,' Pisano said loftily.

Croucher asked: 'And when you reached the boat?'

'I waited.'

'For what?'

'For the Marchesa.'

'And then?'

'She came with the Lieutenant.'

'Then?'

'The Lieutenant ordered the men to start rowing as soon as the other sailor came.'

'Did you say anything?'

'*Mio Dio!* I pleaded with him to wait for Count Pitti!'

'But,' asked Ferris, 'what made you think Count Pitti could walk?'

Pisano paused for a moment. 'I hoped.'

'How far away were the French cavalry?' asked Croucher, trying to change Ferris's line of questioning.

'Oh—' Pisano was clearly unsure what answer to make. 'It was very difficult to tell.'

'When did you first decide that Lieutenant Ramage's behaviour gave you cause for alarm?'

'Oh – before I met him. His plan was madness. I told everyone so. And I was correct: look what happened: Count Pitti and the Marchesa wounded . . .'

'When,' continued Croucher, 'did you make your complaint?'

'As soon as I met a responsible British officer.'

'I do not think the court has any further questions,' Croucher said in a voice which defied Ferris to say anything. 'The prisoner may cross-examine the witness.'

Pisano stood up at the same moment as Ramage, who said politely to Captain Croucher, 'The witness must still be feeling the effects of the blow on his head. Could he be permitted to be seated again?'

'Oh yes, of course,' agreed Croucher. 'Do please . . .'

Pisano sat down, not realizing for a moment or two that Ramage now had the advantage of looking down at him.

'Count Pisano,' Ramage said, 'both the peasant and the Marchesa explained to you before you came to—'

'A leading question,' interrupted Croucher. 'You must not ask questions that instruct a witness as to the answer he is to give.'

'I beg your pardon, sir.'

He turned back to Pisano.

'When did you know that there was only a small boat to rescue you?'

'The peasant told me.'

'How many were there in your original party?'

'Six.'

'How many eventually decided to come in the boat?'

'You know perfectly well.'

'Answer the question.'

'Three.'

'Why did the others not come?'

'They did not like the plan.'

'But you did?'

'Yes – no, I mean.'

'You did not like the plan, yet you came?'

'Yes.'

'You arrived at the boat first, before any of the rest of the party?'

'Yes.'

'Then what happened?'

'You know perfectly well: you arrived at the boat carrying the Marchesa.'

'After that?'

'She was helped on board.'

'By whom?'

'The sailors – and you.'

'But not you.'

'No.'

'Did I get into the boat then?'

'Yes.'

The man lied so smoothly that Ramage was thrown off his balance.

'You did not hear me ask one of the seamen where Count Pitti was?'

'No.'

'You did not see me wade back and go up to the top of the dunes?'

'No.'

'Nor call out for Jackson, the other seaman?'

'No.'

Croucher interrupted: 'You do not seem to be pursuing a profitable line of questioning with this witness, Mr Ramage.'

No, Ramage thought: he's just going to lie and lie. And all I've done is put Pisano's original story into the court minutes in a more convincing form.

Croucher told Pisano he could stand down, and then had to explain what the phrase meant.

Then Croucher looked straight at Ramage: there was a look of triumph in his face, and he said, 'The prisoner will make his defence.'

Ramage was just about to speak when Croucher said testily, 'Haven't you written out your defence? Don't say we have to waste time while you dictate it to the Deputy Judge Advocate? Surely you know by now you should read it and give him a copy?'

'If you will allow me, sir . . .'

'Well, go on then!'

'Regarding the loss of the *Sibella*, I do not feel it necessary to re-call the Bosun and the Carpenter's Mate to give evidence on my behalf: the evidence they have already given in support of the charge makes it clear I did the only thing possible in the circumstances.'

'That is for the court to decide,' commented Croucher.

Was it worth calling Jackson? What could he add? Ramage decided he would not bother. Instead he said:

'Of course, sir. But Count Pisano's evidence introduces another aspect of the case not referred to in the charge, and I wish to call one witness in my defence.'

He paused deliberately, knowing Croucher expected him to call Jackson, and waiting for him to get impatient.

'Well, name the witness, then!'

'Call the Marchesa di Volterra.'

Barrow hurriedly whipped off his spectacles and Croucher banged the table to stop the Marine sentry opening the door and repeating Ramage's words outside.

'You cannot call the Marchesa.'

'Why not, sir?'

Croucher waved a piece of paper. 'She's not on your own list of witnesses.'

'But the court has already decided it has the authority to call a witness not listed.'

'The court, yes: but not a prisoner.'

Ramage glanced at Barrow and saw he had stopped writing and was watching Croucher.

'With all due respect, sir, I think this should be recorded in the minutes. I have asked for only one witness. Am I to understand the court refuses to call her?'

'You understand correctly, Mr Ramage. The Judge Advocate General ruled that a person could be called if the *court* thought that person "capable of giving material testimony". The Marchesa has already told us all she knows; indeed, you insisted her words should be entered in the minutes. The court does not think she can add any further "material testimony" to what she has already said.'

Ramage rubbed the scar over his forehead. The noose was round his neck now: he'd placed it there himself, and now Croucher was hauling in the slack.

In writing, set down in the minutes, Croucher's decision would sound reasonable enough . . . if only he'd – oh, the devil with it.

'Very well, sir, I would like to call a witness who is on my list. Thomas Jackson.'

Any port in a storm, he thought.

'Carry on, Barrow,' said Croucher smoothly. 'Call the witness.'

When Jackson came into the cabin Ramage felt less lonely; yet he knew his anchors were dragging. The court would pass a verdict involving cowardice, and anyone reading the minutes would agree with the sentence.

The American was smartly dressed: he would have made a favourable impression on an unprejudiced court. Taking the oath and answering Barrow's routine questions, he spoke in a clear voice which had only a slight American accent.

Ramage felt a twinge of conscience as he remembered the American had deliberately made Probus arrest him so that he could be available as a witness, and only a few moments ago Ramage had decided not to call him. . . .

'You may begin your interrogatories,' Croucher told him.

'Thank you, sir,' said Ramage automatically – for a moment his mind had been a complete blank. The *Sibella* – yes, he'd fill in a few blanks there.

'After Captain Letts had been killed, when did you first see me on deck?'

'As soon as you dragged yourself up, sir.'

'Dragged?' repeated Ferris.

'Yes, sir: he was very dazed and bleeding from his wound.'

'From then until we left the ship, for how long were you not at my side?'

'Only a few minutes, sir.'

'What instructions did I give you prior to leaving the ship?'

'Several, sir, but you told me to get the charts and logs, and I helped you find the Captain's order book and letter book.'

'If you had been left the senior surviving rating, what steps would you have taken to keep the ship afloat?'

Would Croucher allow that?

'There were no steps that could be taken, sir: she was sinking too fast.'

Good: he'd try another one.

'If you had been in command, how would you have safeguarded the wounded?'

'I don't know, sir,' Jackson said frankly. 'The way you did it was the best, but I'd never have thought of it.'

'Now, the night we took off the Marchesa di Volterra and Count Pisano: will you describe what happened from the time we first heard them approaching us?'

'Yes, sir. Well—'

At that moment the door of the cabin rattled violently as someone knocked on the framework. It was an urgent knock; a knock intended to warn Captain Croucher the reason for the interruption was important.

'Give way, there! Come in!' roared Croucher.

A lieutenant hurried up to the table and handed Croucher a note. He might, for the look of anger spreading over Croucher's face, have just cheated him out of five years' prize money.

'The court is adjourned indefinitely,' he announced. 'Barrow, inform the witnesses accordingly. You are freed from arrest,' he told Ramage. 'Of course you must hold yourself ready for when the court meets again,' he added hastily, as if realizing he was revealing his anger a little too openly.

At that moment the dull boom of a single gun echoed across the anchorage – from seaward, Ramage noted.

Chapter 18

RAMAGE HURRIED from the cabin before the captains could get round the table, walked on to the quarter-deck and looked over the side. About a mile offshore a line-of-battle ship was beating into the anchorage, all plain sail set and her bows a flurry of spray. A commodore's broad pendant flew from her mainmast and she was flying a Union flag from the mizen top-masthead: the signal for all captains to come on board. The Commodore isn't wasting any time, Ramage thought.

Was Gianna still on board the *Trumpeter*? A lieutenant, telescope to his eye, was standing by the mizenmast and Ramage called:

'Has the Marchesa gone on shore?'

The lieutenant lowered his telescope in surprise.

'Oh – er, no: she's waiting in the clerk's office.'

Ramage ran back towards Croucher's cabin, from which members of the court were now emerging. The clerk's cabin was a tiny box forward of the Captain's accommodation, and in a moment he was flinging the door open.

She glanced up in alarm: she was sitting in the only chair, her hands clasped together.

'Nicholas!'

'I thought you'd gone!'

'No – they wanted me to but . . .' .

'But what?'

A silly question, but there was too much unexplained for them to be other than shy.

'But – I wanted to wait until it's all over. Is it?'

He held her hands and looked down at her: the eyes were questioning, worried, beautiful.

'For the time being.'

'What happened?'

'Commodore Nelson's arriving. Come and watch.'

'Commodore Nelson! The little captain!'

'Yes – you know him?'

'No – but in Livorno they spoke of no one else. He is a friend of yours?'

'No – I've never met him.'

'A pity,' she said, standing up. 'If he was, he would help you and make everything all right.'

'I need someone—' he stopped.

'Someone?' she prompted, standing very close, looking up at him.

'—someone about as tall as him but much more interesting.'

'Who?' she asked with innocence which made her beauty glow with freshness.

'You.'

'Then everything is all right.'

Her lips were close to his: but a sudden outburst of shouting made her tauten with fear.

'What's happening? And why did they fire that gun?'

'The Commodore's signalled that he wants all the captains to go on board his ship.'

'Let us watch,' she said excitedly.

The captains were impatiently pacing up and down the gangway while Croucher bellowed for a boat. Ramage led Gianna to the quarter-deck.

Although he had been at sea almost continually for nearly eight years – for so long that when rarely he saw green fields, country lanes, colourful birds and flowers it was with the fresh curiosity of a stranger – Ramage always felt the same excitement, almost wonder, watching a great warship thrashing her way to windward.

The sunlight burnishing the sea a bright blue was so strong the colour seemed harsh; and the *Libeccio*, its sharp edge blunted as it blew across the width of Corsica, momentarily stippled the tops of the waves with daubs of white.

The ship, her bold sheerline emphasized by the two parallel yellow strakes running the length of her black hull, came surging in, swooping and plunging over the troughs and crests of the swell waves with the easy ridge-and-furrow flight of a woodpecker. Her powerful rounded bow punched each successive sea, dissolving them into rainbow showers of sparkling diamonds which cascaded over her foredeck or blew away downwind, their moment of beauty quickly past. From the buff-painted masts and yards the great sails arched down in taut curves, catching every ounce of wind, and dark patches on the foot of the courses and headsails showed spray was flying high, soaking the canvas and staining its natural colour – a warm tint of umber, with a touch of raw sienna or perhaps yellow ochre, and which really needed the tones of a rising or setting sun to bring out its richness.

Gianna said: 'Now I know why you are a sailor: I have never seen such a sight.'

There was awe in her voice, as if she understood the raw and naked power of a ship of war and the way it bent the forces of Nature to its own purposes; a hint of awe, too, at the beauty of the ship and the swathe of spray it cut through the sea; and – yes, perhaps even a hint of envy that it was a life in which she could not enter.

Ramage beckoned a midshipman and borrowed the boy's telescope. In the waist of the approaching ship, between the fore- and mainmasts, men were busy round one of the boats stowed there. They would be hooking on the stay-tackle, ready to hoist it out.

Suddenly groups of seamen appeared at the foot of the shrouds of each mast, ant-like in the distance: Captain Towry – for the ship was the *Diadem* – was preparing to anchor, and

216

the topmen were waiting for the order to scramble aloft to take in the topgallants. He's leaving everything rather late, thought Ramage: there'll have to be some very smart sail-handling in the next few minutes.

Suddenly the men began swarming hand over hand up the shrouds until they were level with the great yards on which were set the courses, the lowest and largest of the sails. Without pausing they climbed on past them, and past the topsails set above, until they were at the crosstrees. From the deck the topgallant yards were hauled round until the wind, instead of filling the sails, blew along the length of the canvas so that it shivered ineffectually.

The yards were then lowered a few feet and in a flash the topmen were scrambling out along them while Gianna exclaimed 'Mio Dio!' at the thought of them working more than a hundred feet above the deck on masts which gyrated like stalks of corn in a high wind.

The sails, already hauled up to the yards like curtains, were furled and secured with gaskets. The men side-stepped along the yards back to the safety of the crosstrees and a moment later were scrambling down the shrouds to the deck.

Strange, thought Ramage: what about the topsails? The ship was by now barely half a mile from the entrance to the harbour: in four minutes or less she would have covered that distance. Then slowly the big fore and main yards were hauled round parallel to the wind so that the courses shivered, and at that instant were hauled right up to the yards in huge, loosely billowing bundles by the men on deck. At once more seamen scurried up the shrouds and furled the sails neatly on the yards – the forecourse was made of more than three thousand square feet of canvas while the maincourse was more than four thousand – and at the same moment the jib and foretopmast staysails came tumbling down to the jib-boom and bowsprit.

So Captain Towry was going to heave-to the ship: was she not staying long? What on earth was going on? The Diadem was now inshore of the Trumpeter and only a few hundred yards from the beach. Ramage saw the foretopsail yard being hauled round until it was lying parallel to the wind, and then even farther, so that the wind was pressing the yard and sail back against the mast. Slowly the ship lost speed.

'What are they doing?' asked Gianna.

'Heaving to: stopping the ship without taking in all the sails.'

'But how?'

'You see the foretopsail – that sail on the first mast? Well, that's been hauled round so that it is backed: the wind is blowing on to the wrong side of it – trying to push the ship backwards. But the maintopsail and the mizentopsail – the equivalent sails on the second and third masts – haven't been touched, so they are still trying to push the ship forward. The forward push of those two is roughly equal to the backward push of the other one, so the ship stops.'

'But why do they do it?'

'It's a way of avoiding anchoring. Useful, too, if you want to stop only for a few minutes. I expect they've gone in close to send someone on shore in a boat – you can see they're hoisting out a boat.'

'Yes.'

'Probably Commodore Nelson is in a hurry to send a message to the Viceroy.'

'Does that mean he is not staying?' she asked anxiously.

'I don't know.'

A few moments later the boat was in the water and pulling for the harbour entrance. Suddenly there was a flurry of activity on board the *Diadem*: all three topsail yards were hauled round and lowered as topmen raced aloft to furl the sails, and the ship began to drift to leeward. An anchor splashed into the sea, and her sails were neatly furled by the time she came head to wind and settled back on the scope of her anchor cable, like a dog on a leash.

Already Croucher's barge had left the *Trumpeter*, carrying all the captains.

Gianna asked: 'Are you—'

He turned to look at her: she seemed embarrassed.

'Are you free?'

'Yes – why?'

'Can we go on land now?'

He thought for a moment and noticed that a boat had put off from the *Lively* – Probus had recovered from his illness quickly enough with the Commodore's arrival. Well, no one would want him for an hour or two.

Chapter 19

RAMAGE STOOD on the slimy steps at the quay and turned round to help Gianna out of the boat. She paused because the shoulder wound prevented her using her right hand and she needed the left to lift her skirt slightly.

'Wait a moment,' he said and, bracing himself, picked her up by the waist and swung her out of the boat and on to the step. She was so light that he wanted to carry her up the steps in his arms, but the *Lively*'s boat was waiting. He said to the midshipman in the sternsheets, 'Thank you: return to the ship.'

At the top of the steps she said: 'It's a long walk to the Viceroy's house.'

'Are you sure you are feeling strong enough?'

'Yes, of course,' she said quickly, and he realized – or was it that he hoped? – she wanted to be alone with him.

As they walked along the Quai de la Santé Ramage glanced across the narrow harbour at the great Citadel, its sharply angled walls merging into sheer rock, and noted that like most harbour defences it was useless: completely vulnerable to attack from the landward side.

The hills and houses shielded the quays from the *Libeccio* and the heat rose up from the stone blocks, solid and invisible. Fishermen wearing leather aprons and canvas smocks were pulling nets and lines up on to the quay from their gaudily painted boats. Here and there, sitting on the cobbles, backs against the wall, were their wives, nets across their legs, and each with a bare foot protruding from her skirts, using a big toe to hold the mesh taut as her hands looped and dived with the flat wooden needle, repairing holes. The women had fixed

219

expressions on their faces which, despite the cowl-like hoods over their heads, were tanned deep brown by the sun and heavily wrinkled. None looked up; for each one there was no horizon, no existence beyond the torn nets.

Ramage and Gianna reached the end of the quay and turned right into the narrow street leading to the Viceroy's residence. The houses on each side were so high that it was like entering a chasm and the street was packed with groups of people gathered, gossiping vociferously: no one listened – each waited impatiently for the other to pause in order to take over the conversation.

Most of the men here were obviously shepherds: they wore thick woollen stocking caps or broad-brimmed, round-topped hats that shaded their faces. Some argued, bartered or quarrelled while still astride their tiny donkeys, feet almost touching the ground on each side, and sitting on angular wooden saddles shaped like the sawing horse used in England for cutting up firewood, and which chafed bare patches on the animals' backs. Ramage noticed that every man – fisherman, shepherd or idler – had a musket and cartouche box slung over his shoulder, and a pistol or knife in his belt.

There were several old women in the groups, some sitting side-saddle on donkeys, their long hair black from the smoke of fires in their huts and covered with a black scarf. Black, black, black – everyone seemed to be in perpetual mourning. Black hair, black hats and headscarves, black breeches on the men, black skirts and blouses on the women. . . .

Everywhere there was an all-pervading stench: a nauseating blend of *brocciu*, the harsh goat's milk cheese hanging in every house, of stagnant sewage, excrement and urine, garlic-laden breath, the sweat of people unused to washing, and rotting vegetables. Ramage, thinking of the island's beauty from seaward, and then looking up the street, recalled a remark of Lady Elliot's – 'All that Nature has done for the island is lovely, and all that man has added filthy.'

Unlike the fishermen's wives on the quay, who were completely engrossed in their work, the women and men stared at the two of them as they walked up the street, stepping round large piles of refuse, across small ones. They stared as they approached and Ramage could feel their stares even after they had passed. As always in a Latin country it was impossible to guess whether the glittering eyes showed curiosity or hatred.

Occasionally they passed a few British soldiers, smart but perspiring in red coats and pipeclayed cross-belts, gravely saluting Ramage while careful not to step into one of the heaps of rotting rubbish.

Once clear of the houses the street became wider and tree-lined.

'How did you know about the trial?' he asked suddenly.

'Boh!' she said with a grimace: the Italian way of saying 'Who knows?'

'But someone must have told you?'

'Of course they did!'

'But who? Who have you been speaking to?'

'Speaking to no one!'

'Then someone wrote to you.'

'Yes, but I promised never to say who it was.'

'You don't have to,' he said, suddenly remembering Lord Probus's remark the previous evening, 'I've another letter to write.'

'But this person,' he continued, 'told you your cousin would be giving evidence at the trial?'

'Yes.'

And, he thought to himself, better leave it at that: she was content, almost matter-of-fact, about what she had done. God knows, even for an impulsive girl of her age it was a brave thing to do; on the other hand, few girls were the head of such a powerful family. Yet there was something else he had to know.

'Gianna—'

'Nee-cho-lass,' she mimicked.

She was smiling, but it was not a smiling question.

'—Did you do this – I mean, why did . . .' Cursing himself, he tried to phrase the question carefully. She gave him no help: they just walked on, side by side, towards the Residency, neither looking at the other.

'You know what I am trying to ask?'

'Yes, but why ask it?'

'Because I want to know, of course!'

'Nicholas, it is strange how you know so much – and yet so little: so much about ships and guns and battles and how to lead people ...' She seemed to be thinking aloud rather than talking to him. '... And yet so little about the people you lead.'

He was so taken aback that he said nothing.

Ramage recalled with a shock that barely three hours earlier Gianna had burst into the court on board the *Trumpeter*. Now he was a guest in a magnificent palace, sitting in a comfortable cane chair on this terrace, overlooking a garden flanked by myrtle hedges and ablaze with the last of the season's oleander and roses, with small, pointed cypresses scattered about like sentries among the orange trees and arbutus.

From the terrace, looking across the blue Tyrrhenian Sea towards the distant mainland of Italy, he found it hard to believe there could be war in any part of the world, least of all just over the horizon: the line-of-battle ships, frigates and smaller craft at anchor in the Roads at the bottom of the garden were, in this sharp clear light, and against this background and atmosphere, things of grace and beauty, not specifically designed to kill, sink, burn and destroy.

The far horizon to the eastward was beginning to turn a faint mauve in the late afternoon while behind him the sun would soon dip behind Mount Pigno and draw a shadow over the town and port of Bastia. To his left the outline of the island of Capraia, dissolving in the haze, would soon be invisible like Elba directly in front of him and tiny Pianosa on the right. Out of sight over the horizon, British frigates were blockading Leghorn to prevent twenty or so privateers in the port from getting out. But to little purpose.

While Lady Elliot and Gianna sat close by him in the shade of parasols clipped to their chairs, Ramage was still trying to absorb the extraordinary news Sir Gilbert had given him ten minutes earlier: during the night the French had landed several hundred troops at the north end of Corsica, and they were marching southwards on Bastia. How they evaded patrolling frigates was a mystery; but they had at most nineteen miles – but more likely only fifteen – of extremely mountainous countryside to cover before they reached the town.

Over there, mused Ramage, behind that pearl-grey band along the horizon, is Italy, where Bonaparte's troops are marching, his cavalry patrols out ahead scouring the Tuscan hillside. As they arrive in each town square, they give a few hearty cheers for the Red Cap of Liberty, plant a wrought-iron tree of liberty, and then, from all accounts, set up a guillotine or two near by to show the local people just how free they are to be under their French liberators: free to rest their heads above the basket and below the great blade; or free to watch the flash of the blade dropping to decapitate one of their friends. . . .

Ramage noticed that a boat which had earlier left the *Diadem* and gone to the *Lively* was now heading for the harbour: he pitied the poor beggars at the oars – it was hot weather for rowing with such a lop on the sea.

By now Lady Elliot had finished describing Ramage's father and mother to Gianna and launched off on a description of each of her own six children, the youngest of whom had been ordered to play at the front of the palace to leave them in peace.

The garden swept down to the water's edge and Lady Elliot pointed out the children's little sailing boat. What would happen to it, Ramage wondered, now the French were actually on Corsica: now that Bonaparte's troops had at last landed on the island of his birth?

A steward came out through the glass doors and told Ramage the Viceroy wished to see him in the study.

The furnishings of the palace's big, marble-floored study showed Sir Gilbert to be a cultured man who bought wisely and with taste during his extensive travels in Europe. A Roman amphora standing on a deep mahogany base in one corner still had the barnacles and thin white veins of coral sticking to its surface, showing it had been dragged up from the sea bed by fishermen's nets, the remains of the cargo of some Roman galley shipwrecked possibly a couple of thousand years ago.

The Viceroy saw Ramage looking at it and said, 'Remove the stopper.'

Curious, Ramage walked across and, holding the narrow neck firmly, pulled out the wooden bung. The inside of the neck was stained, as if oil had darkened the red pottery. He bent down and sniffed: indeed it was oil – aromatic oil, probably intended to be rubbed into the body of a luxury-loving centurion stationed in a far-flung camp of the Roman empire.

'Yes, myrrh,' said Sir Gilbert, 'Oil of the Sweet Cicely.'

The Scotsman's voice brought Ramage back to the study with a jerk: in a sudden wild and erotic train of thought he had seen himself massaging myrrh into Gianna's warm body.

'Her Ladyship,' the Viceroy added, 'thought it was a delightful smell until I told her what it was. But to her the very words frankincense and myrrh are synonymous with unnamable debaucheries, so the innocent amphora has been relegated to my study.'

Sir Gilbert apologized for having to cut short their talk half an hour earlier: the news which Commodore Nelson had brought from the north was serious . . . But, he asked, how were his old friends, the Earl and Countess? Ramage could give little news of his parents: no letters had arrived for several weeks.

The Marchesa, Sir Gilbert said, seemed to be making a good recovery: did he not think so?

Ramage agreed.

'We are grateful to you, my boy,' the Viceroy said. 'You had a difficult task: far more difficult,' he added, obviously with intentional ambiguity, 'than was anticipated, even allowing for the loss of your ship. In a way I regret ever having suggested to Sir John Jervis that he should send the *Sibella*, so that use could be made of your knowledge of Italian.'

'Oh – that was why I was named in the orders!'

'Yes – and of course you knew the Volterras.'

'The mother – not the daughter: she's grown up since then!'

'Of course; but since the *Sibella* was available, it seemed a good idea at the time.'

Ramage suddenly realized Sir Gilbert was blaming himself for what had happened.

'Indeed, sir, it was a good idea: we were just unlucky in being caught by the *Barras*.'

'Well, I'm glad you think so. By the way, I gather that to-day's – er proceedings – were somewhat interrupted, and not concluded.'

'Yes: interrupted finally by the Commodore's arrival.'

'Well, I trust all ends well. You are three headstrong young people.'

'Three, sir?'

'Yourself, the Marchesa and her cousin.'

'Oh – yes. I suppose so.'

'I was unaware of what was going on this morning. In fact my wife and I assumed the Marchesa was in bed until the doctor called, and we found she had – er, gone visiting, leaving a note in her room.'

Ramage did not know if Sir Gilbert genuinely did not know, was being diplomatic, or simply indicating that he did not intend being involved, until the old Scot added:

'I suppose you know we too are old friends of the Marchesa's family?'

'Yes – her Ladyship mentioned it a few minutes ago.'

'Perhaps you think this influenced my request that the refugees should be rescued?'

'No, sir: I hadn't connected the two.'

'In fact, if we are ever to free the Marchesa's unhappy country from Bonaparte, we'll need something with which to rally the people – rather as Bonaparte uses crude standards for his troops, as though they are the Roman legions of old ...

'Well, we shall need people, not emblems. Many regard the Marchesa's family – particularly the Marchesa herself and the cousin who was killed, Count Pitti – as the progressive element which the Grand Duke of Tuscany has been trying to crush. The Grand Duke has behaved oddly, to say the least of it, in treating with Bonaparte. And what could be a better standard, a better inspiration, than a beautiful young woman?'

'The modern Joan of Arc!'

'Indeed! Well, let us join my wife and our graceful standard.'

He led the way back to the terrace.

They barely had time to sit down before a steward came out, whispered something to Sir Gilbert, and hurried indoors again.

'Someone has called to see you,' the Viceroy explained.

Ramage felt guilty: Probus was probably angry because he'd left the ship for a few hours, although Jack Dawlish said he'd explain they could not let the Marchesa return to the Residency unescorted. . . .

The steward led out a young midshipman who paused by the glass doors and looked round in bewilderment: the transition from the midshipmen's berth in the *Diadem* to such a terrace clearly bewildered him.

Ramage beckoned.

'I am Lieutenant Ramage.'

'Casey, sir, from the *Diadem*. I've to' – he hauled a letter out of his pocket – 'to deliver this to you, sir. There'll be no answer, they said, so if you'll excuse me.'

Ramage thanked him and put the envelope in his lap, politely affecting unconcern, but desperately anxious to read it. Was the court martial to reconvene? Was he to return to the ship and remain under close arrest?

The Elliots had seen too many official documents delivered to regard the midshipman's arrival as anything unusual, and Sir Gilbert, noticing Gianna's worried glance at the oblong packet, said: 'Carry on, Nicholas.'

Ramage broke the seal, and read the letter – orders, in fact – twice. The first time he was unable to believe his eyes; the second he read in amazement. He folded the letter and put it in his pocket. He searched across the anchorage, looking for a small cutter: yes, there she was. She looked trim enough – about 190 tons, cost about £4,500 to build, a crew of about sixty men, carried ten carronades, and had a snug sail plan – about 1,700 square feet in the mainsail, about a thousand in the topsail, another thousand in the jib, and half that in the foresail. Draught – not that it mattered in these waters – about eight feet forward and fourteen aft. She'd be about seventy-five feet long from taffrail to stemhead with another forty feet for the bowsprit. With a good breeze she'd make nine knots, providing her bottom was clean – which would be unlikely: it'd be encrusted with barnacles and weed.

Glancing up, he saw Gianna looking at him with barely concealed anxiety and he realized she was afraid the letter meant he would be leaving her. He smiled but could not explain: the orders were headed 'Secret'.

Leaving her ... the idea flickered lightly across his mind, then jerked back violently as the two words took on a harsh reality. He felt the smile fade from his face; now he could understand why she was looking at him like that: her eyes were speaking, her lips silently pleading; it seemed her whole body was trying to cling to him; yet the Elliots noticed nothing.

To an idle onlooker the Marchesa di Volterra was sitting elegantly in a cane chair, beneath a silken parasol, a glass of lemonade on a small table beside her, a fan folded in her lap. Ramage realized the same cold fear now sinking into his stomach must have been gripping her for the past five minutes: the fear of parting with a loved one in wartime. The first parting could be the last – yet it could also be the prelude to many happy reunions.

She was sitting six feet away yet she seemed a part of his body: a part of his very existence was contained in her. He knew that wherever he went, wherever superior orders sent him – to the East Indies or the West, to the North Sea, to blockade duty off Brest – he would never be complete again; a part of him would always be with her, wherever she was, whether she was alive or dead.

Would a landscape ever be beautiful again if she was not there to share it? Would life have any colour, taste or interest when he was alone? Or any purpose – except to get back to her?

Would he ever again willingly risk his life on some mad enterprise, knowing what he now had to lose? Would he fret for her when he should be thinking of the Service? Old Sir John Jervis was notorious for his views on married officers: he reckoned anyone who married was lost to the Service and never hesitated to tell them so, either.

Ramage could now understand why: a few days ago he did not care over-much about risking his life – certainly he was frightened of being killed, but he did not think too much about it since no one depended on him for money or security. But now – well, he'd certainly 'given a hostage unto fortune'.

He was just going to say something to reassure her when Sir Gilbert rose.

'Well, if you'll excuse me, I have some papers to prepare for the Commodore. By the way, my dear,' he said to Lady Elliot, 'the Commodore will be dining with us tonight.'

'Oh, what a pleasant surprise,' said her Ladyship. 'The Marchesa is longing to meet him.'

Ramage also stood up. 'Will you excuse me, too? I must go to my ship.'

My ship, he thought and touched his pocket to reassure himself the packet was still there; that he had not been dreaming.

Lady Elliot said, 'We shall be seeing you again soon, Nicholas? Tomorrow, perhaps?'

'I am afraid not, Madam: I have orders to sail almost at once.'

He avoided looking at Gianna, who reached out for his hand.

'You will return here?' She spoke in a whisper.

'I hope so, but – *qui lo sa?*'

Lady Elliot, quick to sense the tension, said, 'You can leave her in our care, my dear. And I'll write to your parents to say we've seen you.'

Ramage found Jack Dawlish waiting for him on board the *Lively*. 'Salaams,' Dawlish said mockingly, 'I trust you've had a pleasant dalliance on shore?'

Ramage grinned and bowed: 'Yes, thank you, my good man: be good enough to unsaddle my horse and give it a good rub down.'

'Talking of saddles, his Lordship's sitting on his high horse waiting for you.'

'Upset?'

'No, not really: came back from seeing the Commodore

expecting to see you on board, and took a round turn on my throat when he found you weren't – until I explained you were on escort duty.'

'Sorry.'

'That's all right. By the way,' Dawlish added, 'I've got my sword back!'

Ramage's face fell: when the court broke up he'd forgotten to retrieve it from Blenkinsop, the erstwhile Provost Marshal.

Probus was sitting at his desk when Ramage went in.

'Sorry I wasn't on board, sir.'

'I gather you had urgent business on shore,' Probus said dryly. 'You've presumably received orders from the Commodore?'

'Yes, sir: bit of a surprise.'

'You don't sound very pleased: getting command of a cutter – even tho' temporarily – used to be a young lieutenant's dream when I was your age.'

'I didn't mean that, sir: I just wondered why.'

'Oh Christ,' exclaimed Probus, obviously exasperated, 'this isn't an appointment by Rear-Admiral Goddard. Do your best and say your prayers like the rest of us. Now listen carefully – here,' he said, pushing pen, ink and a block of paper towards him, 'sit down, and make any notes you want.'

With that he stood up and began walking up and down the cabin, head and shoulders bent to avoid banging his head.

'The Commodore told me to explain this to you. First, the French have landed troops about twenty miles up the coast, between Cape Corse and Macinaggio, just south of the Cape.'

'Yes, I know.'

'Oh?'

'The Viceroy . . .'

'Hmm. Well, they are advancing towards Bastia. Second, the frigate *Belette* was on her way round here from San Fiorenzo Bay with news of the landings when she came up with two privateer schooners just off Cape Corse. They were full of soldiers which the *Belette*'s captain guessed they intended landing somewhere round there.'

'When was this, sir?'

'Yesterday, in the forenoon. Anyway, the *Belette* chased 'em southward – remember that, always get between the enemy and his objective – and they made a bolt for a little port farther down the coast.'

'Macinaggio?'

'Yes, it's very small and hardly any depth of water. The leading schooner managed to get in but the *Belette* was inshore of the second one and forced her to carry on southward. The *Belette* then bore away to get offshore of her, trapping her between the *Belette* and the coast. A good move, eh?'

'Yes, sir: the shore is as good as another frigate.'

'Exactly: cuts down the alternatives open to the enemy. Then the *Belette* caught up with her. What would you have done then – boarded or sunk her?'

'Sunk her, sir.'

'Why?'

'If she was full of soldiers they'd outnumber the boarding party. Not worth risking trained seamen.'

'Hmm ... well, the *Belette*'s captain chose to board, but each time she closed the schooner edged inshore, until finally they came up to a small headland with sloping cliffs and a tower on top – the Tour Rouge.'

Ramage nodded.

'Either the privateer had a very shallow draught, or the French deliberately led the *Belette* on to an outlying rock or small reef – I don't know which – but anyway the frigate hit, drove over and wrenched her rudder off. Before they could get her under control she'd run up on the rocks just below the cliff and under the Tower.

'She hit the rocks with her starboard bow and finished up lying nearly parallel with the cliff and almost touching it. The impact sent her masts by the board but they fell against the cliff and ended up like ladders.'

'No chance of towing her off, sir?'

'None at all: a rock as big as a carriage and four is sticking up through her starboard bilge.'

'Where do I come into it, then? My orders say to go to her assistance.'

'Wait a minute,' Probus said testily. 'Her commanding officer realized the French troops had probably advanced well past where the ship was stranded; but apparently they hadn't bothered with the Tower, which is in sight of the ship and only three or four hundred yards away.

'So he sent the Marines up the cliff – they climbed most of the way along the masts – to occupy the Tower; rigged up tackles and managed to sway up a couple of brass six-pounders, powder and shot, food and water; then moved the whole ship's company into the Tower.'

'So I have to rescue them from the Tower.'

'Exactly.'

'That doesn't sound too bad, sir.'

'I haven't finished yet. While this was going on the schooner came back, had a good look, and obviously made all speed for Macinaggio to raise the alarm. One of the *Belette*'s lieutenants and a seaman were sent off to Bastia for help.'

'Where are they now?'

'The seaman's dead – he fell down a ravine – and the lieutenant is in hospital: his feet are raw and he's utterly exhausted.'

'So I—'

'So you sail before daylight tomorrow with the cutter *Kathleen* and get the Belettes out of that Tower.'

'Sounds more like a job for soldiers, sir.'

'Oh, certainly: you can see we've hundreds to spare in Bastia.'

'Sorry, sir: I was thinking aloud.'

'Well,' said Probus, 'you'd better think better than that. You can take it from me, as far as the Commodore's concerned, you're still on trial.'

By the time the boat took him over to the *Kathleen* the sun had dropped below Mount Pigno and Bastia and the anchorage was almost in darkness. Ramage thought of Lord Probus's last words. He'd already a plan in mind for the rescue, and his remark about soldiers – which Probus had taken as lack of enthusiasm – was meant as a joke.

Towers seemed to be looming large in his life these days:

231

the Torre di Buranaccio, and now the Tour Rouge. Why red? Probably the colour of the stone used to build it. Towers and trials. Did Probus mean he was on trial in the sense the Commodore was trying him out, testing him? Or that he was expected to make a mess of this job as well and so ... he deliberately stopped himself thinking any more about it: if he wasn't careful he'd soon think every man's hand was turned against him.

Chapter 20

'WILLING AND requiring you forthwith to go on board and take upon you the charge and command of captain in her accordingly; strictly charging and commanding all the officers and company of the said cutter to behave themselves jointly and severally in their respective appointments, with all due respect and obedience unto you, their said captain ... Hereof, nor you nor any of you may fail as you will answer to the contrary at your peril ...'

Ramage finished reading his commission in as loud a voice as he could muster without shouting, the wind whipping the words from his mouth, and rolled up the stiff rectangle of parchment. He looked at the fifty or so men standing in a half-circle round him on the cutter's flush decks. Both he and they had heard a captain 'read himself in' many times before, legally establishing himself as commanding officer; luckily they'd never know his schoolboyish elation now he was doing it himself. Even the sonorous words took on a new significance – particularly the phrase about failing 'at your peril ...'

Well, they looked an efficient ship's company. The Master, Henry Southwick, was middle-aged and tubby; he had a jolly face and seemed popular and competent, judging by the way the seamen responded when he'd ordered them aft as Ramage came on board. The Master's Mate, John Appleby, was a former midshipman waiting for his twentieth birthday so that he could take his examination for lieutenant. A cutter did not rate a bosun, but the Bosun's Mate, Evan Evans, was a thin and doleful Welshman whose nose, bulbous and purple, obviously had an unerring instinct for pointing into a mug of grog.

After reading himself in, it was usual for the new captain to make a little speech to the ship's company which, depending on his personality, was full of threats, encouragements or platitudes. Ramage could think of nothing to say, yet the men expected a few words – it gave them a chance to size up their new captain.

'Well, I'm told you're good seamen. You'd better be, because in a few hours' time the *Kathleen*'s going to try something which'll either give you a good yarn to spin to your children or make 'em orphans.'

The men laughed and waited for him to continue. Blast, that was supposed to be the end of his speech. Still, now was the chance to explain why they were going to risk their necks: it might well make them work that much faster when the time came. He described how the Belettes were marooned in the Tour Rouge and ended by saying: 'If we don't go and take 'em by the hand and lead 'em home, the French'll make butcher's meat of 'em – and if we make any mistake we'll be put down as "Discharged Dead" – that's if I remember to send the muster book to the Navy Board before I drown.'

With that the men roared with laughter and gave a cheer – a spontaneous bellow of enthusiasm and amusement. The fools, he thought; already, on no better evidence than flatulent claptrap, they'd put their trust in him. But before sunset to-morrow, if he misjudged a certain distance by as much as a foot, they'd all be dead ... But fools or not, they were willing and loyal, which was all that mattered.

'Very well,' he said. 'Fall out the ship's company. Carry on, Mr Southwick!'

He walked aft a few feet to the companionway and went down the narrow steps to his box of a cabin. Even with his neck bent so much that he was forced to look down at the deck he could not stand upright. The small lantern in gimbals on the bulkhead showed the cabin was furnished with a cot, a tiny desk, cupboard and rickety chair.

He opened the only drawer in the desk and found the *Kathleen*'s muster book. Looking at the names he saw they were the usual mixed bag – the column headed 'Where born' revealed a couple of Portuguese, a Genoese, a Jamaican, a Frenchman and, last on the list, an American. He glanced across the page at the name and saw it was Jackson's – he'd already been entered as cox'n, just above his own name, 'Lieutenant Nicholas Ramage . . . As per commission dated October 19th, 1796 . . . Bastia.' The Master had made sure the paper work was up to date, Ramage noted with relief: the *Kathleen*'s previous commanding officer had suddenly been taken to hospital several days before.

Glancing through the captain's order and letter book, he saw they contained only routine matters. Later he'd have to sign receipts for them and signal books, inventories and a host of other papers; but for the moment there were more important tasks. He called to the sentry at the door, 'Pass the word for the Master and tell him to bring his charts.'

Southwick was with him in a moment, a roll of charts under his arm.

'What's the condition of the sails and standing and running rigging, Mr Southwick?'

'Typical Mediterranean, sir,' Southwick said bitterly. 'Can't get a scrap of new stuff. All the running rigging's been turned end for end half a dozen times. Sails are as ripe as pears – and more patches than original cloths. The whole bloody outfit ought to have been condemned a year ago. Masts, spars and hull are sound though, thank God.'

'What about the ship's company?'

'First-class, sir, and I mean it. Being as we're so small, we've mostly been on our own and always at sea. None of the hanging around in harbour that rots the men.'

'Fine,' said Ramage. 'Now let's have a look at the chart for this coast to the northward.'

Southwick spread it on the desk, putting the muster book on one end to prevent it rolling up.

Briefly Ramage outlined their task while taking a pair of dividers from a rack over the desk and measuring off the distance to the headland on which the Tour Rouge stood, and comparing it with the latitude scale at the side of the chart. Fourteen minutes of latitude, so it was fourteen sea miles. The wind was now west and by dawn he could reckon on half a gale. Sails and rigging not too good; but the rescue was urgent. He needed daylight for the operation. A couple of hours from weighing anchor should see them off the Tower, allowing for a tack or two at the headland to size up the situation.

'Right, Mr Southwick, we get under way two hours before dawn.'

With the ship under-officered – he was short of a lieutenant and a second master – all the work would fall on Southwick, the young Master's Mate, Appleby, and himself.

'You'd better get some sleep,' he told Southwick.

For the next ten minutes Ramage studied the chart, converting it into a mental picture of the contours of the coast and the sea bed. He was cursing the sparseness of the soundings when he heard someone coming down the companionway and a moment later, after knocking on the door, Jackson came in carrying a letter and two parcels.

'Boat's just come out with these, sir, addressed to you. A shore boat, sir.'

'Very well, put them on the bunk.'

As soon as Jackson left, Ramage picked up the longer parcel, guessing its contents from the shape. He tore off the wrappings and indeed it was a sword. He unsheathed it and the blade was blue in the lantern light, except for its cutting edge, which glinted cold to the eye, the steel sharpened and then polished. The blade itself was extravagantly engraved – but solid and well balanced; the basket handle was finely carved, but strong. It was a magnificent fighting sword; not an expensive, light-weight piece of elegance for ceremonial use.

In the other parcel he was surprised to find a brass-bound mahogany case of pistols. As soon as he opened it he recognized a pair of duelling pistols which he had last seen only that afternoon, on a rack in Sir Gilbert's study: they had looked such a fine pair that he had commented on them. They were deadly accurate, although the hair-trigger meant they were not ideally suited to the rough-and-tumble of boarding an enemy ship; but they were as perfect an example of the gunmaker's art as anyone could wish for. The case was complete with a powder horn, extra flints, mould for casting shot, and cleaning brushes.

Ramage then opened the letter. It said simply: 'Please accept these three stalwarts who will, I hope, prove as reliable to you in an emergency as you have to – yours truly, Gilbert Elliot.'

He called to the sentry, 'Pass the word for my cox'n.'

When Jackson came down, Ramage gave him the case.

'Check these over, please: fine powder, good flints, and ready for me in the morning, loaded.'

'Phew!' Jackson exclaimed. 'They're a rare pair of barkers!'

Ramage thought that now was as good a time as any to talk with the American.

'Jackson – thank you for what you did over the trial: you took a tremendous risk.'

The American looked embarrassed and said nothing.

'But tell me, what evidence did you think you had that wouldn't be given by the Bosun and Carpenter's Mate?'

'Only the part while we were in the boat, sir.'

'But that was all spoken in Italian.'

Jackson looked puzzled.

'Well, sir, about going to the peasant's hut, and the Tower business, and how you carried the Marchesa, and how the other chap came to be killed – that sort of thing.'

Ramage glanced up quickly.

'How the other chap came to be killed?'

'Why yes, sir: you know, Count Pretty.'

'Pitti.'

'Count Pitti, then.'

'What do you know about that?'

'Only that he was shot in the head.'

'How do you know he was shot in the head?'

Jackson flushed, as if angry because he thought his word

236

was being doubted, but for the moment Ramage was too eager for the man's reply to explain the question.

'Well, sir – you know when you carried the Marchesa and I frightened the horsemen?'

'Yes.'

'Then a few minutes later you called me to come back to the boat?'

'Yes, yes – go on, man!'

'Well, as I ran along the top of the dunes, I dodged in and out of the bushes: there were still some Frenchmen dashing around, and I didn't want to bump into them.

'I just came to an open patch between the two lots of bushes when I saw a man lying on the sand, face downwards. I turned him over and saw his face was blown off. I guessed it must have been Count Pretty.'

'Oh Christ,' Ramage groaned.

'Why, sir, have I said the wrong thing?'

'No – no, on the contrary. It's just a pity Commodore Nelson didn't arrive a few minutes later – after you'd told that to the court.'

'But what difference would it have made?' Jackson was completely puzzled.

'I mentioned I was being accused of cowardice, didn't I . . .'

'Yes, sir.'

'Well, the accusation was that I pushed off in the boat and deliberately left Count Pitti behind wounded. It was even said that as we rowed away someone heard him calling for help.'

'But didn't you come up and find him after putting the Marchesa in the boat, sir? I saw footprints in the sand from the boat to the body and back: I thought they were yours.'

'They were, but no one saw me go back. Nor was there anyone – as far as I knew – who could corroborate that I found him with his face blown off.'

'Except me, sir.'

'Yes, except you. But I didn't know you knew – and,' Ramage gave a bitter laugh, 'you didn't know I didn't know you knew!'

'Trouble was, sir, you were all talking in Italian. I knew

you were having a row with that other chap, but none of us knew what it was about ... Still, I can square that when the court sits again.'

'Maybe – but I'm afraid the court might not believe you now: they might think we made the story up.'

'They could, sir; but they've only got to ask the rest of the lads in the gig. They can vouch that I told them what I'd seen soon after I got in the boat: before the lady collapsed.'

'Well, we'll have to see. You'd better take the pistols and check them. And tell the steward to get me some supper.'

'Man the – er, windlass,' Ramage told the Bosun's Mate, and at once the shrill, warbling note of his call pierced the ship, sounding eerie in the darkness.

Ramage was tired; his eyelids felt gummed up, and he cursed himself for not making an inspection of the ship the previous evening: handling a small fore-and-aft-rigged cutter was a vastly different proposition from a square-rigged frigate: apart from the sails, the little *Kathleen* had a tiller instead of a wheel and a windlass instead of a capstan: he'd nearly made a fool of himself with almost his first order, just managing to change 'capstan' to 'windlass' in time.

The foc's'lemen and the ship's half dozen Marines ran to the foredeck and a couple of them disappeared below: they would stow the cable as it went down into the cable tier.

There was plenty of wind; too much but for the fact that the sea would be calm close in, where the mountainous coast formed a lee. He'd have to watch out for the tremendous gusts funnelling along the occasional valleys which ran down at right-angles to the sea: that was how many a ship lost her topmasts. . . .

Despite her ripe sails, he saw the *Kathleen* had a solid enough mast, thicker than a man's waist and made of selected Baltic spruce – well, no doubt the Admiralty contractors swore it was selected. The long boom, just above him as he stood on the quarter-deck, projected several feet beyond the taffrail, like a gundog's tail. The heavy mainsail was neatly furled along its full length, secured by gaskets, and the gaff lashed down on top.

Jib and foresail were in tidy bundles at the foot of their respective stays: the big jib on the end of the bowsprit – which stuck out horizontally beyond the bow for forty feet, like a giant fishing rod – and the foresail at the stemhead itself.

'At short stay, sir,' Southwick shouted from the fo'c'sle. The anchor cable was now stretching down to the sea bed at the same angle as the forestay.

'Right – keep heaving.'

Now to hoist the mainsail. Jackson passed the speaking trumpet, and Ramage bellowed, 'Afterguard and idlers lay aft!'

A group of seamen ran towards him.

'Ease away downhauls and tack tricing lines ... Off main sail gaskets!'

Swiftly some of the men slacked away ropes while others scrambled along the boom to untie the narrow strips of plaited rope holding the gaff and mainsail to the boom.

'Up and down, sir!' called Southwick from the fo'c'sle. With the anchor cable now vertical, the anchor had no bite on the sea bed: blast, he'd left it a fraction late: the anchor wouldn't hold, yet he had no sail set to give him control.

'Anchor's aweigh!' yelled Southwick.

'Man the topping lift – haul taut and belay ... Overhaul mainsheet ... Man throat and peak halyards.'

The men tailed on to the ropes that would hoist the heavy gaff and sail up the mast. As soon as he saw they were ready he shouted:

'Haul taut – hoist away! Handsomely, now!'

Slowly the sail crawled up the mast, the canvas flogging in the wind.

'Man and overhaul the mainsheet ... Look alive, there! Right, tally aft the mainsheet.'

He turned to the quartermaster and seaman at the tiller. 'Up with the helm – now, meet her ... That's it – steady as you go.'

The topping lift was slackened away so that the mainsail

took up the weight of the boom. Hmm – it was patched but sat well.

It was good to be under way again, even if getting a cutter out of a crowded anchorage presented plenty of problems. He'd never commanded one before and didn't know how long she took to react to various combinations of rudder and sail. Some fore-and-aft-rigged ships preferred the headsails hardened in and the mainsail trimmed fairly free; others just the opposite.

But he was damned if he was going to ask Southwick – it'd very soon be obvious which the *Kathleen* liked. The only gamble for the moment was how quickly she'd gather way and give the rudder a chance to get a bite on the water, so he could control the ship. If she was slow, making a lot of leeway before picking up speed, then there were enough ships anchored to leeward – including Commodore Nelson's – to make a collision inevitable.

The anchor and cable were still hanging vertically and dragging in the water under the bow like a brake, but judging from the increased speed with which the men were working the windlass, in a few moments the anchor itself would break the surface. He rattled out a series of orders as the ship's bow paid off to starboard, and first the foresail and then the jib crawled up their stays as men sweated at the halyards.

Both were quickly sheeted home and at once the ship came alive: no longer was she inert in the water, pitching and rolling to her anchor cable like a lumbering ox at the end of a rope: the sea gurgled round her straight stem and swirled along the hull before tucking under her quarter and bubbling aft in the wake.

On the foredeck men hooked the cat to the anchor and hauled it up the last few feet to the cat-head, the beam of wood sticking out on each side of the bow like a tusk of a wild boar, where another tackle clapped on one of the flukes hoisted the whole anchor parallel with the ship's side.

Because her bows had paid off to starboard he'd been able to hoist the headsails with the wind on the larboard side; and

it was the larboard tack that would take the *Kathleen* northward towards Macinaggio.

Like a trotting horse breaking into a gallop, the *Kathleen*
surged ahead: her stem sliced through the sea, flinging up a
foaming white bow wave. He saw the shadowy outline of a
big transport anchored ahead and promptly ordered the sheets
to be hardened in and the helm put down to bring the *Kathleen* hard on the wind.

As she heeled well over under the increased pressure on her
sails, with the sea swilling in at the lee gun ports, Ramage
noticed a nervous glance from Southwick, who had just come
aft: the Master wasn't used to passing close to windward of
big ships, when the slightest miscalculation – or even an extra
large wave – meant all the difference between clearing by a
few feet and colliding. Southwick was, of course, quite right:
it was safer to pass to leeward, but it wasted time because the
sails of a tiny vessel like the *Kathleen* would be blanketed by
the sheer bulk of a big ship and lose the wind for several valuable moments.

Ramage told the quartermaster to bear away slightly,
ordered the sheets to be eased, and gradually brought the
cutter round on to the course which would take them up to the
wreck of the *Belette*. There was a lot of weight on the tiller for
just two men. If the wind increased he'd have to use relieving
tackles. Should he set the jib topsail? No, nor the gaff topsail:
the cutter was already making a good eight knots and clapping
on more sail would only make her heel more without adding
to her speed. It was a mistake many people made.

Bastia was sliding astern. Gianna would not have seen him
leave in the darkness, although the *Kathleen* must have passed
within half a mile of the bottom of the Viceroy's garden. Ramage had been so absorbed in handling the ship he hadn't even
glanced that way.

'Mr Southwick, hand over the conn to the Master's Mate
and come aft with the Bosun's Mate.'

'Aye aye, sir.'

As the *Kathleen* thrashed her way northward Ramage felt
a sudden exhilaration: a cutter might be one of the Navy's

smallest warships, but she was one of the handiest: her fore-and-aft sails allowed her to sail so much closer to the wind that she could outmanoeuvre a far bigger square-rigged opponent, her ability to dodge helping to make up for the enemy's overwhelmingly superior guns. It was the story of the terrier and the bull – the terrier was safe enough as long as he dodged the sweeping horns and the violent kicks.

Ramage went over to the weather rail abreast the mainmast, where he could use one of the *Kathleen*'s carronades to steady himself if the ship gave a particularly violent roll, and talk to the Master and Bosun's Mate without everyone overhearing.

Hellfire, those shrouds and runners looked old: if appearances were anything to go by they should part any minute and let the mast go by the board. The mainsail, bellying upwards above him, had more patches than a Neapolitan beggar's cape; even the darkness couldn't hide that.

'Oh yes,' he said, suddenly noticing Southwick and Evans waiting. 'Oh yes, there are a few things I want to go over.'

Swiftly, for Evans' benefit, he explained how the *Belette* was lying at the foot of the cliff.

'It's no good making detailed plans until we get a good look at her. But if she scraped over the reef losing only her rudder, then with our draught the reef's no danger to us. We can go in on the same course as the *Belette*. All we want is deep water close along her larboard side.'

'How shall we get the men off, sir?' asked Southwick.

'I want to luff up alongside and hold on long enough to get them all on board. Holding on is your responsibility, Evans.'

'Grapnels, sir?'

'Yes, but first of all, protection for ourselves: I can't luff up suddenly and slap our bow alongside her because we'd lose the bowsprit: we've got to do it gently. On the other hand I don't want to scrape down her side – her chainplates and davits would tear our rigging to pieces. So make up three long sausage-shaped fenders: boarding nets stowed with hammocks, old rope – anything. When I give the word, sling one forward, one amidships to protect our own chainplates, and the other right aft, on our quarter.'

'Aye aye, sir.'

'And I want half a dozen boarding grapnels ready, each with at least ten fathoms of line. Pick six of the best men and detail off one for the bowsprit and the rest along the starboard side – cat-head, main chains and so on. They've got to give a good heave when I give the word and hook on to the *Belette*.

'Make up some heavier lines to hold ourselves alongside if necessary,' he added. 'The grapnel lines may not be strong enough.'

Southwick said, 'There'll be a lot of men coming on board . . .'

'Yes: as soon as they arrive, send 'em below: the *Belette*'s officers are the only exception – unless we're under fire, in which case I'll need their Marines to help.'

'Are the French likely to be making trouble?' Evans asked.

'Yes, but probably not at first: they'll be attacking the Tower, I imagine.'

'They could set fire to the ship, sir,' Southwick pointed out.

'Yes, they could; but soldiers won't know how badly she's damaged, so I think they'd probably leave her for their own people to salvage.'

'Now, our carronades won't elevate enough to be much use covering the men's escape from the Tower to the wreck; but our Marines can have a bit of target practice. Pick half a dozen seamen who are handy with muskets to help them. Get all the spare muskets loaded and stowed, with powder and shot, somewhere dry and easy to get at, ready for the *Belette*'s Marines.

'That's all: any questions? No? Right, carry on, then.'

Ramage went down to his cabin after glancing round the horizon. The wind had not increased and Appleby, the young Master's Mate, was keeping the men busy trimming the main and headsail sheets, slackening and tautening as occasional valleys and headlands varied the wind's direction.

At the bottom of the ladder he acknowledged the sentry's salute, crouched as he went into the cabin and sat down on his cot, letting it swing as the *Kathleen* rolled.

He was enjoying himself. He listened to the rudder creaking on its pintles, and occasionally a sea surging up on the quarter hit the tuck of the stern with a thump. His nose reminded him that just below the little cabin was the breadroom, stowed with sack upon sack of hard biscuit and, judging by the musty smell, none too fresh. And also beneath him was the magazine, filled with barrels and bags of gunpowder. It was often said, as an illustration of the pitfalls facing a captain, that commanding one of the King's ships was like living on a powder barrel. A cutter was one of the few types of vessel where this was not just a simile.

The Tower and the wrecked *Belette* were hidden beyond another small headland until they were almost abeam of the *Kathleen*. Ramage was relieved to see the frigate lying roughly as he expected, like a huge whale thrown ashore in a gale. But blast her lieutenant for not mentioning in his report that there was this second headland to the south, barely a couple of hundred yards from the one on which the *Belette* was now stranded. The chart did not show it, but Ramage saw that after the *Kathleen* turned to come alongside the wrecked ship, if he made a mistake and overshot slightly, the cutter could easily run on to the second headland before she could bear away to seaward and get clear....

'Mr Southwick!'

The Master hurried over. 'Make a sketch in the log of how she's lying in relation to those two headlands: you can modify it in detail later. It'll be useful if someone else has to come in to salvage or burn us!'

Ramage looked at the Tower again. Magnified several times in the telescope, it appeared to be only a few hundred yards away. Sixteenth-century Spanish in design and in good condition, it stood a reddish-grey circular column a short distance from the edge of the headland, its only entrance a hole in the side some fifteen feet above the ground.

A puff of smoke from the top of the Tower drifted away in the wind, looking harmless enough, then another, followed by several smaller ones. The *Belette*'s crew were busy with

244

their brass six-pounders and muskets, but he could not see their targets.

The Tower did not seem damaged, so presumably the French hadn't been able to bring up field pieces – hardly surprising since it would be tough going even for a mule across this sort of countryside.

Ramage looked again at the *Belette* herself. As the *Kathleen* continued northward, the bearing of the frigate had changed and he could now see she was in fact lying at an angle of about thirty degrees to the cliff, her stern to the northward, just as Probus had said. Her masts, snapped off close to the deck and leaning against the cliff, looked like three steep catwalks.

What on earth was that on top of the Tower? Pieces of bunting? No, three signal flags! They were lashed to a pole which someone was waving violently, though careful to keep his head below the parapet.

'Jackson! The signal book, quickly.'

But his days as a midshipman were close enough behind for Ramage to read the flags and remember their meaning. Blue, white and blue vertical stripes; plain red; and a French Tricolor. The first two were signal number thirty-one, which meant '*Ships seen are—*'. The Tricolor indicated the ships were French.

A puzzled Ramage glanced round the horizon, but there was not a vessel in sight, except for the stranded *Belette*. The signal could mean 'ship' or 'ships' – ah, yes! They were warning him that French soldiers were on board the frigate.

'Jackson, acknowledge that signal.'

The American hurried to the flag locker.

'Master's Mate!' Ramage snapped, 'help with the signals. Mr Southwick! Take over the conn for the time being.'

Blast the signal book: in trying to explain his intentions to the *Belette*'s captain in the Tower, Ramage was limited to a couple of hundred words or routine phrases listed in the book with the corresponding flag numbers: signals such as 'Furl sails', 'The Fleet to moor', 'Caulkers with their implements to repair to the ship denoted'.

Let's hope the *Belette*'s captain has some imagination, Ramage thought to himself and glanced through the signal book to refresh his memory.

'Jackson, a yellow flag from the ensign staff – yes, yes, I know: ship the blasted thing, I only want it up for a couple of minutes!'

He'd anticipated Jackson's protest that it was dangerous to ship the ensign staff while under way because the boom might smash it: that was why at sea the *Kathleen*'s ensign flew from the peak of the gaff.

It took a moment to get the yellow flag streaming out astern over the taffrail, and he was relieved to see the signal acknowledged from the Tower. As he glanced round to tell Jackson to lower the flag and stow the staff he saw the puzzled look on the faces of the Master and various other men who'd seen it hoisted. Hardly surprising, Ramage thought, because they knew that normally it indicated someone was about to be flogged or hanged. The clue was in the precise wording of its official meaning in the signal book – 'Punishment going to be inflicted'. Its significance ought to be obvious to the men in the Tower.

'Beat to quarters, Mr Southwick. The French are in possession of the frigate,' he added.

The Master had hardly bellowed the first part of the order before the rat-a-tat-tat of a drum sounded out from forward. The Carpenter's Mate and his crew bolted below to collect their tools and prepare shot plugs; the Gunner's Mate followed him to unlock the magazine and issue locks and cartridges for the carronades; the Bosun's Mate had seamen half filling shallow tubs with water and placing them near the carronades, ready for the slow matches – in effect slow-burning fuses – to be stuck in notches round the brim, the lighted end hanging over the water, for use in case the flintlocks misfired. Other seamen scattered wet sand along the deck and down the companionways, so the men's feet should not slip and, more important, the friction of shoes or the recoil of the guns would not ignite any stray grains of gunpowder.

Men who had followed the Gunner's Mate down the ladder

to the magazine and powder room soon came running up on deck again carrying a hollow wooden cylinder in each hand. Safely stowed in the cylinders were flannel bags filled with gunpowder – the cartridges ready for loading the first broadside.

'I'll have the guns loaded but not run out, Mr Southwick. Make sure the tompions are replaced, and the locks covered.'

Ramage glanced at the signal book again. Trying to convey his intentions to the men in the Tower was like playing some elaborate game of charades.

'Jackson, get this signal bent on, but don't hoist it until I give the word: one-three-two. As soon as it's acknowledged I'll want one-one-seven ready for hoisting. Have you got them?'

He repeated the number and saw Appleby, the young Master's Mate, scribbling them on the slate used to note the ship's courses and speeds.

'Appleby,' he called, 'go round and tell each gun captain on the starboard side that we'll soon be opening fire on the *Belette*: we'll pass her close but I'll try to wear round slowly. Each gun is to fire individually as it bears. I want to rake her, so aim only at the transom.'

What else was there to remember? On the face of it, raking a stranded frigate manned by French soldiers to drive them off was simple enough: it should take up one line in his written report. Going alongside the frigate afterwards and getting the Belettes on board – another two lines. In fact the whole operation, from leaving Bastia and returning with the men on board, should take up eight lines at the most.

Yet, if he failed in any particular – touched a rock and holed the cutter, had an unlucky shot from the French send his mast by the board or damaged the ship getting her alongside – he'd face yet another trial. The Navy was a harsh judge. In time of war, with hundreds of warships always at sea, an operation like this had to be routine for a captain. Success didn't enter into it: he either carried out the task or not. If not, then he had to face the consequences, and it was the same in battle:

judgement was based first on the knowledge that luck and determination were almost as important as the weight of a broadside, and secondly the tradition that one Briton was equal to three Frenchmen or Spaniards.

But if he overshot and let the *Kathleen* range alongside, and the French soldiers knew how to handle the *Belette*'s guns properly, then he'd be lucky if they didn't sink the cutter – yet no one would normally expect a small cutter armed with ten small carronades to attack a frigate carrying twenty-six 12-pounders and six 6-pounders: it would be suicide and a cutter's captain who bolted for safety would be justified and probably complimented. But if the same frigate was stranded ... that was a different story: she was a wreck, and wrecks were regarded as helpless.

Yet the *Belette* was far from helpless: Ramage knew the French would fire the whole of the frigate's larboard broadside into the *Kathleen* if he took her into the frigate's arc of fire: thirteen solid shot, each more than four and a half inches in diameter and weighing twelve pounds, and three more each of six pounds. For they could use grape shot, with the 12-pounders firing more than 150 grape – iron balls weighing a pound each – and the six-pounders eighteen more at half a pound each.

'You are still on trial . . .'

Probus's phrase came back to him: to have the cutter sunk by a wreck: that would just about finish me, Ramage thought: he'd be the laughing stock of the Service: he could hear the gossip – 'Have you heard? Old Blaze-away's son was sunk by a wreck!'

Through the telescope he thought he could see faces peering cautiously from one or two of the *Belette*'s gun ports. The French would be gambling he didn't know they were on board: they'd laid a neat trap and were just waiting for him to get within range. But they didn't know he'd already been warned. Moreover, he knew just how far aft the *Belette*'s broadside guns could be trained, so that until the cutter reached a certain bearing on the frigate's quarter, she would be safe from their fire: it was as if the arc of fire of the guns was a huge fan poking out sideways from the centre of the ship. But if the *Kathleen* passed into the fan, then it needed only three guns to be fired accurately to smash the little cutter into driftwood.

Ramage tried to do a quick calculation in his head: if the *Belette*'s guns were trained as far aft as possible and he took the *Kathleen* in at about seven knots and passed a hundred yards off her quarter at, say, forty-five degrees to the frigate centre-line and then wore round . . .

He cursed his unreliable mathematics and then stopped calculating: if he overshot and could not bear away in time he'd be fired at anyway. Yet he had to get in close – and thus risk overshooting – if the pelting from the grapeshot of his carronades was to do any harm: at much over a hundred yards the little iron eggs would scatter too much: he had to be close enough to ensure they were still grouped together as they blasted their way in through the *Belette*'s transom and, he hoped, cut down the French soldiers in swathes.

Ramage felt his previous elation disappearing: the task ahead was far more difficult than anyone had appreciated. If a cutter was caught by a frigate at sea she could use her greater manoeuvrability to avoid the frigate's massive broadside, and there was a slight chance a lucky shot from the cutter's guns would damage the frigate's rigging and allow her to escape. But the *Kathleen* had no such chance: the wrecked *Belette* was in effect a fortress, and the French gunners, admittedly firing at a moving target, had another great advantage – their guns were on a steady platform, while the cutter was rolling.

Ramage looked over the *Kathleen*'s larboard quarter: from his present position the *Belette* was foreshortened: he could see her stern and part of her quarter: it was time to tack, to sail in towards the headland on a course very similar to the one that the *Belette* had taken when she ran aground.

'Mr Southwick: we'll tack now, if you please.'

The Master roared a string of orders and seamen ran to the jib, foresail and main sheets, while others overhauled the lee runners, ready to set them up.

Southwick glanced forward along the deck and then aloft to check everything was clear.

'Ready ho!'

He turned to the men at the tiller. 'Put the helm down!'

The cutter's bow began swinging to larboard, towards the shore. She came into the wind's eye and both jib and foresail started to flog as the wind blew down both sides; then the big main boom swung across overhead.

'Helm's a lee! ... Let go and overhaul lee runners ... Aft those sheets!'

Seamen who had let go the starboard sheets for both jib and foresail moved unhurriedly – or so it seemed: in fact they were fast but, being well trained, used the minimum of effort – to the larboard sheets and began hauling them in, bellying both the headsails as the wind once again blew life and shape into the canvas.

'Look alive, there,' called Southwick. 'Meet her,' he snapped at the two men at the helm. They eased the tiller a fraction to let the ship pay off and gather speed, so that her bow would not be pushed too far round by the punch of the waves.

Ramage said, 'Thank you, Mr Southwick, I want her hard on the wind.'

'Tally aft jib and foresail sheets,' bellowed Southwick. 'Aft the mainsheet! Quartermaster – starboard a point!'

Ramage watched the *Kathleen*'s sharp bow come up into the wind. The alteration was only a few degrees but she responded instantly. From the time they left Bastia until she tacked the cutter had been on a reach, with wind and sea abeam, and she had hardly pitched at all: the waves coming in from the larboard side slid under the ship and thrust at her deep keel, but the wind in her sails balanced the thrust so the cutter slipped along well heeled and with easy grace.

But now, beating to windward, she was meeting the seas at a sharp angle; her bow rose up and crashed down diagonally on to each advancing line of waves, shouldering the solid crests and smashing them into showers of sparkling spray which flung up over the weather bow and soaked everyone forward of the mast.

Ramage balanced himself on the balls of his feet without even realizing he was doing it, and the muscles of his legs alternately slackened and tautened to keep him standing upright.

He looked at the *Belette*: she was fine on the starboard bow, and the *Kathleen*'s course now converged slightly with the coast. Without realizing he was doing it, Ramage worked out the ship's leeway, saw she would pass too far off, and ordered, 'Quartermaster, come on the wind until the leech begins to shake . . . Right, steady as you go.'

'South by west a half west, sir,' the man said automatically.

'Right, Mr Southwick – a swig aft with the sheets, if you please.'

And that, Ramage thought, is just about right: the *Kathleen* should shoot up to the *Belette* as if she was going to poke her bowsprit into the windows of the captain's cabin. It was going to require perfect timing for him to bear away at the last moment, yet if he was going to give his gunners a chance, he could not bear away too quickly.

Fortunately any big warship's most vulnerable part was her stern: the great transom was flimsily built compared with the sides. If the *Kathleen*'s grapeshot could smash in through the transom they'd sweep the whole of the after part of the ship. The effect on the French soldiers would be terrifying: the fact they weren't used to the half-darkness and low headroom of a frigate's gun deck put them at a disadvantage; if they heard the transom being smashed down and then saw their target spin on her heel and sail out to sea again without ever getting anywhere near the arc of fire of their cannon, it would make them nervous. And the steps from nervousness to fear, and fear to panic, were very small . . .

'Bosun's Mate! Pass the word down to the Carpenter's Mate that we'll probably be under fire on the starboard side in less than five minutes' time.'

That would make sure the Carpenter's Mate's crew would be ready with shot plugs, sheets of leather and of copper, and liberal quantities of tallow, ready to stop up any holes. Because she was pitching violently, the chance of a shot hitting the underwater section of her bow as it rose in the air was considerable; and with the wind coming off the land the *Kathleen* was also heeled to larboard, showing a lot of the copper sheathing along her vulnerable starboard bilge below the waterline.

Up and over: the *Kathleen*'s bow lifted to a wave, sliced off the top in spray, and sank into the trough. Suddenly an extra strong gust of wind heeled her right over so that the sharp wedge of the stem cut into the next crest at a much sharper angle, scooping solid water over the weather bow and sluicing it aft along the flush deck. Seamen grabbed handholds on guns and rope tackles as, a moment later, they were knee high in water which cascaded along like a river, snatching up everything loose on deck – including thick rope rammers and sponges used for loading the guns, and some of the match tubs.

Southwick bellowed to the men at the aftermost guns on the lee side and they grabbed the flotsam before it swept out through the gun ports.

Ramage just cursed to himself. Thank God he'd ordered the tompions to be put back in the carronades to seal the muzzles.

'Mr Southwick – make sure the guns' captains wipe the flints and the locks.'

Ramage could now see every detail of the *Belette* quite clearly without the telescope. He called Southwick over, quickly ran through the plan and told him again, emphasizing each word: 'As soon as we're in range I'll begin to pay off to bring the guns to bear. The minute the last gun's fired, we wear ship to get clear to seaward.'

'Aye aye, sir: I understand.'

'And overhaul all the sheets and runners.'

'Aye, aye, sir,' Southwick said cheerfully. 'We'll do it just as if the Admiral was watching.'

'Better than that,' Ramage grinned. 'It's a lot worse being blown up by a Frenchman than rubbed down by an Admiral.'

At that moment Ramage thought of Gianna: what was she doing? He deliberately pushed the thought from his mind, otherwise he'd start wondering if he'd ever see her again. A reasonable enough question, though, looking at those 12-pounder guns whose snouts were already sticking out through the *Belette*'s ports.

Something over half a mile, with four or five minutes to go, and the cutter sailing too fast and rolling too much to give the gunners a real chance.

'I'll have the guns run out, Mr Southwick. Leave the tompions in.'

He watched the carronades being hauled out on their slides, ordered a slight alteration of course, and suddenly decided on a brief few words with the men. He put the speaking trumpet to his lips – what a beastly taste the copper mouthpiece had – and shouted:

'D'you hear there! Mr Appleby's explained what we are going to do. Remember – every shot through the captain's cabin! And look lively at the sheets when we wear round or those Frenchmen will knock off your heads and the *Kathleen*'s stern!'

The men yelled and waved: they were soaking wet from spray but cheerful.

The cutter was finding calmer water in the lee of the cliffs: now he had to watch out for sudden unexpected gusts of wind. He wanted to reduce last-minute rushing about, and anyway she was still heeling too much.

'Haul down the foresail, Mr Southwick, and check the main sheet a fraction.'

The men at the mast let go the foresail halyard while others slackened away the sheet. After flapping for a moment or two it slid down the stay. At the same time other men eased away the mainsheet and, with the mainsail holding less wind, the cutter slowed down, her motion at once becoming less violent.

Damn . . . as usual he was leaving things too late; but still, the less time anyone – including himself – had to think about the *Belette*'s guns the better.

Jackson was standing near and Ramage said: 'Hoist the first signal – number one hundred and thirty-two.'

The American hauled one end of the light halyard, keeping tension on the other by letting it run through his legs.

Ramage had been watching the men at the tiller: they were good helmsmen, and it'd be easier to tell them where to go than try to give a course.

'Steer as if you were going to put us ashore three hundred yards this side of the frigate.'

By now the signal flags were streaming out in the wind and through his telescope Ramage saw the acknowledgement waved from the Tower.

Would the *Bélette*'s captain understand when it was reported to him that the cutter had just signalled, 'To exercise guns and small arms'? Ramage wanted him to make a diversion; but even if he missed the significance, it would not spoil the plan.

The *Belette* seemed to be deserted, but Ramage knew hidden telescopes were watching him and seeing the exchange of signals with the Tower.

'Lot of shooting from the Tower, sir,' reported Jackson.

Ramage looked up at the cliff, yes, the British had taken the hint and were doing their best: puffs of smoke were squirting from the top of the building and vanishing quickly in the wind.

Looking forward along the deck, Ramage saw the cutter was still smashing into an occasional larger-than-usual wave and throwing spray over the weather bow.

'Ease her to the big ones,' he snapped to the men at the tiller: he did not want more water over the guns.

The cliffs were getting very close now and the *Belette* was end on.

'Stand by to ease sheets, Mr Southwick! Quartermaster – steer as though you were going to lay us alongside!'

The Master shouted an order.

Ramage was suddenly worried that he might have taken the cutter too close, so the carronades couldn't be elevated high enough. Southwick saw his expression, misinterpreted it and, glancing up at the cliffs, said with his usual cheerfulness:

'If we hit a rock, sir, it'll be just a bit o' bad luck: should be ten fathoms under our keel with cliffs like that.'

Ramage nodded: steep cliffs usually meant deep water

close in, while a low coastline normally went with shallow water.

With the *Kathleen* racing down on the frigate Ramage was conscious of a stream of impressions: the sea was much calmer, though the cliffs weren't blanketing the wind nearly as much as he'd expected, and he could see only the top of the Tower – the edge of the cliff hid the rest.

'You are still on trial' – whatever Probus meant, the next trial wouldn't lack witnesses but if he made a mistake they'd lack someone to charge.

God, but they were approaching the frigate quickly! He saw Jackson looking at him and realized he was rubbing the scar on his forehead. Damn that American! Self-consciously he clasped his hands behind his back, telescope under his left arm. Once more unto the breach, dear friends. . . .

Now he could see the panes of glass in the frigate's stern lights – they'd need re-glazing soon. And there was the jagged remains of the rudder post where the rudder had snapped off close under the tuck of the transom. Curious how the masts had fallen in just the right position against the cliff.

Three hundred yards to go; no, less, much less.

He put the speaking trumpet to his lips, then took it away and wiped the mouthpiece free of salt water – he was thirsty enough already.

'Remember, you men: every shot must count! Don't hurry – and remember I'll be bearing away slightly as you fire, so don't worry about training the carronades. Out with the tompions!'

Now he could see some details of the gilt scrollwork on the *Belette*'s transom and quarter galleries. A face appeared for a moment where a pane of glass was missing.

'For what we are about to receive, may the Lord make us truly thankful,' Jackson said blithely.

Two hundred yards to go to the firing point: the cutter was creaming along like a yacht – one needed a few beautiful women on deck, laughing and joking. . . One hundred and fifty yards . . . Women like Gianna, asking questions, mis-pronouncing unfamiliar words, her voice like music, her body . . . One hundred yards: the quartermaster was balancing at the windward side of the tiller, easing it a fraction this way and that, the other man pushing or pulling in unison.

'Stand by to ease sheets, Mr Southwick.'

An unnecessary order – he'd just said that. Ramage rubbed his forehead again, not giving a damn whether or not Jackson noticed, and glimpsed the face at the window again.

From where he was standing it was sixty feet to the *Kathleen*'s stemhead and her bowsprit stretched out another forty feet beyond: a little over thirty yards altogether.

Then a momentary spasm of terror gripped Ramage: he realized that it was impossible to rake the *Belette* and then wear the cutter round in time to avoid passing through the field of fire of the frigate's aftermost guns. He'd misjudged both his course and the curve of the *Belette*'s quarter; but it was too late to do anything about it.

Fifty yards to the point where he could begin to bear away. Half these men now tensed by the guns would be dead in a couple of minutes' time.

'Quartermaster – bear away slowly now! Mr Southwick – sheets! Sand by at the guns!'

Slowly the cutter's bow, which had been heading almost directly at the frigate's stern, began to turn away to seaward. Ramage thought he'd never seen a ship turn so slowly and was just going to tell the quartermaster to put the helm hard up when he saw the captain of the first carronade drop down on one knee four or five feet behind the gun and peer along the barrel, the trigger line taut in his right hand.

Steady, he told himself . . . But God Almighty, a frigate was a damn big ship viewed from the deck of a cutter.

A sudden crash from forward as the first gun fired made him jump, but instinctively he glanced at the target; a complete section of the *Belette*'s stern lights where the man had been standing disappeared in a cloud of dust: strange how shot hitting light woodwork always sent up dust. Some rusty-coloured pockmarks round the hole showed where a few scattered grapeshot had smashed through planking.

Another crash as the second carronade fired, and the grapeshot blasted into the starboard side of the transom. Most of them hit below the windows, sending up more dust, showers of splinters, and sparks where they ricocheted off metal.

The third gun fired, punching in the centre section. But the *Kathleen* was still swinging seaward and Ramage could now look along the side of the frigate. He saw the ugly short muzzles of her broadside guns poking out of the ports, trained round as far aft as possible. He could imagine the Frenchmen, their hands taking up the slack on the trigger lines, waiting for the cutter to sail into their sights. . . .

The smoke from the *Kathleen*'s carronades drifted aft and although Ramage was not watching it, the smell was there, acrid and biting in the back of his throat. The noise and smell of battle: the combination drove many men temporarily crazy, transforming them from quiet, amiable sailors into blood-thirsty killers. This was the moment – particularly with board-ing parties – when officers had to be alert to keep the men firmly in the grip of discipline. They rarely if ever did; but success needed no excuses, and in case of failure dead officers could not reproach themselves.

'Mr Southwick – stand by to wear ship!'

The fourth carronade fired: one more round to go: he looked at the fifth gun, the last of his puny broadside. The Gunner's Mate, Edwards, was kneeling down aiming it: even now he was calling for a slight adjustment in elevation.

The trigger line was tight in his hand. Would the damned man never fire? He looked along the barrel, glanced through the port to make sure no large waves were coming, paused a moment for the roll – and then jerked the line.

Ramage was hardly conscious of the crash of the gun: but saw the smoke spurting from the muzzle.

'Wear ship!'

The Quartermaster and his mate swung the tiller; seamen hauled desperately at the main sheet to ease over the main boom; others heaved at runners and jib sheet. The cutter's bow began to swing seaward, but slowly, hell, how slowly. Ramage watched the big boom bang across, then glanced astern.

He was looking right into the muzzles of four 12-pounders on the frigate's main deck, and four smaller guns on the deck above: staring straight at the proof of his error of judgement. Because the *Belette*'s fat hull curved round to her narrower quarters, the aftermost guns could train farther round: he'd misjudged the extent of that curve, and even now the French gunners must see the *Kathleen* filling their sights.

Jackson was muttering, 'Jesus . . . Jesus!'

The muzzle of the aftermost gun on the *Belette*'s lower deck winked a red eye and spurted yellowish smoke. A split second later there was a crash overhead and Ramage glanced up to see the *Kathleen*'s topmast slowly toppling down. He could not stop himself looking back at the frigate.

The next gun forward winked and breathed smoke.

A sudden sound like ripping canvas warned him the shot had passed within a few feet, but a hideous metallic clanging and the shrieks of wounded men told him, even before he could glance round, that it had ploughed down the line of guns on the starboard side.

But as Ramage's eyes were drawn back to the frigate the aftermost gun on her upper deck fired, followed a moment later by the second.

He waited for pain and noise; instead there was a splash in the sea thirty yards astern of the cutter and a vicious whine as the shot, ricocheting off the water, spun away overhead. The second shot must have been too high.

'One man aiming the upper-deck guns,' commented Jackson. 'Don't know where he sent the last one, though.'

The third of the upper-deck guns fired, followed by the third on the main deck. A heavy thud and splintering wood warned a shot had smashed through the *Kathleen*'s taffrail, but a quick glance at the tiller showed the steering had not been damaged: then he saw the men hauling in the mainsheet had dissolved into a bloody tangle of bodies: the shot had landed in the middle of them.

The *Kathleen* was heading north-eastward and still swinging fast. Ramage waited for the fourth of the lower-deck guns to fire. With a bit of luck the rest still could not be brought to bear.

Southwick was already sending men aloft to clear the wreckage of the topmast and he came over and reported.

'We can cut the topmast away without difficulty, sir: hasn't damaged anything else. Three of the starboard side guns dismounted. At a guess, a dozen or so of the lads killed, and maybe a couple of dozen wounded.'

'Very well: see the wounded are taken below at once.'

A bloody mess – but it could have been a lot worse. What now, though? How the devil was he going to get the men from the Tower on board if he couldn't use the frigate as a landing stage? All right, all right, he told himself: don't panic. Itemize, Ramage; itemize carefully.

Hmm ... Item: only two guns left out of the five on the *Kathleen*'s starboard side. Very well, if I want to attack again on the starboard side, shift over larboard side guns to take their place. That'll take time, though, with the ship heeled.

Item: all three of the shots fired by the *Belette*'s lower deck guns hit the *Kathleen*; so if I have a whole broadside fired at me, I can reckon on at least ten hits out of thirteen. Ten hits would leave the *Kathleen* as so much driftwood.

Item: the *Belette* is impregnable so far as the *Kathleen*'s concerned: despite being raked with grapeshot, her aftermost guns had fired, and fired accurately. The guns' crews might have been killed, but others quickly replaced them.

Item: the – a sudden thought struck him: although the *Belette*'s impregnable *so far as the cutter is concerned,* what about the *Belette*'s former crew in the Tower? Supposing they made a sally and recaptured her by boarding, using the masts as ladders?

Short of the *Kathleen* boarding, which is impossible because we can't get alongside without being blown out of the water, that's the only chance. The more Ramage thought about it, the more convinced he became.

It left two unknown factors: how many French soldiers are there in the *Belette*; how many French soldiers are besieging the Tower?

Ramage reckoned there were at least six score seamen and Marines in the Tower; and he'd have to chance that most of them had muskets or cutlasses. If he organized it properly, the

Belettes would have a vital ally – surprise; often the most decisive factor in any battle. A horde of British seamen suddenly yelling and whooping their way out of the Tower and making a bolt for the cliff top might well get them through a French cordon of twice their number. And in the *Belette* herself, the seamen would have all the advantage of fighting in a ship they knew intimately, while the French soldiers would be tripping over everything.

That settled it. Ramage rubbed his forehead: how could he convey the idea to the *Belette*'s captain, marooned in his lofty Tower? There's no signal in the book to cover it.

Meanwhile the *Kathleen* was still running north-eastward, wasting time. He glanced up and saw the men lowering the last few pieces of the shattered topmast to the deck, and Jackson was walking towards him.

'All the wounded have been taken below, sir. Ten dead and three won't last long.'

Thirteen men killed unnecessarily, Ramage thought bitterly.

'How many wounded altogether?'

'Fifteen, sir.'

Twenty-five killed and wounded out of a ship's company of sixty-five: more than a third – nearly a half, in fact. Enough to satisfy anyone who rated a ship's effectiveness in battle by the size of the butcher's bill, even if her captain was still 'on trial'.

Yet he was lucky – Southwick, Appleby, Jackson and Evans had all escaped.

'Mr Southwick – a moment, if you please.'

The Master came striding over, a cheerful look still on his face: a man who thrived on difficulties, Ramage noted thankfully.

'How long before I can tack? We're wasting time standing out to sea like this.'

'Give me two minutes, sir. I'm just making sure all the halyards are free to run and checking the shrouds and stays.'

'Very well.'

He said to Jackson: 'Signal book, please.'

Ramage flicked over the pages, glancing at the numbers of the signals on the left and their meanings on the right.

First, he would hoist 'Prepare for Battle'. The Belettes will understand that easily enough. They'll have seen the damage to the cutter and the captain's no doubt wondering what Ramage was going to do next.

Ah! Ramage jabbed the page with his finger – he should have thought of that: the 'Preparative' flag, followed by the signal to board the enemy. The actual wording was 'To lay the enemy on board as arriving up with them', but when hoisted with the 'Preparative' flag, the *Belette*'s captain would not obey it until the Preparative flag was hauled down.

He'd just told Jackson to get the flags bent on the halyards in readiness when Southwick came aft to report that the mainmast was now clear of wreckage.

'Right,' snapped Ramage. 'We'll go about at once.'

Three minutes later the *Kathleen* had turned and was plunging in towards the shore again, hard on the wind, sluicing spray washing away the dark stains on the deck by the dismounted guns and farther aft, where the men at the mainsheet had been killed.

If the French gunners had used grape or caseshot instead of ordinary round shot ... Grape would have done much more damage aloft than just smash the topmast; case shot – forty-two iron balls each weighing four ounces – would have fanned out to kill just about everyone on deck. Ramage shivered.

He'd better give the Belettes as much time as possible to get ready – it would be no easy task giving orders to four score or more seamen crowded into that Tower.

'Jackson – hoist both the signals, but make sure you've got the "Preparative" before the second one.'

'Aye aye, sir.'

Ramage watched a red flag followed by a flag quartered in red and white squares soar up the halyard.

To Prepare for Battle, one of the most exciting signals in the book. . . .

Through his telescope he saw the Tower acknowledge.

Then, on another halyard, Jackson hoisted a flag divided horizontally into five blue and four white stripes: 'Preparative'.

Finally the American hauled away at a two-flag hoist, the first a blue cross on white, the second horizontal stripes of blue, white and red – 'To lay the enemy on board . . .'

Once again the Tower acknowledged.

Everything depends on the timing . . . everything depends on the timing . . . Well, not everything: if the men in the Tower failed to carry the *Belette* by boarding, no timing in the world would save the *Kathleen* from being blown out of the water because he wouldn't know of their failure early enough to get clear.

Looking round the deck, Ramage saw the rolls of hammocks in boarding nets which he had ordered the Bosun's Mate to prepare for when the *Kathleen* went alongside – before he knew the French were in occupation. It'd be worth getting them rigged over the side. And the hands for grapnels – had any been killed? He walked over to Southwick and gave him the necessary instructions.

Perhaps the wind was easing off after all: earlier he had noticed momentary pauses, as if the *Libeccio* was occasionally holding its breath. He had often seen half a dozen pauses like that herald the change in ten minutes from a strong wind to nothing, leaving a ship becalmed and wallowing in a nasty sea, with everything aloft thumping and slatting and everything below jumping up and down as if it had St Vitus' dance. Supposing he was becalmed a hundred yards short of the *Belette*, after the seamen had left the Tower . . .?

Ramage swayed in time to the cutter's rhythmic roll: the *Belette* was a mile ahead and he was steering the same course as before. The 'Prepare for Battle' and 'Board' signals were flying, the latter qualified by the all-important 'Preparative'. The main and jib sheets were eased so that both sails were spilling a lot of wind, reducing the cutter's speed to about five knots. They'd be alongside the *Belette* in about twelve minutes.

Ramage walked over to the quartermaster, who was standing on the weather side of the tiller, with a seaman to leeward.

'You understand your orders?'

The quartermaster grinned confidently.

'Yes, sir: same as before, only this time I luff her up and lay alongside the *Belette,* so our transom is level with theirs.'

'Good: do your best: mind the bowsprit – we don't want to harpoon the *Belette* with it.'

Both the quartermaster and seaman laughed.

Ramage was thankful he'd hove-to and shifted over the larboard-side carronades to replace the damaged ones to starboard: it had been hard work, but worth it. He walked over to the crew of the aftermost gun. Their cutlasses and boarding pikes were stuck into the bulwark on each side of the port, ready to be snatched up at a moment's notice. The gun was loaded, and the tompion closed the muzzle against spray. A gaudy yellow and red striped rag – judging from the grease one of the men had been wearing it round his forehead – covered the flintlock, and the trigger line was laid on top. To one side of the gun was a grapnel, its line coiled down. The once-smooth planking of the deck was deeply scored where the shot from the *Belette* had flung aside the carronade that this one replaced.

'Who's the man for the grapnel?'

A burly seaman in grimy canvas trousers and faded blue shirt stepped forward.

'Me, sir.'

'And you know where I want that grapnel to land?'

'If we get alongside like you said, sir, then I pop 'im over the bulwarks just above the second gun port from aft.'

'And if we stop short?'

'Over the taffrail, sir.'

'Fine. Don't forget to let it go when you throw: I don't want you to fly across to the *Belette*.'

The rest of the gun's crew laughed and a moment later the seaman, who had not at first understood Ramage's joke, joined in.

Ramage walked forward, having a word with the crew of each gun. He checked how the sausage-shaped fenders had been lashed over the side and made sure they were clear of the muzzles of the guns.

Standing by himself near the stemhead, Ramage found a

small, thin and almost bald seaman waiting patiently with a grapnel and coil of line at his feet.

He seemed hardly the right man to heave a grapnel, yet the Bosun's Mate had chosen him to be in the most important and difficult position of all – at the end of the bowsprit, clear of the jib.

Ramage asked him: 'How far can you throw that?'

'Dunno, really, sir.'

'Forty feet?'

'Dunno, sir: but a deal farther than anyone else on board.'

'How do you know?'

'Last cap'n had a sort of competition, sir. Got meself an extra tot.'

'Good,' Ramage smiled. 'Heave like that again and you'll get a couple of extra tots!'

'Oh, thank'ee, sir, thank'ee: John Smith the Third sir, able seaman. You won't forget, sir?'

The man's eyes were pleading. For all he knew, in – well, about eight minutes' time – he would be out on his lonely perch facing a murderous fire from the French, and the prospect left him unworried. But the chance of an extra couple of tots of rum – that made his eyes sparkle and brought with it a sudden anxious fear, that the captain might forget.

'I'll remember,' Ramage said, 'John Smith the Third.'

'Akshly, sir, I just remembered it's "the Second" now, sir: one of the other two dragged his anchors at number four gun.'

Ramage looked ahead at the *Belette*. So three John Smiths had sailed from Bastia. With luck two would return. The other, as his namesake had just phrased it in seamen's slang, was dead. Bastia . . . Gianna was doing – what?

He strode aft again along the weather side of the deck, calling to Jackson for his telescope.

'Might as well have these, too, sir,' the American said, offering him the pistols Sir Gilbert Elliot had sent on board.

'Oh – yes, thank you.'

He undid the bottom buttons of his waistcoat, pulled the flaps back and pushed the long barrels into the top of his breeches.

'And this, sir.'

Jackson handed him the sword.

Ramage waved it away. 'You keep that: I've enough already.'

He bent down and eased the throwing knife so that it was loose in its sheath in his boot.

Southwick came aft, beaming.

'Satisfied, sir?'

'Perfectly, Mr Southwick.'

'If you did it like you did last time, sir, we'll be all right.'

Ramage glanced up sharply and was just about to tell him to watch his tongue when he realized the man was serious: the fool really thought the first attempt was well done. Well done – with ten corpses already bundled over the side without ceremony and fifteen men below wounded, three of them – in John Smith's phrase – dragging their anchors for the next world. . . .

He put the telescope to his eye and looked at the *Belette*, judging the distance. He waited and then without looking round called to Jackson, 'Haul down the "Preparative"!'

'Aye aye, sir.'

Half a mile away: that'd give the Belettes six minutes to get out of the Tower and board the frigate. God, it had been a temptation to give them ten minutes, so there would be no risk to the *Kathleen:* in that time they'd either have captured the ship, or the survivors would be jumping over the side in confusion, giving him plenty of warning of their failure.

But by allowing them six minutes he was gambling on the *Kathleen* coming alongside a couple of minutes after they had boarded, just as the French quit the guns to fight them off. The *Kathleen*'s carronades barking at their heels might tip the scales, showing the French they were trapped between the boarders from the Tower and the guns – and possibly more boarders – from the *Kathleen*.

He looked at the *Belette*'s transom and was surprised to see the damage done by the *Kathleen*'s carronades. Realizing it would do the Gunner's Mate good to see the result and tell the men, Ramage called: 'Edwards – take the glass and have a look at the damage. I want the next broadside to be as effective, if we have to fire it.'

The man ran aft and took the telescope, steadied himself, and gave a whistle. 'Well, we certainly wrecked the cabin!'

A typical reaction, thought Ramage, smiling to himself: the idea of smashing up the captain's accommodation in one of the King's ships while acting under orders obviously appealed to him.

'But sir—' exclaimed Edwards, and then stumbled as the ship gave a violent roll. He steadied himself and again looked through the telescope. '—Yes! By God, sir, more men are going on board!'

Ramage snatched the glass: Edwards was right, but the men were British: dozens were lining the edge of the cliff and jostling their way down a few feet to swarm across the fallen masts, and the masts themselves were already thick with sailors.

'Run out the guns, Mr Southwick! Quartermaster! Steer as if your life depends on it!'

The Belettes had quit the Tower and started to board much more quickly than he'd allowed, blast it: now he had to increase speed to help them – just when he wanted to make his final approach as slowly as possible: a cutter took a lot of stopping.

He swung the telescope downwards again to the root of the masts: there was no sign of smoke, so perhaps the French in the ship had not yet spotted the seamen scrambling down towards them. Ramage said a silent prayer that the men were not yelling, so they could benefit from surprise.

Looking back along the edge of the cliff he could see the seamen were thinning out: a good half of them were on the masts or already on board. Why were there no French uniforms on the cliff? The break-out from the Tower must have taken them completely by surprise.

Ramage shut the telescope with a snap: the *Kathleen* was so close he could see enough with the naked eye.

The cutter's quartermaster was watching the leeches of the jib and mainsail like a hawk, reacting with the tiller to every gust of wind. The ship was so close under the cliffs that the wind was fluky, much of it blowing down at an angle, and changing direction slightly.

'Mr Southwick – I want those men in position with the grapnels and heaving lines. Tell the foredeck men to be ready to back the jib.'

The frigate's stern was looming up large: now he could see right along her side: the guns were run out and again trained as far aft as possible. He could see that her chainplates, thick boards sticking out edgeways from the hull and originally supporting the shrouds that held up the masts, would be a problem. No, maybe not – they might be just a bit too high to tear at the *Kathleen*'s shrouds.

He saw seamen, each with a grapnel in his hand, stationing themselves along the side of the cutter, and John Smith, lately the Third and now the Second, was already out on the end of the bowsprit, partly hidden by the luff of the jib.

Six men with grapnels, another half dozen to handle the jib sheets and halyard, ten more to get the mainsail down – well, there were very few left to handle the guns.

The most dangerous time will be after the Belettes are on board the *Kathleen* and she's getting under way again: if the French manage to get the guns and fire even a couple of rounds. . . .

Ramage rubbed his forehead as another idea came to him.

Since his own carronades would not do much good – firing them into the ship risked killing Britons as well – he decided to gamble on the *Belette*'s guns having been left while the French tried to fight off the boarders.

'Jackson! Pick a dozen men and as soon as we get alongside, board her and cut through as many of the breechings and side tackles as you can. Then do what you can to help the Belettes.'

If the French fired a gun without the thick rope breeching – which stopped it after being flung back a few feet by the recoil – the gun would career right across the deck, killing anyone standing in the way.

Jackson grinned with pleasure, drew the sword presented to Ramage by Sir Gilbert, and ran along the guns picking his men.

Two hundred yards to go ... How much way did this damned ship carry? Blast, a wave punched her bow round to larboard, but the quartermaster quickly put the tiller over for a second and the cutter came back on course.

Yet Ramage was in a better position than he thought: he could now see the full length of the frigate's side and the *Kathleen*'s course was parallel to and fifteen or twenty yards to seaward of the frigate's centre-line.

A hundred and fifty yards ...

'Mr Southwick – ease the mainsheet.'

That began to slow her up handsomely.

'Overhaul the mainsheet and the weather jib sheet.'

That ensured the ropes would be clear for the moment he ordered the jib to be backed, when the wind against the canvas would try to thrust the bow to leeward, away from the frigate. But hardening on the mainsheet at the last moment and putting the tiller over would push the bow up into the wind towards the frigate. The two opposing forces should balance and cancel each other out, leaving the cutter hove-to right alongside the frigate, close enough for the men to throw the grapnels and hook them over the bulwarks.

A hundred yards, maybe less, and the blasted cutter was going along like a runaway coach: damnation, he had to risk it. If she stopped short of the frigate they were all in trouble, whereas if she was travelling too fast as she came alongside there was at least a chance of stopping her with the grapnels, or banging her hard against the frigate's hull with a sudden luff.

'Mr Southwick – we'll heave-to alongside. As soon as the grapnels are over, pull us in. I'll pass the word when to let fly the main and back the jib.'

Seventy-five yards at a guess, and it was a rough guess at that.

No one looked worried: Southwick's face was placid, the quartermaster was concentrating on steering, and Jackson was making some swipes with Sir Gilbert's sword, testing its balance.

'Mr Southwick, back the jib!' Ramage snapped.

Blast, he was going to overshoot. What's that popping noise?

Muskets! And he could hear yelling on board the frigate.

'Starboard a point! Aft the main sheet!'

He'd overshoot by thirty yards at least, probably more. No, maybe only twenty yards – less if the grapnels held.

The backed jib trying to shove the bow to leeward was fighting its own battle with the mainsail trying to thrust the bow to windward; but, more important, the resulting stalemate was slowing down the cutter better than he'd expected and closing the gap.

A few yards to go now and they'd pass ten feet off; already the *Kathleen*'s bowsprit end was passing the frigate's stern.

'Quartermaster, hard down with the helm.'

Once the rudder was over more than about thirty degrees it acted as a brake. Now—

'Let fly jib and main sheets, Mr Southwick!'

Southwick bawled out orders. The jib flapped and the great main boom swung off to larboard, the sail slatting with the wind blowing down both sides and exerting no pressure.

Ramage realized Southwick was shouting, 'Neat, oh very neat, by Christ!'

Snatching up the speaking trumpet, Ramage yelled, 'Get those grapnels over!'

He watched John Smith the Second poised on the bowsprit, the grapnel swinging from his right hand, body slack, apparently nonchalant; but then he stiffened, swung his body round and his right arm back. Suddenly the arm and shoulder shot forward and the grapnel soared up, the line momentarily forming a bow in the air. The grapnel disappeared over the frigate's bulwarks and Smith let go of the line, leaving men in the bow to haul in the slack. The *Kathleen* had stopped so close it had been an easy throw; but Smith was in credit to the extent of two tots.

One after another the remaining grapnels soared up and disappeared over the *Belette*'s bulwarks. Hurriedly the seamen hauled and a moment later the *Kathleen* thudded alongside the frigate.

'Away boarders!' Ramage bellowed into the speaking trumpet and saw Jackson leap from the cutter's bulwarks in through one of the *Belette*'s gun ports with more men following him.

On a sudden impulse Ramage flung down the speaking trumpet, dragged the pistols from the waistband of his breeches, and jumped on to the aftermost carronade, intending to follow Jackson, but at that moment several men appeared along the bulwarks of the frigate's poop, high overhead.

Ramage, off balance, knew he could not raise his pistols in time and waited for a volley of musket shots. Instead he heard cheers – British cheers.

He scrambled down from the carronade, feeling sheepish. He put down the pistols, retrieved the speaking trumpet, and shouted:

'Come on, you Belettes, get on board, fast!'

Someone was shouting down at him with an authoritative voice and he saw a hatless officer with an epaulet on each shoulder standing at a gun port: a captain of more than three years' seniority.

Amid the din of flapping sails, musketry and shouting, it was difficult to hear, so Ramage jumped back on the carronade. The captain shouted: 'Give us five minutes – we want to finish off these Frogs.'

'Aye aye, sir.'

Thank Christ for that, thought Ramage, the Belettes have the upper hand. But—

'What about the French on the cliff, sir?'

'Don't worry – we can stop 'em coming down the masts: that's all that matters!'

Even as he spoke there was a popping of muskets from the other side of the ship and Ramage saw that French soldiers had appeared along the edge of the cliff, but they dodged back almost at once.

Captain Laidman of the *Belette* was as good as his word: in less than four minutes seamen – among them Jackson and his party – were climbing down her side on to the *Kathleen*'s decks and Laidman shouted from the poop:

'Everyone's off except the Marines: are you ready to get under way?'

'Ready when you are, sir.'

'Right.'

Laidman disappeared from the port and a minute later red-coated Marines, still clutching their muskets, began scrambling down the frigate's side. As soon as they reached the *Kathleen*'s decks, and before Ramage had time to give them any orders, their lieutenant had them lining the cutter's bulwarks, loading their muskets and ready to fire. In the meantime the rest of the Belettes had been bundled below, out of the way.

Jackson, who had been waiting an opportunity to report, said:

'All breechings cut on both sides, sir.'

'That was quick work.'

'Some of the Belettes gave a hand, sir, but I checked every gun myself.'

'Very well, stand by here.'

Finally Captain Laidman appeared again at a gun port and climbed down to the *Kathleen*.

'Welcome on board, sir.'

'Thank you, m'lad: sorry there were uninvited guests on board the *Belette* when you first arrived.'

Ramage laughed. 'At least you announced them! But if you'll excuse me, sir—'

Captain Laidman nodded, and Ramage looked round for the Master.

'Mr Southwick – sheet the jib aback and hoist the foresail.'

As she lay alongside the frigate, the *Kathleen*'s bowsprit pointed at an angle towards the cliffs on which the *Belette*'s bow rested, and Ramage saw the only way to sail out was to let the wind swing the cutter's bow round while her stern was held against the frigate. That would take her clear of the rocks at the foot of the next headland.

'Evans,' he called to the Bosun's Mate, 'cut away the for'ard four lines, but hold on to the aftermost two. Pay out and snub if need be, but keep our stern in. Quartermaster, put the helm down.'

By now the jib had been sheeted in aback so that the canvas was as flat as a board. The wind began to push the cutter's bow round to seaward, but her long, narrow keel diverted some

271

of the effort into a fore-and-aft movement so the *Kathleen* began to move astern.

Ramage glanced aft: the frigate's stern gallery, looking very battered from the *Kathleen*'s earlier assault, was drawing level with the cutter's transom. Evans was directing seamen and alternately paying out the grapnel lines to allow for the movement astern, and then snubbing them, to keep the cutter's stern against the frigate and help lever the bow round.

Ramage watched until the *Kathleen*'s stem was well clear of the outlying rocks ahead. The foresail had by now been hoisted and, like the jib, sheeted aback.

'Mr Southwick, I'll have jib and foresail sheeted home, if you please.'

As soon as they started drawing, the *Kathleen*'s sternway would be checked and she would start moving ahead but, without the mainsail drawing, would still pay off to leeward.

'Quartermaster, tiller amidships.'

A sudden crackling of muskets made him glance up at the cliff: a group of French soldiers were kneeling, muskets at their shoulders. Almost at once the Marines along the *Kathleen*'s bulwarks fired back and the French promptly ducked.

The *Kathleen* heeled slightly as the wind filled the head-sails, and gradually started gathering headway.

'Evans, cut away those lines! Quartermaster, meet her! Mr Southwick, aft the mainsheet!'

Ten minutes later the *Kathleen* was broad-reaching along the coast heading for Bastia, and Ramage handed over the conn to Southwick while he went over to Captain Laidman who had, he realized, been tactfully keeping himself to the lee side of the quarter-deck.

'My apologies for not giving you a proper welcome, sir: I am Ramage.'

'Laidman,' he answered gruffly. 'Damn' fine piece of seamanship, m'boy: y' can rely on me to make that clear in m' report. Now, meet m' officers. They're at your disposal. Use what men you like: you're pretty short-handed, aren't you?'

Without waiting for a reply he called over his lieutenants, master and Marine lieutenant, and introduced them.

'By the way,' Laidman said. 'If you can get your galley fire lit, none of us have eaten for some time. . . .'

'Of course, sir, I'll see to it.'

Ramage called to Jackson, 'Tell my steward to arrange some food for the officers.'

He looked round for the Bosun's Mate. 'Evans – tell the cook he can have as many hands as he wants from the Kathleens and the Belettes, but I want both ships' companies to have a meal within an hour.'

Then he walked over to Southwick, who simply held out his hand. Ramage shook it.

'Thanks. I'm just going below to have a word with the wounded. The galley fire's being lit. In the meantime, every man on board is to have a tot, but serve two to John Smith the Second!'

Chapter 21

RAMAGE COULD see the tall spire of Sainte Marie Church sticking up from the centre of the citadel of Bastia, and several seventy-fours were at anchor off the town, among them the *Diadem*, still flying Commodore Nelson's broad pendant.

The great bulk of Mount Pigno was sharply outlined in the setting sun, but the peak was almost completely hidden by *balles de coton*, the stationary clouds which always appeared with the *Libeccio*. He watched the surface of the sea between the *Kathleen* and the shore for the sudden dark pewtering which was the only warning he'd get that one of Bastia's notorious squalls had rolled down the mountainside and was roaring out to sea.

Since he had nearly three times the normal complement of seamen on board, Ramage was determined that no one in the whole squadron would be able to fault the way the *Kathleen* anchored.

For the last half an hour, Southwick and Evans had been selecting various men from the *Belette*'s former crew and

273

allotting them stations for sail handling and anchoring. All the men had eaten a good meal, sunk their tot of rum, and cleaned up the ship after the action.

Half an hour earlier the last of the three badly wounded men had died, and Ramage had conducted the first funeral service of his career. Although he had attended dozens without much emotion, he was surprised to find how moving were the sonorous words of the service when one spoke them oneself.

Jackson was watching the *Diadem* in case she should make a signal and Captain Laidman was walking the deck, making little attempt to hide the fact that he was a worried man: in a few minutes' time he would be accounting to the Commodore for the loss of the *Belette*.

Oh, to hell with it: so far Ramage had deliberately not looked at the terrace of the Viceroy's residence with his telescope, then decided it was an unnecessary act of self-denial. But no one stood there: he could see the big glass doors were shut, the terrace was bare of the usual tables and chairs. Nor was the Elliot children's boat moored at the bottom of the garden. The whole place seemed deserted.

The *Diadem* was not more than half a mile away and lying head to wind athwart the *Kathleen*'s course as she sailed in parallel to the coast. If they were going to be ordered to a special berth, a signal should have been made by now.

Ramage decided to pass under the *Diadem*'s stern, luff up and anchor farther inshore, to windward of the Commodore's ship – which apart from anything else, would mean that the boat taking him and Captain Laidman to the *Diadem* would be rowed with the wind aft and they would appear reasonably smart, instead of dripping with spray.

Laidman looked so miserable that Ramage felt cheered. He wondered how often such a small ship as the *Kathleen* had arrived in an anchorage carrying one commanding officer to have his trial resumed, and another to have his trial ordered.

Well, despite Laidman's remarks, Ramage knew he had bungled the rescue: men had been killed unnecessarily, and Commodore Nelson wasn't the man to overlook that. The trouble is, Ramage thought ruefully, the whole blasted operation looked so simple on paper. It was good of Captain Laidman to say he would give him full credit in his report, but Laidman was already discredited. For this trip, he told himself bitterly, the *Kathleen* is carrying a couple of failures . . . Apart from all that, Ramage had grave doubts about the wisdom of leaving the *Belette* without setting fire to her. He'd suggested it to Laidman as soon as he stepped on board the *Kathleen*, but the frigate's captain had shaken his head, muttering something about salvaging her. Knowing the Commodore – according to Probus, anyway – was aware of the extent of the damage, he'd pressed the point; but Laidman had made no reply.

'Sir . . .'

It was Southwick, an anxious note in his voice: Christ, and no wonder: the *Diadem* was only a hundred yards away, fine on the starboard bow, and he'd been day-dreaming. Every spare telescope in the squadron was probably trained on him. Well, let 'em look: he and Laidman would probably be sent home in the same ship and they could have another look.

'Stand by to harden in the sheets, Mr Southwick. . . .'

The *Diadem*'s stern was flashing past.

'Aft those sheets, Mr Southwick! Quartermaster – bring her to the wind.'

The *Kathleen* turned under the *Diadem*'s great counter and headed inshore, spray once again flying over the weather bow as she beat to windward.

'Mr Southwick – haul taut the topping lifts; stand by all sheets and see the halyards clear for running.'

Ramage had deliberately not looked up at the *Diadem* as they passed and Jackson, noticing this, said in a quiet voice, 'The Commodore's watching, sir, and some civilians.'

'Very good, Jackson.'

Well, let's hope the Commodore's noticed the *Kathleen*'s lost her topmast and that there are only two guns on the larboard side. Ramage had left all five carronades on the starboard side: the extra weight up to windward helped the ship along.

'Are you ready, Mr Southwick?'

'Aye aye, sir.'

'Quartermaster, bring her round head to wind!'

Let's hope the bloody man doesn't shove the tiller over too far and put the ship about on the other tack. No, he was judging it well: the belly in the headsails and main was flattening: the leeches of the jib and foresail began quivering. Instinctively Ramage looked up at the vane on the topmast truck and then realized it was probably floating somewhere in the sea off the Tour Rouge.

Now all the sails were flapping and seamen were hauling in the sheets. Ramage made a sudden downward movement with his right hand – a movement the seamen at the halyards had been watching for.

As if all three were one piece of canvas, the jib, foresail and mainsail began to slide down.

As the jib and foresail reached the bottom of their stays seamen leapt on them to stifle the flogging canvas and secure them with gaskets. Now the great mainsail was down with the gaff on top, and more men were swarming along the boom, folding in the canvas and passing gaskets.

But half a dozen men in the bow were still watching Ramage. He was waiting for Jackson, who had moved over to the bulwark on the starboard side.

'About a knot, sir. . . .'

Ramage lifted his left hand level with his waist, and could see the men in the bow tensing themselves.

'She's barely got way on now, sir . . . stopped . . . making sternway.'

He chopped his hand down to his side and men in the bow sprang to life. The anchor splashed into the water and the sternway avoided the risk that the cable would foul it. A few moments later Ramage could detect a faint smell of burning being brought aft on the wind as the friction scorched the cable.

'Signal from the Commodore,' said Jackson, and, after glancing at the signal book, reported: 'Our number and the *Belette*'s: captains to report on board.'

Laidman walked over and said: 'Well, m' boy, we'd better go over – 'tisn't very often one reports the loss of one's ship.'

'Oh, I don't know, sir,' Ramage said in a flat voice, 'I did it only three or four days ago.'

'Oh? What ship?'

'The *Sibella*.'

'But she's a frigate!'

'I know, sir: I was the senior surviving officer.'

'What happened to you?'

'Captain Croucher brought me to trial.'

'Croucher? Oh yes, in Admiral Goddard's squadron. What was the verdict?'

'I don't know, sir: the trial was interrupted by the Commodore's arrival. I was then given the *Kathleen* and sent up to you.'

'Well, it doesn't sound too bad. But – of course!' he exclaimed, 'you're old "Blaze-away's" son, so Admiral Goddard . . .'

'Exactly, sir.'

'Exactly what?' snapped Laidman. 'Don't put words into my mouth.'

Southwick was waiting near by and Ramage, realizing that as far as Laidman was concerned he had suddenly become potentially more dangerous to Laidman's future than a ship full of the plague, took the opportunity of turning away.

'Boat's ready, sir,' Southwick reported.

Ramage turned back to Laidman and repeated the Master's words.

Once he had climbed down into the boat to go to the *Diadem*, Ramage found that the exhilaration which, without him fully realizing it, had been keeping him alert and active for the last twenty-four hours, with very little food or sleep, had gone, leaving him desperately tired and very depressed.

Up to then, although the *Belette* rescue had happened only that morning, it already had an air of unreality about it; almost as though it had never happened: perhaps a well-told tale he'd heard a few months ago. The *Sibella* affair too, was just a half-remembered dream.

Now, as Jackson steered the boat for the *Diadem* and Captain Laidman sat opposite, silent and morose, the whole business came back into sharp focus, as if he'd made a fractional adjustment to a telescope in his memory.

There was a thump, and Laidman lumbered to his feet: they had arrived alongside the *Diadem* and Laidman, as senior, climbed up first.

At the gangway Captain Towry greeted Laidman and told him the Commodore was waiting.

To Ramage, he said: 'The Commodore will see you in five minutes.'

The young lieutenant standing anchor watch looked at Ramage, obviously wondering whether or not to say something, but Ramage was in no mood for small talk and began pacing the other side of the gangway. He barely noticed Captain Laidman leave the ship.

Eventually a lieutenant came up and asked: 'Ramage?'

'Yes.'

'The Commodore will see you now.'

The lieutenant led the way. Outside the door to the Commodore's quarters a Marine sentry snapped to attention, and the lieutenant knocked on the door, opened it when someone answered, and stepped inside. Evidently the Commodore was in his sleeping cabin, because without walking through to the great cabin the lieutenant said quietly:

'Mr Ramage, sir.'

He turned and signalled Ramage to go in.

'Ah, Mr Ramage!'

The voice was high-pitched and nasal, and Ramage was surprised how small the Commodore was: shorter than Gianna, narrow shouldered, face thin – and, he realized with a shock, one eye had a slightly glazed look. Of course, Commodore Nelson had lost the sight of an eye at Calvi only a year or so ago, but the remaining one was sharp enough.

Nelson might be physically very small, but already Ramage could feel the strength of the little man's personality: he was taut as a violin string, yet perfectly controlled: his face seemed to betray excitement, yet a moment later Ramage realized the features were in fact quite calm. The man was like a coiled spring.

The Commodore pointed to a chair at the foot of the small cot.

'Please sit down.'

Was he conscious of his size? Ramage wondered. It seemed an obvious move to put Ramage at a disadvantage. Why, incidentally, was the interview taking place in the sleeping cabin?

'Now, Mr Ramage, why have I sent for you?'

The question was so unexpected that Ramage looked up quickly, thinking the Commodore was joking; but the single blue eye was frosty and unwavering.

'Any one of half a dozen reasons, sir,' Ramage said without thinking.

'List them.'

'Well – abandoning the *Sibella* ... Trying to carry out the orders to Captain Letts to rescue the refugees.'

'That makes two.'

'And – well, Count Pisano's complaint against me; and the trial, sir.'

'Four.'

Ye gods, thought Ramage, I've jumped out of the Goddard into the fire.

'Oh yes, the *Belette* operation, sir.'

'And the sixth?'

'I can only think of five, sir.'

'Well, now what do you suppose my judgement will be on each of these escapades?'

His voice now had an icy edge to it and Ramage was tired and utterly defeated. Not because he was frightened, but because of all the captains and junior flag officers in the Mediterranean – in the whole Service in fact – he had been most impressed by what he had heard of Commodore Nelson. He suddenly realized he'd secretly hoped, after the trial was interrupted, that if the Commodore only knew all the facts he would clear him of any blame.

But that cold, almost off-hand tone: Commodore Nelson's manner showed that, at best, he had an unpleasant task ahead of him and did not relish doing it and, at worst, he was taking over where Goddard and Croucher had left off.

'I don't know what it *will* be, sir, but I know what it *ought* to be.' Ramage's voice was bitter and, unintentionally, almost insolent.

'Go on, then, out with it,' Nelson said impatiently, 'and be brief.'

'The *Sibella* – we couldn't fight on, sir, and we couldn't treat the wounded because the surgeon and his mate were killed. She was sinking so fast the French'd never keep her afloat long enough to patch her up. What I did meant medical attention for the wounded, as well as giving the unwounded time to escape in the boats.'

'The idea of being a prisoner of the French frightened you into escaping after you had surrendered?'

There was a sneer in the Commodore's voice which made Ramage flush with an anger that he could only just control.

'No, sir! I didn't surrender myself: I deliberately left the ship before the wounded surrendered her. An officer who allows himself and his men to be taken prisoner when he can escape and serve again ought to be tried as a traitor – well, almost a traitor. It's that kind of a man the – the Articles of War are aimed at.'

'Well spoken!' said Nelson with an unexpected laugh. 'That occurred to me when I read your report. An excellent report, incidentally, which is already on its way to Sir John Jervis with my covering letter. Now then, what about rescuing the refugees?'

'We did our best, sir.'

'What made you risk it with just a gig?'

The voice was cold again, and Ramage's heart sank.

'It seemed the lesser of two evils, sir. First, if there was any delay in the rescue, there was the danger the French would capture them. Second, if I tried getting them away, there was the danger we'd run into a gale with an overloaded boat.'

'So you considered a rescue attempt using the boat offered the refugees the best chance of survival?'

'Yes, sir.'

'Why?'

'Well, if they stayed on shore they might be betrayed by peasants. I couldn't do anything to prevent that. But if I took them off in the boat I was reasonably certain I could weather a gale somehow or other.'

'Very well. Now for Count Pisano's complaint.'

'There's nothing much to say, sir. I went back and found his cousin dead, but Pisano doesn't believe that.'

'You've no witnesses.'

'No, sir. Oh yes, I have, though!' he exclaimed, realizing the *Belette* operation had driven all thought of Jackson's revelation from his memory.

'Who is he?'

'The *Sibella*'s cox'n, an American named Jackson. I didn't know he'd seen the body after me. He didn't know of Pisano's allegations and didn't realize he had evidence of any importance. Anyway, sir, the *Diadem*'s arrival interrupted his evidence.'

'When did you find out all this?'

'We were talking on our way up to the *Belette*.'

'A conspiracy? No,' the Commodore said, waving a hand to stop Ramage's protest. 'I'm not saying you two were conspiring. I'm just pointing out that it could be said. Why do you suppose Count Pisano made the complaint against you?'

'To cover himself,' Ramage said bitterly. 'If he accuses me of failing in my duty by not going back, everyone forgets to ask him why he didn't go himself.'

'Not everyone,' Nelson said shortly. 'Now – what about the *Belette*? You've lost a lot of men?'

'Yes, thirteen dead and fifteen wounded. An error of judgement on my part, sir.'

'In what respect?'

'I decided to rake the *Belette* and then wear round before her guns could bear.'

'And—'

'We raked her all right, but I found I couldn't wear round in time: we were raked ourselves by her aftermost guns – I didn't allow enough for the curve on her quarter.'

'And what do you think will happen to you now?'

'To begin with, I imagine the court will reconvene and finish my trial, sir.'

'You seem remarkably ignorant of the Court Martial Statutes, Lieutenant, and remarkably unobservant.'

Ramage looked puzzled and the Commodore said, 'Once a court has dispersed, it can never be reconvened. And you have failed to notice that the *Trumpeter* is not in the anchorage.'

'Well, I suppose you'll order another trial, sir.'

'Perhaps. Follow me,' he ordered, walking through the door and into the great cabin.

Gianna was standing against one of the great stern lights. She was wearing her usual black travelling cloak thrown back over the shoulders to reveal the red lining, and a high-waisted pearl-grey dress. She was watching him anxiously, her lips moist and slightly parted.

On her left a heavily built man with a short, square beard sat in a chair, clasping a walking stick between his knees. The stick was thick – he must be lame, Ramage thought, and then noticed that the left ankle appeared to be in plaster. The man was handsome, but the finely cut features did not hide that he was hard, tough and possibly ruthless. He was Italian: that much was certain from his face, but the clothes he was wearing – a dark grey coat, yellow waistcoat and pale-grey breeches – were not his, or else he had a bad tailor.

At that moment Ramage, speechless with surprise, looked at Gianna and saw she was glancing at the man with affection, almost adoration. The man was smiling at her with love in his eyes.

The shock was, for Ramage, almost physical: this must be a *fiancé*. Where the devil had he come from? Gianna had never mentioned him – yet there was no reason why she should, he thought bitterly.

The Commodore, apparently blissfully unaware of the tension gripping Ramage, was talking. He'd apparently introduced the seated man, who made an attempt to stand up, but Ramage motioned him to remain seated and walked over and shook his hand. The grip was firm; the smile on the face was friendly and genuine.

Ramage turned to Gianna, took her hand and lifted it to his lips, and then swung round to face Commodore Nelson without looking at her again.

The Commodore was obviously in jovial mood: he slapped his knee and exclaimed:

'How about that, Ramage, eh?'

Ramage looked puzzled.

'Bit of a surprise, eh? Dead men do tell tales after all!'

The other three were laughing. Was the Commodore one of these blasted practical jokers?

The Italian said, 'We have almost met before, *Tenente*.'

'You have the advantage of me, sir,' Ramage said coolly.

Everyone seemed to be talking in riddles. It's Gianna's turn to have a dig now, he thought sourly, involuntarily glancing at her.

She looked as if he had just slapped her face.

'Nicholas! Nicholas!'

She almost ran the four or five paces separating them, and gripped his arm with her left hand. 'It's Antonio! Don't you understand?'

She was almost in tears. No, he didn't understand, nor did he care about Antonio: he simply wanted to kiss her, but instead gently pushed her away.

'Antonio, Nicholas! Antonio – my cousin: *Count Pitti*!'

The cabin slowly began moving round him; in a moment it was spinning and Gianna held him tightly, otherwise he would have fallen. A few seconds later the Commodore and Gianna were helping him to a chair while Pitti, now standing helplessly and leaning on his stick, kept repeating, 'What happened? What is wrong?'

Ramage saw that exploded face, the shattered bones and remains of the teeth silvery-white in the moonlight, the torn flesh and slopping blood, black and caked in the sand. Yet Pisano had been right: Count Pitti was alive after all. God – no wonder no one believed he had gone back. But Jackson ...

God damn and blast them all: he dragged himself out of

the chair, conscious his brow was wet with cold perspiration, and asked the Commodore:

'May I return to my ship, sir?'

Nelson looked puzzled but promptly said: 'No – sit down.'

Ramage almost slid into the chair: there was no strength in his knees and tiredness was adding its quota to help fuddle his brain. If only they'd leave him alone.

Suddenly he realized Gianna was kneeling beside him, talking softly, and the agony and bewilderment in her face stabbed into his consciousness like a dagger.

'But it is all right now,' she was saying. 'It is all right, Nico – *e finito, cara mia!*'

The Commodore interrupted:

'Mr Ramage has received a shock. My little surprise seems to have misfired and he deserves an explanation. Count Pitti, perhaps you would oblige – and please be seated,' he added, pushing a chair towards him.

Pitti sat down heavily.

'*Allora, Tenente*, you remember you met us on the track leading to the Tower? Well, when you and Gianna ran over the dunes towards the sea, my cousin Pisano and I, with the two peasants, went on to the Tower along the track and then up on to the dunes.

'I was worried about Gianna and stopped on top of the dunes to look back. I saw several French cavalry galloping along the beach towards you. It seemed impossible for either of you to avoid being killed. Then suddenly, at the last moment, a man ran out of the bushes and down the side of the dune, charging the cavalrymen and shouting so loud he frightened the horses.'

'Yes,' Ramage nodded. 'That was my cox'n, Jackson.'

'Well, I watched you pick up Gianna and run towards the boat at the end of the dunes. But at that moment two or three French soldiers, who must have galloped along the track and left their horses by the Tower, suddenly appeared behind me – between me and the Tower.

'I ran into the bushes and the soldiers followed, but they had to split up because the bushes were so thick.

'I had almost reached the end of the dunes, running in and out of the bushes like a rabbit, when I slipped in the sand as I crossed a clearing – you remember how soft it was – and broke my ankle. I managed to crawl under a bush a few moments before a French soldier appeared in the clearing. He stopped – I think he saw the marks I had made in the sand.

'There was a shot behind him – from the direction he'd come – and he fell down; but almost at once there were more shots and much shouting in French, and the rest of the soldiers went back towards the Tower. I think he was shot accidentally by one of his own people because he was in front and the rest of them mistook him for one of us.'

Ramage asked: 'Which way was he facing when he was shot?'

'Towards the boat: the ball hit the back of his head. Ah – I see why you ask. Well, I stayed under my bush for two or three minutes; then I heard someone calling in English from the direction of the boat. Then a man ran into the clearing and turned the body over – it was lying on its face.

'The man was you, was it not? I recognized you when you came into the cabin: you have a particular – how do you say, a particular stance.'

'Yes, I came back. But I didn't realize the body was of a French soldier.'

'I am not surprised: he was a cavalryman and wore a cloak, as I did. He was not wearing a hat – I expect he lost it. He wore white breeches and boots – just as I was wearing.'

The Commodore said, 'The uniforms of Revolutionary France are very sober now: none of the old trappings.'

'*Allora*, I was going to call you, but I knew my ankle was broken and that it would take a long time for me to get to the boat. I also knew any delay would risk everyone else's life. So I stayed under the bush and you went away. Then a few minutes later someone else came running through the clearing, from the same direction that the French soldier had come.

'He too looked at the body and swore in English. I realized it was a sailor and guessed he was the man who charged the cavalry. Well, that's all.'

'But how did you get here?'

'That was not too difficult. You told the two peasants that I was missing, and ordered them to escape. They crossed the river – to please you, incidentally – and as soon as you had gone off in the boat came back to look for me. After the French soldiers fired at you from the beach they galloped away.'

'Then what happened?'

'The peasants took me to a hut near the village of Capalbio, and bribed a fisherman from Port' Ercole to take me to Elba – to Porto Ferraio. He would not risk crossing to Bastia, and so we went along the coast at night. At Port Ferraio I found a British frigate, and went on board. The next day Commodore Nelson arrived and until yesterday I was his guest.'

Ramage looked at Nelson. 'So Count Pitti was on board when you arrived here, sir?'

'Yes, my boy.'

'Well, sir, I do think—'

'No,' interrupted Nelson, 'not if you think a little harder. When I read the minutes of the trial which my arrival interrupted, I needed a lieutenant to take command of the *Kathleen*. In view of the circumstances surrounding the trial, I thought it wiser you should leave Bastia for a short while. I asked Count Pitti if he would mind if the Marchesa was kept waiting for a few more hours before she was told that he was safe, and he agreed.'

Ramage said, 'I am sorry, sir: I didn't realize ...'

'Oh, don't thank me,' replied Nelson. 'I don't want cowards serving under me. I was bound to send a report to Sir John Jervis about the rather – er, inconclusive – proceedings here involving an accusation of cowardice. If I could later forward a report from the same young officer describing how he had successfully rescued the crew of the *Belette*, then neither the Admiral nor myself need have any further doubts about his courage – or qualities of leadership for that matter.'

'But sir, you had no idea that it would be any harder rescuing them than picking them up from a quay!' exclaimed Ramage.

'Oh?' Nelson said, raising his eyebrows. 'On the contrary.

An offshore wind, another headland to get in your way – and I guessed French troops would be on board. I believe Lord Probus made some reference to you to the effect that you were still on trial?'

'Yes, sir.'

'That was intended to be a warning. Now let's change the subject. You have probably realized we may have to evacuate Bastia?'

'Yes.'

'Well, Count Pisano and Lady Elliot left this morning for Gibraltar. The Marchesa and Count Pitti are also going to Gibraltar, but they wanted to await your return, so they leave tomorrow night.'

He watched Ramage's face fall and said sympathetically, 'Yes, it is very sad: I for one shall miss their company. However, I hope we shall all meet again soon under happier circumstances. Are you tired, Mr Ramage?'

'No, sir,' lied Ramage.

'Very well, perhaps you would care to join us for supper?'

The supper had been a great success: Nelson had kept them all amused, teasing both Gianna and Ramage, and in turn being teased by Pitti, who was obviously fascinated by the little man's vivacity. They had all drunk bumpers to the downfall of Bonaparte, the safety of the two charcoal burners, the health and happiness of Gianna, and a safe voyage for both her and Pitti.

Finally the supper had ended, and Nelson had taken his farewell of the two cousins, and suggested Ramage did the same, explaining that they were returning to the Viceroy's residence and Ramage might not have time to call on them next day.

So he had said goodbye. Pitti had said very little; in fact he was almost formal. Nor had Gianna seemed upset at the prospect of being parted from him. Her eyes had twinkled, but when a moment later he kissed her hand it had been limp: there was no secret pressure, no hidden message in its touch. The rescue, he thought sourly, was at last completed: the

287

cousins were reunited and Lieutenant Ramage's role had ended.

Just as he had turned to leave the cabin – he wanted to be the first to leave the ship, so that he did not have to watch the boat carry Gianna to the shore – the Commodore had handed him a sealed packet.

'Your orders,' he said shortly. 'Let me have your written report on the *Belette* operation in the forenoon tomorrow.'

Now, as Jackson steered the boat back to the *Kathleen* in the darkness, Ramage sat in the sternsheets, eaten up with bitterness. It was all façade, all pretence with these Italians. One minute she was on her knees beside him; the next minute she was saying goodbye with about as much emotion as she would display to a guest who had overstayed his welcome.

A hail came from the cutter and Jackson shouted back, '*Kathleen*', warning them that the captain was on board.

As soon as he reached his tiny cabin, where the steward had a moment before hooked a lantern to the bulkhead, he unhitched his sword, flung himself into the chair, and stared down at the deck. The canvas stretched across it as a carpet was worn where the door scraped and needed painting again. Hell, he was tired. How lucky was a piece of canvas, he thought sleepily: a coat of paint would cover all the old marks and make it like new.

He pulled the sealed linen envelope from his pocket. What did the Commodore want him to do now? Some dam' fool errand: that's all cutters were meant for. Probably deliver despatches to Sir John Jervis at San Fiorenzo, or take letters for the Ambassador in Naples.

He broke the seal, opened the envelope and began reading.

'You are hereby required and directed,' it said, 'to receive on board His Majesty's ship under your command the persons of the Marchesa di Volterra and Count Pitti and to proceed with all possible despatch to Gibraltar, being careful to follow a southerly route to avoid interception by enemy ships of war . . . On arrival at Gibraltar you will report forthwith to the admiral commanding to receive orders for your further proceedings.'

Ramage grinned: no wonder Gianna's eyes had twinkled.